ACCLAIM FOR ANN BEATTIE's

Another You

"A novel of distinction. . . . Beattie's complexities make us more alert to the layered complexities of our own lives."
—*Los Angeles Times*

"A master novelist of our brave new world."
—*Chicago Tribune Book World*

"Beattie writes out of wisdom and maturity that are timeless."
—*The New York Times Book Review*

"Beattie can capture a particular kind of moonlit melancholy of the soul with a near singular sheen . . . a writer of seamless technique and great authenticity. . . . The ending of her story here is wonderful, full of sorrow, revelation, and sweet impossibility."
—*Boston Globe*

"*Another You* is rich in detail, sympathy, and chiaroscuro."
—*The New York Times*

"Enlivened by all of Beattie's trademarks at their very best: an ear for contemporary speech as unerring as Elmore Leonard's; an unblinking eye for the gloriously absurd details of American life in the fast lane; and, best of all, a gift for hilarious yet sympathetic satire."
—*Washington Post Book World*

"Beattie's vision of contemporary middle-class society is as penetrating as radar . . . truthful and compelling."
—*Miami Herald*

ANN BEATTIE

Another You

Ann Beattie has published four previous novels and five collections of stories, among them *Chilly Scenes of Winter, Falling in Place, The Burning House, Love Always,* and *Picturing Will.* She lives in Maine with her husband, the painter Lincoln Perry.

BOOKS BY ANN BEATTIE

Another You

Ann Beattie

ANOTHER YOU

VINTAGE CONTEMPORARIES

Vintage Books

A Division of Random House, Inc.

New York

FIRST VINTAGE CONTEMPORARIES EDITION, SEPTEMBER 1996

Copyright © 1995 by Irony & Pity, Inc.

The Library of Congress has cataloged the Knopf edition
as follows:
Beattie, Ann.
Another you / Ann Beattie.
p. cm.
ISBN 0-679-40078-8
I. Title.
PS3552.E177A56   1995
813'.54—dc20   95-2667
CIP
Vintage ISBN: 0-679-73464-3

Random House Web address: http://www.randomhouse.com/

Printed in the United States of America
10 9 8 7 6 5 4 3 2

FOR ANDREW BORNSTEIN

Second-Growth Pine

1

_____

THERE SHE WAS, swaddled like an oversized infant in her white parka with its pointed hood pulled tight by a drawstring, turning at intervals to face oncoming traffic, extending her hand and pointing her thumb. Marshall went by so fast, and was so preoccupied—how many times do they play Marianne Faithfull singing "As Tears Go By" on the radio these days?—that he flinched as he sprayed her with dirty snow and kept going, hardly registering her presence. As the receding baby's bunting blip came into focus in his rearview mirror, Cheryl Lanier transformed into a real person. Marshall moved his foot slowly onto the brake, his eyes flicking up to the rearview at the same instant to make sure the car behind him wasn't going to ram his car. He touched the pedal, eased up, tapped again until the flashing lights caught the other driver's attention. The driver of the other car, frustrated that he could no longer tailgate, swerved to pass on the right, racing the motor and sending a heavy spray of slush onto the windshield as Marshall squinted to see, pulling off onto the shoulder.

Though there had been no near accident, so much had happened in a few seconds that as Cheryl Lanier ran up to the car, he had not yet recovered enough composure to greet her in the mocking mode he generally used with the young. "Cheryl," he said simply, as she threw open the passenger door. "Omigod," she said. "It's you." Her long black scarf trailed to her knee on one side; the other end formed a small epaulet of fringe that dangled from her left shoulder. As she thumped down into the passenger seat, the scarf slid to the floor. They almost bumped heads as they leaned forward to snatch it up.

But too late: it was soaked from the puddle her boots made as she stepped into the car.

He fingered his own long maroon wool scarf from England, which had been his sister-in-law Beth's birthday gift to him. As if it were a laurel, he removed his scarf and draped it around her neck. He winced, looking at her red cheeks that had chapped to the texture of an emery board, while her eyes brimmed with tears from the wind. "Smiling faces I can see," Marianne Faithfull sang. *But not for me,* he sang in unison, silently, to himself. Was that the way it should be? Should he let his restless impulse coast to a stop as his car had? Should he keep the needle unwavering at 40 m.p.h., be as upstanding as the needle until he dropped her where she was going, then continue off into the darkening afternoon, the wheels tracing the familiar back roads to his house as if they had a life of their own?

She was fingering the scarf, saying she couldn't possibly accept it; his voice overlaid Marianne Faithfull's soft, uninflected singing: she must take it; it was already hers. Hearing the flatness of his own tone meld into Marianne Faithfull's haunted voice—she, a former heroin addict, a lover in her golden-haired youth of the now fifty-year-old Mick Jagger—brought him down. When Cheryl Lanier said, "Who's that?" it snapped him out of his reverie. My God: he was on his way home from an English department meeting, driving his car along a slick winter road in a place he never intended to live, this damp, pretty young girl seated at his side, and she had just asked who Marianne Faithfull was. It was like not knowing Nixon had a dog named Checkers. Though she was probably born the year Nixon resigned. Nixon, Mick Jagger, the resignation, the Stones' almost annual comeback tours, the "elder statesman," Jumpin' Jack Flash boogeying back to the mike. What a world it was. What a world, in which people got recycled—or conveniently recycled themselves—long before it became politically correct to recycle newspapers and glass bottles.

Cheryl Lanier was still in a dither about accepting his scarf. He heard the words *Woolite* and *too expensive* before his thoughts drowned out the rest of her protests. *What do you think, Cheryl? Elvis Presley, shaking the hand of Tricky Dick Nixon, and not a Republican cloth coat in sight: just two guys in suits, big smiles, shaking hands for the camera in front of a row of limp flags, Nixon having deputized the Pelvis as an official agent in the war against drugs. This, shortly before Elvis died in the bathroom, after having ingested so many drugs a cough from him could have derailed the* Montrealer. *Either Tweedledum or Tweedledee had doubts about the administration being made the butt of a grotesque joke and advised against granting Elvis this power, or at least against the photo op — but the moment happened anyway, like so many moments, it happened anyway, and afterward Tricky no doubt sauntered upstairs, sat by the fire, which he ordered lit even in the middle of summer, tossed down a few scotches, then went around and told the gentlemen painted in the portraits on the walls what he thought of them. Think about it: Can you imagine Margaret Thatcher weaving down the corridors of Number* 10 *Downing, giving Gladstone and Disraeli the what for? Mitterrand posing rhetorical questions late at night to an oil painting of le Roi Soleil? But in our country we have a bunch of clowns; the circus continues, the band strikes up the music, the balloons rise toward the ceiling from the convention floor. Later, Ford will walk into walls and Reagan will fall off his horse: clowns. Kissinger, court jester, is ordered down to his knees in prayer and plops down at Nixon's side, while up in heaven J.F.K. jumps from one cloud to the next, as if they're so many rooftops under which his sleeping lovers lie.*

She said she would be glad to have a cup of coffee with him. She looked at him, her hood thrown back, his scarf around her neck. She had been telling him about her roommate's drinking. Wasn't it her roommate she was talking about? His thoughts had drifted; the best he could do was to paraphrase what he thought she'd said.

"You think now that when she's been on crying jags, your roommate has been drunk?" he said.

"Yes," she said. "But the thing is, she went to see somebody about what happened, and the counsellor told her to forget it. She wouldn't really listen to her, she just told her to forget it. Livan wasn't drinking before that—or not that Timothy and I knew about. And the thing is, what happened was pretty awful. I can't tell you what, but trust me. I feel like calling that woman, the counsellor, and asking her if she has any idea what harm she's caused, though I don't suppose she's going to take the call, number one, and if she did, why would she admit she was incompetent?"

The white bag she had produced from her coat pocket was from the pharmacy: Valium, prescribed for another girl Cheryl knew but destined for Livan. This was why she was out at dusk, hitching in the direction of home, having spent most of her month's food allowance filling the prescription. He had said that instead of coffee, they should have dinner. It was so early, he could eat something with Cheryl at the tavern he sometimes stopped at—a place frequented by farmers and other locals, rednecks, unemployed kids, very few people from Benson College ever went there—and still go home and pick at dinner with Sonja. As he drove, the sky darkened to steely gray. The moon already shone, a half parenthesis. For a certain period in his life, his brother, Gordon, had taken Valium, and this much he remembered: you weren't supposed to take Valium and drink. If her roommate was drinking, it was not a good idea to give her the pills—and, if she was as distraught as Cheryl said, it wouldn't be a good idea to provide her with the pill bottle. He cautioned Cheryl as he drove. Eyes wide, she looked at him. He was causing her to doubt her solution. Her expensive, magic solution.

"I never thought she was so upset she'd kill herself," Cheryl said. She spoke grudgingly, hiking up her shoulders like a cat.

He decided to push a little. "Why don't you tell me what the problem is?" he said. "I'll never meet her. Maybe I could give you some advice."

More of the big eyes. A deep sigh as her shoulders relaxed. Her hands nervously rearranged her hair. She said, quietly, "I shouldn't have said anything."

"What do you think? I'm the Big Bad Wolf and I'm going to blow down her door?"

"It's my door, too," she said.

What a strange answer—as if the discussion had been about the possible destruction of personal property. But she had become quite petulant. He saw it in the minuscule, sulky protrusion of her bottom lip. Perhaps, in her fantasies, he had already walked through the apartment door. In his own, just now, as his mind raced, he certainly had. Once he found she did not live in one of the dorms, one of those ugly towers put up in the late '70s that looked like gigantic smokestacks which bordered the campus, he had wished her to live without roommates, in a cozy apartment he could walk into, shutting the door on the cold winter afternoon. From what he gathered, though, there were two roommates. On the radio, the theme music of *All Things*

Considered began. Marshall had friends who had, as a joke, used that same music instead of the wedding march. In a flash, the program about to follow was summarized first by a female voice, then a male, the two seesawing between sound bites on the famine in Africa to the results of a study analyzing sudden, strange changes in bones removed from an Indian burial ground. He did something he never did: he turned off *All Things Considered.*

"Somebody hurt her," Cheryl said.

"Hurt her in what way?"

"What do you think I'm talking about? Her emotions?"

"Hurt her physically?"

A nod. Her head quickly turned away as she looked out the side window.

Just when she had finally coaxed him into curiosity about her roommate, forcing him into the present moment, Cheryl intended to drop the subject. It made him a little angry. He thought about Sonja, the night before, turning out the bedside lamp while he was finishing the last paragraph of an article he had been reading, Sonja saying, "Oh, I'm sorry. I thought the light was still on on your side." Her quizzical look: Could he really have taken offense at such a simple, sleepy mistake? The room suddenly lit up again. He had gotten out of bed and gone into the bathroom, where more things had displeased him: a copy of *International Wildlife* magazine tossed on the bathroom floor, curl-edged from humidity; the towel thrown over one side of the bathtub instead of draped over the towel rack so it would dry. Lately, Sonja kept house the way Paul Delario ran the curriculum meetings: the inconsequential quickly overwhelmed anything of importance. The theorists were allowed to engage in endless rhetorical debates. But what did it really matter? The students were accepting of anything, while the faculty wanted to do as little as possible to keep their jobs. Everybody lived for sports and any new restaurant reported to be good, where they could deconstruct their broasted chicken. Frowning in consternation, he looked at Cheryl and was startled to see her young face superimposed on his wife's—this face that looked back at him with Sonja's narrowed eyes.

He took Cheryl's hand. As he had taken Sonja's hand when he returned to the bedroom, sliding into bed beside her, the night-light burning in an outlet just above the baseboards: a three-inch-high visage of Donald Duck, his big, protuberant lips glowing yellow, plastic hat jauntily tilted atop his head.

You need a vacation, Sonja had said, going limp-wristed as he slid into bed beside her, took her hand, and tried to nuzzle his way to a reconciliation. Now, through Sonja's limp hand, rose the slight pressure of Cheryl Lanier's smaller, gloved hand, returning nothing of his strengthening grip, but not withdrawing, either.

Well past the college now, he turned onto a smaller, winding road, knowing there was a tavern near the end, before the road looped back past the dairy farm onto the highway.

"I appreciate your concern," Cheryl was saying to him.

"Ms. Lanier," he said. In his head, he was mocking youth, in general, as if he had things figured out, as if he had things under control, when really his inadequacies could make him feel slightly faint, when he focused on them. Which was what he was doing at the moment, and no wonder: Did he think Sonja might be out riding in someone's car, with her hand in another man's? Any possibility that Sonja would be off having a drink with some handsome client? Possibly there were advances she warded off that she never told him about, but what he really thought was that since she gave out no signals of availability, most men simply got the message. At the tavern, he would call Sonja and tell her he'd be late—maybe even say he was giving a student a ride home. It was turning into a bad night, with rain falling on already slick roads. He wondered whether the tavern would be empty or crowded and decided it would be crowded; by this point in the winter, everybody was woods crazy. A beagle wandered onto the road, and he braked, thinking it a raccoon, at first, later realizing it was someone's dog that had a high-hipped swagger. He kept his eyes on the dog, transfixed by the animal though he couldn't say why. It was a fat beagle, old, probably used to crossing this road, because it was suddenly gone, disappearing through a hole in the fence and vanishing into the darkness.

"I don't think I should," Cheryl Lanier said.

"You don't think you should what?" he said, playing it cool about the meaning of his hand holding hers.

"Tell you," she said. "I mean, Livan made me promise."

"Well, you don't have to," he said. "But if you want to, the secret's safe with me."

"Secrets never stay safe," she said.

A cliché, but it gave him a moment's pause. "You mean," he said, "you've never confided anything that has stayed confidential?"

"I'm not sure," she said. "How would I know? The next person who was told wouldn't be likely to repeat it to me, would they? They might tell somebody else, but they wouldn't tell me." She sank lower in the seat. "You know Professor McCallum?" she said.

Jack McCallum. Nice looking, Harvard man, interested in literary theory, managed to get his salary raised every couple of years because he was always hunted by other colleges. A mean softball pitch, a brown bagger, a recent convert to Catholicism. "Bless you," McCallum had said to him, earlier that week, when Marshall loaned him Gide's *Strait Is the Gate,* a book McCallum had had trouble getting. Did he know him? No, he didn't really know him, but that seemed an unnecessarily oblique answer.

"Livan's his research assistant," Cheryl said. "They went to Boston in November, over Thanksgiving break, to do research at the Boston Public Library."

"I don't assume that's all that happened?"

Another beagle darted in front of the headlights, moving dangerously close to his car. *That's all I need,* he thought, *to kill a dog.* He wondered if it might be the same beagle: if the dog might have circled around at a greater speed than the car in order to tempt fate one more time. Not likely, yet it reminded him of being a young child, having no sense of distance or time, thinking the craziest things might be possible. That if you sat on your horse on the carousel and kept waving your arm with your fist forward, you could catch up with the other horses. There had been a carnival in their town when he and Gordon were young, and the two of them had gone constantly, their pleading so frenzied their father had simply given in, and he and Gordon had made up a series of rituals they thought would make their desires materialize: if you could blink fifteen times before you passed the devil's face in the ride in the dark, you'd find money on the ground when you exited; if you said "Whirl" out loud every time the Tilt-a-Whirl circled, the ride would last longer. But, he thought, this wasn't a ride on a gilded horse, and he wasn't seated in a metal cage that would twirl around a tipping disk; here were two people in a car, about to have a conversation in which would be revealed—no matter what ritualistic incantation he might try to banish the announcement—that sometime after Thanksgiving, McCallum had screwed Cheryl Lanier's roommate in Boston. He turned his head sideways to receive this information. As he did, Cheryl reached up with her gloved hand and touched him briefly, lightly, on the jaw. It was so unexpected, and so intimate, that his mouth dropped open. It was the way a person would touch you if they loved you, or perhaps if their own sadness was inexpressible except through touch. Was she this sad? Was he?

In front of them was the tavern, the deeply rutted entranceway lined with cars and trucks, the string of half-burned-out lights casting a yellow haze under the roof. As he guided the car through the deep mud ruts, he realized he had both hands on the wheel. When had he let go of her hand? He turned left, where he saw parking space at the end of the lot. He turned off the ignition and thought: *Only in some stupid Hollywood movie would the man lean over, now, and kiss the woman.* What woman? Cheryl Lanier was nineteen years old. The woman he had been holding hands with, the "woman" he had been about to kiss, was his student, though for a few moments he had entirely forgotten that. What did Cheryl Lanier want, or expect? Certainly not McCallum's treatment, if she was so upset by what McCallum had done. McCallum with his peanut-butter sandwiches and the huge apples he shined on his pants leg, then tossed in the air with his hearty "God bless" if you passed his open door and had even the briefest exchange with him.

He opened his door, meaning to go around to her side, but she opened her door at the same time and stepped out, standing on tiptoe as she surveyed the mess she'd have to maneuver through. She'd walked a straight line as perfectly as a tightrope performer by the time he caught up with her—he'd forgotten to lock the car and had to go back—and when he did catch up, he took her elbow, though she was already maneuvering with no trouble. Her parka was so thick he could barely feel her elbow beneath the padding.

He steered her to a table away from the jukebox. The table was round, small, covered with a red-and-white-checked cloth. Salt was sprinkled around the salt and pepper shakers. He put his thumb into the salt spill and shifted it into a straight line, then brushed it into the palm of his hand. He dropped it on the floor, and as if he'd rung the dinner bell, a large waitress with dyed yellow hair appeared, her hair clipped back with a butterfly barrette, the butterfly motif echoed by a silver butterfly pin above her name tag, which said MYRTIS.

"Let me have a Jack Daniel's on the rocks," he said.

"A Heineken, please," Cheryl said.

The waitress was preoccupied; she didn't register Cheryl's age. Marshall wished that Cheryl had ordered a double, in case the waitress eventually snapped to and noticed. But how could you do that? How could you order a double beer? He called after her, "Let me have a draft as a chaser." Myrtis nodded and kept going.

"You know," Cheryl said, "when I was in your office the other day and you were recommending poems to read in that anthology? It took me a minute to realize that sometimes you were telling me the title of a poem, and other times you were saying the poet's name. When you said 'Orr,' I thought you were contradicting yourself about my reading Roethke. *Or* someone else, I thought you were saying. And 'Wright.' I thought you were, you know, corroborating what you'd just said— that you'd given a title correctly. That you were *right*."

"You're avoiding the subject," he said.

"I don't even feel good about telling you what I've told you," she said.

"Let me make a phone call," he said. "Take a look at the menu. Let's go ahead and order." He pulled the plastic menu out from between the napkin holder and a bottle of ketchup and put it in front of her as he got up to call Sonja. There was someone on the phone, so he went into the men's room and peed, standing next to a balding man in a black motorcycle jacket and blue-and-green-striped pants. As the man zipped his fly, Marshall heard the man humming "Rock of Ages." Outside again, the phone was available, and he reached in his pocket for a coin, then dialled his number.

"I'm glad you're okay," Sonja said.

"I'm listening to some kid's problem," he said. "I'm giving him a ride back to his dorm, but the weather's gotten so bad, we're going to have coffee and sit it out for a while. You didn't have to go out in this, did you?"

"No," she said. "I've been home all afternoon."

"Good," he said. "I'll see you soon." Then: "Love you."

"I love you, too," she said.

"I'm actually with a girl, not a guy. We're drinking. She's telling me about her roommate's problems, which I'm about as interested in as reading random names in the phone book."

"Marshall," Sonja sighed. "Why do you make fun of me for being paranoid when I'm not paranoid?"

"I love to tease."

"Well, so do *girls* love to tease, so be sure it's her roommate she's talking about while you drink, not herself."

It had never occurred to him. What Sonja had just said was absolutely correct: she might be having such trouble talking to him because she was making a personal confession. There might not even be a roommate.

"Marshall?" Sonja said. "Has my brilliant warning struck you dumb, or do you have something else to say before you go back to your boozing and flirtation?"

"I love you," he said. It seemed the simplest thing to say.

"What's the kid's name?" she said.

"Henry," he said. That, too, seemed the simplest thing to say. It was written beside the phone, in green ink: "Henry gives Alex good head."

When he hung up, he walked slowly back to the table, turning sideways to give their waitress more room. She was holding a big oval tray loaded with bowls of spaghetti and meatballs. It smelled wonderful, but as he inhaled he realized he'd been breathing shallowly because he had a headache. The glossy, wet roads, the same winter itchiness everyone else had, a lying phone call to his wife, whom he *did* love, something happening between himself and a young girl he hardly knew that was not entirely in his control—why bother to wallow in your midlife crisis if you were going to clamp down on your itchiness by exerting control?—and now, the idea had been planted that there might not be a roommate, that Cheryl Lanier might be making a personal confession.

"I drank your Jack Daniel's," she said, as he returned to the table.

He looked at her empty beer bottle. He looked at the empty glass. "I see you did," he said, trying not to sound as surprised as he was.

"Because you've got a beer anyway," she said.

"Should I have stayed gone longer?"

She smiled at his little joke.

"I could turn my head," he said. "I'll count to ten, and if the beer's still there, I'll assume you didn't want to take the opportunity."

"I also took a Valium."

"You did?" he said. His thoughts raced: Sonja was right; this girl was someone to beware of; she wasn't just revealing herself to him, she was flirting with real danger. Mixing Valium and alcohol, let alone tossing down a generous shot of Jack Daniel's. . . . Good he'd come back to the table in time to stop her from drinking everything from every glass, her desire for him turned suicidal, or—less flattering to think, by far—her suicidal desire provoking a desire for him.

"Like to order anything?" Myrtis said. "Another J.D.?" she said, before he could answer.

"I'll have another beer," Cheryl said. She turned to Marshall. "Are we going to eat?"

"Sure," he said.

"Sure you want another, or sure you're eating?" Myrtis said.

"Both," he said. "I'll have a burger. Medium."

"And for you?" Myrtis said to Cheryl.

"The same," she said, "but well done."

"Fries with those?"

"Yes, thanks," he said.

"I'll eat some of his," Cheryl said.

As the waitress left, Cheryl took a sip of his beer. When she saw how upset he looked, she laughed. "You're not one of those people who are territorial about food, are you?" she said.

"Listen," he said, "be serious. It's a very bad idea to take Valium and drink."

"One pill's not going to kill me. I've never taken Valium. Are you worried I'm going to become a rag doll and embarrass you, or something?"

"Will you stop after this next beer?" he said.

She saw that he was serious. "Yes," she said. "Now can we talk about something else?"

"Yeah," he said. "Your roommate's problem?"

"I shouldn't," she said. Then, suddenly, she said, "You know, I know quite a few students who think you're a prick. Because of the way you seem to have all these in-jokes with yourself when you talk to them. You call the guys by their first names. Or if you really like them, by their last names. But you always call women 'Ms.' The 'Ms. Lanier' bit. But I think you're very nice. So I'm saying this as a friend. I think that you should tone it down."

Myrtis put a plate of french fries on the table, along with the Jack Daniel's and another Heineken. She moved the ketchup bottle to the side of the plate. "Enjoy, enjoy, for tomorrow . . . we enjoy!" Myrtis said, picking up Cheryl's empty bottle.

"It's so nice not to see students everywhere," Cheryl said. "It makes me crazy, sometimes. They think they're so radical, but they all talk about the same things. The environment. The reefs dying. Clear-cutting. They move around in a little pack and they talk about forests in Oregon and polluted reefs, and they act so self-righteous, like they'd never flush their toilet if they lived in Florida."

"You're not worried about the future?"

"I'm worried, right now, about Livan. I think she needs to talk to somebody about what McCallum did to her and also what that stupid woman at student health said. You know what the woman said? She said, 'Can't you see past this situation? What exactly do you think it's done to your future?' "

"It's difficult to say anything, because I don't know what the situation is," he said.

"He tied her to the bed and had sex with her."

"One burger well, one burger medium. How are you doing with that drink?" Myrtis said to Marshall. He looked at his glass. It was half-full. "In a while," he said. Myrtis nodded and walked away. He looked at Cheryl. She was looking at him intently.

"Is it possible . . . just possible, I mean . . . maybe it was something they were doing and then she freaked out? Or felt bad about later?"

"She had to piss in the bed," she said.

He looked at his hamburger. It looked like the strangest thing in the world. He looked at the drink. It was half-empty. He took a sip and put the glass down. Cheryl picked up the glass and finished it, the ice sliding, causing a small rivulet of bourbon to splash down her chin. She wiped it away. She pushed back her bangs.

"He asked her to piss in the bed?"

"No, he didn't ask her. She was tied up so long that she had to piss right there. She was humiliated."

"Cheryl," he said, "wouldn't it make sense that if they were there in a hotel, she'd scream for help? That . . ." He broke off. Jesus: McCallum tying up some kid in Boston. What had he done, polished his apple while she struggled? "God bless" indeed.

"It wasn't a hotel," she said. "It was in Revere. Somebody's triplex in Revere. When they got there, there were other people, but the next day the place was empty. She had sex with him the first night. She wanted to. I mean, she didn't go to Boston wanting to, but she agreed. And when she agreed, it made him mad. She said she knew she'd done something wrong. And the next morning the whole house was quiet, and when she woke up, he tied her wrists to the bed."

"And you're telling me some counsellor in student health only wanted to know what impact this was going to have on the rest of her life?"

She nodded yes. He sensed Myrtis approaching. At least for the moment, she was occupied by people complaining about the blueberry pie; then, at the same table, someone wanted directions for driving the back roads to Portsmouth. *Go up to the Texaco station,* he heard. And: *quarter mile, maybe just a bit over.* The song on the jukebox was "Where the Boys Are." Connie Francis. Good God—Connie Francis. Hadn't something happened to her, hadn't she been raped herself, when someone broke into her motel room? *I'll wait im-pa-tient-ly,* Connie Francis sang.

"I just saw that on the tube," Cheryl said. Cheryl was looking beyond him, nodding, signalling yes to Myrtis. Rubbing her hamburger around in the grease on the plate. Cheryl said, "That movie. *Where the Boys Are.*"

"It's so depressing," he said.

"Unbelievably depressing," she said.

"Your roommate," he said. "I meant your roommate."

"I'm glad you've forgotten her name," Cheryl said. "I never should have told you."

"She needs to see somebody else at student health. I'll go with her if I need to. You're right. Of course she's got to get help."

"Go with her!" It was almost a yelp. "She would kill me if she thought I told anybody about this, let alone a teacher. She would never trust another human being as long as she lived."

He thought about it. "Then I'll go to student health myself and talk to whoever's in charge and they can contact her."

"Isn't that—I mean—you mean you can just go over there and tell them to call her, and they will?"

"I assume so," he said. He was beginning to think more clearly.

Sonja had a friend who was a doctor at student health—a woman who was in her book discussion group.

"Can you find out the name of the therapist?" he said. "Get the name. My wife has a friend who works there and she can be sure that person won't see her again."

"But you swear you won't go there?" Cheryl said. "I mean it: if she found out, she would kill me. She trusts me totally."

"You've done the right thing to tell me," he said. "I'll give you my phone number, and you can call me tomorrow night. I assume my wife can get in touch with her friend by then. But wait a minute. Wait a minute. . . ." What he was thinking was that, if Cheryl called the house, Cheryl might say something and Sonja might find out that he had, indeed, been out the night before with a female student. If only he hadn't said "Henry" on the phone. If only he'd laughed and side-stepped the question. But no: he had to blurt out a man's name.

"I'll call you," he said. "That's better."

She reached in his shirt pocket and took out his pen. She wrote her name on a napkin, and her telephone number. It was a young girl's writing. Naturally, he thought, since she was a young girl. Even the piece of paper would have to be hidden from Sonja. Or maybe that was ridiculous. Sonja wasn't paranoid; she'd believe him if he said this was the name of the girl who was the roommate of . . . Livan. That was the girl's name. How was he going to look McCallum in the eye?

He looked at the red smear of ketchup on his plate. He had wolfed down the rest of his hamburger as Cheryl wrote. Now all he needed was . . . *thank you, Myrtis* . . . the last drink of the evening, which he meant to hold on to tightly so Cheryl couldn't get the glass away from him, and maybe a glass of water . . . *thank you, Myrtis* . . . to swallow aspirin with. He asked Cheryl if she had aspirin, knowing that if she didn't, he could buy some at the cash register. But she did have them, and she produced them from her fanny pack, unzipping it and taking out a small bottle of Bayer, even opening the top and shaking two into the palm of his hand. He thanked her and washed them down with the last inch of her beer.

"So does a little part of you think that people my age invite trouble?" she said.

"I think what happened was horrible, if that's what you mean."

"Marshall, you've never been anything like a prick with me, and I appreciate it," she said.

He tried not to reveal his surprise that she had called him Marshall. But why not, for heaven's sake? He'd been in the restaurant with her for more than an hour, drinking and listening to the troubling story she'd needed to tell. He'd held her hand in the car. Who should he be, if not Marshall?

"Don't give her Valium if she's been drinking," he said. "Promise?"

"Okay," she said.

"And don't take it yourself, either."

"It didn't do anything," she said.

"Just don't do it," he said.

She nodded.

Myrtis gave them the check, her name and the word "Thanx" written on the back, three horizontal lines under "Thanx."

"Thanks," Cheryl said, as he reached for his wallet. "I have five dollars, but I don't suppose you'd take it."

He shook his head no.

"I'll hold your hand when we get to the car," she said.

He looked at her, embarrassed. He'd hoped what happened before wouldn't be directly addressed. He'd counted on it. "Ms. Lanier," he said, speaking quickly to cover his surprise. "Can I truly count on such an exceptional pleasure?"

"But that's all, *Mr. Lockard*," she said. "First date, and all that."

He could feel himself blush.

"See what it's like to be mocked?" she said. "You don't have to do that so much. Really. I advise you to tone it down."

She slipped her hand into his as he reached above her one-handed to open the restaurant door. That way, ducking their heads against the wind, they hurried to the car in the lightly falling snow.

Dearest Martine:

It seems we are always days and weeks away from seeing you. Every time I count the days, Alice reminds me that what I am really counting is weeks: 16 days should not be considered days, but more than two weeks, properly speaking, and then I realize I must write.

The trip to New York has been quite wonderful, and of course we have eaten wonderfully well. We thought of you when we had chicken stuffed with roasted peppers and porcini. Have two creative chefs coincidentally invented that, or did you sneak a look at a cookbook?

There is a slight chance Ethan Bedell will stop by quite soon after our arrival. If he should call before we arrive, please try to put him off as I'll need time to lay in the port he always expects (and appreciates, dear soul!), and to try to encourage sympathy toward him from Alice. We must all three join hands and recite together that we will not be drawn into his unhappiness when he arrives. When people are united in their intolerance of his gloominess, he quickly snaps to and becomes a much happier fellow.

Martine. We speak of you so many times a day. Alice said last night she hoped you were planting carrots so the rabbits would be attracted to the garden. What a feeling: to so love seeing them, yet they devour the garden greens as if our hand-clapping was only musical accompaniment to their munching.

Please plant lemon verbena.

Don't work too hard. We both mean this. Alice looks over my shoulder. She says to tell you she is living vicariously, through you, enjoying the beautiful spring.

With affection,

M.

2

SONJA AWAKENED EARLY to see Marshall, wrapped in a bath-
robe, an afghan draped over his shoulders, his sleep-crushed hair
sticking up in an Ed Grimley, sitting on a chair he'd pulled close to
the window, hands on his knees in the gesture of a small boy being
told a story. What story might Marshall be imagining? The familiar
story of Old Mister Whiteflakes taunting everyone because he could
snow all winter, whenever he wanted, however much he liked? Or
perhaps he was hearing more personal stories. Internal stories. A moment in his mother's life, as previously recounted by his father. Something about her knitting, constantly knitting, as if she could make
ordinary things, such as scarves and mittens, become magical because, unlike life, they would not unravel. Who had she been, really,
that woman dead so many years, whom Evie, her successor, still
talked about so adoringly, that young woman kissing her children's
gloves with her lipsticked blessing and embroidering the wristbands
with forget-me-nots?

Marshall's head was tilted back enough so that his eyes could connect with the moon, yet from across the room, from the bed, from
which she could see only the tipped-back crown of his head, she felt
sure his eyes were closed, that he had brought his chair close to the
window not to look at the sky but to bask in the presence of darkness,
the glimmer of starlight, the opacity of the moon. And then, in her
sleepy reverie, she contradicted her thinking: one could describe, to a
blind man, what the starbursts and showers of light were like. Oh
really? How could one do that? With an illuminating analogy?

Through the charm of synesthesia? She had been watching her husband, thinking, *Thank God he's not blind,* certain that she would be a terrible guide for anyone who could not see exactly what she saw. Yet what foolishness that was: objectivity. Even little children knew that a thrice-whispered word metamorphosed to another, that no tadpole restrained itself from transformation to a frog, to say nothing of individual perceptions, which made a puddle a pond and a lake an ocean.

Marshall shifted in the chair, the afghan slid to the floor, she put her fingers to her lips as if she feared something. Then, in startled confusion, he rose from the chair, disoriented—there: she knew he had been asleep—and, in a kind of sleepwalk, started toward the bed.

Marshall curled on his side, on top of the covers, his face windowpane cold. She tried to tug the sheet and blanket from underneath to cover him, but it was no use. He stayed the way he had first fallen on the bed, the twist of afghan a half chrysalis binding his torso, his lips open, robe bunched around his chest. She touched his shoulder. If there had not been enough light in the room for her to see that this provoked a frown, even in sleep, she would have persisted, but it was too cruel—and where, exactly, would she begin explaining to him her irrational thoughts? *Oh, darling, wake up: I've been thinking about tadpoles and puddles and lakes, and I'm very happy you aren't blind.* They were so bizarre that she tried to forget them herself, nestling against him, pulling covers up from behind to warm her back, then trying to catch the rhythm of his suddenly quieter breathing, as if, even in sleep, he had made a bargain with her: *If I don't have to listen to you, you don't have to listen to me.*

She was not going to get back to sleep, so she went downstairs and looked for something to do. Actually, it came as a relief that Marshall had so captivated her attention—that she had seen him as vulnerable, that she had felt close to him as he struggled through the night. Because she had been struggling through quite a few difficult nights herself lately, stung by guilt over the affair she was having with her boss, Tony Hembley, trying to deny the fact that in such situations, now that the '60s were long gone, eventually she would have to decide.

Beside the stairs was a basket of things that needed to be ironed, including her favorite pillow shams that wrinkled like crepe paper but could be quickly steamed into satiny softness. But she was too sleepy to iron. Instead, she went into the living room and curled up, pulling an afghan Evie had knitted for her over her lap, turning on the reading light, and scanning Sunday's still-unfinished crossword puzzle. She saw that Marshall had written in a couple of words she'd missed in pencil, and also that he'd doodled as he thought about the answers, drawing circles that became ovals, then what looked like a fried egg, its albumen spreading out lacily from the yolk. Or maybe it was no such thing; maybe she was just hungry. For another few minutes she gave thought to "Poet translated by FitzGerald"—wouldn't Marshall have known that?—yet Marshall was always preoccupied, so possibly he had not even glanced at that part of the puzzle. Even when he was supposed to be asleep, he often moved around the room, sleepwalking or just plain drifting, quietly walking part of the night away. It was to her advantage that he was so often in a world of his own, or distracted, she thought, and then, instantly, felt ashamed of her thoughts. Gordon, Marshall's brother, was apparently a restless sleeper too; at least, his new wife—the only one of his wives she had ever had a real correspondence with—often remarked on Gordon's insomnia, or his troubled sleep. The brothers were at once physically similar and also dissimilar: both had unusually colored green eyes, deeply hooded; both had large feet and hands, though only Marshall's had a sculptural delicacy. Of course, working with his hands had toughened and abraded Gordon's hands in a way Marshall's behind-the-lectern gestures had not. Also, the difference in age between them, which was not great, would not explain Marshall's almost unlined skin, the tiny crow's-feet at his eyes drawing attention to one of his best features. Marshall was six feet tall, though he slumped so much he didn't appear particularly tall. Gordon was shorter by several inches, though he held himself ramrod straight, shoulders squared—perhaps the carriage he'd learned in the army, while Marshall was pursuing his Ph.D. She lifted the photograph of herself and Marshall off the side table and rubbed the dusty frame. It had been taken in Boston many years ago by the teenage son of a woman she'd worked with. What had happened to the woman and her talented son, who had been so passionate about his photography courses? She'd lost track of so many people, and so had Marshall—though he'd never had as many friends and acquaintances as she. He maintained that men didn't socialize the way women did, but lately he didn't socialize at all, and she hardly did, herself: just the book discussion group, or an odd evening out when Marshall taught his night class. In the photograph, Marshall's hand clasped her shoulder, and he nuzzled her hair, which was much longer, falling below her shoulders. His eyes were half-closed, his thoughts turned inward, but she hadn't been relaxed at all: her eyes a bit too wide, her smile slightly artificial. Still, the tenderness between them showed. Then and now, when he wasn't thinking about three things at once, going in one direction looking for his briefcase and another to find the pile of papers he'd just graded, meanwhile forgetting his watch on the dresser and leaving the lunch bag on the kitchen counter, he would look at her appreciatively and his gaze would calm her. She knew he loved her, but she was often surprised to see that he was looking quietly at her simply because he liked her. She didn't mind at all that it was the same way he would look at the covers of certain books, or the way he'd look out the window and appreciate, for a brief second, the sight of branches blowing in the wind, or be amused by squirrels cavorting on the telephone wires.

Thinking fondly of her husband—relieved that she did, because for quite a while her thoughts had habitually turned, instead, to Tony—she went into the kitchen and made pancake batter. No assurance he'd have time to eat pancakes, unless she was unkind and woke him up after his stressful night sleepwalking, but if he did wake up, the batter would be there. Cracking an egg into the powdery mixture, she thought again about his doodles, and about the inked and pencilled puzzle, slightly sorry that instead of going to foreign films or going dancing—well, a few times, years ago in Boston, they had gone dancing—they now sat so many nights in front of the fire, settling for nothing but relaxation and wordless connection with one another. Strange, really, that while she felt comfortable with their pleasant domestic routines most of the time, at other times the sameness seemed oppressive. Just a day or so ago, she had complained to Tony about their evenings at home, yet when he had commiserated, calling them "your quotidian quotient," she had become defensive. She had actually found herself talking about the solitary beauty of the second-growth pine, and of the birches, lit by the backyard spotlight, and if Tony hadn't laughed, she would probably have continued: the mesmerizing fire in the fireplace; the complex patterns the shadows cast upon the wall. "I'm here to save you from your life of happy pretense," Tony had said to her, clinking the rim of his coffee cup to hers. One thing about Tony was that he never minded overstepping his bounds—and when he had, he registered his glee by making a silent toast, or by flashing the V-for-victory sign. It was a mistake to confide in him, but also, for some reason, irresistible. Now she forced him out of her mind and finished stirring the batter.

She supposed she should be grateful she could keep such odd hours at the real estate business, communicating essentially by Post-it notes and taped messages, though the more she thought about it, it was possible she might appear both organized and brilliantly improvisational to Tony: certainly he had realized he was hiring an unconventional person, someone with a zigzagging past that slalomed his own. She had finished law school, flunked her exams the first time around, gotten sidetracked taking night courses in literature while keeping the books for a Boston electronics store for almost two years, then enrolled in a Harvard summer program she thought would teach her about new computer technology, which instead resulted in her retreat into the works of Jane Austen, followed by the rather unexpected promotion of Marshall to full professor at Benson College, their joyful decision to leave their apartment for a real house, followed by their having the good fortune to meet Tony Hembley at a friend's summer wedding in the Adirondacks, where she spontaneously joined him at a rickety piano to accompany his accordion-played Cajun rendition of "Bosco Stomp." More than half the guests were too drunk to understand what a weird spectacle was transpiring, though she and Tony had gotten it entirely: the inexplicable oddity of finding a soul mate in the unlikeliest place at the unlikeliest time, a kind of obligation, naturally, required of those thus blessed. ". . . Too stupid to pass the law boards," she had said. ". . . So couldn't imagine the rest of my life fastening suspenders to my pants and tying a noose with a rep tie. Just had to switch from Dean Witless to real estate," he'd replied.

The house Tony found for them was half an hour from Tony's own house, twenty minutes from Marshall's job. The first time she had gone to Hembley and Hembley (Tony's little joke; he was the sole owner of the business, but he felt he should acknowledge he was a

Gemini) it had been as a client, the second as a buyer, the third as a prospective employee. "Why don't you study and take the law boards a second time?" he'd said to her. "Why don't you get rid of your trust-fund guilt and expand out of your parents' converted garage?" she'd said. Checkmate: she passed the exam on her second try, then turned her attention to the next challenge and studied to become a real estate agent; he moved into a gargantuan church put up for auction by the Feds that sold far below market value. He had placed two gargoyles above the entranceway, painted the interior with richly pigmented Benjamin Moore historic colors, then written a long letter which was printed in the *New York Times,* indicting himself, as well as the system, for allowing people to take advantage, at the taxpayer's expense, of expedient fire sales to unload properties following the collapse of the savings and loan industry. This resulted in his real estate business's instant notoriety, plus the interest of a local congressman who took the occasion to speak for his constituents as being scandalized by the FDIC practices. The whole business became such a cause célèbre that the first day Sonja went to work for Tony, cameras recorded the employees' entrance while TV reporters identified her as "a disaffected lawyer moving on to other things in the nineties." The program ended with a close-up cut to the gargoyles, as a recording of Tony's Cajun swing played in the background. Truth was, she was not so much disaffected as the repository for other people's anxious desire to change their lives by moving from one place to another. Many clients appeared in extremis, the hysteria of selling and buying taking on a life of its own, people projecting wildly onto her so that she became their censorious parent, their skeptical employer, the devil himself if she questioned their financial stability. She forced Tony and the business out of her mind and walked upstairs to awaken Marshall.

"What's the matter?" he said sleepily, as she rubbed her hand across his shoulders.

"Why should anything be the matter? I just thought you might want to get up and have some pancakes with me before I go off to work."

"Winter," he said.

"What?"

"No blueberries. Winter," he said.

"This means you're rejecting them?"

"Rejecting you and every idea you've ever had," he said, reaching up and pulling her forward, so her face was close to his. He snuggled into her neck.

"You were sleepwalking last night," she said.

"Wasn't," he said.

"You were."

"You were dreaming," he said.

How was it he could make her laugh just by contradicting her? Because he made her see that everything wasn't so serious, she supposed. On the other hand, wouldn't he be disturbed if he awoke to find her sitting by the window—wouldn't he find it a little spooky? She did not do such things, he had already told her teasingly, because she exhibited good manners even in sleep. As he struggled up, she thought how young he seemed sometimes, hair awry, creases in his face made by lying on wrinkled sheets.

"Blueberry pancakes," Marshall said. "It's July. Seventy degrees out there, temperature climbing. Nice day to go rowing on the lake."

"Are we going to do that this summer?" she said. "Last summer we only did it one time."

"Next summer I build you a tree house, put in a grape arbor, don't let the grass dry out, we go rowing at every opportunity."

"I don't want a grape arbor," she said.

"You want a tree house?" he said, slightly surprised.

"What if I did? A sort of home office."

"You like working at the House of Gargoyles too much," he said. "I don't believe you."

"Do you believe I made pancakes?"

"You didn't?" he said, rolling out of bed.

"I did. Big thrill, huh?"

"Yeah," he said. "Now I'm hungry."

She watched him walk to the bathroom, thinking how amazing it was that after all those years they had lived with the bathtub in the kitchen, now there was a large bathroom off the bedroom. It was only the fun—the mindless fun of those days she missed. Not the poorly heated, badly insulated apartments. Not the doctored canned spaghetti sauce, or the jugs of red wine that would taste, at best, as if they had no taste at all.

Downstairs, waiting for him, she poured glasses of orange juice, started the coffee machine. A tree house—what a nice thought. Why not take advantage of being in New Hampshire? If they'd had a child, Marshall probably would have built a tree house. Or was that hopelessly old-fashioned? The child would have had to unlace Rollerblades to climb up. And would it be worth the climb, just to sneak a joint? A joint—probably now it would be crack. Or something new—some tranquillizer used on cows that had been discovered to make you feel powerful and highly accomplished, the biggest cow in the field, a cow who was going places. Well: that speculative cynicism was the way Tony thought, and not dissimilar from the way Marshall saw things. Tony never passed up an opportunity to announce that the world had gone to hell, and that you could never outguess the next ludicrous happening. So, if Tony was even half-right—and you couldn't work with Tony day after day without at least half believing that he might be half-right, which would still account for accepting a lot of skepticism—would this be any sort of world to bring a child into?

Out the window she saw the tracks she had made in the snow the night before, taking out the garbage. Snow had drifted in, softening the impressions, making it seem someone delicate and narrow-footed—certainly not a large, shivering person wearing her husband's heavy rubber boots—had trod in the snow. The outside world was made both simple and lovely by the snow. You could become fascinated, if you forgot you had seen it the day before, and the day before that. Like a sad situation, or a problem, it could seem quite captivating if you were thinking it through for the first time, not the ten thousandth. And what good did it do to think about it? Now that she was forty years old, did she really want to undergo surgical procedures done with no guarantee of success to risk having another miscarriage? The snow that had drifted into her footprints seemed to have already answered the question, but she would have to be a poet to explain, metaphorically, how the question and the observation were related. Just the sort of thing Marshall would present to his class, exciting them with strange new connections, implied complexities. He liked to shake them up; he'd admitted that.

As if some such far-fetched poem really existed, and had already been shared by the two of them, he came into the kitchen smiling.

Dear Martine,

I begin this note with a comma after your name, having been corrected previously by Alice, who tells me that a colon should be reserved for business correspondence. A comma is apparently a more pleasant way to begin.

I enclose a brochure of wicker rockers, which I mentioned before I'd try to get to you as soon as possible. Alice cannot decide between the ones on p. 4 and the larger ones, p. 16. In my experience, Macy's may well be out of both styles, and if one is in stock and the other not, that solves our problem right there. But I think either would be fine and leave it to you to cast the deciding vote.

Let me change my mind about something I told you to mark on the calendar before we left for New York. I don't think, after all, that it would be a good idea to have the dinner on July 4th, even though that is the only day the Burks can be with us. We recently viewed a performance during which several flares were shot into the sky, and I could tell that Alice was very unnerved. I suddenly envisioned us out on the back porch, having dinner, and realized how upset she would be to see fireworks in the distance. I am trying as much as possible to keep her happy, and also to see that she enjoys the house again. Frankly, if she did not think of it in conjunction with your presence, I'm not sure she'd be eager to return. You may already know more than I; surely it cannot always be easy to keep everyone's confidence and not feel that sometimes, in your silence, you are misleading someone else. These awkward situations arise often enough in business. I've had to smile through recitations of situations-in-the-works when I've already been the recipient of privileged information about the outcome; I'm all too aware that people's private circumstances are often the exact opposite of the way they are presented. I'm not above sneaking off a letter to you behind Alice's back, as we see! Something must be done so that she does not equate private gestures with possible betrayals, though.

Item #2. Do you think we should get a dog? I think you are the best person to ask, because dog owners always tell you to get a dog (though they're full of warnings), and people who don't have dogs seem to feel you shouldn't even take on a house plant. Alice has often reacted with immediate warmth when she sees certain dogs, though in thinking back, it doesn't seem to me that this has been true lately. But please do not worry: I am not sending you off to find us a dog, just asking you to order a set of rocking chairs. We can discuss the dog when I get there. Maybe whispering as she leaves the room. . . . Oh, I should not make fun. Or I should make fun of myself for being so unsure of what would please my own wife that I feel I must consult you.

I don't say this to burden you, but you do realize how we both depend on you. Nothing could come as more of a surprise to me, because I think of myself as rather reluctant in matters of true friendship.

With affection,
M.

3

WHEN MARSHALL WALKED into the house and checked the answering machine, he found three messages: the first was from Emmet Llewellyn, President of Benson College, asking Marshall if he would be available to have sherry, late in the afternoon, with a wealthy woman whose daughter had graduated from Benson. The girl's mother was now considering sponsoring an annual poetry prize, which the President understood would be the first step toward working with the college and offering an endowment to bring in visiting poets. "I hate these machines," Emmet Llewellyn said, with much more conviction in his voice than when he asked Marshall to appear on short notice to help entice a rich woman to donate money. The second message was from Sonja; she had called to say that Dr. Llewellyn's secretary had called her at work because they were trying to track down Marshall about something very important. "Sherry and a hit up," Sonja said with a sigh, telling him to call her if he hadn't already received Llewellyn's message, or if he needed further clarification. Was she exasperated with him, or with them—she should only blame them—because they'd called her at work about something that was clearly not an emergency? The third message was from "Barbara. Secretary to President Llewellyn. The President would appreciate your calling him as soon as possible regarding the visit of Mrs. Adam Barrows." She pronounced the last three words very slowly and distinctly, as if she were saying "I need help" in a foreign language she was unaccustomed to speaking. She left the President's phone number at the beginning and end of the message. As he picked up the phone to return the call, he briefly considered telling the secretary that he was sorry he hadn't called back sooner, but he had some trouble finding the phone number. What the hell: he had tenure. And if you didn't keep yourself amused at Benson, certainly no one else was likely to amuse you, unless you still had a taste for students' outrageous stories about why work was late or enjoyed tracking the course of the plague that inevitably killed numerous family members during the time the students were scheduled to take final exams.

"Thank you so much for calling," President Llewellyn said. "And I very much hope you can make yourself available for about an hour this afternoon."

The one thing Marshall liked about Llewellyn was that he had a big pig of a dog, a rottweiler–black lab mix, he thought it was—that he brought to school with him. Why not send in the dog? It would be just as charming as anything he could muster.

"Yes," Marshall said. "But in your note to me, when you thought Mrs. Whatever-Her-Name-Is—"

"Mrs. Adam Barrows. She refers to herself that way. Keeps us guessing about her first name, but not about what generation she's from," the President said.

"Yes. You thought she was coming at the end of the week. I said—"

"You said you didn't remember her daughter, but let me tell you, Professor Lockard, that girl remembers you, and as you must realize, our college would be most pleased to have an endowment that would allow us to bring in a visiting poet. No need at all to state what you don't remember."

"I'll pretend that I'm being tortured," Marshall said. "I'll just state my name—"

"Good one," President Llewellyn said. "I was in Korea. You?"

"Flunked the physical during the Vietnam War," Marshall said. "Mental illness."

"That aside," President Llewellyn said. "I can count on you?"

"Sir, where Spanish sherry is poured, I am never far away."

"We have red wine, too," President Llewellyn said, sounding more on the offensive than he had when he spoke about serving in Korea.

"Beaujolais?" Marshall asked.

"Good one. Three-thirty, in the Irving T. Peck Room. I appreciate it."

He hung up.

For a while, Marshall considered taking some poetry books with him, reading aloud from them whenever he could pretend a stanza or so was pertinent, watching the President squirm. To add to the impression of preoccupation and self-absorption, he could wear the black beret Sonja had found—something that had been mysteriously left hanging on the car aerial in the grocery store parking lot, she said. She had thought about putting it on someone else's aerial, assuming that it must be a lost hat someone had wanted to call attention to, but as she was walking toward the nearest car with an antenna, she realized that a man was sitting inside, watching her. She had pretended to be looking for someone, then quickly returned to her car with the hat still in her hand, feeling as guilty, she had said, as if she'd been caught about to spray graffiti. So: the poetry books; the beret. And perhaps he could bring a bottle of Beaujolais, if there was one in the house. Draw a mustache over his top lip, call her Madame. Such ideas were what Sonja called *not funny* and also *self-defeating.* "You're not one of the college kids," she often reminded him. "Why do you have to let the nonsense get to you so much?"

Because it was what he did for a living. Because he hadn't published a book when he should have, which would have been his ticket out of Benson College, and the possibility of a serious academic career. And now it was too late, because all anyone cared about was theory. No one read books and got excited about them anymore; they argued that transparent plots were murkily opaque and incomprehensible, they projected political interpretations onto literature, then decried the offensive political implications. The day before, while he was getting a drink of water, Susan Campbell-Magawa had tucked a pamphlet in his back pocket—hey: what if he cried sexual harassment?—announcing a conference she knew he wouldn't want to attend: Natty Bumppo and the Postmodern Predicament. Susan Campbell-Magawa and her husband would be renting a Rent-A-Wreck to drive through Southern California in order to go to an air-conditioned conference room in a windowless building, to express outrage, with other academics, concerning the improper politics and convoluted neoconservatism of a fictional character named Natty Bumppo. Mr. Magawa did not live in New Hampshire. He lived in Ann Arbor, where he had a job at the University of Michigan. He and his wife commuted: one weekend a month he would fly to New Hampshire; one weekend she would fly to Michigan. With their frequent-flier miles, they vacationed every summer on Maui, where this year, no doubt, they would continue their discussion of Natty Bumppo while walking the beach with leis around their necks, and eating suckling pig, as Susan Campbell-Magawa continued to try to conceive a child. He knew this because Susan Campbell-Magawa, who had no use for him, was fond of Sonja. They had talked in September, at the welcoming party for new faculty. Mr. Magawa, who applied every year for a job at Benson and who was inevitably rejected because he was overqualified, was not in attendance. One year, he had distinguished himself by fainting while talking to President Llewellyn and later sending a note of apology, saying that his hectic life of commuting had recently begun to cause his physical collapse. Behind Susan Campbell-Magawa's back, Jack McCallum and Darren Luftquist had worked up howlingly funny imitations of her husband passing out. The idea was to enact this as soon as possible after Susan Campbell-Magawa left the room, to try to make whoever remained in the room laugh, which usually meant that she would return to see if they were laughing at her. Once, Jack McCallum had almost been caught. From the floor, he had pretended to be tying his tennis shoe, and Dr. Gerold Ziller (as he always signed his memos) had appeared peculiarly cruel, to be laughing so hard at a man down on one knee, having trouble tying a shoelace, as Susan Campbell-Magawa reappeared and stood frowning in the doorway.

When Marshall first got the job, he had worked harder and been more collegial. But his real friends had moved on, publishing books that got them better jobs, or dropping out of teaching and going to business school, and as far as he was concerned, the serious study of literature had gone out the window when the theorists marched in. As he got older, the students got younger. Enrollment fell, and more local students began to enroll. Now he routinely taught a course in composition, as well as his poetry seminar and his survey course on modern American literature. He was considered stodgy, but admirable. The newer people taught Third World literature and women's studies. McCallum taught a seminar on the unreliable narrator in twentieth-century fiction, as well as offering a course in popular fiction, informally known as "shit lit." Well, he thought: as one student had recently written, "It's a doggy dog world." He was a mutt, and the purebreds were at Stanford or Columbia or Harvard. So, he wondered, who else would be at the sherry fest? Dr. Gerold Ziller was only on campus one day a week, on the orders of his proctologist. Susan Campbell-Magawa had probably already left for the City of Angels, to fly among her airheaded own. McCallum. Would they bring out that wild card? Or would it be other people in the department, or people from the administration? Someone from campus parking, perhaps, to explain why Mrs. Adam Barrows had had to park half a mile away, since the mudflat that was once visitor parking had been paved over to provide an area for safer Rollerblading?

At exactly three-thirty, his hands empty of books, his head bare, Marshall walked into the Irving T. Peck Room. Barbara, the voice on the phone, was there, emptying ice cubes into an aluminum ice bucket beneath the portrait of Professor Emeritus Irving T. Peck. In the portrait, Peck's long neck stretched high, like a chicken or turkey looking for a way out. The folds of skin, relentlessly detailed by the portrait painter, added to the impression of the man as a startled fowl. He had retired the year before Marshall came to Benson, though questions about his sexual preferences still remained, indelibly, in the men's room.

Barbara greeted him with delight. She was younger than he'd thought from her officious voice on the phone—young and, it turned out, quite pleasant. The President was showing Mrs. Barrows around the library, she told him. He wondered aloud whether Mrs. Barrows would be shown the easily jimmied-open window in the history stacks, through which books could easily be dropped from the second floor. Barbara blushed, as if she had personally arranged the book drop. She emptied the ice cubes into the bucket, shook the ice cube tray over the floor, and dropped the tray in her backpack. She set the sherry bottle in place—there was no red wine—and put out plastic glasses and paper napkins on the mahogany drop-leaf. Today, the table was protected by a series of place mats imprinted with pictures of wolves running along under grapevines or through snowy fields, or leaping in midair, about to pounce on a frightened rabbit. Barbara surveyed everything and announced that she would take her leave, lifting the backpack from the floor, shrugging her shoulders to center it on her back as she inserted her long, thin arms.

"I won't drink it all before they show up," he said.

"Oh. No," she said, blushing again, as if she'd actually had such a concern.

Then she was gone, relieved to be away from him, no doubt. He looked around. The barometer on the wall indicated rain or snow, the needle right on the line between the two. Outside, the sky was gray. It didn't look like a snow sky. He sat in one of the brown leather chairs, thinking how inelegant all of this was. The room was a shabby, cheap imitation of an English library, with bookshelves that contained more magazines than books, and a rug that looked like Jackson Pollock had been recruited, in the last thirty seconds of the rug's creation, to drizzle some color over its grayness.

"Hello, hello," President Llewellyn said, extending his hand. "It's just terrific that you could make time in your schedule to see us. Marshall, may I introduce Mrs. Barrows. She's the mother of Darcy Barrows, whom I know you remember fondly. Mrs. Barrows, Marshall Lockard."

"Oh, this is such a pleasure," Mrs. Barrows said. "All of it. The library. Dean Llewellyn's lovely office with that magnificent sunlight streaming in. I hoped it would last, too, but the weather can't be trusted this time of year. Hello, Professor Lockard. You have inspired my daughter and made her the art-conscious young woman she is today. Not a day passes that she doesn't read to me and to Adam from her poetry manual."

"That's—"

"It's a wonderful thing. That's what it is," President Llewellyn said, gesturing for Mrs. Barrows to sit. "What's that song?" President Llewellyn said. " 'It's a great big wonderful world we live in'?"

"But it isn't!" Mrs. Barrows said, as excited as if it were. "How does anybody get along now, with so many pressures from within and from without?"

Marshall looked at President Llewellyn. President Llewellyn looked at the sherry bottle and moved so quickly Marshall had the feeling the bottle might be knocked out of the field if the President didn't stop it. It was a quick catch. In seconds, the cap was unscrewed.

"Ice, Mrs. Barrows?" the President asked.

" 'Some think the world will end in fire, some think in ice,' " Marshall recited.

The President shot him a dirty look, but it faded when Mrs. Barrows said, "Robert Frost!"

" 'Stopping by Woods on a Snowy Evening,' " Marshall said, as if Frost's name were an association test.

" 'My little horse must think it queer!' " she called out.

" 'Whose woods are these? Whose woods these are I think I know,' " President Llewellyn said, not to be outdone.

But what he said ended the exchange. Marshall sat with his hands on the chair arms, smiling. He had decided to pretend that this was a 1940s movie and that he was a famous, wealthy man in his study, and that two mad people had come to call. The movie would be a comedy.

"Now tell me," Mrs. Barrows said, turning to Marshall, as the President put a glass of sherry on the table near her chair. "Harvey sucks" was carved on the tabletop, but Mrs. Barrows didn't see it, because Barbara had placed a doily over the scratched words. "Tell me if there is even a teeny, tiny chance that you remember Darcy Barrows."

"Do you have a photograph?" he said.

The President glared at him, slightly upset, slightly encouraging. It was the look of someone who had bet a lot of money on a horse, watching that horse mysteriously and improbably come to a complete stop.

"She used to say that Bob Dylan was a poet, but I never did believe that," Mrs. Barrows said, nodding as if she had adequately answered Marshall's question.

"Then whom do you most like to hear sing?" Marshall said. (Butler! Please show these delightful people out now.)

"Kiri Te Kanawa," Mrs. Barrows said.

She went up a notch in his estimation. As did the President, for dropping out of this Theater of the Absurd conversation as quickly as possible.

"And what do you think of the plays of Harold Pinter?" he asked, gesturing behind him as if they were shelved in the bookcases, instead of what truly interested college students: old *Time* magazines and books of Garfield cartoons.

"The inability of people to communicate," Mrs. Barrows said. "It is a challenging problem."

"If you were to offer us the funds to hire a poet," Marshall said, "I would insist that you, personally, introduce that poet at the reading he or she would give when they arrived on campus."

"My goodness!" Mrs. Barrows said. "Why, I have no training. I only know what I like."

"Then I'd be happy to help you focus your ideas as you're writing the introduction," Marshall said.

President Llewellyn watched this volley as if he were watching a tennis match in slow motion. His own glass of sherry was empty.

"Tell me the truth now: Do you remember my Darcy?" Mrs. Barrows said.

"If you don't have a picture, I don't have a story," Marshall said, smiling, as if he'd made a great joke.

She shook her finger at him and picked up her purse. She unsnapped it and unzipped a pouch inside. From the pouch she took a small leather folder. Inside, behind the plastic on the first page, was a photograph of a rather plain, round-faced, brown-haired girl. It was only her headband that made him remember her. Darcy Barrows: that tall, shy girl who sat front row center, never speaking unless called on. The girl who wore headbands with little plastic animals on them, or sparkling stars. Five or six years ago: Darcy Barrows.

"I see from your eyes you remember," Mrs. Barrows said. "The eyes can never hide a lack of recognition."

"She sat in the first row. I guess she did like my class," he said.

"And do you know, she lives one and one quarter miles from my husband and me, and every day she doesn't visit—with my grandchild, I might add!—she phones and reads us a poem."

"You couldn't ask for more as a teacher," he said.

"Inspirational," the President said.

"I think Darcy Starflyx should give the introduction!" Mrs. Barrows said.

"Her married name?" the President said.

"Her stage name?" Marshall said.

She ignored the President and poked her finger at Marshall: her sign that he was being funny, but naughty.

Which he continued to be for another ten minutes, before the

President, who was still puzzled about how things had gone so well when they had seemed so bizarre, stood and announced that they must "firm up the details" in his office and have Mrs. Barrows on her way well before dark.

(Butler! See that these people are pointed in the right direction.)

On the way out, Marshall picked up his mail. Maybe he should be an actor, he thought. But his performance had only been so good because Mrs. Barrows had been so good. Probably, if he had tried this act without her, he would have been about as funny as the Marx Brothers with no foil. In her way, Mrs. Barrows had been as charmingly perplexed as Margaret Dumont. All in all, a surreal afternoon. He looked at the junk mail and decided that no, the perfect finale to the day would not be having radial tires put on the car at a 10 percent faculty discount.

"Hey, Mr. Lockard, way to go," a student said as he passed him on the stairs. The things the students said in greeting were formulaic, but didn't really mean anything. The English language could be abandoned entirely. People could communicate by grunts. The graffiti were already everywhere, the new hieroglyphics. Words could be restricted to bathroom walls. Texts could be dispensed with. *All right!* as the students said. All fucking right.

In the parking lot, a girl in sweatpants and a blue parka was running in a widening circle, guiding a yelping puppy on a leash.

"Take it easy you don't exhaust him," Marshall called.

"He's doing!" the girl laughed, continuing to run.

That wasn't exactly what the girl meant, either, he thought. But if he thought too much, he'd be in a state of despair.

"Way to go!" he hollered, with false cheer.

"I'm like wiped," the girl screamed back.

So was he. And he would be glad to return to his house, and to his adult wife, Sonja, who was so fluent in English.

Dearest Martine,

What was I thinking of? I do not, myself, want a dog! That is the simple truth. Lately I have found myself engaged in speculative thought that later seems quite perplexing.

Apropos my last letter: Do you think that sending a note to the Burks might persuade them to come to dinner another night? Might they return to the area specifically to see us, even though they will have relocated to Washington? I would ask them myself, but I know that she, in particular, is so fond of you that I think you might succeed better.

Am I being too overbearing, planning so far ahead? If so, ignore this note entirely, and I will contact the Burks myself once we've returned.

Fondly,
M.

4

WITH THE NEW aluminum snow shovel in the trunk, her felt-lined boots pulled off and placed to drip on the floor of the passenger's side, wearing wool socks and flats with crushed heels that she kept in the car and used as driving shoes, Sonja pulled out of the driveway and bumped carefully into the narrow channel cleared by the snowplow, reaching up to flip down the visor, moving her hand to the tape deck to click in the cassette and hear the rest of the Claudio Arrau recording she had begun to listen to the day before. On the seat beside her was a canvas bag filled with things she thought Evie might want or need: lotion, magazines, new underpants, cookies. The drive to the nursing home took about an hour, and though Marshall had offered to drive her to see his stepmother this coming Saturday, she decided she'd been housebound too long; the drive would do her good, as well as cheering Evie. And now she was being rewarded by Claudio Arrau playing Chopin. The music was as clear and direct as the channel the snowplow had pushed open—the sort of music, she thought, that made you aware that other possibilities surrounded it, music that suggested a physical place, where unheard tones might be as real as heaped snow.

Evie had smoked three packs a day until she had a stroke. Six cigarettes a day until, a year later, she had the second. Now she begged an occasional cigarette from the male night nurse, entered into somber-faced agreements with the doctor that such transgressions would stop. It was so difficult to come to terms with: fashionable Evie, with her once neatly permed hair, become a streaming-haired witch in layers of clothes as odd as the things teenagers wore at the mall: pleated skirts over skinny trousers; tights with rolled anklets; mismatched cardigans and blouses that dangled beneath the sweaters. Her conversations were equally dishevelled: ragged references to things in the present; slightly strange diction, so that the Queen of England became the London Queen, as in: *What do I care how I look? It's not as if the London Queen's coming for a visit.* *Annus* became "anus" as Evie summarized the London Queen's travails for Sonja: O bad year of fires, marriages gone wrong, the doe eyes of her middle son's babies bug-big in the camera's flash, their redheaded mother smiling, her white teeth orthodontically straight, though her life had wavered. Much cleavage; a cuckolded husband; publicly nibbled toes.

Sonja, herself, was certainly not the London Queen. In fact, though her blue earmuffs had become her favorite winter hat, they were not coordinated with her camouflage boots and, unlike the Queen's old-lady handbags with their small handles—handbags ladies hold the way children hold buckets of wet sand at the beach—the black leather bag with the drawstring Sonja carried slung over her shoulder had lasted over fifteen years. Once, among the sunken treasures on the handbag's linty bottom, there had been a rather large zippered makeup bag, now replaced by a smaller quilted bag. When the black mascara dried up, Sonja had not replaced it. The bronze eyeliner had gotten lost somewhere; when she could not find the same shade, she had replaced it with dark blue. Now the makeup bag contained only a small bottle of aspirin, a stub of blue eyeliner. Tampons had taken over. Once the handbag had been a treasure trove of things she found necessary and interesting: compact corkscrews; miniature bottles of perfume; keys to many people's apartments; photo books crammed with pictures of herself and her boyfriends, later a small foldout book of her wedding pictures, soon overlaid by pictures of friends' children. Now the purse contained a travel-size package of Kleenex, and usually a few coupons floated around like buoyant bits of driftwood, along with deteriorating peppermint Life Savers and rumpled bills she'd forgotten to mail. The Mont Blanc fountain pen she had practiced writing her married name with over and over was long gone, lost somewhere, replaced by a felt-tip. Her wallet contained a single photograph of Marshall. On the flip side of the rectangle of clear plastic was her AAA card. She also had one credit card—one more than she vowed she would ever have—which she kept tucked in a separate compartment in her wallet so she wouldn't be tempted to pull it out. On one corner was a hologram of a bird that flashed spectral colors and appeared to be flying as you jiggled the card. It seemed more suitable as an element of a mobile that might dangle over a child's crib than as a plastic symbol of your own potential flights of fancy that could dazzle all the while you were depleting your bank account.

She was, she realized—with the notable exception of her involvement with Tony Hembley—rather conservative. A practical person who thought that if something was serviceable, it didn't need to be replaced. And she had believed in recycling long before it became popular. Old tie-dyed T-shirts had been stitched into colorful foam-filled animals and donated to the church bazaar; trading beads she would no longer wear had been unstrung and added to light-pulls; embroidered free-flowing dresses had become summer nightgowns. Though maybe, come to think of it, it wasn't judiciousness so much as a desire to make the past fit in with the present. Though it surely couldn't be dovetailed, perhaps the past could at least unapologetically sidle up beside the furniture or clothes or philosophy of the present moment.

What, she wondered, had put her in this suddenly philosophical mood—especially on a day when the music she was listening to perfectly augmented the melting world outside, when she was driving familiar roads for familiar reasons? She thought, as Arrau softly played the notes whose near echo of sameness was the ending of the piece, that she must have subconsciously selected music that sounded haunted. It was the sound track for the morning after, music to soothe the sometimes-mad, adagio as antidote to a difficult day.

She passed the dry cleaner's and forgot until she was at the intersection that she'd left clothes there she needed to pick up. She envisioned her recent progress in reverse: she couldn't stop the mental image of her car turned back past the dry cleaner's, retracing her route on Locust Avenue, which curved into Daymer Drive, then the turn onto snowy Hollowell Road, backtracking all the way to her driveway. And then what? Reenter the house and retrace her steps, return to the point where she was still curled in bed, snug and sleepy—act as if she had no obligations? After the visit to the nursing home, she would be driving to UPS to mail a box of clothes to the family in

Appalachia she and Marshall sponsored, and after that she would try to get the car washed before buying groceries. One good thing about winter was that groceries could be left safely in the car for long periods while she did other things. She could leave them there and get on the highway and drive half an hour to Hembley and Hembley, find out if she was scheduled to show a house, then listen to the phone messages, hope that the one contract she had in the works was progressing without trouble, check the listings to see if anything had sold (not likely; in her position, it wasn't necessary to keep posted on all the hysterical cover stories in the magazines, informing everyone that the boom days of '80s real estate were over).

She turned into the parking lot outside the nursing home. Three places were reserved for doctors, six for staff, two for the handicapped. There were five cars in staff parking. The rest of the places were empty, though a motorcycle was parked horizontally at the back of one of the doctor's spots. A red pickup was parked in visitor parking and a blue Chevrolet with Florida plates. She pulled her white Toyota in between the truck and the Chevy, thinking: how patriotic.

At the station inside the entrance she was greeted by a pudgy woman sausage-stuffed into a pastel-green uniform, who immediately announced it was her first week on the job, so she didn't recognize anybody. The woman entered Evie's name on the computer and, reading the screen, told Sonja everything was much the same; Evie was continuing to progress in physical therapy, her conjunctivitis was cured, and she had resumed sleeping normally. The woman spoke brightly, as if anything merely normal could be viewed as amazing progress. Evie had been such an active person all her life, and now she was only a person about whom things were said: she did this; she did that; this is cured; another day passed uneventfully. *How slowly they must pass,* Sonja thought. How very slowly they must pass. As Sonja sniffed a gardenia in a vase on the counter, the woman complimented Sonja's blue earmuffs, which hung around her neck like Walkman headphones. In such settings, there were always so many things left unsaid, Sonja thought: the tacit understanding that we're-okay-they're-screwed was like an eyewink that didn't have to transpire.

Evie and the other residents were at Time with Tots, a weekly visit from a neighboring preschool. Getting off the elevator, Sonja could hear the squeals. First the hospital staff had tried bringing pets in to cheer the nursing home patients, but that resulted in petty jealousies and despondency when the pets were trotted off; then they decided on children, which, surprisingly, the patients seemed not to project onto so much and from whom they did not expect so many things.

Sonja stood in the doorway of the large sunny room at the end of the hallway, the place where patients snacked or talked between scheduled activities, watching the thin-as-a-rail nurse flicking her fingers on a tambourine. Other tambourines had been passed out to the patients. As children tumbled through cartwheels or various contortions on a big rubber mat, under the direction of their preschool teacher, tambourines jingled out of sync, shaken by a woman in a wheelchair and a tall man who sat on a sofa, methodically patting another man's hand, his free hand madly jingling the tambourine, his knee jumping nervously. Evie sat in a small chair—small Evie in her small chair—and Sonja was happy to see that today Evie had sufficient strength to sit there without being tied in. There were about twelve patients in the room, half seeming to enjoy the children's tumbling, the other half sleeping or staring somewhere else. Evie was one of the patients staring somewhere else. For a few seconds, before she took a deep breath and walked into the room, Sonja reflected that Evie's look of hazy concentration had been constant throughout her life: the slight frown, the stigmatic gaze, her mouth the only sure giveaway as to whether she was happy or sad. Today Evie was sad. Drooplipped, she looked at the action, frowned, and looked away—though who wouldn't intensify her wince in the cacophony of the tambourines? Sonja made her way carefully around the room's perimeter, smiling in response to the thin nurse's half smile, stopping to shake the hand of a man in a wheelchair who extended a bony hand in greeting. "I'm not senile," the man said, as they shook hands. Loud jingling drowned out her response of "I'm sure you're not." "It's music and tumbling," he said.

Evie saw her coming, and her mouth eased into a surprised smile. Her speech had been thick since the last stroke, so Sonja's name sounded like "Toada." Sonja smiled at the idea of herself as a toad-woman, some absurd creature in a sci-fi movie—Toada, with supernatural abilities to . . . what? Swim through air, webbed feet kicking behind her, swimming for the distance. No amount of kicking would change this fact: after half an hour Sonja would leave and Evie wouldn't; it was Evie who should have the supernatural powers, Evie who needed empowerment to escape. After she asked how Sonja was, the second question would inevitably be about Marshall. She had stopped asking about Gordon, but she always inquired about Marshall. Why did he call but not visit? Was he still so dissatisfied with academic life? Was he taking care of himself?

From the pocket of her housedress, Evie brought out a card. It was from a childhood friend, who now lived in California—a card meant to be humorous that depicted two old crones with fur coats over their pajamas and Barbarella hair, each drinking champagne, the message easily paraphrasable as "You're only as old as you feel." "Hairy," Evie said. She meant "very," but at first Sonja thought Evie was wryly commenting on the hairdos. Sonja left Evie to get a wheelchair so they could talk privately in Evie's room. The wheelchairs were lined up just outside the door: new wheelchairs with red leather seats, all marked on the back FLOOR 2, quite a few with bumper stickers on the back: I'D RATHER BE WRITING MY NOVEL; I SKIED POTRERO HILL.

As they left the room, the children were holding hands and circling, beginning to sing. Their shrill voices, reciting a poem they'd memorized, seemed grating—and what did the poem, about the coming of spring, have to do with going in a circle? The nurse and the teacher recited the poem: something about crocus popping up with pink heads. . . . Sonja was glad she and Evie could escape the room. As she wheeled her down the hallway, Evie inspected the contents of her gift bag, took out the cookies, planning a hiding place for the cookies once they got to the room. Underpants and cookies always disappeared. Maybe it was the Tooth Fairy gone mad, become the Underpants and Cookies Fairy, a malevolent goblin who stole instead of giving. Sonja discussed the possibility with Evie; Evie told her she wouldn't joke if she had to spend as much time as she did listening to senile imaginings. They settled themselves in the room, which had a hospital bed, but which was furnished with Evie's own furniture. Though it wasn't a depressing room, Sonja was depressed to think that, for Evie, it had come to this—a little room down a little corridor, where she would swallow little pills from little cups that would be of little help.

"I thought about our talk last time," Evie said. "Thought" came out "taught."

"About Tony? Whether I should tell Marshall?" Sonja said.

"I still think what I thought last time. I don't think you can gain anything by telling him. He wouldn't show his emotions, and that would be hard to accept."

"Maybe he'd go crazy. First he'd slug me, then he'd buy me candy and flowers."

"He'd miss when he took a swing at you, and he'd buy the flowers but leave them somewhere. That's what he'd do. He'd come home with his books."

This was the way Evie usually talked about Marshall when he was absent. When he was there, though, she doted on him. Sonja took her hand, nodding in silent agreement, and changed the subject. She told Evie what she hoped were amusing stories about how neurotic some people had been recently as she'd shown them houses. "You know what the kids say now? 'Get a life.' They say it if somebody's fixated on something stupid. 'Get a life.' I was getting gas a few days ago, during the storm, and a guy who was paying for his gas was insisting on telling a joke to the attendant. Cars everywhere, wind blowing, snow coming down, and this jerk was trying to buttonhole the attendant to tell him a joke about the Pope and Frank Perdue, and finally the attendant just walked away, saying, 'Get a life.'"

"Everybody's so rude," Evie said. "It would be funny if everybody wasn't already so rude."

"Nobody's rude to you here, are they, Evie?"

"Marshall," Evie said. "He could visit more often." She bit into a cookie. "I wonder what it was about the Pope and Frank Perdue," she said. "Remember that joke the nurse told me? 'He doesn't write, he doesn't call.'"

Sonja did remember the joke—it involved a woman raped by a gorilla, bemoaning the fact that afterward, "He never writes, he never calls"—but she wasn't much in the mood for jokes. She had talked to Tony just before she left the house that morning, about a house sale that was slipping away, and interspersed with that morning's sexual fantasies, he had communicated his own anxiety about relaying bad news by telling one inappropriate joke after another. And Evie—what must the world seem like to Evie, now that nothing was taboo and there were so many jokes, told by everyone from the nurses to the cleaning crew? She felt stuffy—stuffier than Evie, by far. She was also sorry that Marshall did not pay more attention to his stepmother, though if anyone could understand his habitual preoccupation, it would be Evie. The week before, when Sonja visited, Evie had quizzed her about Marshall. Did he help her with housework? She had taught him how to make a bed, how to iron, how to bake. Did he do any of those things to help out? "You know Marshall," Sonja had said. "He's very distractible." "Well, are the beds even half-made, then?" Evie had wanted to know. Some part of Sonja took secret delight in Evie's high estimation of her. If she had answered honestly, she would have said she'd stopped making the bed herself. Not only that, but she'd been cavorting in beds in motel rooms with Tony. On the last visit, she had given Evie the impression that the affair was winding down, though that was untrue. She had misled her, hedging her bets: she'd confessed in order to be forgiven, though in case Evie didn't seem inclined that way, she'd tried to deemphasize the importance of the affair, hoping that would also result in her feeling less pain if Evie did censure her.

"It was quiet here last night," Evie said. She spoke suddenly, as if she had just realized something. "No one was complaining, and I didn't hear one dinner plate dropped on the floor, and the television was broken, which almost gave Mr. Goldman Saint Vitus' dance, so they played music for us. One of the aides went out to her car and brought in Frank Sinatra music. There's a record—a tape, I guess I should say—of him singing duets with new singers" (it came out "pinging duets with new pingers"), "and you know, it was still nice to listen to him, but of course he'd lost that beautiful voice. The way he once sang 'This Love of Mine.'" She smiled apologetically at Sonja. "I never had a crush on him the way most people did. I was just thinking that when he was young, he could sing and seem to make the world go quiet. I think people in the nightclubs did settle down. They paid attention even when he was singing an up-tempo song. They couldn't help but listen, the way you can't think of anything else if there's a bee behind your head." "Bee" came out "tree," and it was only when Evie made a spiralling motion with her finger that Sonja understood what she was pantomiming. "And if I was like some of the others here, I'd take the occasion to talk about the beautiful gardens I used to have, and to tell you about all the bees that would come for the purple flowers on the oregano plants, but that drives me crazy: they say one word, like 'bee,' and they're off and running about every time they ever saw a bee and how funny and meaningful and important it was, like you'd never seen one yourself. I could get bothered by it, but I don't." She shrugged. "I am bothered by it. But that doesn't mean I'm going to tell you about every other time in my life when I was bothered." Evie fidgeted with the ring on her finger. "And another thing they do is make complete non sequiturs," she said, "so maybe I'll take a hint from them there. I wanted to ask you to unwrap some more of that Yardley soap you brought last time. At my age, I'm not going to wash with little shards of soap anymore. It's not like we're still back in the days when all of America was told to 'Use it up, wear it out, make it do, or do without.' Of course, they tell you whatever they want to tell you. Look at the so-called gas crisis, not so many years back."

Sonja could not be in Evie's room long without feeling trapped, and Evie knew it, so she asked her to do things for her: straighten the clothes on the hangers; unwrap new soap. When Sonja finished, it was always her cue to leave—Evie expected it and acted as grateful as if she'd served her all morning.

Downstairs, though she had forgotten to sign in, Sonja signed out. Meal trays were being wheeled onto the elevators for the patients who ate in their rooms instead of going to the common room. The sausage woman was standing by the elevators, joking with one of the men pushing the carts. She waved to Sonja to acknowledge her leaving, but did not return to the desk. Her task was left unfinished at the computer; fish swam across the screen as the machine awaited her return. The smell of gardenia was strong in the air, an oppressive smell of near-cloying sweetness that stuck in her nose as she stood in front of the automatic door and emerged into the suddenly much colder day, the sun having disappeared behind clouds, the snow as discolored as candle wax rubbed between dirty fingers.

As she started the car and backed out, she had a sudden memory of the children circling. She heard again the chanted poem and wondered whether it would have amused or dismayed Marshall—Marshall with his love of Yeats and Pound and Shakespeare's sonnets. Though she did not always know his thoughts, she usually knew which issues he was thinking about, and, after so many years, she could formulate arguments for or against, which—to tell the truth—she often invoked not as a matter of principle but to get a discussion going. As winter wore on, Marshall went into his own form of hibernation. He could become as silent as drifted snow.

Martine, dear:

A quick note to ask that you do me a couple of favors. I enclose E. Bedell's business card and wish you would call and say it would be better for him to visit in late June, when some fellow is coming from Yale to fund-raise, so by joining our forces we might escape paying through the nose. He will already know what this is all about. I believe he will be in Stonington, but someone should answer at any of the numbers.

Also, the owner of Heatherfields has told me there is a slight possibility of getting some trees planted before the summer is over — you would think they'd try harder to please in this bad economy, but they're as vague as ever. The other favor is that Alice has taken quite a dislike to Mr. Perry's painting in our bedroom, and though it hurts me to part with it, I think if it could be taken down for the present and put in another room, that would make her happier. I try to walk the line about what is an indulgence of Alice and what is simply common courtesy. I suspect I am overreacting to her overreaction, but if you would put it in my study — just lean it against the wall, I mean — I'd appreciate that.

Alice firmly refuses to phone Dr. St. Vance, whom she formerly thought quite brilliant and helpful, and I am wondering if I would be asking too much to put you up to calling his office and letting him know she will soon be returning to Maine. He is so tactful, he may wish to phone to welcome her, or something like that, and I feel sure that when she hears his voice her resolve will change. If this is an imposition, do nothing and I will try to handle it when I arrive. I suppose this is going behind Alice's back, but she still seems very sad to me, quite irrespective of circumstance, and I know that previously you shared my belief that . . . oh, I am lecturing you, and twisting your arm besides. Do what you think best.

Until we meet, Fondly,

M.

5

IN A DISTURBING DREAM, the beagle that had run into the road when Cheryl Lanier had been in his car took flight just as he was about to hit it, his attempts to brake in time futile, the car like a heat-seeking missile targeting its object. Marshall was asleep and aware that he was dreaming, but someone or some situation had forced him to be asleep, so it was with the mixed emotions of a person unwittingly drugged, or perhaps hypnotized, somehow kept in a dreamlike state against his will—well: he couldn't articulate it, but if he'd been forced to describe the way he felt, he could have said only that he felt slightly anesthetized and that while he knew the out-of-control car might cause serious harm, there was a simultaneous awareness that he could relax, because he was only a dreamer in a dream. Then his perspective shifted, and what he saw was a car in the snow, a car that might drive forever, a snowstorm that would continually fall, and beside him in the car was Cheryl. He had thought, within the dream: *I'm dreaming,* but then he had felt her hand in his and been sure that he was in real time, that whatever was happening was real. Somehow he and Cheryl had gotten out of the car, and they stood on an embankment, ankle-deep in snow, looking down on a miniature car running on its own, as if they were watching a slotcar someone else held the switch for. He felt momentarily pleased, in the dream, like a child taken to look inside a department store window at Christmas, seeing a train whizzing around a track, mounds of cotton sprinkled with glitter approximating fallen snow, small lights warming the interiors of each small cottage. Everyone

was old-fashioned: the women in their wide-brimmed hats and floating scarves, hands plunged into furry muffs; the men in fedoras, holding aloft tiny children who were replicas of themselves. Everyone was
waiting—as those at the store window waited—for Santa's sleigh. He
was clasping Cheryl's hand in childish excitement as the teetering
sleigh on its nearly invisible wires began its transit across the night
sky, the sound of bells heralding its passage, Santa's face seen in profile, until the sleigh with its shaky runners disappeared in a denoue-
ment of tinkling bells, while down below the automated figures,
whose movements had not been well synchronized to correspond to
the arrival of Santa's sleigh, looked up just after he disappeared, their
hats falling backward, the children held aloft to gaze upward at absolutely nothing.

   None of which Marshall remembered until, standing with his bare
feet on the cold bathroom tiles, he glanced out at the snowy morning,
looking through the window to where one long icicle seemed to di-
vide the glass in two. He crossed the floor to rub his pajama sleeve
on the smudge of frost inside the window, peering up to see where
the icicle originated, peering down to guess the depth of snow. He
saw a dog sniffing near a bush. Seeing his car in the drive transformed
to an R. Crumb mound, he remembered that not long ago he had
been out in the snow, standing on a hill with Cheryl. No, he hadn't;
he had dreamed they stood together in the snow, but actually, the
time they had been together, they had been inside his car, or in the
tavern. They had not stood in the cold night air and observed any
winter wonderland, any department store's miniature animation of
village life on a wintry night. He had heard about her roommate's
problems, she had flirted with him—to give her credit, what she had
done was certainly a rather forthright, innovative version of flirting—
and driving home he had thought again about the necessity of getting
adequate counselling for Livan, about the surprising stupidity of so-
called counsellors who should not have been able to keep their jobs
if they could only question the victim about how abusive sex might
affect her future. For a while he had successfully displaced his hostil-
ity toward McCallum onto the counsellor, whoever she was—that
would be up to Sonja's friend from the book discussion group to find
out for him. But exactly which one was Jenny Oughton? Though
Sonja had tried to describe Jenny, the women were not very differenti-

ated in his mind: they were mostly women who had vaguely mannish haircuts, geometric earrings, and proper New England clothes, sitting in the living room shoeless, their socks individualizing them as pragmatic or mischievous. Though anyone could surprise you, those particular women, who were all about the same age, about the same height, either unnaturally thin or twenty pounds overweight, seemed, except for their feet, to hold no surprises. Sonja was the prettiest. She was also—from the few times he had overheard them discussing books—one of the most articulate. He was probably guilty of taking her for granted, though she never accused him of that. He saw from a note she'd left for him that she had gotten up early to visit Evie and then, hopefully, to show a house. Instead of writing the last word, she had drawn a rectangle and perched a triangle atop it: a house without doors or windows, the two geometric shapes meant to symbolize "house." Maybe it was a form of superstition: if she didn't say the word, if she didn't refer to the house as what it was, maybe she would get the sale. Sonja was afraid of Friday the thirteenth and would not walk under a ladder. A ladder: he thought of the concluding lines of Yeats's brilliant poem "The Circus Animals' Desertion," then of the imaginary ladders he'd leaned up against his childhood home to frighten his brother, Gordon, inventing scenarios to scare Gordon about burglars climbing shadowy steps in order to pounce on him in his sleep. Instead of Santa with his bag of toys, the intruder would carry a bag containing ropes to bind Gordon's wrists, gags to snake through his mouth. Marshall's vivid imagination had transformed every branch blowing in the wind into a footstep, while the tree shadows were squinted into precarious burglars' ladders leaned against the house in windstorms. He had hated to let one imaginary scenario go to accommodate a revision, so that if whoever was imagined to be entering the house by ladder was not frightening enough in his own right, the intruder would hold a cage in which a wild coyote paced, a coyote that would be set free on Gordon's face, where he would devour him by first eating his brain. Marshall had such a talent for storytelling that even though he was younger than Gordon, Gordon could be made to shriek muffled cries of terror into his pillow. And Marshall was so good at pretending, that if their father came into the room, he could feign sleep convincingly. His father never doubted it, while he'd hiss in Gordon's ear that he was going to pull him out of bed and make him sit upright in the living room with all the lights on if his ridiculous night terrors didn't end immediately. That was the punishment for too much carrying on at night: back in your clothes, out into the living room chair, and not the one with the footstool, either, hands in your lap, the overhead light burning. You could fall asleep if you were able to. If you stayed awake all night, well: that was your problem. Caused by you. Because of being ridiculous. So think about it.

He turned off the electric razor and placed it in the recharging stand toward the back of the counter. The image of a bound Livan cycled through his thoughts just as the memory of his cringing brother, hiding from burglars, faded. Having no image of Livan, in his mind he had made her look something like Cheryl Lanier: that height; those eyes, clear of makeup; the girl's smooth, unlined face still settling into its final bone structure. When he'd returned home after being at the tavern with Cheryl, he had told Sonja he needed information from her friend at student health. In only the sketchiest way, not naming names, he had told her that some faculty member had apparently mistreated a student, and that the student's visit to a psychologist at student health had only compounded the problem; what was the name of the woman in her book discussion group who worked at student health? He did not want the poor student to blunder into an inadequate counsellor a second time.

"Jenny Oughton," Sonja had said. "I can't believe you've forgotten the name of my best friend." She flipped open her address book to write down Jenny's work number. "She's hard to get in to see, though, because she's in charge of a yearlong research project—which I've told you about and you've no doubt forgotten. So be sure to remind her that you're my husband. Never thought I'd be so helpful, did you? Knowing me is like knowing the doorman at a hip new disco."

Were there still discos? Did anyone use the word "hip" anymore? He'd wondered that when Sonja said it, and he wondered again as he pulled his robe off the hook on the back of the bathroom door and walked downstairs, heading toward the kitchen telephone. Raves, that's what the students talked about: going to a rave. He had no image for raves, except that the idea of them made the kitchen look ridiculously banal, bleached as it was by morning sunlight, crumbs on the floor, white dishtowel dangling from the handle of the refrigerator so that the refrigerator seemed to be offering itself in surrender. He called student health and asked to speak to Jenny Oughton.

"Dr. Oughton?" the young woman who answered replied. "She's not available. May I take a message?"

"I know she's involved in research," he said. "I'm the husband of her friend Sonja Lockard. I teach at the college. I need to speak to her about"—how to phrase it?—"a private matter."

"Certainly," the voice said. He could almost sense the young girl drawing herself up to full height: responsive; businesslike. "Let me put you on hold."

He waited. He pulled up a stool and sat at the counter by the wall phone, resting his arm on a pile of newly laundered underwear Sonja had not yet taken to their bedroom. He found himself wondering if the women's socks corresponded to their underwear. Perhaps, because Sonja's usual socks, navy-blue knee-highs, seemed a practical accompaniment to her white cotton pants. She had gotten rid of her bikini briefs, she had told him when he asked, because she could easily tuck the T-shirts she wore under blouses and sweaters into her pants when the pants rose to her waist, but the T-shirt would work its way up if she tried to keep it in place anchored under bikini briefs. It shocked him, sometimes: how mundane, but how compelling, were the things his wife told him. Was it because he loved her that he could retain such information—even conjure it up apropos of almost nothing, while sitting on a stool and glancing over his shoulder, thinking about eating a banana? He wondered, idly, if there was any poem that contained the word "banana." "Peach," certainly: what Magritte had done for the green apple, Eliot had done for the peach. For a moment he thought how different, how absurdly different, the whole poem would be if Prufrock had wondered whether he dared to eat a banana.

"Sonja's husband?" a woman's voice was saying on the phone. "Hello, Marshall. I'm on a speakerphone; that's all there is in this room, and several people are here with me. I just wanted you to know."

"That's fine," he said. Was he talking to the woman with the socks patterned with roses, or the heavy-duty gray ones that men and women alike wore, with the band of red around the top?

"What can I do for you?" Jenny said.

The gray ones.

"I'm actually wondering if there's any time today I could stop by to talk to you briefly. It's about a student—a slightly complicated situation, and I'm calling to ask you a favor, having to do with her seeing someone at student health."

"If this has to do with psychological counselling, I'd need to refer you to someone else. Sonja may have told you that I'm involved in research right now." There was a slight echo on the line as she spoke the last word of each sentence. "Now," he heard, in a quiet tinny waver.

"Still, could I drop by?" he said.

"Certainly." Gray socks; he was right. "I usually take a break around two, or you could come when we close at five."

"Thanks," he said. "I'll be there at five."

As he replaced the phone, it rang almost immediately. It was Sonja, calling from Littleton, ten miles away, wanting to know whether she had left her gloves in the basket by the door, or whether she'd forgotten them at the house she'd shown earlier that morning. He sprinted into the hallway and saw them there: the long suede gloves. "Weren't you cold without them when you walked out the door?" he asked.

"I was sleepwalking," she said.

The second call—it was probably best the calls hadn't come in reverse order; it would have been difficult to withhold the news from Sonja—was that Evie had had some sort of seizure, not a stroke, a seizure, and was awaiting transfer to the hospital. For a long time he'd known this was coming, and yet he hadn't known, had done nothing to prepare himself. He had conveniently pretended that Evie's situation wouldn't worsen; he had seized upon whatever encouraging news Sonja gave him after her visits: that Evie had laughed at a joke; that she'd suggested he might help out by baking cakes, which Sonja thought might have been a subtle joke on Evie's part. He knew he had let her down in big ways as well as small. He wished, foolishly, that he had baked a cake for Evie. He wrote down the name of the doctor and the hospital's phone number, thanked the person who had called, then stood with his hands in the pockets of his robe, looking out the back door at the white lawn, the white bushes. The wind was gusting, blowing the fine, dry snow upward as the sky sent down more in a gradual sift. If Evie died, he was going to be filled with regret, and Sonja was going to be very, very sad. If she died, he was going to feel guilty that he hadn't accompanied Sonja on her many visits to see her: he was always secretly pleased when Sonja made the trips alone, relieved that he wouldn't be expected to relive the past with Evie or, worse, be asked to read to her from her anthology of poetry: insipid, rhymed poems that were a travesty of the genre, as if he, a professor, were inseparable from the drivel any uninspired fool had written. A seizure: What did that mean? You lived in your body, but when something went wrong, you had to consult a doctor to tell you what had happened. It was absurd, how little everyone knew: it was like inhabiting a house while at the same time suspecting that if you peeked under the rug, you would realize the floor sagged because the supports had rotted, and what that meant was that you had several options. Inspect for termites, first off, everyone in agreement. Then, if termites could be ruled out, what? Surgery? The various degrees of pain imagined and computed, rarely referred to directly. Except that if the problems were bad enough, you could always—at least hypothetically—exchange one house for another, while the body was the only house you would ever inhabit, inescapable, the decor dealt out hereditarily, the gradual deterioration nothing you could do very much about. From his robe he took the note he'd pocketed earlier, in the upstairs bathroom, and looked again at Sonja's simple house. It seemed, like all symbols, evocative and also mysterious—a serviceable image that would communicate simply at the same time it implied complexity: there was no such thing as a winding road that was only a winding road (thank you, Robert Frost; thanks, Beatles). As he pocketed the note on his way upstairs to dress, he wondered why he had fixated on the little drawing, decided that it had provoked his thoughts because Sonja's hand had drawn it; he was appreciating not so much the drawing as the creation of his wife, his wife who simplified complexities, or who tried to. Come to think of it, the drawing was not much different from what she did all the time: keeping things running smoothly; assuming responsibility and not talking about all the trivia involved in getting so many things done—including her ability to deal with emotional issues he'd just as soon sidestep. Sonja remembered birthdays and anniversaries, Sonja dispatched flowers and thoughtful notes, Sonja got in the car every week and drove to visit Evie regardless of the weather, as long as the roads were passable. Though that particular drive might be one Sonja would not be taking in the future. It was slightly strange, he thought, that the bad news had shaken him so little; he worried more for Sonja's sake than for Evie's, imagined himself dutifully accompanying Sonja through the formalities of hospital visits or attending the funeral, saying the proper things, paying whatever bills needed to be paid. When Evie first went into the nursing home, he had gotten power of attorney. One of the first things he had had to do was get his name put on Evie's checking account so he could pay her bills. The newly printed checks had come with Evie's name and his printed double-decker at the top, with both addresses, but only his phone number. The checks themselves astonished him. When he ordered the new checks they printed the information on Evie's former choice of decorative checks: faded images of pirouetting ballerinas at the barre and larger dancers in the foreground swirling behind the line to write in the name and amount, their pastel tutus and long-legged pink torsos reflected in a rectangular mirror, the whole surface of the check filled with torna-does of clashing colors so that only the deepest black ink could effec-tively overlay the pandemonium. With these checks he had sent payment for Evie's diapers (payment made directly to the diaper ser-vice, not included in the regular monthly expenses at the nursing home), payment to the phone company for Evie's monthly service (she dialled their number exclusively, he saw), payment for a tweed jacket she had asked Sonja to order from a catalog, and which he first had seen worn backward, like a straitjacket, because Evie had gotten con-fused dressing herself the morning he and Sonja visited. Looking at her in the chair, soon after receiving the gaudy checks, he had imag-ined the ballerinas surrounding her in her strange, Ivy League tweed bondage, seen them the way, in certain light, he had sometimes been sure he could see the currents of the air, shimmering at the edge of the shoreline or far in the distance, wavering above the mirage of a lake his car approached across long distances of hot asphalt. Those visits to Evie had seemed interchangeable with taking a long drive: time passing slowly, the speed of the car seeming slower than what the speedometer indicated, a drowsiness overcoming him until he found he needed caffeine, yearned to stretch.

Evie had always loved him, but it was so clear whom she had come to love most, the light in her eyes sparkling when she looked from him to Sonja. He was at a disadvantage with Evie, of course, because when she became frail, it frightened him, and he backed off. And what did he know about women that age? Young women he did know something about, because he came in contact with them, but he never imagined his students old; it was not that he really thought of them as forever young, but that beyond a certain point, he knew whatever effect he had had on their lives would dissipate. There were not very many Darcy Barrowses. He would be mixed in with other memories, perhaps existing only as a person who provided a footnote to the fondly remembered campus. Or they might remember his name but not much else about him, as they remembered a line of a poem— time would erode the body of the poem and let linger, at best, a line or a phrase. He would no longer be as tall or as handsome, as original or funny, because they would have spent their adult lives inflating and deflating their husbands and lovers. Some would inevitably remember with embarrassment the silly gifts they had bestowed on him, the curlicued calligraphy written on cards with implied messages or, worse yet, cards that seemed humorous because they'd been young and had not yet heard all the jokes. Sometimes—a few times—students had tried to do it over again. The girl who had given him the dumb card of a pig flying over a rainbow writing a real note, years later, about how difficult her life had become and acknowledging what had once been her adolescent crush on him. The person who had given him a cute little plastic lion cub inside a geode now apologizing, in effect, by knitting and sending a conservative blue scarf. The strange cookies, studded with things no adult would want, like chopped Reese's peanut-butter cups, or miniature marshmallows, replaced by a simple chocolate bar mailed from Paris. Though he got quite a few cards at Christmas—at least for a few years after they'd left, from those students who had particularly liked him—they usually thought of him not at holidays, but at odd times, such as when the line of a poem they'd studied with him was suddenly clarified by what they'd experienced, or when, in their travels, they finally saw a particular painting or sculpture that had been nothing but an allusion in a poem until the moment they stood in front of it and it shimmered. So many of his former students were out there, the ones who grew to his height, but who still thought he was taller than he was, the ones who would always see him running an impatient hand through bushy hair, though his hair was thinning, those who against all evidence continued to believe that he had unique insights, and that he had been speaking to them, personally. And this one thing was always true: in the letters and postcards they sent, they never thought to ask if he remembered them. No doubt that would have been as absurd, considering what he represented, considering their projections onto him, as beginning a letter, *Dear Father: As you may remember, I am your son.* Well—it was probably true that he simplified their young lives the same way they romanticized his. Or at least he had, until recently, when—without his at first realizing it—his students had begun to seem strange; strangers who were not recognizable, very young people whose motivation he didn't understand, or feel at all drawn into. The gap had widened. Still, those who cared about him cared about him, but now there were limits to his concern, or even to his infrequent, vague affections. They weren't even his children; they were somebody else's children, who would go off and do whatever they did, and after so many years of teaching, he might as well admit he wasn't doing it because of them, but for personal reasons—personal reasons, plus his salary. He was passing time among them because he liked to read books. Also, the lecturing made for a little excitement; he gave himself credit for impassioned yet overstated appreciations of poets' rather ordinary terrains, for his dense explanations of matters just slightly opaque. And then he would turn his attention to the students who took the bait, to those whose eyes widened with incredulity. Continuing, just as outrageously, he would then smile slyly at Cheryl Lanier, or anyone else who caught on, at once acknowledging his outrageousness, but also making clear that he had favorites in the classroom, to whom he was speaking directly.

He watched as Sonja's car came slowly into the drive. It was not until he saw her car that his eyes filled with tears. The neighborhood boys had shovelled the drive early in the morning; otherwise, it would be impassable. They'd be around for their payment as soon as school was out: the big-eared boy the girls called Mickey Mouse and his younger, towheaded brother who was so diminutive they taunted him as Tinkerbell. They had their routine down, Mickey and Tink: Mickey shovelled first, followed by Tink, who widened the path by throwing snow off to the left and right, having the more difficult job but working fast enough to keep up with his brother.

Sonja stepped out of the car, the wind lashing her hair across her face, her bare hand reaching up to pin it back. *I have been standing around the house, staring out one window or the other all morning,* Marshall thought. *Now I'll have to stare into my wife's face and tell her Evie has had a seizure.* He frowned as he thought of it. Maybe it wasn't true. Maybe it was made up, invented for effect, as someone in his class had recently accused him of doing when he gave a Marxist interpretation of one of Robert Frost's poems. Maybe Evie was fine. Maybe Sonja would tell him that.

"I think I got a sale," Sonja said as he came down the stairs into the front hallway to greet her. "Cross your fingers and hope this one goes through. The housing inspector goes there tomorrow, and I don't think these people are kidding about being able to pay cash."

He embraced her, realizing as he did that she would misunderstand and think he was happy about the upcoming sale. He was stalling for time, though what help could a few seconds be? He pulled Sonja tightly to him and told her there was bad news: Evie had had a seizure. He could tell from her suddenly rigid body that Sonja believed this entirely. "But Marshall—I just saw her," Sonja whispered.

"They've taken her to the morgue," he said, the word out of his mouth before he realized what he was saying. "To the hospital," he said quickly.

"Which is it?" she said, looking at him as if he were mad.

He was so surprised at the stupidity his awkwardness produced that he didn't dare speak again. He looked blankly back at her.

"You think I can't handle it if she's dead?" Sonja's eyes had filled with tears.

"She isn't dead, she's fine," he said.

"Fine?" Sonja echoed.

At that moment, all he could think to do was to throw himself into Sonja's arms—this time he was not embracing her so much as he was pleading with her to embrace him. Which she did, standing there sniffling, her head against his chest. Finally, she said, "Why are we just standing here?"

. . .

It wasn't until five-thirty that he realized he'd forgotten to call Jenny Oughton, and when he did call, from a pay phone in the hospital lounge, he left his message, his apology, on the answering machine. The clinic was closed for the weekend. He would have to ask Sonja for Jenny's home number, call her there, and explain why he hadn't shown up. As he stood talking to the answering machine, he realized that he was looking at what had by now become a very familiar face: the face of a coyote on the wildlife magazine that always seemed to be thrown somewhere in his bathroom, the magazine that was also thrown on a tabletop in the hospital lounge.

As a child, it had been his responsibility to keep the house tidy. Gordon was called upon for other services—the more difficult things, actually, such as fixing the toaster or planing the bottoms of humidity-swollen doors—but it had been expected of Marshall that he put things back in their places, replace burned-out lightbulbs, sweep. Evie had hated the sound of the vacuum, so most often they had swept, in unison, Evie accelerating the pace to see how long it would take him to catch on. And it had always taken too long: he had quickly fallen in step, and would have worked frantically if she had not eventually leaned on her broom handle and told him to relax, that they weren't sweeping to win a race. A clean house had simply been expected: shelved books; straight hall runners; pots and pans in the proper place. He knew that now he had become disorganized. Most days he lost his keys, forgot to put money in his wallet, wrote notes about errands that needed doing that he then left behind. Sonja would shake her head in disbelief when he attempted to make the bed, the sheet hanging low on one side and the blanket hanging almost to the floor on the other, the bedspread with its design off-center, both pillows mashed together, half under the bedspread, half-exposed. He knew that Sonja and Evie laughed about his ineptitude, though now that he thought about it, that, too, might be rooted in an unconscious protest against having to straighten up the mess after a night's chaotic tossing and turning, or—though it had become less frequent—lovemaking. What a thought: lovemaking. So very long ago: his father and Evie. The night sounds. The wordless activity he had drowned out, when necessary, by whispering made-up stories to frighten his brother. How anxious he had once been for silence, wanting both to hear them, and then to hear them become silent.

There was a *Time* magazine with Bill Clinton on the cover. A coloring book left behind by some child, called *Coloring China*. He opened the coloring book and saw a Chinese man in a straw hat, running along pulling a rickshaw in which was seated an American family: Dad's face was blue; mother's orange, beneath a pale-pink pillbox hat; the children's faces were uncolored, except for a mustache and goatee that had been added to the little girl. The Chinese man had not been colored in, either, but whoever had been working on the picture had added a few Keith Haring–like bursts around his figure to indicate movement. Marshall stared at it, enjoying the brief, imaginary transport of this travesty depicting a visit to China. It was better than thinking about Evie, whose face was also blue—though such a pale blue it seemed frighteningly translucent.

Chère Martine,

I write with bad news. At the end of a lovely evening dining with old friends from Boston days, Alice experienced dizziness and had to be taken to the emergency room at Lenox Hill. She is fine now. It was an ear infection that caused her no pain but that disturbed her sense of balance. After EKG's and other tests, the unusual but rather simple problem was diagnosed, and we were able to return to our hotel with a prescription for antibiotics and a prescription for a sedative, as she was extremely upset — more from the embarrassment of not being able to sit upright in the restaurant and having to be supported on the way out than from any physical distress, I'm convinced. Back in the hotel we were both fine — she'd had a pill and seemed sleepy — when suddenly she began to pace the room, again holding her hand to her heart and trying to breathe steadily. At this point I must stop and assure you that everything is in fact perfectly fine now. Several times I led her to the chair or to the bed, though when it was clear that walking provided her some ease I simply walked with her. Eventually we opened the door and walked in the corridor, because there was no way to pace comfortably in the room. At one point I made a joke, stealing a rosebud from a vase on a room-service tray outside someone's door, and I thought as she paused to laugh that she would momentarily be fine. Yet she held the rose to her side with the bud pointing downward like a dowsing rod. She said aloud, to a perfect stranger who passed us on his way to his room, that she was ill, and he stopped to see if he could be of assistance. To my chagrin, she told him about the tragedy, as if it had just happened, and he was of course at a loss for what to do, looking at me for some cue which I dared not give because she can become terribly angry if she thinks I'm giving any look behind her back. Fortunately the man was quite a nice fellow — he also had a suite that had been booked by his company, and he asked us to come in and sit for a minute. I was so astonished at her behavior that I was happy to think of sinking down into a chair myself. Inside the room she did seem calmer, but

I found it odd that while in the restaurant she had been so embarrassed, with a total stranger she seemed to brighten. It ended with the three of us drinking port from a decanter on his desk. I must move on from this description and make a couple of points, lest I forget them. One is that as she became more composed, Alice mentioned that her dear friend Amelia was unhappy in New York and was looking for a way to move to San Francisco. Then she spoke glowingly of S.F. and told the man she and I had discussed a similar move, though I assure you we have not. There it seemed they had something in common, as both had stayed at the same hotel near Union Square, she on a shopping expedition many years ago, he on business. I felt uncomfortable, as she asked him rather personal questions: if he enjoyed practicing law, etc. All the while, she was clasping my hand or letting go of it to glance in the mirror and smooth her hair, which I'm afraid her friends and I had quite wrecked by dabbing her face with a wet napkin in the restaurant.

Martine—only between the two of us: her demeanor changed so that she seemed to me almost flirtatious, so focused was she on the man's every word. All of it was so curious, though—and after a bit I realized that I was completely exhausted, that the strain had gotten to me, and that if we did not leave the room at once, I might never be able to rise. By then, though, the two of them were firm friends. To my relief, Alice seemed willing to move along quite soon thereafter, so we stood and thanked him for his most generous hospitality.

In our room, she insisted I call to find out how to reach this man in the future. I told her that if she found him so interesting, she should place the call herself, since she had not minded at all dragging him into our affairs in the first place, and we had something of a row. She said I was not receptive to new friendships and then—with a clarity I couldn't deny—she said it would be far better if I called than she, because he would see that what we wanted in the future was a social interaction, whereas if she called it might seem improper. As it was, neither of us called. I thought I could be much more coherent about Alice's strange behavior and our odd encounter, but details already slip my mind as I write. That night, I had a dream of trees being planted. In the dream, I realized they would not take root because concrete lay below the grass. The whole house rested on concrete, which extended far beyond the house's foundation, and what that meant was that we would never be able to dig but so deep, and then things would be impossible. (Clearly, your point about my visiting Dr. St. Vance myself, about which I was once so perturbed with you, is not a bad idea.)

This is so sentimental, Martine, but I keep having an image of you when you'd only recently arrived in our home, running from Alice around the dining room table because you did not want her to braid your hair, sunlight streaming into the room — more of the nonsense you and Alice often engaged in. That particular day, the sun bleached out your features, so that you seemed quite surreal. I felt very distant from the two of you, much older than I should like to feel.

Affectionately,
M.

6

"THERE WAS A COUPLE I was showing houses to last winter who'd adopted two children," Sonja said to Jenny Oughton. "They let both kids rename the dog. Don't laugh—it's true. The wife explained to me that when they adopted the first child, they wanted to give him the same name they'd given the dog. The dog's name was Jonathan. The husband changed the dog's name to Sparks, because he said when it ran across the floor, sparks flew from under the dog's toenails. Then when the kid was five, the father told his son about renaming the dog, and the kid went ballistic, pleading with them to restore the dog's name. The parents disagreed with each other—I think he wanted to let the dog have its initial name back, but she thought it was a terrible idea—anyway, it happened, and the dog became Jonathan again, nicknamed J. Then they adopted a little girl, and eventually Jonathan told her about the naming of the dog, and she thought she should also name it. By then the dog was ten years old. She named the dog Cinderella. And the father said okay. He accused his wife of having a lower estimation of girl children than boy children because she wanted to overrule the little girl. Through all of this, there had apparently only been minor confusion, with the dog responding to its new name pretty quickly. Maybe because it was old, or maybe it had a will of its own, I don't know, but the dog wouldn't respond to Cinderella and stopped eating its food. They decided she'd have to think up another name, because the dog had simply rejected Cinderella. She cried and took it out on the dog, going wherever the dog was and saying, 'You should be Cinderella, you're Cinderella.'

Everybody else called the dog Jonathan, or J. And then the dog died. It developed asthma, and none of the medicine did any good. The wife said she thought the dog just knew it was leaving time. The kids were heartbroken, and on the headstone was every name the dog had ever had. The wife adamantly refused to get another dog. They could have cats, gerbils—she even let the boy have a snake. They had turtles and goldfish. They could call any of them anything they wanted, so there were a million names. She told me this whole story while the housing inspector was explaining to her husband why it would be so costly to switch from electric baseboard heat to oil. The housing inspector had brought his dog—this silly Pekinese or whatever the thing was, with a bow on top of its head. Anyway: at the end of her story—I was trying to show her through the house but she wasn't paying attention—her husband appeared at our side, and do you know what he said? 'We have had a slightly fuller life than my wife is suggesting.' I'll never forget that: the housing inspector, with his little dog in his arms, and the husband's barely disguised fury at his wife. I had the feeling she'd told the story a lot of times before, and that she'd tell it again. I just happened to be the one that day, showing them through a reduced-priced colonial."

Jenny Oughton turned into Trevi's parking lot, shaking her head. In the summer there was valet parking, but the rest of the year no one was there to park cars; the valet parking sign had been covered with black plastic. The owner, Vincent, had sunk the parking sign, on an enormous pole, into concrete the second time the sign had been stolen. "Some hippie asshole wants it pointing at his toilet, I don't know," Vincent had told Sonja the last time she'd eaten there.

Having dinner at Trevi had been Sonja's idea; Jenny had offered to cook, but Sonja felt better about eating at a restaurant and not putting Jenny to any trouble. Walking from the parking lot to the restaurant, Sonja said to Jenny, "I probably shouldn't have told you that story. It's probably more of the same, for you. Or it was, before you switched from people to research."

"That was particularly good," Jenny said. "I assure you."

Vincent was not behind the reservation desk. A young blond woman in an off-the-shoulder black dress greeted them, showing them to a table beside a window, as Sonja had requested. Though it was too dark to look out on the water, you could still sense that it was there, see it, almost, beyond the spotlights that tinged the frozen ground an eerie blue. In summer, it was lovely to walk in the gardens after dinner. This was the restaurant she and Marshall had come to on their last anniversary. Now she was here with a friend, with the ulterior motive of telling Jenny about her affair and finding out whether Jenny thought she might be . . . what was the euphemism for "cracking up"? Or was that the euphemism? So how had she gotten off the point so soon, telling the story about the strange family? Sonja wondered. Her best guess would have been that while she knew Jenny liked her, she sometimes felt she needed to establish with other women that she was a real presence, as if her being there, and talking casually, weren't enough. That was what made her an intermittent raconteur. Tony, unlike her, was always self-assured, which allowed him to be quite direct, in business as well as in personal relationships. Once you'd gotten involved with Tony, though, he seemed so authoritative that you forgot to question him, and then he was actually able to act the way he felt most comfortable, operating not by direct lies, but through lies of omission. "Let me tell you some things I would be concerned about if I were buying this property," Tony would say to prospective buyers, adding a winning hey-we're-in-this-together smile, putting himself and the client on one side of the fence and the seller on the other. Then he would discuss the house's more obvious superficial defects, which would deflect attention from potentially complex problems. With young couples who were obviously workaholics, he would stress the availability of interesting things in the community, mentioning scuba-diving classes they would love at the community pool, lying about "the best class I ever took in my life" (tango lessons given by an imaginary local Argentinean couple), suggesting that an exciting life could come with acquisition of the property, deliberately missing the point about their boring lives. Ah, Tony. "You see through me," he'd said to her early on, cueing her that she should, making a preemptive strike in case she had and had some reservations. The attention would be deflected from Tony onto the other person—what an intelligent person, he implied, who saw through him. And then you were hooked and you began to talk about your life.

Sonja suggested the Cakebread Cellars chardonnay when the waiter came to the table. "We could also order by the glass," she said.

This was the P.S. everyone added after suggesting a bottle, made guilty by other people's health-conscious abstemiousness. But Jenny didn't let her down.

"A bottle of Cakebread," Jenny said. "Great."

The waiter returned and put wineglasses in front of them. The busboy stood still until the waiter moved away, then poured water from a silver pitcher tied with a linen napkin into the tall, thin water glasses.

"We've all missed you since you left the book discussion group," Sonja said. "Not only do I miss you, but I always feel slightly guilty that while we're sitting around talking, you're still in the lab." She took a sip of water. "Not that we weren't all happy your project got funded."

"But I've been overdoing it." Jenny sighed. "I finally realized that part of it was a retreat from my ex-husband. I knew if I was home, he'd be phoning me. We finally had a long talk, and I told him things had to change. I made him understand that from my perspective, it was over."

The waiter showed Jenny the wine bottle, although Sonja had ordered. When Jenny pointed to Sonja, the waiter turned the bottle toward her.

"It's good to take a hard line," Sonja said. She said it emphatically, because she wanted to know not only what it would be like to speak so bluntly to someone who loved you, but to see if she could convince herself that such a confrontation might be good. She continued to think that she might tell Marshall about Tony. Though she wavered, thinking one day about breaking it off with Tony, thinking the next day that she'd continue, but quit her job. Or that she would tell Marshall and he would insist she leave her job.

"I was glad you called," Jenny said. "After I exerted all my authority on my husband, my ex-husband, I was lying low. It's a mistake to withdraw from your friends, though. Just like it was a mistake to get so involved in things at the clinic. Because I wanted to tell you"—she looked up, her blue eyes outlined with brown pencil, the lashes carefully brushed with mascara—"I'm going to be moving to Santa Fe. I know that's the last thing you expected to hear, because it's almost the last thing I expected to do, but I went there for a long weekend and I fell in love with the place. I wanted to talk to you about putting my house in Dover on the market. Sonja, you look *so* surprised. You look like one big exclamation point."

"You're moving?"

"I went for Halloween. It was quite the celebration out there. Blue margaritas and pumpkin burritos. When the hot-air balloon we were in inflated, a huge orange balloon shot up over our heads, with black eyes and a black mouth, and there we were: amazed little people flying over that endless expanse of land, riding in the bucket of a big billowy jack-o'-lantern. I know this seems impulsive. It was impulsive to go there, so this is just the rest of my impulsiveness."

"Really?" Sonja said. "What are you going to do in Santa Fe?"

"I majored in art in undergraduate school, not psychology, and I don't know why I gave it up, because it's so challenging, it's so fascinating to see how forms play off against one another, which you really do sense out there because you have to strain for perspective; everything's so far in the distance, you have no idea of actual size. I don't want to paint landscapes exactly, I want the landscape to inspire abstract paintings. I was a figurative painter in school, but the place doesn't make you want to paint people; they seem unimportant in all that natural beauty."

"I've never picked up and gone anywhere," Sonja said. "I think it's very courageous of you. But I guess if a place strikes you that way, you respond to it intensely."

"That's it, exactly. The only other place I was ever in awe of in the United States was the Northeast Kingdom, that really rugged part of Vermont near the border."

"When are you going?" Sonja said.

"I'll actually be living with a few other people, in a tiny dot on the map outside Santa Fe called Ojo Caliente. There's a big place under restoration now, and one of my friends is living in a wing of the house supervising the work. I've already kicked in my share for the rebuilding. I'm going to have a fireplace in my bedroom. Does this sound like bragging? Or madness?"

"No," Sonja said halfheartedly. "It sounds terrific."

"So terrific that you'll visit?"

She looked at the spotlit lawn, the shadowy sculpture near a fieldstone wall casting a dark shadow within pale shadows. She had sat on the wall and dangled her feet, Marshall jumping up beside her on their anniversary. They hardly went anywhere. Certainly, she never went anywhere alone. It was rare enough that she even had dinner with someone other than Marshall. It was an exciting and slightly startling prospect—that she might have a life separate from his. Though she had certainly moved in that direction by having an affair with Tony.

"The place was a peach farm," Jenny said, finishing her glass of wine. "The Rio Grande is right there, just across a field. At night there are more stars than you can imagine. I thought New Hampshire was starry until I went there."

Sonja nodded. "You know, tonight I was going to ask you if you thought I might be cracking up," she said. "I was going to give you some information first, of course. But hearing this makes me think what people should do is think about themselves in relationship to something else, instead of thinking of everything else as things that attach themselves to you. Does that make any sense?"

"What exactly are you talking about?" Jenny said, pouring wine into her glass and Sonja's. Before Sonja could answer, Jenny said, "Don't think of me as a shrink. Don't be analytical to get the jump on the doctor. Just tell me as your friend."

The waiter pretended not to hear this. He came to the table as if he were gliding in on ice, hands clasped behind him. He recited the night's specials and asked if there were any questions.

"Bruschetta," Jenny said. "We'll eat that while we read the menu."

"Excellent," the waiter said. "Brushed with the finest extra-virgin olive oil," he said to the air, as he walked away.

"No, no," Sonja said, slightly embarrassed. "I want to hear more. You're going to be living with other people on what used to be a peach farm?"

"There's a flagstone patio connecting the main house with the new addition. They've transplanted lots of old rosebushes that were here and there so that now they line the patio."

"And you have the money to just . . . do this?" Sonja said.

"Pretty much," Jenny said. "I also took out a personal loan, just in case, while I'm still gainfully employed and a good credit risk."

"I envy you," Sonja said. "Evie—my mother-in-law, who's so sick. She always wanted to move back to Canada, but it got more and more built up, and she got older, and it never happened. I guess I'm thinking of that because—why am I thinking of it? Because I suppose it's good to act when you first know you should, to go someplace at the exact moment the place calls to you."

"You've talked about Evie a lot," Jenny said. "I'm sorry I never met her."

"I'm sorry, too. I hope she gets through this, somehow. I hope you can meet her."

"Ladies," the waiter said, "any questions about the menu?" There were no questions. Jenny ordered veal. Sonja ordered chicken.

"I'm glad you're enthusiastic about Santa Fe," Jenny said. "I was worried about your reaction."

"I think it's great," Sonja said. "I can't wait to visit and float over the desert in a pumpkin balloon. Santa balloon. Whatever."

"My son's going out with me. He's trying to get me to agree that if he stays, I'll buy him a highrider. He's crazy about lowriders and highriders—anything but Dad's geeky car. Of course, Dad's not such a geek that living with him and his new wife and the babies isn't preferable to living with a bunch of pond scum lesbo dykes. He's just checking out Santa Fe, according to him, to eat some good food, see Los Alamos, and figure out whether he could hack the place even if he had a highrider. 'It would have to be way cool for me to stay,' he told me. Completely skeptical that his mother would ever discover *anything* cool." Jenny bit into the last small bruschetta toast.

Sonja had stopped listening. She had stopped one second—one delayed second—after Jenny let her know she was gay. She was so surprised, the silence must have echoed for Jenny as much as it did for her. She simply could not think what to say. Jenny shrugged her shoulders. "Okay, I knew you didn't know," Jenny said. "I suppose I've been leading a somewhat deceptive existence: the research I'm involved in indicates that certain personality types respond positively to skepticism—but how do I live? As a sort of glorified housemother to whoever drops by my house in Dover, validating their experiences whether they're an introvert or an extrovert. And then my sexuality: I give off vibes I'm heterosexual, actually I'm attracted to women. I do put out clear signals that only women are welcome at the house, though. And my vanity: the sin of pride. I like it when they imitate me. Hell—if somebody goes out and buys clothes that I have, I'm flattered. I know it's insecurity, but it pleases me. If they buy gloves like my gloves, it pleases me. I've created a commune for myself. All my research about how people can best get along, and what I really want is my own little world. A secret society of women."

"What about your husband?" Sonja said.

Jenny shrugged again, poured wine into Sonja's glass, gesturing for her to drink. "He's straight," Jenny said.

"It's none of my business. I'm sorry," Sonja said.

"He knew I was bisexual when we got married. I got pregnant, and he really, really wanted to marry me. So we got married."

Two waiters put their dinners down in unison, lifting the warming lids and handing them to the busboy, who held them straight in front of him like two headlights of an old roadster.

"Ladies," the waiter said. "Anything else?"

"No thank you," Sonja said. Sonja was glad to be able to eat, sure anything she said to Jenny would come out wrong. There was no way to pretend to any sophistication now—her silence had blown it.

"Oh, eat your dinner," Jenny said, as the waiter moved quickly away. "See: gay or not, I'm just a Jewish mother." Jenny picked up her knife and fork and cut a slice of veal.

"It never occurred to me. Am I really dense?" Sonja said.

"What do you mean? You mean, have I been playing footsie with some woman and you didn't see it? That right this minute, the jewelry I'm wearing sends a signal to everyone in the gay world?"

"Isn't there something about which ear is pierced?" Sonja said. She realized as she spoke that she was a little drunk.

"Now everybody's ears are pincushions," Jenny said.

Sonja looked up. Jenny was wearing small diamond studs. A gray turtleneck. A man's watch, but many women wore men's watches. A crepe skirt.

"Boo!" Jenny said, and Sonja jumped.

"Oh, I'm sorry. That was cruel," Jenny said.

"Well," Sonja said, taking a deep breath and exhaling, "I've been having an affair with the man I work for. We let ourselves into houses that are up for sale and chase each other—we take turns chasing each other. Sometimes we play hide-and-seek and duck into closets, or Tony will double up under the kitchen sink. He can wedge himself in places so tiny most kids wouldn't attempt them. We always take off our clothes immediately. This only happens naked. Lately I've had an irresistible urge to tell Marshall."

Jenny's eyes widened as Sonja spoke. She had leaned her knife and fork against the edge of her plate. "A person with her own surprises," Jenny said.

"All those bruises, and Marshall never asked. He hardly ever noticed. Once he was running his thumb up my thigh, and I winced, and he said, 'Oh no. I hurt you.' The bruise was already there, yellow and green, days old from a tumble I'd taken when Tony made a flying leap to catch me."

Jenny raised an eyebrow.

"I was going to ask you if you thought I'd snapped."

"Clearly," Jenny said.

"Really?"

"Well, yes. Don't you think so?"

The waiter glided to the table, poured the wine.

"Dinners like this are a lot more fun than book discussion groups," Jenny said.

Sonja, suddenly hungry, picked up her fork and pierced slivered zucchini. She nodded.

"Do people have . . . I don't know what to call it. *Episodes* and then they regain their equilibrium?"

"Of course."

"You don't seem particularly worried."

"You seem okay. Is there something you're not telling me?"

"No, I mean, is this what you'd say if I came to you as a patient?"

"You haven't. You haven't because you know you don't need a shrink. You're having an affair with your boss. Why tell Marshall?"

"I think because I'm angry with him. His life, the way he loves routine, his isolation. I guess I wanted him to know his isolation isolates me, too. You know, I look at Evie and I think time shouldn't be wasted. People should act on their impulses. Is that sane, or reckless?"

"Reckless," Jenny said, summoning the waiter. "Two glasses of chardonnay," she said. "We're working up to brandy."

The waiter nodded.

Jenny shrugged. "Listen—if you need a vacation from everything, I mean it about Santa Fe. I know how upset you are about Evie being hospitalized. I mean, that's enough to have to deal with right now. Don't add to your problems by telling Marshall. It should go without saying that nobody in Santa Fe would misunderstand what you were doing there."

"Thank you," Sonja said.

"What book would we have been talking about this week if I hadn't dropped out of the group?" Jenny said.

"*Last Letters from Hav,*" Sonja said. "Jan Morris wrote it."

"*The Scarlet Letter* drove me out," Jenny said. She ate another piece of veal, lifting her eyebrows to indicate its deliciousness. She put a piece on Sonja's plate. "Wasn't it interesting we'd all forgotten Hester's husband was a real presence in the book. None of us who'd read it back in high school remembered he'd gone to haunt poor Hester."

"High school," Sonja laughed. "What did we know about men haunting women in high school?"

Jenny looked up, perfectly serious. "What's made Marshall withdraw from you?" she said.

"Withdraw? What makes you think that?"

Yet it was a perfectly simple question, based on the reasonable assumption that that explained part of what was happening. Sonja had to question herself when she did not have an answer. Was it possible that not only had Marshall failed to see her bruises, she had failed to notice his?

The waiter placed the glasses on the table, his lips puckered.

The chardonnay was the same bright yellow as a large bruise on the side of her leg she'd gotten in a struggle with Tony, but it was deliciously cold when she took the first sip.

Martine des Fleurs (as Alice says) —

If a comma is more familiar than a colon, then what is a dash? A running start?

I write, having recently concluded our conversation of an hour ago, to say that my plans have changed. I am terribly distressed that I must stay in New York until the end of the week. I have done my best to convince Alice to proceed to Boston and have you pick her up, but she feels that until her nausea subsides, she does not want to travel. I have offered to drive her myself and return the next day. Amelia's doctor has been to see Alice, and she has kept her last appointment to see him, though until the last minute she was insisting that she would not go to his office. Alice has become skeptical of any doctor, including Dr. St. Vance (in absentia). The New York Dr. feels it is only fatigue, and the combination of wine with the tranquillizer that made her dizzy a second time the other night. She is finishing the course of antibiotics for her ear, but has been feeling fine in that department almost from the minute she began taking those pills. The N.Y.C. doctor is always quite worried about medicines that conflict, and in fact seems not much to like medicine at all, but I've known enough doctors of whom this is true not to be surprised. It did distress me a bit that he all but suggested that Alice's having taken one calming pill after a party during which she'd ingested several glasses of champagne was not only unwise, but potentially life-threatening. I took him aside in the corridor and asked whether he seriously thought that one calmative taken two hours after drinking one or two glasses of champagne in the course of an evening was suicidal, and he looked at me as if I'd poured the champagne down her throat and then handed her a pill bottle. Then he said, "I examined her. She did not drink only two glasses of champagne." Well, Martine, I was at her side the entire evening. Even if she had three, this would be the absolute maximum, and she was by no means drunk either at the party or afterwards. The doctor asked me, "Do social occasions make your wife nervous?" At first I thought it the oddest question, yet perhaps her indecisiveness is a response to social pressures. It has grown worse of late; I know the two of you chide me about how easy it is to pull on one of my "uniforms," but her trouble in arriving at a decision is now much worse than when last you saw her. If I see him again, I mean to reopen the discussion, but correct me if I'm wrong here: I assume he meant to imply either that she was generally in not very good shape, or perhaps that in point of fact she was sneaking a drink in the hotel room, or something of that nature, in which case I can swear this was not so. I am probably being overly analytical here because it is a sensitive point—that she might not be doing very well, that is. Nevertheless, I am glad I did not take issue with him at the moment, and of course he is a concerned man, having come out initially on a very rainy night to a hotel to see a patient whom he'd never met before.

The party, by the way, was for my godson, Neil, who sends you his best regards. He has just passed his bar exam. He says to tell you that you should send flowers! Neil, Alice tells me, goes rollerskating in Washington Square Park on the weekends.

We cannot wait to see you. Living in a hotel is only fine for a couple of days. We are both sorry that the company has not yet decided on what to purchase as a corporate apartment. Why did they let the old one go? Real estate prices are going to begin rising again the nearer we get to the election.

It was lovely to hear your voice. I hope to soon hear you humming, as you so often do, arranging the flowers, which by now must be quite plentiful.

Until Friday,
M.

7

———

"I TOLD HER I told you," Cheryl said. "At first she was really upset I did this behind her back, but now she's agreed to talk to you. But the thing is, she says she absolutely will not go back to student health. I'm sorry to lay this on you. I really am. She just—she seems to want to talk to you to see if you think Professor McCallum was deranged or something. My guess is that she wants to think the closest thing she can to its not having happened, which would be that it was some momentary aberration."

God, McCallum, he thought. *You are an insane fucking fool.*

"Are you—I hate to dump this stuff on you, but she and I were just watching the weather, and when the weatherman talked about snow and pointed to asterisks over Boston on the map, she leaned forward and puked on the floor. And it was the first time that day we'd gotten her to eat. I know this isn't your problem, but—"

"I'm sorry," he said. What was he sorry about? Was he sorry that for almost a week, Sonja had gone to the hospital to see Evie every day, while he had dropped out days ago? Sorry he had picked up the telephone just now to get Cheryl's call? Or was he simply sorry that McCallum had done such a thing? Sorry to be involved in this, that was for sure, yet he sympathized with Cheryl. She'd been dragged into a messy situation, and he was about as useful, right now, as McCallum's hearty, but ultimately dismissive, "God bless." He hadn't gotten in touch not only because he didn't want to be kept posted on Livan Baker's sad situation, but also because he didn't want his own life to become a sad situation: a middle-aged man paying too much attention to a teenage girl, himself not so unlike McCallum in being another opportunist, a person who barged into another person's life just because the opportunity was there. Tonight, Cheryl's voice was weary, the fatigue barely disguising real alarm. Just thinking about what happened to Cheryl's roommate made him so depressed he was tempted to personify the weather, to see it as pathetic, this long winter of cold asterisks with diagonal slashes moving in behind and dark puffs of cloud streaming over Boston like steam escaping from a train, obliterating what clarity there was in the sky. McCallum and some kid: *Goddamn.*

"If somebody can't talk sense to her, I don't think she's going to recover," Cheryl said.

"I understand," he said. "I've put in a call to my wife's friend at student health, but there's been something of a crisis here, and I wasn't able to keep the appointment."

"She's not going to eat tonight," Cheryl said.

"You're doing what you can," he said, realizing as he spoke that he was deliberately missing the point: the point was not that Cheryl felt bad, but that her roommate was losing ground. He was aware of that, but he was sitting on a stool by the phone, about to cook a package of Ramen noodles and eat them in front of the fire he'd just started in the fireplace in the living room—the simple, sensual pleasure of it almost made him laugh: as a young man, would he ever have thought an ideal evening would be sitting cross-legged by the hearth, slurping up twenty-cent noodles, reading an essay in *The New England Review* by McCallum deconstructing Arthur Bremer's diary?— when suddenly the quality of his evening, already under a gloomy cloud of anxiety because of Evie's critical condition, was yet again being tempered by a big dose of reality, the asterisks falling on Boston like footnotes offering bad prognoses about sexual aggression, the devil's face more ominous than usual, seen on the fireback through flames crackling off burning logs. McCallum's face . . . stupid, deranged McCallum, who earlier in the week had walked past his office, flanked by several students, raising his hand in a distracted, two-fingered wave, an odd gesture as if he were speaking in sign language to his troops: *There it is, guys; destroy it.* That was, of course, what Marshall feared: that somehow, once he was dragged in, it would be war and he would become McCallum's enemy. Opening the package of noodles, he flinched at what a coward he was, saw himself (chin wedging phone against his shoulder) as self-absorbed, a middle-aged man dodging responsibility in order to eat some fast food while basking by a pleasant fire. He should be interrupting his evening to talk to Livan, if only as a token adult, someone whose sympathetic presence might in some small way mitigate the aftershock of the dreadful trip.

". . . at your apartment," he heard himself saying.

"I would really appreciate it," Cheryl said. "I would really, really appreciate it."

He scribbled directions to her apartment on the back of an envelope. He put the package of noodles with its torn corner back on the shelf, turned off the boiling water, walked to the living room doorway and looked briefly at the already dwindling fire, and with as many misgivings at leaving the fire unattended as with dread about what he was setting out to do, he pulled on his coat, picked up his car keys, wrote a note to Sonja saying he'd explain where he'd been once he was back, then went out to the driveway. In spite of the snow and slush, a boy was riding by on a bicycle, and for a moment he remembered the springtime rides he'd taken with his father and brother, his father's exercise program meant to keep demons at bay and also to wear the two boys out, because of course, in those days, no one jogged, and if his father had gone running, what would anyone have made of the two of them running behind? He watched until the boy grew small and disappeared in the graying distance. The kid on the bicycle made him feel out of shape and out of sorts, so that as he settled himself in the car, he had to remind himself that winter always got him down, that he was going off to do a good deed, that Cheryl Lanier had a crush on him, that, ridiculous as it seemed, he took a little pride in not being the sort of jerk who would exploit those feelings, let alone take a student off to where the hell had it been? Revere. It didn't take much imagination to think of someplace classier than a triplex in Revere for a seduction, though McCallum had probably been cynical enough to do what was convenient. Sort of like opening a package of Ramen noodles when your wife was keeping a vigil at the hospital—anything would do. Sex as Ramen noodles. He remembered, again, McCallum's wave, which had come just as he'd lifted his eyes from a very beautiful poem about a forever-missed moment by Jay Parini, more of the words that rose in front of his eyes every day, as inevitably as the fog that now hazed his windshield. McCallum's wave had been a slight acknowledgment to a colleague already greeted too many times that day, more a gesture that acknowledged one should make a gesture than the gesture itself. An allusion to a gesture that would allude to their complicity in not speaking meaningfully. A postmodern gesture, he thought, amused at his own bemusement. In fact, of the people who were predictably around the department, conversations devolved into sound bites, most often attended by vague kidding or chiding, a tacit admission of I-know-what-you're-interested-in/you-know-my-own-preoccupations. Where did a person go from there? Into a corridor, a real and symbolic corridor, where any connecting or reconnecting would be done between teacher and student, not between teacher and teacher, a hierarchical system in which adults played king-of-the-hill, with their knowledge a caveman's club to keep those wishing to ascend far below: *I'm saying this as a friend. I think that you should tone it down.* He heard her words as he drove down the hill, aware that his anxiety about the house's catching fire was displaced fear, more certain as the seconds passed that he was a coward, whether or not he'd been lured out of the safety of his house, a coward for not having taken McCallum aside when he'd first heard about the outrage he'd perpetrated, instead of looking up, blank-faced, letting McCallum walk by the door simultaneously greeting and dismissing him. Marshall had swivelled his chair to look at the empty space left behind McCallum, finding in it the ghost of a question. Wasn't it at all possible that Livan was hysterical, or crazy in some way, a liar, a young girl who wanted to destroy her professor because . . . because what? Because he had what she didn't have: a mate, a home, a life. Money and vacations. What if McCallum hadn't done anything to her? What if there had been no trip to Revere, what if her boyfriend had gotten her pregnant and she decided McCallum could be the fall guy, maybe because they had gone to Boston together, even visited Revere, but they'd been in a hotel: room-service strawberries and quadruple-priced California champagne, a quick night of laughing at old movies on TV, Livan knowing none of the actors' names, McCallum having remembered wrong, for years, all the famous lines, feeding each other expensive morsels, the two of them slightly tipsy.

He was trying to find a way to blame the victim, he realized. Why bother? If McCallum didn't know to keep his hands off undergraduates, this was exactly what he deserved. But was it really possible that McCallum, striding along in his black sweater and his gray-and-white-striped jeans that were so out of fashion they could quite possibly be of-the-moment, hipper than hip—was it likely that he had tortured one of his students, then returned to campus to deconstruct coming-of-age novels, walking and talking the same way, offering passing waves to colleagues, his vampire fangs retracted into small, slightly buck teeth he self-consciously covered with his hand when he spoke? That was it: there was something about his embarrassment about his protruding teeth, there was some awkwardness in the way McCallum carried his body because of his shame about his teeth, that made him question whether the events in Revere were as unambiguous as Livan made them out to be.

Thinking this, he noticed, sadly, a cluster of dead elm trees as he pulled into the parking lot of a convenience store and tried to think what to do. There was an outdoor phone, over by the pyramid of stacked soft drink cartons—what did they do, disassemble the pyramid every night, so the Cokes wouldn't freeze?—and he eyed it, wondering whether he should call Cheryl and tell her they needed to talk before he got to her apartment, or whether he should simply call home (if the house hadn't burned, his house would be right where he'd left it) to ask Sonja's advice, or even whether he should call McCallum to ask for his side of the story. Of the three possibilities, calling McCallum seemed the most upsetting, so he decided he would, indeed, call McCallum. He would at least give the man the benefit of the doubt so he could address the accusations.

A teenage girl came out of the store, her arms thrown around a boy's arms, pinning them to his sides, giggling. She had on a cap with a tassel, and on her feet the same camouflage boots Sonja was so fond of, though purple leg warmers rose from the girl's boots to just below her knees. Even in her padded jacket, he could see that the girl was scrawny—a word his father had used, which he realized no one used anymore—scrawny and full of enthusiasm, teasing the boy about something and laughing. They got in their car, a beat-up Ford of some indeterminate color that reminded him of the walls in a house he had toured recently, when it was first listed with Sonja's agency. What had

Sonja said they were called? Sponged and glazed. The half-rusted, sun-faded car looked like the sort of paint job rich people wanted on their walls now. He watched them climb into the car, and then, as the headlights went on, noticed a strange blur of movement inside the back window: cats, it was—kittens, five or six of them, their legs slipping out from under as the boy abruptly gassed the car, many of them thrown back against the window, or, Marshall guessed, spilling onto the backseat, one or two dark shapes remaining as tires squealed and the Ford lurched onto the road, bucking as if it were about to stall, then shooting into the far lane. What was the story behind that? Two teenagers with kittens from some stray cat they'd taken in. It was sad, but at the end of every school year, abandoned cats and dogs—even turtles and snakes—would prowl the campus looking for their owners, growing gradually thinner as they tried to find a new friend, many of the dogs and some of the cats following everyone and anyone, in desperation. Once, an obviously malnourished yellow lab had jumped in Marshall's car and sat hopefully in the passenger's seat. He had found a starved cat dead in front of a Coke machine outside the gym. But McCallum's having found a box turtle, HIS HIGHNESS MR. TURTLE painted on its shell with red paint . . . wait: McCallum had been dismayed and angry to have found the turtle upside down in the center of the sidewalk—a football; he had taken it, at a distance, to be a football—did it stand to reason that a man who rescued a turtle would take a student to another city and tie her to a bed? Of course, Hitler had been a painter, a vegetarian. Too many people were bored with what they were doing, and also passionate about something else they did: the internist a lepidopterist, his nurse a blackjack player, the accountant in the waiting room a collector of Byzantine coins. Most of the time Marshall found such things wonderful, but in a way such situations also made him sad—his suspicion that so many other people were not pursuing those things they really loved, as if only the young had immunity from society's questioning a person's desire to be a doctor who catches butterflies and who enjoys discussions about ancient coins, with a few other interests thrown in, such as figure skating, raised-bed gardening, an attempt to read the complete writings of Henry James, plus an interest in the occult and a passion for rappelling. Which, in fact, was true of the doctor Marshall had seen for five or six years, who had finally left the area to study neonatal surgery, while attending whatever performance art was happening in Seattle, as the blackjack-playing nurse, who had become his wife, began to think seriously about adopting a second Rumanian baby. With this multifaceted man, he had once discussed a burning feeling when urinating. A peculiar stiffening of his knee. A rash behind his ears. Those odd yet invigorating office visits: a shot of cortisone for the knee, but how could Marshall, a professor, not have read *The Golden Bowl*? An ointment for the rash, but had Marshall thought about the possibility of learning to scuba dive instead of settling for snorkeling? He felt a kind of hero worship toward the doctor, while at the same time being in the man's presence too long could exhaust him. They'd kept in touch, exchanging books and Christmas notes, and Marshall felt that if the man had stayed in New Hampshire, they would probably have become friends. In fact, for all his colleagues and in spite of Sonja's love, he sometimes felt that he had no friends: they would be, like Sonja, more than friends, or, like McCallum—*God, McCallum, you insane fucking fool*—people who gave intermittent signs of being a friend, but were not.

He parked and went inside the store, where he poured himself a cup of coffee and paid with a dollar bill to get change for the phone. Sonja might be back at the house, and he could ask her advice, tell her about the visit he was about to make. He deposited the money, hunching his shoulders against the wind. The line was busy. As he redialled, the amusing thought crossed his mind that calling home to explain his whereabouts was not something Shelley or Keats would ever have worried about. Yeats. Could anyone imagine Yeats chatting on the phone? The beautiful closing line of Yeats's "An Irish Airman Foresees His Death" passed quickly through his mind. Here he was, in a rather ridiculous situation, suddenly contemplating life and death, which could only mean that he was very anxious, he thought the stakes in his mission were high, or feared they might be. Sonja, of course, would think his involvement in this was a big mistake. Maybe not the involvement so much as the way he was handling things. Though how was he handling things? So far, by conjuring up lines of poetry written by Yeats, while loitering around a convenience store and wondering about the lives of people who got in their cars, by sipping coffee which would keep him awake later that night, by being on sensory overload.

He got McCallum's number from information. The phone was answered by a woman, and in the long time it took McCallum to pick up, Marshall thought seriously about replacing the phone in its cradle, driving to McCallum's, and asking him to take a ride with him, confronting him in person.

"Yes?" McCallum said.

Yes, instead of hello?

"McCallum," Marshall said. As he spoke, he was struck, for the first time, that while everyone called McCallum by his last name, they almost all called each other by their first names. "McCallum," he repeated, as if by repeating the name, he could build up steam. "It's Marshall. I'm at a phone booth outside a convenience store."

Why had he felt that was a necessary detail?

"Hello, Marshall. What can I do for you?"

Marshall detected a tenuous tone to McCallum's voice. Perhaps because of the mention of where he was calling from, or the Coke can clattering across the parking lot, sent rolling by a sudden gust of wind. "I'm on my way somewhere, and I have to talk to you first," Marshall said.

"Isn't that true of all of us," McCallum said. "All of us, on our way somewhere."

There was a long pause, as though McCallum thought he had answered the implied question. Though even McCallum seemed wearied by his oddities tonight; you could hear the fatigue in his voice. He could also hear, above the racket of the Coke can that never stopped rolling, a squeal of brakes in the distance and, from people coming out of the store carrying a boom box, the escalating volume of Whitney Houston, singing about what she would always do. Sometimes the ordinariness of the world he inhabited made him yearn for more excitement. Except that, like McCallum, he was fatigued; maybe that was why people stayed where they were, doing what they were doing: because few people had the doctor's energy.

"The reason for your call, Marshall?"

Hadn't he told him?

"I need to see you about something."

"Tomorrow? Bright and early?"

Very sarcastic, that "Bright and early." As if being up early, on a bright day, were inherently ridiculous.

"I'd prefer to see you now," Marshall said.

"Well, the thing of it is, Marshall, we're sitting around rather stunned, at the moment, because a blue ring has appeared in the little pee jar, which seems to have confirmed that Susan is pregnant. In fact, she was just naming the blue ring when you phoned. I believe she has selected the name of a distant relative, Gemma, off in the kitchen, doing a sort of dance with the pee jar—a sort of twist, if you remember the twist. 'Let's twist again, like we did last summer,'" McCallum said. "That twist."

"Do you know a girl named Livan Baker?" Marshall said.

A missed beat on McCallum's end. "Baker. Yes, slightly."

"She's your research assistant, right?"

"Do I want to be dead?" McCallum said. "Is this a phone call asking whether I wouldn't rather be dead?"

"What?" Marshall said.

"Do I know, and would I rather?" McCallum said. "I do— slightly, as I so circumspectly stated—and would I? I might rather. Yes. Because when I think about it, the weather is dreary, and our jobs don't mean much in the long run, and Susan and I already have a child who poses considerable problems, and now she is overhearing me to say—on this night when she has farmed out the beloved boy to the Luftquists, so we can have a glass of champagne and celebrate, all cautionary warnings about alcohol consumption aside for this last fling, while doing the twist on the new kitchen linoleum—she is overhearing me to criticize the direction my life has just taken, on top of which you call with this disturbing question, wanting to probe something I do not want probed, whether or not Elavil may now mitigate my downward mood swings."

Marshall found McCallum's response so bizarre, so discomfiting, that he said the first thing that occurred to him: "Do you find it impossible to talk like a normal human being?"

Something crashed to the floor in McCallum's house, the noise overlaying the slammed car door to Marshall's right, a tall blond woman in a scarf looking murderous as she stalked into the store, a red handbag clutched in her hand like a brick. Was there ever truly a time when Marshall and Gordon and their father, bicycling through the streets, had rung the bells on their bikes to warn people of their approach, to ward off danger? Bicycling—it seemed like pushing hoops down cobblestone streets.

Following the crash, McCallum had said, "Signing off. God

bless," and hung up. So: it had been the wrong thing—certainly the wrong moment, probably even the wrong thing—to try to talk to McCallum directly. Maybe he should take that as a signal against calling Sonja, also. Maybe it was best he simply proceed to Cheryl's apartment, talk to Livan, get at least the preliminary things over with. *She won't eat,* he remembered Cheryl saying with McCallumesque resignation in her voice.

Knowing it was wishful thinking, he went into the store and picked up a bag of Oreos, a six-pack of Cokes. In front of him, the blond woman was checking out, the clerk placing a bottle of Pepto-Bismol and *Soap Opera Digest* in a plastic bag and pushing the bag toward her. He refilled his coffee cup and handed the clerk a ten, from which he received change arranged as if by a mad origami master, so it was impossible to grasp the money the clerk placed every which way in his palm all at once: dollar bills pointing left and right, coins on the man's fingertips, more scattered on top of wildly splayed dollars. He pocketed it, losing several pieces of change on the counter as he disturbed the balancing act. It was the clerk's routine, meant to be troublesome. If a manager had been there, Marshall might have complained, but the only other person who seemed to be in a position of authority was mopping up a broken bottle of Gatorade, the swamp-green liquid trickling away in rivulets amid shards of glass.

He drove to Cheryl Lanier's, pulling into the safety lane once to turn on the overhead light and recheck the directions scribbled on the envelope. For the first time, he also examined the front of the envelope and found that it was a letter addressed to both of them, from his brother. He opened it. The letter had been typed. It read:

Chers Bro and So:
   Thank you very much for passing on the book on Kissinger. Beth is reading it and says that the man was an unconscionable monster. You know me—I don't read the paper, so thought Nixon and Checkers were still together shitting in the White House. Beth says K. was in no way spiritual. She's read some of the stuff aloud to me, and what I say is—that man needed to drink a few beers and lighten up. Cross your fingers that Watanabe-san decides to buy the dive shop. Hope he doesn't think you have to put on a tank and go

fifty feet down to muff dive. Ha! Can't wait to see you in the Conch Republic.

Love, Gordon

"Won't eat," Marshall had written on the envelope's other side, and underneath that, a list of roads, left turns and right turns noted, plus a doodled star and some crosshatching.

He found the roads, but not the star. The night sky was empty of stars, though there was a blur of moon he looked at, wishing it could be the sun in Key West, where Gordon and Beth lived. As he walked toward the apartment building, which was as anonymous and dreary as he'd remembered from the night he dropped Cheryl off, he wondered what other objects were now broken at McCallum's. Here he was, going up a flight of stairs carrying a package of cookies, his thumb looped into a six-pack of Cokes, about to try, absurdly, to atone for some other adult's mistake, some other adult's pathology— whatever it had been that McCallum so mercilessly displayed in Revere. He was glad he'd made the call in one respect: it had convinced him that McCallum almost certainly had done what the girl accused him of doing, and he was slightly dismayed at himself that for a few minutes he'd tried to give such an unpleasant person the benefit of the doubt. But what was his scenario now? To sympathize with the victim, to pretend that Oreos could do some good? Maybe part of the reason he was doing this was pride: a sort of preening for Cheryl Lanier. And if that was so, did that make him much different from McCallum—leaving aside the fact that kinky sex had never interested him, but even if it did, would he ever do such a thing to Cheryl?

Cheryl was on the second-floor landing, sitting in a lawn chair, as if she were sunning herself at the beach. Instead of a bathing suit, though, she wore a sweaterdress. "Thanks for coming, Marshall," she said, "but I'm here to head you off. This is pretty unbelievable, but she's got a boyfriend from Chicago who just came into town. I don't know why she couldn't have told us she was engaged, but half an hour ago we found out he existed, then that he was coming, and believe it or not, he's in there now and they've called out for pizza."

What a confusing, pointless night. And how stupid that he was standing halfway up the stairs in Cheryl Lanier's apartment, holding cookies and Cokes. Though what the hell? What the hell, really. Banished from her apartment to the chilly hallway, the other roommate . . . where was the other roommate? . . . the situation being what it was, maybe he should just sit on the landing, open a Coke, take a breather before turning around and going home. As if she'd read his mind about the missing roommate, she said, "Timothy thought he'd better go back to the library. I thought I'd sit here and wait for you and apologize. She's in there all cheered up, and suddenly it's like I'm the problem, like I was overreacting all the time she was crying and waking me up at night screaming with nightmares. I mean, Timothy was sort of upset, because she'd been crying on his shoulder all day, and now he thinks she's been using us. That *she* overreacted. But I mean, McCallum did those things. He's a sick man." She looked inside, then looked back at him. "I don't know what's going on anymore."

"Coke?" he said.

"Oreo." She smiled.

The absurdity of getting involved in young people's problems. All this drama over what was probably nothing, while a responsible husband would have been at his wife's side as she sat in the hospital with *his* dying stepmother, but instead he was having a little late-night party on the dimly lit landing of an apartment house, sitting on the dusty floor atop a flight of stairs like a servant at the beck and call of the Queen, who happened to be sitting not on a throne, but in a lawn chair. He barely knew Cheryl Lanier. She was the one who had the crush on him. She was the one who had mentioned a "date," taken his hand in the car, tried to involve him in something. As he sat on the landing, the rushing around of the past hour making him feel suddenly more defeated than truly tired, the door creaked open behind Cheryl.

"That the pizza?" a man's voice said.

"No. I'm here with a friend of mine," Cheryl said. She sounded more defeated than Marshall. She said it with the matter-of-factness of someone saying, *I give up.*

"You can come in, you know. I don't know why you won't stay in the apartment with us." It was a girl's voice; Livan's voice.

"Aren't the pizzas free if they don't get here in half an hour?" the man said. Still, there was only the cracked door, a pale zipper of light.

It was clear that Cheryl didn't mean to answer the question. Nor did she have to, because a few seconds later, while the door was still ajar, a car pulled up and a delivery boy got out, racing into the apartment with the pizza in an insulated silver bag, taking the steps two at a time.

"Twenty-seven minutes," the man said, opening the door. He was a man, not a boy: thirty or so, Marshall guessed—short, bad skin, wearing aviator glasses and a fisherman's sweater that sagged low over his jeans. Clearly none of it looked strange to the deliveryman, who decided to hand the box to Cheryl, though it was the man who reached into his pocket and took out folded dollar bills, counting the money twice and telling him to keep the change. Who could imagine what the deliveryman saw every night? To him, they were just a bunch of perfectly normal people standing around waiting for food. What would it even matter that one was a professor, another a student, and that the pock-marked man had just arrived from Chicago? Marshall watched him disappear, taking the steps three at a time, staring after him until he heard the front door bang shut.

Beside the man now holding the pizza box—the man who looked through Marshall with complete indifference, as if he didn't exist; no greeting, nothing—beside the man rolling his eyes comically, as if enjoying a little joke with himself as he held the box to his nose and inhaled the pizza's aroma, stood a girl, a tall girl, about five-foot-ten, her eyes swollen from crying, her hair dishevelled, a clump gathered back in a ponytail, the rest tangling free. She was wearing sweatpants, an orange pullover sweater, and fuzzy slippers made to look like rabbits. Unlike her friend, who had turned and gone back into the apartment, she looked at him, then at Cheryl, with what he could only think was disdain, as if they were squatters camping in the hall. She stood before them, a girl looking with empty eyes at her roommate and then—too much appraisal creeping in for her look to be described as dispassionate—looking once again at the stranger who sat at Cheryl's feet. He could see himself through her eyes: a teacher, a man who now, by definition, was to be distrusted; perhaps he was also a fool for rushing over, or at the very least ineffectual. It was the last thing he would have expected: that he would dislike Livan, feel no sympathy for her. For a while, he had intended to be judicious— hadn't that been his plan, such as it was?—to feel her out, see if she was convincing as she talked about McCallum, and then, assuming she was convincing, to begin to persuade her that she must get help. Apparently, help had been a phone call away, all along. And he and Cheryl, neither of them in that moment feeling anything but exploited, were behaving, by their silence and with their dropped eyes, as if she had a right to judge them. His sympathy was for Cheryl— Cheryl, out on the landing—and for himself: no dinner; a tiring ruined evening, his valuable time wasted because he'd convinced himself he must go on a mercy mission.

"Get your coat and we'll get out of here," he said to Cheryl.

"Thanks," she said, "but you've done enough."

"Let's go," he said, standing. He had tried that line with Sonja so many times during Evie's hospitalization, but all she'd agree to do was to step out of Evie's room while they worked on her. He couldn't do anything for Evie, but maybe he could do something for Cheryl Lanier. "Don't blame yourself," he said. "Come on. Let's go."

"She's got a student loan they're not renewing unless she gets her grades up. Maybe that's all she's really upset about," Cheryl said.

"I spoke to McCallum on the phone tonight," he said. "Apparently he's got something to feel guilty about." He remembered the sound of something crashing in the background, heard McCallum's voice asking, "Do I want to be dead?"

"I've got a friend I can stay with in Dover," she said. "Would you mind giving me a ride?"

"Sure," he said. "I'll drop you in Dover."

She folded the chair and leaned it against the wall. Now, from inside the apartment, he could smell the marijuana Cheryl had talked about, hear muffled laughter above the rock and roll.

"I spent a lot of time sitting in stairwells when I was growing up, when my father started in on my mother. He never hit her, but he'd scream like one of those people they pay to start things shaking at rock concerts. You know, one of the foxes." She tried again: "A plant."

"You mean that isn't just unbridled enthusiasm?"

"Sometimes, sure. But they pay people, too. They did when the Beatles first came to the United States. Did you know that?"

"Did the Beatles know it?" he said.

She shrugged. "What do you think: they were such upstanding lads they would have objected?"

"You assume I'm inextricable from my generation? That naturally I'd have great reverence for the Beatles?"

They were on the verge of really arguing, to his surprise. It must be that they needed to blow off steam, both of them feeling used, both feeling foolish, but left for the moment with only each other.

In the downstairs hallway she reached in among the coats and pulled her down jacket off a peg; underneath the jacket hung the scarf he'd insisted she take in the car, which surprised him for a second because he'd forgotten he'd given it to her. Instead of wearing it, though, she straightened it on the peg, then zipped her jacket, still without speaking. What did this mean? That they'd had an argument and that now she was renouncing him by renouncing his gift?

"I'm sorry for dragging you into this," she said coolly, sitting primly in the car.

"Well, my stepmother is in the hospital. It gave me something to think about other than that," he said. If she was going to tell him about her family, he'd tell her something about his.

"Is it serious?" she said, after a pause.

"She had a stroke. The third one. At first they thought it was a seizure, but it turns out it was another stroke."

"I'm sorry," she said.

At the intersection, he headed toward Dover. He asked if she wanted him to stop so she could call her friends before they got there. "No. That's something people from your generation do," she said. It worked, too; until he whirled around to look at her and saw her sly smile, he had taken her seriously, aghast at how cryptic she'd suddenly become.

"Don't worry. I'm not your worst fear," she said. "I'm not mean, and I'm not down on older men. If they're attractive."

"Cheryl," he said, "I admit that flirting is more interesting than arguing, but let's drop it, okay? Think about this from my perspective: I've just been trying to do the right thing. I guess by now it's clear that in some way, we've both been had."

"We're a great team," she said.

"We're not a team," he said. "I have a wife."

She looked at him. "Would you be more comfortable if I got out and walked?"

"You're the one who's been trying to provoke me," he said.

"Does that make me your worst fear? A woman who's provocative?"

"Worst fear? What are you talking about? That's like a question on a psychological exam: 'Often I feel that other people are . . .'; 'My worst fear is that. . . .'"

"Often I feel that other people are going to succeed, and I'm not," Cheryl said. "My worst fear is that for reasons I don't understand, I'm trying to antagonize someone I want to be my friend."

Think of something to say; she's opened up to you, he kept thinking, all the way through the town, past the empty factory buildings, past used-book stores and out-of-business boutiques, up the dirt road she directed him to, thinking it still as he coasted to a stop outside a large clapboard house bordered by a second-growth pine forest. *Say something,* he told himself as she opened the car door, but urgency only paralyzed him further. If he hadn't reached over and grabbed her jacket and pulled her back and pressed his forehead against hers, closing his eyes, inhaling the smell of her shampoo, his lips parting slightly against her cheek, his lips trailing down to kiss her lips, she would simply have gotten out of the car and disappeared into the house in silence.

Martine, Martine, Martine, Martine —

How often in the two days since we last spoke has your name echoed in my mind, as if by incantation I could conjure up your strong spirit and derive strength from it. I have been almost unable to look anyone in the eye since Alice's admission to the hospital in Connecticut. They are not so much polite as exceedingly businesslike: every time I admit to my stupidity, they tell me there will be plenty of time to discuss it later, treating me like a child being told to play inside on a rainy day, because the next day is sure to be sunny. They're very skeptical — with reason, I suppose — of a man whose wife is addicted to drugs and alcohol and who claims to have noticed nothing out of the ordinary. Well, Martine, what has been "ordinary" about Alice since M's death? And if this might have been the situation when he was alive, did you have the slightest indication this was so? How amazing I didn't ask you that when I phoned, and how equally amazing that I am ashamed to call again, half because I suspect you, also, must think me a fool, and half because if you do not, and pity me, I would be undone. I know the truth is that you were so horrified by the facts I laid out that you never recovered yourself during my call. Also, I was in the administrative office when I called — just a few big antique tables with typewriters and vases of flowers on them, in the Greek Revival building that is on the hospital grounds — and there was nowhere to sit, the recorded Vivaldi was maddening, a doctor came in and began to argue with an insurance company representative — it wouldn't seem that in such a moment of crisis I could be so distracted, but I find I hardly remember what I said to you, and what you said to me I remember almost not at all. I felt I knew nothing of the world and that I never have, standing in a room that looked exactly like a room in someone's private home, yet this was a hospital, my wife was in another similarly antique studded building across a vast Gatsbyesque lawn, and I was expected to sign forms agreeing to pay them any amount they demanded and disappear without seeing her again and to return only after several days had passed, believing that it would take that long to detoxify her body from an assortment of drugs, most of which I had never heard of, that she had presumably washed down with various liquors ingested right under my nose? Fortunately, I was able to reach Dr. St. Vance at once, so at least his overseeing of the situation will begin immediately. Once in the office, I simply ignored the young doctor and managed several calls before the noise level got so loud I gave up. I realize that the welfare of spouses is secondary at such a time, but I find it astonishing that no thought is given to the shock we may be experiencing. On my way out, one of the women sitting at a desk asked if I wished to buy a raffle ticket! It did not instill confidence about the hospital, which Amelia tells me is very fine, and which Dr. St. Vance also seemed to feel would be a good enough place for Alice to be at present. But still, Martine: no one wants to think about winning a bicycle when their wife has been found passed out. It was so annoying as to drive me almost mad.

I am in Amelia's apartment now, waiting for her to return from work so I can talk to someone friendly and understanding, instead of someone who wants me to sign away all rights to my money and/ or buy a raffle ticket. I cannot at this moment stand to go back to the hotel room after the shock of entering it and finding Alice passed out on the bed, the sickening stench of vomit in the air. As coincidence would have it, kind Amelia had phoned the hotel and left a message for me, begging me to find time in the evening to see her and to tell her about Alice, so here I am—let in by her landlord—sitting in her apartment, which I find I have so often imagined, and imagined wrong. It is rather dilapidated, and any movement seems to result in more paint flaking from the walls. Alice always spoke of her fondness for the place by calling it a good place to nest, though I, myself, feel it's more like the scrap from which a nest could be assembled. I find it difficult to imagine you, so tidy and so given to beautiful arrangements, spending time here without damage to the spirit. I am thinking of the time you occupied this apartment when Alice and I went to Key Largo the fall after M's death.

I know what is going to happen now. The baby's death is going to be the starting point for every diagnosis, every possible solution, every recommendation about how Alice and I should live our lives. The thing I have tried so hard to put out of mind is going to be paraded out like an enormous float at Mardi Gras, all the doctors and nurses reaching up their cups for coins. M's death and Alice's sad state are going to be paraded by me time and again, and I will no doubt be expected to explain what truths lie beneath the masks. It seems quite excessive punishment for something I did that was not so sinful, really. At least, since we do not speak of it, I assume you don't think my actions were a sin, or that if they were, you have implicitly forgiven me. That's why I was so glad you came, and even happier that you stayed.

Ever,

M.

8

SONJA OPENED THE DOOR as Marshall was still fumbling with his key, and he sensed immediately that something was different. Perhaps she smiled slightly more than she would have ordinarily; perhaps she was just a touch too formal in the way she stood before him, as if whoever was behind her might have the ability to stare through the back of her head and see her expression from the front.

Sonja was in her gold sweater, but it was not worn over the black thermal underwear she was so fond of lounging around in. The camouflage boots were gone, and she was wearing white wool socks with her ballet flats. He stared at her in the brief information-gathering moment available to him before he would have to go into the house, looking for a clue. There was none, but none was needed: immediately upon entering he saw McCallum, sitting in a chair by the fire and—incredibly!—McCallum did not rise, but raised his arm and gave him the by-now-familiar two-fingered wave acknowledging that Marshall had just walked into his own house.

"Apparently you've both had quite an evening," Sonja said wryly, as she hugged him, her body not slackening at all as it touched his: formal Sonja, entertaining company.

"My apologies," McCallum said. "My apologies for having ruined so many people's lives, though I hope I haven't dragged you into this thing too far, Marshall."

"We've been discussing his depression," Sonja said. "The new medicine he's been taking."

"After your call, which was certainly within your rights, and I appreciate your attempt to help in this difficult situation, Marshall—after your call, though, Susan broke several items and ordered me out of the house, and since you seemed to think it was crucial to talk to me, and since I found myself with no place to spend the night, I thought I'd drop by."

"What has he told you?" Marshall asked Sonja, hanging his coat on the coatrack, walking into the living room intent upon giving McCallum no more pleasant a greeting than McCallum had given him. McCallum had taken the chair closest to the fire. His feet, in black socks with gold toes, were splayed on the footstool. On the table next to him was a coffee mug. Sonja went to the sofa and sat down, picking up a pillow and clutching it to her stomach.

"I think it would be a little difficult to begin at the beginning," she said.

He was sure it would. "How's Evie?" he said. Let the intruder see that they had other things to think about in their lives besides him. If McCallum had told her about Livan Baker, had she told him anything about their own problems? He knew Sonja. He was sure she had not.

"I don't feel you're on my side," McCallum said to Marshall.

"Then what made you decide to come to my house?"

"Because I thought if our unspoken suspicion of one another could be brought out in the open we might have a real exchange."

Marshall sank down on the sofa next to Sonja. He said to her: "You know about Livan Baker? The trip to Boston?"

"He says she's psychotic," Sonja said.

"It never happened?" His eyes went to McCallum.

"It didn't happen the way she says it happened. Nor did she ever state the—how should I say?—unexpurgated version to me, only to her roommate, Timothy, who tore into my office ready to murder me and left an hour later apologizing."

"When did Timothy do that?" Marshall said. Almost the minute he spoke, he realized how ludicrous this was, his asking after somebody who had been at the library as if he knew him.

"Days ago," McCallum said, picking up the mug and sipping. He replaced it on the coaster. He ran his hand over his forehead. "She's had an eating disorder since puberty," he said. "I have, in my wallet, several hysterical notes she's written me, accusing me of progressively more horrendous crimes. When I show you, you'll see they're more than a little self-incriminating. On the now disastrously mythologized Boston trip, she didn't have proper winter clothes, and I felt sorry for her and bought her a coat and a hat. It seems this is a 'mistake' her godfather once made, buying her a coat and then, according to her, spreading it underneath her and screwing her on top of it the same afternoon. In Chicago, when she was nine or ten. Why she doesn't cut up her clothes instead of eating and vomiting, I'll leave to the experts to decide. Why men feel they should buy shivering waifs proper clothes I understand completely. Also, whether the godfather, if that's what he was, did anything more than I did, I must also leave for them to decide, though I hope whoever *they* are, they will factor in my own account of the day that has now grown so monstrous in her recollection."

"She's apparently quite crazy," Sonja said.

"As is my own wife, at the moment," McCallum said. "She feels that in not telling her I had a research assistant, I have somehow made a mockery of our marriage vows. She also feels that our son, who has attention deficit disorder, is a misunderstood genius whom I, and his teachers, in collusion with the doctors, are trying to destroy, in wanting to provide him with medication that will mitigate his behavioral problems so he might sit still, keep quiet, and follow a line of thought." He looked at Marshall. "By the way," he said, "I agree with you. I am incapable of talking like a normal human being. When I try not to be derisive, I am inevitably derisive. Though I've heard the students say the same of you, Marshall. I wonder whether it might not be a pitfall of the profession."

"Leave me out of it."

"You're going to spend the night, is that right?" Sonja said to McCallum. Marshall could see that Sonja realized how unstable the man was; that she was prompting him, cueing a disturbed person about what he wanted to do.

"I could go to a motel," McCallum said, staring into the distance between the two of them.

"McCallum, it's fine if you want to stay," Marshall said, "but right now I've had enough of being dragged into your problems, and I would like to go to bed myself. Without dinner, and having just driven all the way to Livan Baker's apartment, only to find that she's no longer hysterical. She has reunited with her boyfriend. He's come to visit, and she's having a pizza with him. In the morning, when we've all had some rest, we can discuss this further."

"Just like that, you believe I didn't do it?"

"I'm not sure what you did, but Livan Baker didn't impress me, and if you have crazy letters from her, I'm willing to consider that we've both been had."

"Can it be that I'm going to have an ally?"

"You're going to have the guest bedroom," Marshall said. "I'll see you in the morning."

"You two won't whisper behind my back?"

"McCallum, while we whisper, you can talk to yourself and have a running commentary mocking whatever you've just said."

"I did kiss her," McCallum said wearily, getting out of the chair.

"Keep it to yourself," Marshall said.

"But apparently the girl is quite crazy," Sonja said, to no one in particular. She was almost out of the room, tired enough, herself, not to bother saying goodnight to McCallum as she left.

"So she's got a boyfriend," McCallum said, standing with his hands in his pockets as Marshall silently probed the fire, turning over one glowing log, poking the hot ash tip off another.

"Not the friendly type, either," Marshall said.

"Sweet on Cheryl?" McCallum asked quietly.

"No," Marshall said.

"But you did go to a bar with her."

Marshall looked up at McCallum, surprised. "How did you know that?" he said.

"Oh, it's all over town," McCallum said.

It was only when McCallum smiled wickedly that Marshall realized that about that, at least, he was kidding.

"I found out during a moment of male bonding with Timothy," McCallum said.

"You try to make yourself unlikeable, don't you?"

"Bad self-image."

"But the thing is, I don't have much invested in our getting along," Marshall said. "I guess what I'm saying is, I'm not looking for friends."

"Not the currently socially approved attitude for males," McCallum said. "Supposed to be out bonding in the woods, beating the drums."

"McCallum," Marshall said, "I know what things you find absurd and ironic. Is it fair to assume there are also at least a few things you think of as serious?"

"Bad self-image," McCallum said again. "Easier to negate than to accept."

"You kissed her?" Marshall said. The large log glowed with a core of deep orange. It was not about to burn out, and it always made him nervous to turn in when a fire was untended. "Why the hell did you kiss her?"

"You continue to ask serious questions of a man you know habitually dodges them?"

"Try," Marshall said.

"Oh, because we were walking past Boston Common and there was a bag lady on the sidewalk, poking around in a shopping cart filled with all kinds of junk. As we walked nearer I started thinking, What if that were me? What if I were standing around presiding over a heap of rubble? What if Beckett were prescient and knew his characters in their ash cans were literally what our cities would become? What if he were a simple realist slightly ahead of his time? As we passed the bag lady, she looked up and said, 'In the summer I'm a swan boat,' pointing to the pond. Livan started walking faster, but I'd just been struck by the amazing idea of reincarnation, not reincarnation after death, but being one thing in one season, and another thing in another. Isn't that true? We're one thing in winter and another in spring. But Livan had gotten ahead of me, and I rushed to catch up with her, catching hold of her so we'd be in step again— don't you love it?—and when I touched her sleeve she stopped, instead of walking she stopped, and do you know what? I could see the bag lady was watching. She expected to see something romantic; she expected me to kiss the lady. Then something told me that for whatever reason, Livan wanted to be kissed for the bag lady's benefit. Then do you know what I thought? That I was an old guy, compared to Livan, and if I kissed her, the bag lady might say something terrible, and Livan might be hurt, I might be humiliated. And then the kiss just happened. The bag lady seemed to be watching for a split second, and then she lost interest. I was thinking about Boston Common in the spring, the flowers, all that green grass, the swan boats out on the lake."

Perhaps it was the heat of the fire and the cooling temperature of the room that made Marshall shiver. Perhaps, he thought, but not likely: more likely he had realized McCallum was someone he was going to have to take seriously. Talk to longer. "Do you have classes tomorrow?" Marshall heard himself asking.

McCallum hiccupped a dry laugh. "Don't think I'd be my bright-eyed bushy-tailed best up there at the old lectern?" He ran his hand through his hair. "I don't have classes on Wednesday," he said.

"I'm glad," Marshall said.

"Tell the truth," McCallum said. "You came into the house and I was the last person in the world you wanted to see, right? In all the world, I was probably the most unwelcome. Your life was going along fine until you got involved in this. You went over there, and what? You thought you could race in like a bunch of soldiers at the end of a Shakespearean play, restore order. So where does this leave us? If you'd asked me I could have told you Livan was trouble and that the only thing I had to feel guilty about was the impurity of my thoughts, the irrationality of my desires. But Marshall: I didn't have anything else. We're talking about a day, part of a day, taking a walk in a city. We're talking about enjoying walking down the street when for once I was with someone who'd talk to me, not just complain about what the kid did wrong that day, someone who'd ask my opinion, who liked me. We're talking about a grown man who suddenly perceives of a bag lady as his guardian angel because he needed a guardian angel so goddamn much: exiled from my house because there was nowhere to goddamn sit, nothing but ladder-back chairs we inherited when my mother died, the sofa carted off, taken to the junkyard because the kid had broken the frame jumping on it, a man without a sofa, and then this random person who was assigned to me through financial aid, suddenly there the two of us were in Boston, and I was listening sympathetically, as is our goddamn job, correct me if I'm wrong there. I'm listening to her tales of woe, noticing she doesn't have a winter coat, just a windbreaker, a flimsy nylon thing, and I'm thinking that at the very least I can take her to Filene's Basement and buy her a coat, and then the two of us can get on with things, such as research at the library. At the moment, it seemed like an epiphany:

coffee; sympathy; a seventy-buck coat; a hat picked up later in the day from a street vendor. This was not done with a stiff prick, Marshall. It was done with simple good intentions. And as I say this, I don't want you to think that I haven't registered what you said. I heard you loud and clear when you said you weren't looking for friends. But try to see the awkwardness of my position: how can I apologize for driving over here, bending your wife's ear, for not going home when I should, accepting your hospitality, me sitting here like a stalled snowplow that can't roll through another foot of muck. I'm stuck, and you two act the way friends act, even though you're not my friends and you don't want to be. You nevertheless extend yourselves, and the pathetic truth is, I want your goodwill. I want you to believe me when I say that what Livan says happened in Boston did not happen."

"Let me ask you," Marshall said. "Where do you suggest we go from here? I'm not your audience, I'm your colleague."

"Elavil," McCallum said, taking a bottle out of his pants pocket and turning it around in his hand like someone holding a facetted stone, turning it to catch the light. "Connotes 'elevator,' as if you're ascending through space." He plunged the bottle back in his pocket, got up abruptly, and started to walk out of the living room, the afghan he'd pulled over his shoulders slipping to the floor, his unbelted pants so loose they were almost sliding off, his shirt crushed from his having sat slumped deeply in the chair. He was just an overgrown child, Marshall thought: somebody who'd gotten in too deep, who had too many responsibilities, a person who had one too many problems.

"Right here," McCallum said, suddenly reversing direction, holding out a folded envelope. Inside was the note from Livan Baker: a young person's handwriting, a little red-ink drawing of heart-shaped balloons floating away above the words:

I don't ever want to have any secrets from you. I want you to see my secrets as clearly as the things you see looking in a mirror. My secrets surround us. I have a secret for you. It's that there's a way we can be so close, you can be me and I can be you. I'm going to be your secret.

Love, Livan

"That's only the most recent," McCallum said.

"She's written you other things along these lines? You don't know what she's talking about? Can't you take this to a shrink at student health, or to the police?"

"How is that going to help me?"

"If nothing else, you could go on record that she's, you know, unbalanced. It's unwanted attentions, or something. To tell you the truth, I already called a friend of Sonja's at student health a few days ago. We'll go there tomorrow and get her advice, get this put down on the record somewhere."

"'The record'?" McCallum said. "What is 'the record'? Is it like 'the Force'?"

"Maybe you should take a shower and go to bed. You look awful. You can borrow a clean shirt tomorrow. Try to . . ."

"Look the part," McCallum finished. "Look like somebody who isn't a rapist and a sadist. What do you think we're going to do? Have somebody in some position of authority write down what—a complaint, or a—maybe it's a misgiving. Maybe you and I are experiencing misgivings about the mental state of a student at the college. And we're going off to have the grown-ups tell us what to do."

"I sure as hell don't know what to do."

"No, I don't either," McCallum said. He sat in a kitchen chair, ducking his head into his hands, looking up again. "You don't think our going to student health would fan the fire? If they get in touch with her, she's going to tell the same lies to them she's told everybody else."

"She's already been there. She's already talked to somebody, but then she freaked out and didn't go back." As he spoke, he began to wonder whether Livan hadn't gone back because her story hadn't been believed. How could Cheryl be sure, and why had he been sure, that the counsellor's words were what had been reported? Maybe she had picked up on Livan's deceit; maybe that was the reason Livan hadn't returned to press her point. Maybe someone had seen through her, called her bluff. This thought made him slightly optimistic, but it wasn't anything to tell McCallum. It was best—wasn't it best?—to speak to student health, let them contact the dean, get this thing out in the open. Since McCallum had done nothing but kiss her, what could be the harm? At worst, he'd be reprimanded, but if Livan spread the rumor and she was believed . . .

"You know that scene when Redford and Newman are high up on the cliff, and Newman wants them to jump? And Redford has to say he doesn't know how to swim? *Butch Cassidy.* I loved that movie: an all-time great buddy film. So tomorrow we're going off like two characters in a buddy film. Come spring, everything will be fine again, we'll be splashing in the old swimming hole, right? Safe. Doesn't sound right, does it? I don't know if that's really going to happen. Listen to me: I must think this is a movie, not my life. I must think we're both just a couple of characters."

"Well?" Sonja said, looking up from the bed, where she sat, still fully clothed. Marshall, who had finally followed her into the bedroom, was momentarily startled: for a second it seemed she had read his mind, that she wanted him to sort through the possibilities that had been going through his head and give her a definitive answer about how and where this would end. Instead of answering, he sat beside her. It was ludicrous, the amount of time and thought that had gone into these students' problems. Anyone who'd spent any time in the profession knew that being a teacher had more than a little in common with being a doctor, and that you needed to keep professional distance. So is that what he'd tried to do—keep professional distance—in the car, outside the big house in Dover?

What else could he have done? He was offering comfort.

Kissing Cheryl Lanier?

Never again.

Truly?

"I don't know," Marshall said. "I don't know, I don't know, I don't know."

"You must be surprised he came to the house."

"I'm astonished. We don't—" He almost said *We don't like each other,* but instead said, "We don't know the first thing about each other. How I got dragged into this, I'm not quite sure."

"Happens," Sonja said.

She had begun to pull off her clothes, tossing them piece by piece to the bedside chair, missing with the sweater, scoring a hit with the pants. He stood and undressed also, tossing his shirt in the hamper, draping his pants over the doorknob, stripping down to his underwear, which he did not remove. Then he edged close to her in the bed, thankful that he had a kind, sane wife, half wondering what

McCallum had said to her but too tired to ask. If he thought about McCallum, down the hall, about his having to get up and deal with the old McCallum or even the new surprisingly forthcoming McCallum, it would create such anxiety he might not be able to sleep, and as much as he didn't know, didn't know, didn't know, he was tired, tired.

Dearest,

My indebtedness to you is vast, eclipsed only by my affection. Hiding from my responsibilities, conducting myself as if I am entitled to bow to every inclination — because that is what it is: inclination, not a true sense of duty — I have stayed gone too long, choosing to convince myself that the urgency of Alice's present situation supersedes all else. And yet when you did not respond to my letter, but only folded a piece of paper to contain the pictures of the children — my wonderful, so well cared for children who have nevertheless become orphans to their parents, though they are so central to your life, Martine, I do not know what I can ever do to repay you for your diligence, your charity toward us all, though I see us some days as mere pretenders, pretenders to living a proper life, simple cowards in the face of adversity, when actually we are moving in a circle of the damned. Oh, I do so hate to admit to such self-loathing, to such cynicism and such cowardice, yet you are my conscience and whether I confess or not, I could not hide from you.

Let me be blunt and say I despise her for her weakness, for her ability to deceive me, whether it be about a secretly ingested drug or what she makes seem a random fascination with a man in a hotel corridor, whom I know she has met before — a man she has probably been with, as the two of them go about enacting a charade for my benefit. But tell me this: which came first? My highly cultivated ability for self-deception, or Alice's ability to see that whenever something goes wrong, she can play on my guilt? It is my superiority, my damnable feeling of superiority, that affects me so deeply I try every way to hide it from others, including my own wife. Here I am now, at her side — or I would be, if the doctors would allow it, though they feel, at present, she must be separated from me — here I am in limbo, trusting another person to keep things on course, conveniently forgetting that although one child is dead, other children remain, and that they need their parents as well as your superb care.

Yet they seem gone from me. To be honest, limbo is preferable

to the pain of attempting to re-connect with them, which of course
I must soon bring myself to do, as the disappearance of two parents
must be quite traumatic, however much they adore you.

This morning, I stood with the snapshots by the window in my
hotel, the strong sun giving their faces a Bela Lugosi glow,
distracted by the beauty of the trees, the beauty — in my self-pitying
mood, I saw it as the beauty of ordinary people walking to and fro,
doing and thinking ordinary things, or even thinking terrible,
unknowable things, yet nevertheless walking, moving, making
progress, while I stood, as if two snapshots weighed so heavily in
my hands they might as well have been enormous barbells that
allowed me to hold them and raise them once and lower my arms
again, yet after that rooted me to the floor so I could not move.

Something has been wrong with every part of me since his
death. I say "his" because today even the name is too painful to
write. Yet I loved him no more than my other children, or at least
not until the moment when it was clear he had died.

What can you think of this long exile? My separation from
house, from children, from you? Perhaps that is what you spared
me with the blank piece of paper, trying to nudge me back to reality
with images instead of words.

Ever,

M.

9

————

MARSHALL SAT ON the side of his bed, dialling Evie's hospital room. He spoke quietly, conscious of McCallum sleeping at the end of the hallway. Sonja had left for work, and would go from there to the hospital to see Evie, she had told him, whispering herself, leaning forward to kiss his forehead, her hair falling forward to tickle his nose, a haze of perfume mesmerizing him—the perfume she'd begun to squirt underneath her hair. A very citrusy perfume that made him think of orange juice, breakfast, the blueberry pancakes he'd imagined not so long ago, the conversation he and Sonja had had about summer.

Sonja thought it was best that Evie have private nurses. She had discussed it with him just before falling asleep and he'd quickly agreed, embarrassed not to have thought of it himself. Unless something really demanded his attention, he didn't often think things through, and somehow the hospital had seemed so functional, the staff so busy and so effective that, as was his way, he had assumed everything would go smoothly. Sonja had had to explain to him that this was not so: the overworked nurses would ignore blinking lights as long as possible; patients who didn't complain were likely to be ignored. And then the unarguable: "You know if the shoe were on the other foot, Evie would do everything in her power to see you had the finest care. She always did." Of course she had: she had taken care of everyone in his family, uncomplainingly, devotedly. It pained him to remember how hard she had worked, and how patient she had always been, humming softly as she dusted, transported by music on the radio as she hung out the wash to dry. That was how he thought of Evie: as constantly busy. In fact, he realized guiltily, that was one of the many reasons why it was always so difficult to go to see her: his inability to reconcile the active, upbeat person of the past with the relatively silent, passive person she had become. Yet when he woke up that morning, the events of the night before still alarmingly clear in his mind, he had reached for the phone as he had once reached for Evie's hand, rationalizing his need to connect with her—even if it was a one-way conversation—as her needing him. Incredible to think of her now, incapacitated, the songs unhummed, thoughts allowed to pass by unstated, like little fish sliding through holes in a net. How little thanks he and Gordon had ever expressed, how withholding his father had been. The nurse picked up the phone on the second ring. As he spoke to the nurse, he was surprised to hear in his own voice some of his father's brusqueness: he was glad she had had a good night; he was happy to hear that she had tested negative for pneumonia; if the nurse would be so kind as to hold the phone to her ear . . . oh, wonderful that she was reaching for the phone with her good hand. Absolutely wonderful (but, of course, to be expected).

What he said to her was more like a nuzzle than a real attempt to communicate; his words were muffled, and he could feel them nudging against her, sound rather than content—because what to make of the chaos of Cheryl and Livan and McCallum, where to begin even if Evie were well and able to take it all in? "Sonja told me to get you round-the-clock nurses," he said. "I hope they make things a little easier. You always . . ." She always what? Who, or what, always did anything? "You did everything you could, you know. I don't think boys express themselves as easily as girls. When Gordon and I were young, I mean. I mean, we trusted you. That's a form of appreciation in boys, I think, but you probably wish we'd just thanked you more often. I forget to thank Sonja. I . . . Jesus, it sounds like I'm accepting an Academy Award and coming apart, dying to tell everyone about the person behind the scenes who made it all possible. It was you. I called . . . You know what I mean. We loved you, but we weren't very effective about communicating it. I don't seem to have gotten better at it with age. We love you, I mean. I didn't mean to say loved."

"Hello," the nurse said. "She's put the telephone on the pillow. I think she's a little tired. She's whispering that she loves you."

"I wasn't very good about communicating," he said.

"You have a nice day," the nurse said.

"Cheryl Lanier, Livan Baker, Jack McCallum," he said, testing to see if the nurse was listening at all.

"I'll give her everyone's good wishes," the nurse said. "I can see your call really cheered her up."

When he hung up, he thought: *I'm laughing because I'm nervous.* What the nurse said was not really funny. What's happened to Evie is so awful I can't focus on it. What did I say to her? *What did I say?*

Cheryl Lanier was not in class. A girl named Sophia, twirling the end of her cellophane-pink braid, was sitting in the seat Cheryl usually occupied, her tongue working a Chiclet into a pearl she would probe with mounting irritation as the hour wore on. The package of Chiclets lay on her table, along with a package of Marlboro Lights. As he looked at her, she moved her fingers toward the cigarette pack and immediately withdrew them—the tentative gesture he remembered Sonja sometimes making a few seconds after plugging in an iron. In spite of her slatternly appearance—bleached denim overalls covering an enormous striped shirt wadded under her armpits, Doc Martens worn with no socks, one shoe laced, the other unlaced, a wrist full of silver bracelets, a red handkerchief tied in the middle of her bangles, a stud piercing her nose—Sophia Androcelli was not unalert or unintelligent. Her papers had been excellent—late, but excellent—and on the rare occasions he bothered to read the campus newspaper, he had seen several stingingly accurate letters to the editor signed with Sophia's name, protesting wasteful monetary extravagances by the administration and questioning the value of legislating political correctness. She usually sat in the last seat in the last row, to the far left—she had become one of his markers, he now realized; he had gotten into the habit of seeing who was bracketing the corners of the first and last rows, eyeballing the class quickly, as if he were registering the correct positioning of the bases at a baseball game—but today she was slumped in Cheryl Lanier's seat, and in the last row her own chair sat empty. The chair to the far right of the row was, as usual, occupied by Judith Levine, a woman in her forties who had returned to college to finish the degree she'd failed to get when she dropped out to become a flight attendant. Front row left was Dominic Ruiz, an ass-kisser of the first order, and front row right Bill Snyder, a round-faced boy with a peculiar, dog-ear hairstyle that made him look like Lucy in "Peanuts."

Marshall had nodded to the class, then set his books and his clipboard with the typed lecture notes he probably would not consult on the lectern, also placing a stack of papers to be returned on the desk he never sat behind, preferring to stand as he spoke—when Ashton Freer opened the door, beckoned for Marshall to come outside, then closed the door again with a delicate click Marshall felt sure would be the last bit of delicacy of the day. Freer was of medium height, but disturbingly thin. As usual, he was dressed in creased trousers, a white shirt, and a cardigan sweater, with a rolled tie, instead of a handkerchief, forming a small lump in his shirt pocket. On his wrist was a medical bracelet. Peering into Freer's shirt pocket, Marshall saw that the color of today's tie was navy blue. Before Freer spoke, Marshall said, "This is about McCallum."

"Forgive my naïveté," Freer said. "I only began to receive information this morning on what is apparently to you a very well-understood situation. Forgive me also if I wonder aloud whether it might not have been better if you consulted with me, as department chair, assuming that you realized there was some probability this situation might be made public?" Freer fingered the tie's point, as if testing the sharpness of a needle. "Marshall—McCallum was at your home last night? Was I wrong in thinking there was not much love lost between you and McCallum?"

"Why do you automatically believe Livan Baker?" Marshall said.

Once again, Freer opened his mouth, then closed it without speaking. After a pause, he said, "Marshall, have you spoken to your wife?"

Instantly, the hallway began to waver out of focus. What was Freer talking about? Where was Freer going? Why were the students clearing such a large path around them in the hallway, he having been about to teach "The Gulf" by Derek Walcott, Freer with his sneering attitude and his steam-pressed creases and his tie folded queerly in his pocket. The question was, had he spoken to his wife. He had not, but wouldn't she have called if something had happened to Evie? If something was wrong?

"You don't know what happened when you left your house," Freer said. It was a statement, not a question.

"What happened?" Marshall said. He tried to catch up with Freer, but his legs were heavy. Something terrible had happened. Something terrible had happened to Sonja. Two policemen were walking toward them in the hallway.

"Is Sonja all right?" Marshall said.

"She is," Freer said.

"Who are they?" Marshall asked, staring at the approaching policemen.

"Who do you think they are?"

"What's happened?" Marshall said.

To the policemen, Freer said, "You doubted I could locate my colleague?"

"We're new to the force. Rookies are known to be antsy," the blond cop said. He had a gold incisor and an acne-spattered chin. He looked to Marshall the same age as most of his students. The other policeman was handsome, except for green eyes that narrowed to slits as he looked at Marshall. "How ya doin'?" he said, extending his hand.

"He doesn't know what happened," the blond cop said to his partner.

"You haven't spoken to your wife?" the other cop said. His eyes were gone. The green all but disappeared. Marshall wanted to ask if Sonja was all right—or had he asked that before, had somebody said yes?—but he could only echo, "My wife."

"She's not hurt is she?" Marshall said. He had reached out to brace himself by putting his hand on Freer's shoulder.

"Sonja's okay," Freer said. "McCallum's wife went off the deep end this morning and went over to your house and attempted to stab him to death."

The blond cop's nod corroborated this.

"This is a terrible thing to find out," Freer said to the cops, nodding in Marshall's direction as if he couldn't hear. He could hear, but the sound was wavery; trying to hear distinctly was like what could happen visually when you were driving on a hot day, seeing a mirage in front of your car, knowing it was only heat rising from asphalt. Freer had turned his back and was walking away. Freer was walking away: he'd been a mirage.

"He isn't dead, is he?" Marshall said.

"If it was known, we'd know."

What was this, some Zen riddle?

The other cop saw his confusion; he said, "He's in surgery. Got knifed pretty bad."

"He got knifed in my house?" Marshall said. It was beginning to register. McCallum had had a fight with his wife. She must have found out where they lived and gone there. What was he expected to do, try to remember the story about the bag lady near Boston Common? This was like one of those nightmares, one of those anxiety dreams in which he wasn't prepared for class, all he could do was fill time, stand there making a fool of himself and suffering intensely as the students realized he didn't know what he was talking about. A bag lady? What was that about? The class was to be on Derek Walcott's "The Gulf." Every thought he had ever had about Derek Walcott rushed out of his brain. Thank God he was not in the classroom.

"We'd like to take you down to headquarters and have you describe the previous twenty-four hours," Green Eyes said.

"Twenty-four hours," Marshall echoed. How could he begin to remember it all? And what was he to do if only irrelevant, inappropriate things continued to subsume his thoughts, such as the slightly minty smell of Cheryl Lanier's shampoo, the now-vivid image of the pizza delivery boy, every detail of his face suddenly clear, the bruise-like bags under his eyes, the lock of hair curving over his forehead. He could hear the boy's footsteps on the stairs, see the square silver pad from which the pizza was slipped—that familiar magic prop of our time, the sort of top hat from which a rabbit would be pulled—smell marijuana seeping from the apartment, from which Livan Baker and her boyfriend had suddenly materialized.

Both cops were looking at him, frowning, neither one speaking.

"How ya doin'? This comes as a shock, I know," the green-eyed cop said. "You left for school this morning, next thing you know you're walking down the hall with two cops, hearing about an attempted murder in your house."

"Do you think he's going to die?" Marshall said.

"Those surgeons try very hard. If he dies, it's not because they didn't try," the narrow-eyed cop said. "I personally have a lot of respect for surgeons."

"It's not the greatest sign if we get beeped here," the other cop said. "Though to tell you the truth, they've beeped us for nothing. You stop thinking it's necessarily going to be something crucial after the first hundred or so stupid beeps."

All right, then: McCallum's wife had stabbed him, but he would be fine. McCallum was not by any stretch of the imagination a friend of his, except that when you didn't really have any friends, it was difficult to disallow acquaintances. He had been thinking that, something like that, not too long ago, on a day when Cheryl Lanier came to his office to borrow a poetry anthology, and when she had left, he had looked out the window and seen her, seen a dog, as well, and he had reflected that there was every possibility he didn't love anyone, although that was absurd. Absurd, but a thought he had had two or three times before, remembering that he'd thought it before only when the idea hit again. Now he concentrated on thinking otherwise. He loved his wife. He loved Evie. He loved his brother, Gordon.

"Freer wanted to tell me himself?" Marshall said.

"Yeah, but it was our obligation to proceed directly. We told him that and gave him five minutes," the blond cop said. "I don't know what this stuff was about his bringing you to the station. Delusions of grandeur, or something."

"People don't know how the law works," the other cop said.

"Rest assured, there are no charges against you," the blond cop said. "Nobody thinks you stabbed your friend, Professor." Was this happening? "Mrs. McCallum walked into the post office and told the clerk she'd done it, blood all over her," the blond cop said. "You know, gas station attendants are getting confessions all the time. People pull in and roll down their window and it's like a drive-through confessional. Or they buy a candy bar inside and spill the beans, they just blurt it out while the guy's giving them change. Go figure."

At the station house, Marshall drank a cup of lukewarm coffee. He was simultaneously videotaped and tape-recorded, while the blond cop took notes in shorthand and his partner asked every third question. Marshall was tormented about how much to say, how much to tell them about Livan Baker and whatever McCallum's involvement had been with her. He was surprised to see how withholding he could become; he volunteered nothing, half out of sympathy with McCallum, who might be dying as he sat in the station house talking to the cops, half because he felt sure the cops would do nothing to clarify matters for him, and he thought now, deep down, that McCallum had been telling the truth, that Livan Baker's involvement with McCallum had been far less than she claimed.

The questions they asked him were easy to answer, though they zigzagged backward and forward in time so that eventually he began to assume there must be some underlying logic to the way they pitched the questions that he didn't understand—or were they trying to get him to reveal something besides his own genuine confusion?

McCallum appeared at the house while he was out on an errand?

Out getting milk.

What year had he met McCallum?

Whatever year he was hired. . . .

How would he characterize his personal relationship with McCallum?

Oh, as a colleague. You know: bantering. He had trouble with his wife, trouble at home.

Trouble at home.

The wife was pregnant and McCallum didn't seem pleased by that.

How well did he know McCallum's wife?

Oh, not at all. Not . . . perhaps he'd seen her across a room.

What time did he leave the house that morning?

Nine-thirty.

And he had gone out on an errand the night before to get—

To get milk. Sonja was showing some prospective clients a house; I realized we were low on milk, Marshall filled in, surprised that he felt slightly giddy, an odd mixture of pleasure at pleasing, filling in the spaces, saying something informative: the good student still. Yet he also feared that his nervousness was apparent. He felt himself shifting in the chair, shifting more than someone ordinarily would, when informing people he'd gone out for milk. Well: they didn't need to know anything about Cheryl Lanier. He could forget Cheryl Lanier. Whom he had dropped off at that house, glowing in the darkness, after she had said that she wanted to spend the night with friends, after he had pulled her close to him in the car. *I'm sorry?*

The question was repeated: his wife had been home, she said, for a couple of hours with McCallum.

Yes, Sonja got stuck with consoling him for quite a while. . . . He saw the trap: he could not have been getting milk for two hours. *Maybe it seemed to her that she talked to him for two hours; probably she didn't talk to him for two hours.*

"An hour," the cop said, shrugging. Helping him along. But not believing him. He did not think the cop believed him any longer. He could remember the way his skin felt against the smooth skin of Cheryl Lanier's cheek, smell Cheryl's minty shampoo in the chicory-scented steam from the fresh cup of coffee he had just been handed. He was being asked if McCallum had ever stopped by his house before. This did not seem a good question to answer no to.

I think he meant to, but he never really . . .

To clarify: he left at nine-thirty a.m. and McCallum was sleeping?

Sonja said he was sleeping. This was ridiculous; why were his words suddenly being spoken skeptically? It was true: Sonja had said he was sleeping, they had both gone off, leaving him there. Of course he had been there. What did they think, that his wife had crept in and stabbed him when they were still in the house and they'd heard nothing? McCallum was sleeping in the guest bedroom, he and Sonja went off to work. This was factually true, and a quite simple matter to understand. What was he supposed to do, rouse the man and make him leave, just because they were leaving? It wasn't as if McCallum were going to loot the house. Not as if he didn't know the man at all.

If he had met Mrs. McCallum, it might have been at some large social gathering? Something at the college?

This was difficult to focus on, because he had already said—hadn't he?—that he had not met her, that there was a slight possibility he had seen her across a room, but truly: he had no recollection of McCallum's wife, though the policemen's questioning had made him suddenly imagine her in their house, and as he saw her, she was a tall, brown-haired woman—a woman who must be carrying a knife.

Quite frankly, I have no memory of ever having been introduced. Someone may have pointed her out at a department party, or something like that.

His wife said she did not know Mrs. McCallum either. Therefore, they were only McCallum's friends.

You know, I don't mean to imply that my wife and I are close friends of McCallum. He must have felt close to us — or at least that we'd be sympathetic listeners. You know — to come to the house at all.

Mrs. McCallum said you all knew one another.

You believe a crazy woman who just tried to stab her husband to death?

Two different viewpoints: two people saying they didn't know her, she maintaining that she knows them rather well.

I don't know how I can demonstrate that I, we, don't know her, but the fact is, if I've ever met the woman, which I doubt, it would have been so unremarkable that I have absolutely no memory of that.

Therefore, there would not be any possibility that either he or Sonja knew that she had murderous intentions toward her husband?

No.

Also, in the one or two hours during which he was buying milk, he did not cross paths with Mrs. McCallum or in any way contact Mrs. McCallum?

Well, I . . . I spoke to her on the phone.

She called?

I called.

What time was this?

Oh, nine o'clock, probably. I called from a pay phone outside a convenience store. Because he'd been upset when last I saw him. Because of troubles in his marriage, as we now know. So . . .

So what?

Wanted to see if he was okay. Friendly concern.

This was at what time?

Eight. Nine.

Your wife thought that you returned home about ten-thirty.

What are you suggesting?

I'm trying to get an accurate time frame on everyone's movements the night before the attempted murder. Let me ask: You thought to call from this convenience store instead of from your house?

I wondered how he was doing.

Okay. This is at what time?

This is ridiculous. Am I under suspicion? I'll need to call a lawyer. Are you saying I'm suspected of — what? McCallum's wife confesses to stabbing him, and you suspect me of stabbing him, or something?

I'm still back at the convenience store. You phone him at eight or nine p.m., speak to his wife, though you don't really know his wife, then speak to him. Then time has to elapse before you find him in your living room, because your wife spends one or two hours talking to him, which would mean they sit down together at eight-thirty or nine-thirty, if we assume your wife is correct about your returning at ten-thirty. What I'm getting at is that McCallum isn't Superman, this we know, so if you're speaking to him at eight or nine, by your wife's account, he would already be in your living room. You've gone out to buy . . . what was it?

Two-percent milk.

Much healthier to drink low-fat milk. I'm a very literal-minded kind of guy. You know how it is: you can get fixated on things when there seem to be gaps. The gap in time here disturbs me. I figure you weren't out buying milk for approximately two hours, but hey: a person can have a private life. I notice, though, that you don't volunteer information about what you were doing when you weren't buying milk.

This is all just some confusion — my confusion about what time I left the house, I suppose. In fact, I was going in to school to pick up a book I'd forgotten, but the weather was bad and I turned around. I phoned McCallum. I guess I talked to him longer than I thought.

When the cop shrugged and opened the door without comment, Marshall walked to the waiting room, haunted by the cop's sarcastic words. Bothered that McCallum's wife would lie and say she knew him and Sonja when she didn't, but more upset that because he was unwilling to mention anything about Cheryl Lanier, some cop who prided himself on his professional skepticism had cornered him, revealed him to be a liar, then let him go as if he were throwing back a small fish. The cop had made him feel small, and slimy. He wriggled uncomfortably on the bench, filled with shame, though he knew there was no objective reason why he should feel that way, knew that all he was guilty of was having touched his lips to Cheryl Lanier's in a dark car, and what was that in the long run? What was that compared to people like McCallum . . . ? But McCallum was in the hospital, in serious shape, and he didn't want to think bad thoughts about McCallum. He wanted Sonja to emerge from the room where she was being questioned. It was ridiculous that they were keeping either of them so long, ridiculous because the police had a confession, they must have found fingerprints on the knife, he and Sonja weren't the kind of people who should be questioned about where they were and what they were doing every second of what would have been a perfectly ordinary evening if not for their goodwill, their only involvement in the whole horrifying affair having been a willingness to extend themselves to two people who turned out to be murderers and assholes—McCallum was at least an asshole, whatever self-righteous justification he offered about the time he'd spent with Livan Baker. When Marshall exited the room where he'd been questioned another policeman walking by had told him that McCallum was in intensive care. They had operated for over three hours to repair his damaged kidney. Jesus: the woman had stabbed him in the kidney. She had been hurt herself, also—something Marshall hadn't even thought about. McCallum had fought her off, hit her, but then he had collapsed, and if she hadn't confessed to—could that really be what they said? a post office employee?—if she hadn't confessed, he might have bled to death in the house. That was what Green Eyes was now saying to him; that he and Sonja could not return to the house, because it had been sealed off. The cop was asking him if it would be a problem to find somewhere else to spend the night, and he was saying—realizing as he spoke that he was telling another half-truth—that of course they could stay with a friend. They could stay at a motel, he said. That would probably make more sense, even if they did have friends, but the notion of being in some motel, shut out of their house, which was probably bloodier than he wanted to imagine, depressed him, as if he and Sonja were two stray children with nowhere to go. He tried to pull himself together, he was sinking so fast into self-pity; he began fabricating something he suddenly wanted to be the truth: him and Sonja starting over, united by their having been victims in someone else's drama, McCallum, strangely enough, having done them a service by bringing them closer as his own marriage collapsed. This whole nightmare now seemed so protracted, so ultimately silly; if not for McCallum's wife's frightening insanity, it could simply serve as a lesson in not being dragged into other people's problems. Like falling dominoes, now Cheryl Lanier had learned that lesson from getting involved with Livan Baker's problems, and he had learned that lesson from getting involved with McCallum's problems. Cheryl was young and inexperienced—easy to see how she was taken in—but he had helped no one, had not even been genuinely concerned, as Cheryl had been, about anyone's well-being: in the end, McCallum had pressed himself on him; Livan Baker had interested him only to the extent that Cheryl was troubled by her behavior, and some part of him had wanted to help Cheryl. At least that had been genuine. To what end, though? To settle her problems so he could then extricate himself from the situation, or to try to help so she'd be impressed, grateful— so he might become closer to her? That was the answer, he suspected: otherwise, why was he constantly reminded of the smell of her freshly washed hair, why was he troubled—increasingly troubled—that he had left her off at a house in Dover and driven away? He had instigated something—or had he finalized something—when he drew her to him in the car. She would be horrified when he called and told her what had happened. He should be the one to break the news to her about McCallum; though she didn't know him, he'd come to influence her life, he'd indirectly caused her worry and trouble and pain, and although what had happened to McCallum had nothing to do with what he did or did not do to Livan Baker, still Cheryl should know what had happened to this man she'd been made to think so much about. He could do it now, call her, except that he did not want to be overheard talking to her in the police station.

Sonja came down the hallway to where he sat on a bench in the waiting room. Pale and sullen, she wordlessly slipped her hand in his. He was sure he could read her mind, sure that, like him, she wanted only to be gone from the police station. The two reporters waiting outside came as a surprise to them both. In this small community, two reporters were waiting to interview them? The younger reporter might have been a student at Benson; he was red-haired, his mouth the same color as his hair, which he kept sweeping out of his eyes. "Is Mr. McCallum dead?" the reporter wanted to know. The other reporter was older and wore dog tags with a picture ID, but Marshall did not want to focus on him. The younger man took a photograph of Marshall and Sonja, arms interlocked, with a small Instamatic camera. These people were here because someone's wife had tried to kill him? Didn't that happen every day in Harlem? Detroit? After all, McCallum was alive, his wife in custody—to his surprise, Marshall heard himself telling them that McCallum was alive and well, as Sonja tried to hurry him along.

"Over here," Tony Hembley hollered, beating the side of his car as he shouted out the window. Of course; he'd driven Sonja, who was so terribly upset, and all this time he'd been waiting. His outstretched hand seemed to symbolize their escape. Marshall thought: *Oh yes; of course I have a friend.* Then he and Sonja rushed to the car, away from the still-popping flash on the little camera, ducking their heads as if they, themselves, had something to be ashamed of.

Martine,

Truly, you have been most generous with everything you have thought to do. Please do not think I mistake it for mere duty, as I am quite aware that no check can compensate for your endless goodwill toward the boys, and toward Alice and me. I am delighted that Amelia was able to stop by on her trip North. She reported to me only after the fact that she had made the journey, and I do hope you were not inconvenienced by an equally impulsive arrival on her part. She does live quite simply in New York, but I know from experience that almost nothing can be deduced about people's personalities once they have escaped the city limits. In a way, New York breeds a kind of anonymity. It is not until they are elsewhere that you really come to know them, I think, which is very different, for example, from the way one comes to know people in other large Eastern cities, such as Boston. I know she was eager to report to Alice that all was well, the flowers growing, the children prospering, you, yourself, bearing up well. But she was only able to speak to me, as the doctors continue to refuse her any visitors except— Martine, you will not believe what I am about to tell you now. The doctors, who are quite curt with me, and one of whom always accompanies me when I visit Alice in the sitting room—these men have granted the most ridiculous request Alice has ever made, to my knowledge (when do I not have to qualify my remarks these days, humbled, as I am, into admitting I may know Alice very slightly, indeed?). When the weekly bill was mailed to me at the Waldorf, I scanned the itemization of charges and found a visit from a Madame Sosos who, upon my questioning them, turns out to be a fortuneteller! I find that this defies belief, that men of science would allow a fortuneteller to have exchanges with Alice, while they stand like policemen when her own husband comes to visit. A fortune- teller! It is enough to make one wonder if circus performers would be admitted, if Alice decided a high-wire act was just the thing to lift her out of her depression! I am afraid that I was so aghast, I made the mistake of speaking to the head doctor when I was in a

*rather overwrought state — why, she has never put the slightest stock
in such nonsense, as you know — and the doctor became quite
inappropriately analytical of my overreaction. Then began my
recent travails. I see that while Dr. St. Vance was quite happy to
admit Amelia to his office, on the spur of the moment, he, like the
doctors, has insisted upon taking a firm line with me, insisting not
only that he prefers to communicate in person, but in fact sending
word that he will no longer respond to my letters, as it is necessary
for us to discuss all matters face-to-face. I have explained to him the
difficulty of this, but he is unwavering in his position and has even
written the doctors in Connecticut to inform them that he has told
me this. I am not this man's patient, I am the beleaguered husband
of one of his former patients, yet he refuses to be in any way
flexible, and will correspond not even with Alice, apparently, but
only with the hospital doctors. I am, of course, most unhappy
about this, as I felt he could provide valuable assistance directly to
Alice, but when a doctor makes a decision, other doctors inevitably
rush to their colleague's side to support whatever decision has been
made, as we all know.*

*How I wish I had a happier report, but she seems remote, tired,
preoccupied. I know I am an impatient person, but I am beginning
to question whether she is in the right place, and have phoned a
former Yale schoolmate who is himself a neurologist to see if he
might consult with the doctors in Connecticut to assure me that he
thinks they are proceeding correctly. I thought to tell him about the
fortuneteller, but felt I would hold that card until the last, because if
he pronounces these doctors good professional men, I can then ask
him to consider that opinion in light of my new piece of
information. A fortuneteller! Who has ever heard of such a thing, in
a hospital for disturbed people? It is as if the world's gone mad.*

*My love to all, my thanks, and do, please, smell the roses for
me. Maine has become in my imagination even more of a paradise,
and you the presiding angel.*

With affection,
M.

10

———

TONY HAD GONE to Sonja and Marshall's house earlier that morning and returned to pronounce it "fine, except for a little blood. Not weird, no bad vibes." The night before, he'd driven Sonja and Marshall home from the police station, Marshall's car still parked at the college, her car in the parking lot outside the real estate office, where she'd left it when the call came from the police. She could remember her own puzzled speculation, her pointless chitchat with Tony, the reassurances that everything would be fine, how they'd taken turns telling each other things would be fine—that from such a brief, essentially one-way conversation on the telephone, little could be known about the events that must have taken place after she and Marshall left their house earlier that morning.

Driving to the police station, she had given Tony only the barest outline—not because she wanted to withhold information, but because the information she had just been given did not quite register. She explained the late-night visit of Marshall's colleague McCallum; his odd entanglement with a student who was now accusing him of having done terrible things—whatever he'd done to her quite possibly exaggerated, or who knew? Not exaggerated. A long night of talk, a brief conversation with Marshall once they went to bed—Marshall, who had, as she and Tony talked, already arrived at the station. And then when they had both been questioned, instead of their being able to return to their own home after such a terrible day, the house had been sealed off and they had had to go to Tony's. That was probably just as well, because it allowed them to escape the cars passing by, those incomprehensible people who acted as if, in coasting to a stop in front of the house where something shocking had happened, they could have the same pleasure as turning into a drive-in movie: the place would light up; the movie everybody had been talking about would be magically shown, right in front of their eyes. She agreed with Marshall: *Wasn't* it true that such things happened every day in America's cities? All of it happened every day: domestic discord; the pressure gauge going too high; violence. But let it happen in a sleepy town and gossip would spread and people would leave their homes to take a look, expecting some excitement might still be hovering, something they could absorb into their blood like a vaccine, immunizing themselves against personal danger.

Tony had come up with the idea that Sonja and Marshall should avoid the chaos in their house, along with the bother of the ringing phone, by staying as long as they wanted to in the house Tony now stood in with her, which had been put on the market by friends of his, but which, in the absence of buyers, was currently for rent. This morning, after he had dropped Marshall at the parking lot to get his car, after she had read scribbled directions Tony had taken down about how to find his friends' house, which it seemed, except for briefly viewing it before it was listed, he had never visited, she found herself in a strange house, considering Tony's suggestion.

The water was on, the electricity worked (though there was only one floor lamp; the ceiling fixtures had been removed, and splayed wires capped with duct tape protruded from holes in the ceiling), and the wall-to-wall carpeting had been cleaned by the same company that was now in her house, cleaning the blood from the carpets. She was frightened, fearing, on some irrational level, that McCallum's wife might be there, that she might spring out and do to her what she had done to McCallum. Damn: she had never been very bothered by violence in the movies, had not even been inordinately troubled by *Psycho,* but now she had fanatic-with-a-knife waking nightmares, and as she walked with Tony she took his arm—took it like an old person—because the suspense was too much, the memory . . . what was she thinking? The *description* of the attack was very chilling. Imagining what had happened seemed to have changed her perception of graceful, long hallways (not always an advantage), and of plentiful closets (think what could hide there). A real problem, considering her profession. How was she going to act as tour guide in the future, when today she was so oversensitized that the exposed, taped electrical wires seemed a metaphor for the house itself, revealing its vulnerable, underlying nervous system. Marshall would like that, she thought; he'd like the personification of the house; he'd like it that a metaphor suddenly seemed more apt than reality. "I don't like it," she heard herself saying quietly, moving ahead of Tony to peek into another near-empty room, and Tony, who had been unnerved by everything that had happened, made an instant decision not to treat her misgivings seriously, becoming an even jollier enthusiast about this house that she knew was not to his personal taste either and that might even be spooking him as much as it was upsetting her on this gray winter morning, with overhead lights that didn't turn on and the one floor lamp standing in the corner of the living room like a helmeted sentry at his post.

As she walked through the house with Tony, she remembered the way he had chatted with his friends long distance, very upbeat, clearly a man who had a secret to hide, yet how ridiculous: she was his secret—she had listened as he described his "personal friends in distress. Not financial distress. You know: general distress," Tony had said, as Sonja had sat there hearing herself spoken about as if she weren't present, missing her comfortable ballet flats, which she'd worn for years now as a kind of security blanket, wrapped in Tony's robe, unable to shake her gloominess about being displaced, wanting desperately to be in her own house at the same time she dreaded the moment she would have to return. In someone else's clothes, considering her big, pale feet, she had remembered the awkwardness of being a teenager, felt as humiliated as someone's unwanted date. She had a closet full of clothes at her house, a husband, a lover, a friend— Tony was both lover and friend—yet there she'd been, twisting her body awkwardly, at one instant feeling that she was an unexpected guest in a stranger's kitchen, bending forward to hide her breasts, the next moment wanting to shrug off Tony's robe and be pretty, desirable, anything but the tortured creature she had become as Tony offered his friends a bland account of her current problems. And God: someone lay wounded in the hospital, a man she had just met the night before, a colleague of Marshall's, and now Marshall had gone to see a lawyer—that was what happened when you were an adult and not a teenager—though she couldn't understand why, when they were so obviously innocent in this entire affair, Marshall had become progressively more upset about being questioned by the police, after they returned to Tony's and he fixed them Sleepytime tea and served it to them in the kitchen. *The illustration on the tea box,* she thought. That must explain her dream of the night before, in which a bear noisily clanged pots while gathering honey, tossing buckets of the stuff at other animals. It had suddenly come to her that the golden honey was like blood. Blood on the walls. It made her shiver, as she had shivered in Tony's kitchen earlier, thinking about her blood-spattered walls as Tony joked with his friends on the phone, asking how the Versace renovation of some historic apartment building was coming along, inquiring about the street scene outside various cafés in South Beach. She had noticed the way he mentioned "distress" without giving any foundation for it, the way he'd omitted talking about the way violence had entered into his friends' lives. Though it was probably true: if you wanted a favor, it was better to present your request simply. In general, she thought that men were very good at talking around things—that they communicated with each other in a sort of shorthand, either omitting all specifics or else relying exclusively on them, either way signalling the inherent difficulty of things with a shrug, which was not a gesture women usually made. Ah, yes: the difference between men and women. As if you could generalize. Confused and unhappy, Sonja trailed behind Tony as he toured the house.

"What don't you like about it?" Tony said. "I'm not trying to sell it to you, you know. I just thought you might be happier having a house to yourselves for a while, wait for the gawkers to go away. I mean, if you'd rather come back to my house, we can certainly do that. We can go back to my house."

"Tony," she said.

"'Tony' what?"

She didn't answer him, which made him more nervous.

"But, I mean, if it makes you feel strange being in my house, and if the, you know, this furniture here makes you uncomfortable, then maybe a motel would be best. I think we're only talking about a couple of days. They're shampooing the rug. Marshall thought you didn't need to hear about that, but I don't know: the rug man's a little rattled, I'm not sure what sort of job he'll do. Wanted me to check everything out with the police, questioning my authority and all that. I had to tell him he was expected, because how else was the problem going to be dealt with. I had to say to him, 'You're going to shampoo up a bit of blood. Small bit.' You assume the police have some way of dealing with situations like this, you don't assume the police find a place roughed up and have to thumb through the yellow pages. You automatically assume there's a Department of Blood on the Rug, or something. Well, it's absurd, in a way, isn't it? Really quite funny, though one's not sure on whom the joke's being played."

"Tony, you're losing it."

"Well, about the other matter: I mean, the timing isn't exactly propitious, is it? Here I am, trying to sort things out, and suddenly all this erupts, so of course my inclination, anyone's inclination, is to try to help. I mean, I would have felt like worse than a coward if I dropped you at the station and disappeared, a person I've come to care about very much, just . . . what? Dropped you and then phoned along with every other sensation-seeking son of a bitch to see how you were doing? You could have been in the house; she could have been so crazy she came at you. Is that what's troubling you? That it could have been you?"

"It's true," she said. "Two things are true: you're out of control, and your house makes me uncomfortable." She slumped against a wall in the hallway. Tony leaned against the opposite wall.

She had already begun to walk ahead of him, trailing her finger-tips along the wall. Somebody else's house. The anonymity of houses. "What if it was a sort of warning? McCallum's wife flipping out like that, coming to do something awful to him."

"Are you really being so nonsensical as to say that the McCallums' family drama was enacted on your stage as a comment on our actions?"

"If you're making fun of me, how can I tell you what's bothering me?"

"You've told me what's bothering you, and the only response is to dismiss such insane misgivings."

"Don't try to turn this around so the problem is mine, Tony. Yes, I'm upset. I was trying to tell you what was bothering me, and you stopped me."

"I won't do it again," he said, taking her hand. "Listen: I don't know what the two of us are doing standing around in the Ahlgrens' house with their fucking deco curtains and their fucking marbleized custom paint job streaked up and down the hallways and their Directoire chairs, except that I suppose I felt a little funny about having you two in my house, I assumed you'd feel that way too, you apparently did feel that way, I just—I shouldn't have intruded."

"Did you go to the senior prom?" she said.

"Excuse me?"

"Did you, Tony?"

"No, I did not, in part because I arrived in the U.S. midway through what you call senior year and didn't know anyone well enough to ask, though I lost my virginity at fourteen, if that's relevant to our conversation. Also, I was shy around girls. My mother didn't know what was going on, fortunately. She wanted nothing but to be back in Essex, herself. Some party dance that meant she'd have to rent me a tuxedo and buy me slip-on shoes? My mother wouldn't have wanted to hear about nonsense like that."

"I can be a big girl and go home tomorrow if they'll let me, unplug the phone if that's what we need to do, close the shades. How long can they drive by?"

He let the question hang in the air. He was thinking that he had been unfair to her, snapping at her because she was expressing her misgivings over their affair—"affair" was probably too misleading a way to think of their involvement—the sexualization of their admittedly juvenile, existential angst (what she'd called it from the first) that had led them, a few weeks before, to start having sex in empty houses. It had been a good game, a rather thrilling game, until the impersonality began to seem less thrilling and recently they had begun to retreat to his house. Gradually, even when she was gone, things in his private world had begun to seem slightly altered, to take on some of Sonja's personality, absorb her essence, an essence he would be the first to admit he did not fully understand, so that discovering more and more things about her, trying to intuit her feelings, to anticipate her reactions, was like having the pieces of a jigsaw puzzle spread on the rug with no idea what the final picture was to be. Then one night she had suddenly been there with her husband, and like cigarette smoke clinging to fabric, Marshall's own essence had permeated the house. The scent had made Marshall seem at once all too real and also vaporous, like a ghost who might have been there in spirit, observing all along.

"What are you thinking?" Sonja said. "That if somebody hadn't gotten stabbed in my house, the two of us could be off today playing the game? Or are you not very interested? Did spending time with Marshall sour you on the idea? It's hard not to see me as a middle-aged woman with her middle-aged husband, dealing with other people's pedantic problems, isn't it?"

"You're making it out to be shabby," Tony said.

She looked at the firm set of Tony's jaw, his eyes straight ahead, peering out the back window to the lawn's winter-dry grass, grown long and wind tossed like straw thatching, a sifting of snow drifted near trees, piles of sodden packing boxes sagging forlornly. The former occupants must have thrown their extra boxes onto the lawn. She had only been home twenty minutes, half an hour, before Mc-Callum had come to the door; just long enough to shower, after her romp with Tony in the fake Tudor, the one that had just gone on their list as an exclusive, and then the knock had come on the door and, startled, she had looked through the peephole to see a person announcing that he was Marshall's friend from Benson, that it was very important, he must talk immediately to Marshall, who had just called him. Called from where? She had been surprised, but relieved, to return home and not find Marshall there, but where had Marshall been, and under what circumstances had he befriended such a disconsolate man? After having been chased through rooms of gold wall-to-wall carpeting, with the streetlights outside casting just enough light to transform their nude figures into Modigliani shadows, she had returned home to shower immediately, to consider heating some food for herself, though she'd thought it would be better just to sleep, and to eat in the morning . . . who had this person been, who suddenly spoke to a convex glass eye as if he were appealing directly to God?

"I think we're both under too much pressure," Tony said. "I would suggest that the solution might lie in our being in bed. Elsewhere. After lunch and something to drink."

He picked up their coats from the sofa in the living room and held hers by the tips of its shoulders. Looking over her shoulder at him, she thought about the way Evie had handled her wet wash, years ago, when she still lived in her townhouse, lifting it from the washtub and holding it delicately pinched until she could transport the dripping clothing into the dryer. Tony was holding the coat—her dry coat— for her to back into. He slung his own coat over his shoulder and switched off the lamp and opened the front door, turning to lock it behind them.

She sat in the car like a patient, or at least like a patient passenger, replaying scenes from two nights ago. It had all been strange and unexpected, perplexing but manageable. And then, the next morning, after she had dressed and brushed her hair and sprayed perfume underneath her hair, so she could feel the downy hair underneath tingling, she had bent over the bed, intending to tell Marshall that she thought she loved someone else. She had shivered, slightly, with an almost irresistible impulse to speak, in spite of Evie's having urged her to remain silent, but just as quickly the desire had passed. He had looked at her fondly and the desire had passed. They had both left their house, with McCallum still sleeping, and his wife had come after him and tried to kill him.

She was so lost in her thoughts, it took her some while to realize Tony had been speaking to her. "That new motel. How do I go?" He was asking her for directions, but as he asked the question she remembered the brief blip of a nursery rhyme: *how does your garden grow?* She could remember the singsong rhyme, but not the words, except that the poem ended with the words "all in a row." Everything neat. All lined up. She imagined old-fashioned flowers drawn by some illustrator's pen in the pages of a children's book: a pop-up book, the moving boxes she had just seen in the backyard metamorphosed into a cardboard flip-up garden, hollyhocks and peonies, roses and delphiniums springing to life. Which would certainly be a beautiful sight on such an overcast winter day. Which would be wonderfully magical, no less astonishing because it was not real.

Today's sky was evenly gray, cloudless, so flat in color it provided little incentive to remember the sun. Missing its warmth, she superimposed an imaginary sun on the blank screen of sky as Tony drove: her pretty projection, her analogue to the recently invented pop-up book, the red dots floating in front of her as she rubbed her aching, closed eyes, a burst of rosy suns: her nonsense world. With her eyes closed, it was a nonsense world—virtual reality as observed by the not so virtuous. Eyes open, the suns became the spots of blood on her walls. She turned and looked at Tony, whose face was frozen in concentration: the attempt to remember not a sunny day, but what turn to make; activating the windshield wipers to clear the gritty mist of rain and road dirt that splashed in front of them.

Without too much trouble, Tony found the motel. Moments later, on this odd, odd day that had followed the calamitous day that had gone before, they lay curled together in the king-size bed, candle glowing on the night table, watching a Bruce Lee movie on TV. Sonja drew her feet higher, under the blankets. He felt her stirring and put a hand on her hip. He was sick of talking about her wrecked home, about McCallum, and about the two of them. He was engrossed in watching Bruce Lee.

"The blood wasn't all that bad?" she said, trying to get his attention.

"I lied. It freaked me out. It was very upsetting."

"So why tell me now?"

Bruce Lee's foot connected with a man's ribs, and the man went over backward.

"Because it was wrong of me to mislead you. Your house is a mess. Furthermore, you can live with me, if you want. You can live with me without Marshall, that would be the best idea. Then I could save on motel bills."

"Is all of this a sick joke, or was some of it what you really think?" she said, yanking the covers over her back.

His hand returned to pat her hip. He touched her with the same rhythm, the same intensity, people use when they're in a hurry, drumming their fingers on a tabletop. Bruce Lee was doing very well for himself. Tony was spellbound.

"You know, I almost told Marshall yesterday morning," she said. "Diligent Marshall, suddenly finding out he's been living with someone who's stopped being . . . diligent."

He looked at her. "Are you going to tell him or keep this a secret?"

"Keep it a secret," she said. She waited for his response, but there was none. A commercial for cat food came on, an aging movie actress whose name she couldn't remember stooping to shower crunchy stars into a cat's bowl. The cat sprouted wings and flew to the food. The woman sprouted wings and disappeared through the ceiling.

Tony was propped on one elbow, still watching TV. "Doesn't something horrible like this make you realize that life is short and that, I don't know, maybe nothing good comes of hiding your feelings? I mean, we can't all be as extroverted as Susan McCallum, but it seems quite possible that if any good is to come out of something like this, maybe it's to make the people on the sidelines introspective. What I mean is, maybe you should think about telling him."

"You're not afraid of what he'd do?"

There was a long silence, during which she decided he wasn't going to answer. In another room, she heard someone flipping through the channels, getting mostly static, as she and Tony had earlier.

"No," he said.

"Why?" she said.

"Because he likes me well enough."

"Likes you? I don't think he gives you a moment's thought."

Another long pause. "Well, you said he hardly knew McCallum either," Tony said.

"Tony," she said, "what are we talking about?"

"A teeny, tiny bit of cowardice that might exist on your husband's part," he said.

"You think he wouldn't do *anything?*"

"Well, what are you saying?" Tony said. "That I couldn't stand someone's angry words?" He turned toward her. "You're mad at me for stating something that you already understand completely, which is that Marshall wouldn't be an insurmountable problem."

"What would you have him do?" she said.

"Sonja, don't blame me for his disposition. I would have him do just what he would do: complain, or lecture us, or just go off and lick his wounds, I don't know."

"I can't believe it. You don't think he'd care."

"When did I say that?"

"You want him to come on like Bruce Lee."

"There's been enough violence."

"Tony—"

"'Tony,' nothing. You like it that I don't mind being adversarial. In this case, though, I'm only pointing out the obvious. I'm not saying he's a lily-livered coward. I mean, in his place, what would I do myself?"

She had pulled herself up in bed and was feeling the full extent of her discomfort: the wrinkled sheets, cold seeping underneath from where Tony'd pulled them out from under the mattress, the stiff pillow impossible to pound into a comfortable headrest. Here she was in a motel with her lover, with whom she found herself in frivolous fights all too often, listening to him as if he had a great psychic ability to see the future. His expression implied a kind of superiority: the raised eyebrows letting her know he found her slightly ridiculous; his jutting chin set belligerently, as if whatever position he took was the only possible way to think about something. As he turned away from her to rest on his hip again, exasperated, looking once more at Bruce Lee, it dawned on her that he might have said everything he'd said to provoke her. To provoke her not into telling Marshall about their affair, but to ensure that she wouldn't. Her intuition told her she was right. Wasn't it possible Tony was trying to be disagreeable so she would like him less, so she would measure him against Marshall, conventional, diligent Marshall, and find Tony lacking . . . which would mean that if she chose her husband, instead of him, he could come out of their affair feeling self-righteous, superior to her by making it seem she'd opted for the status quo?

"I'm getting bad vibes," Tony said. "I'm feeling that you're put out with me."

"Isn't that what you intended?"

"Look at me," he said, turning toward her. "That is not what I want. I admit I'm in a little over my head. It's made me feel guilty, having him in the house, relating to him like he's my friend. I know it's not my business to tell you what to do about your marriage, but what I am definitely not telling you is to write me off."

She couldn't tell, for sure; looking straight at him, she couldn't tell whether she'd been subsumed by paranoia, or whether there was at least some truth to her suspicions, until he cleared his throat and said that he'd been thinking he needed some time to sort through his feelings. All he was talking about was a few days in the Bahamas. With his mother, no less. So: Tony was the coward, not Marshall. Tony was the one who wasn't standing up to the sudden changes very well.

"Why did you do it?" she said. "Why did you wait for us at the police station?"

"Because I was concerned about you, what the hell do you think?"

"But you knew he'd be there too, didn't you?"

"Why am I being cross-examined about a good deed? I didn't see what else to do; I'd dropped you there, and it seemed only decent to wait to round you up. Yes, I figured he'd be there. I never really encountered him before, except in passing. I didn't expect to like him. To feel sorry for him. It made me feel guilty. I just told you that."

"Which way did you really feel, Tony? That you liked him, or that you felt sorry for him?"

"Both. He's a likeable person. I don't know why he doesn't have any friends. You say he doesn't. McCallum apparently feels he's his friend, but he tells me, and you tell me, that isn't so. I don't have many friends myself. I let people drift away. I didn't extend myself those times I might have. At the very least, you've got to be my friend. I don't ever want to lose you."

My God: he was telling her he just wanted to be friends. That was what he was telling her.

"Why are you looking at me that way?" he said. "Have I asked for something so impossible?"

"Let me get this straight," she said, but this time she was sure she already had it straight. "You're going to go away from me for a few days, and when you come back, you want us to be friends."

"Well, I want us to be friends. Good friends. Yes."

When she didn't answer, he lay rigidly in the bed, turned away from her. He faced the television, but she knew he wasn't watching: it had become sound and images for Tony as well as for her, any meaning that was there had disappeared, the plot had vanished.

Tony's words hung in the air. Even he wasn't going to pretend any longer that her intuition hadn't been working; he was still registering his own words, and they were false enough to make him grow a wooden nose. He sniffed, testing. He sniffed because he was trying to sniff back tears. Because what the hell: he hadn't intended to lie to her, but suddenly it had seemed he had no room to maneuver. It didn't even seem that he could move an inch forward or backward on the big bed, because the lie had paralyzed him. It really had. He couldn't move at all. He was trying, and he couldn't. He was immobilized, his eyes straight ahead, where Bruce Lee began spinning faster and faster, his raised leg sending masked bad guys flying.

Somehow they got out of the room. He remembered it happening in slow motion, as if Bruce Lee's pace were the norm and they were two zombies, dragging the floor for their clothes, avoiding each other's eyes. Every word she didn't speak brought him closer to tears, so he kept in motion, laboriously slow motion, trying to distract himself so he wouldn't do something horrible and unforgivable, such as falling at the feet of a woman he didn't love, to declare, through tears, that he loved her. Though some of what he'd said to her had been true. It was true he'd let his friends slip away, or true he'd lost them in more painful ways, like fooling around with one friend's wife and getting caught, and getting drunk and offending another friend whom he actually thought very highly of, though that particular night he'd been jealous of him, caused a scene, never managed to be forgiven. He could still patch that up. All it would take was a phone call. He'd moved once because of a lost friendship between him and a woman he'd loved, he really had loved her, and then she'd wanted to marry and have a family and he hadn't, so she had gotten together with someone else, and a few times the three of them had eaten together, or gone to the movies, but he'd begun to loathe her fiancé, for no good reason except jealousy, and he'd ruined what might have been his friendship with the woman by begging her to come back, by saying he'd marry her, that they could have children—all of this a few days before her wedding. Mistake, mistake. And with Sonja? He had pursued her just for the hell of it. Always conscientious about her work, husband's photograph on the desk, the day she sadly confided in him that she had had so many miscarriages she didn't have the heart to try any longer to conceive a child. She wasn't his type, so he thought he might see what it was like to try to fall in love with someone who wasn't his type. To instigate games with her, act differently from the way he usually acted, which was to try to win a woman's love through a combination of the tried and true, flowers and expensive candlelit meals, and the unexpected: a gift of two dozen windup Godzillas with shiny red hearts stuck to their chests. That had been Sonja's valentine: twenty-four of them lined up in the top drawer of her desk, which he had completely emptied of all other contents. But all that had happened was that he liked her. He liked her, and he enjoyed her pleased surprise, her sometimes-impulsive girlishness. The truth was, he would rather be her coconspirator in shrugging off adulthood than try to express romantic love for her. He could see her as a sister, or even as someone else's perfectly nice wife whom he was entertaining and being entertained by. When they made love, he tried to think that she was on his wavelength, that she was entertaining him, not falling in love with him. Though maybe she hadn't been in love with him. Maybe she hadn't. If she had, would that love disappear because of one conversation, would it disappear during a Bruce Lee movie?

He looked over his shoulder at the room and marvelled at how ordinary it was: the messy bed; the generic big-flower curtains; the TV. Then he remembered the scene inside Sonja's house, the blood. Next he superimposed that ghastly sight on the anonymous motel room and shuddered—shuddered as much at what his own imagination could produce as at the memory of the scene of McCallum's stabbing. Because deep inside . . . how to explain? It was as if something small and hard—a marble, say—seemed sometimes to begin rolling in his chest, winding down through his rib cage and giving him a small, sharp thrill as it dropped. As with a pinball game, his fingers would flip up and down his ribs, moving before he realized they were, fingertips trying to track the course of the marble, the little nervous nugget that signalled something had to happen, right away, soon, out of his control, something tickling him inside, shooting up and dropping down, his mood rising and sinking as he tried to track it. Looking at the room, he felt the marble start to form—just the smallest tingle, like the first flick that registers with the oyster when the little grain of sand embeds itself. *Yes!* he thought. *Let's feel something starting, let's really be in love with Sonja, let's run after her and shoot that marble directly into the brain, let's have the lights light up, set off bells, keep it in play, win this game.* But the tingle disappeared as quickly as it had come, leaving him again aware of the emptiness inside him.

She leaned against the car, dejected, sorry for herself, preoccupied with emotions he didn't want to know about. Her feet were crossed at the ankles, her arms wrapped around her chest. She despised him, he knew.

"Where shall I take you?" he said. His voice was ashamed, small.

"Anywhere that isn't hell," she said.

He thought: *An actor like me deserves the melodrama.* He thought: *A week — not a few days, a week — in the Bahamas.* And who was he kidding about taking his mother? Really: Who was he kidding?

Martine, Dearest,

Today I was chased down Madison Avenue by a bee, who must have known that in my mind I was already standing in one of the gardens in Maine. No one else was followed by a bee—only me. It made me think that while others had the pleasure of a fluttering butterfly, say, or the pleasant sight of a small bird flying up into a tree, I alone was on Earth to be annoyed by doctors at the hospital, businessmen who are incapable of understanding conclusions arrived at through the process of using common sense and who are therefore unwilling to join in with my conclusions, and then there was that damned bee, swirling about my head, intent upon making me hunch my shoulders and run. A ludicrous sight I must have been, because who among the crowd on Madison Avenue was going to suppose me running because some tiny creature was in hot pursuit?

I intended to write you an anecdote humorously mocking my vulnerabilities, but in re-reading your recent letter about the evasive answers I have in effect made you give the boys because of my long absence, I suppose I might as well assume that you see my true character all too well. Last night I sat up late in the Algonquin lobby, talking to Ethan Bedell and to Marwell Hopkins, a former professor of ours from Yale days. Ethan had brought him intentionally, to talk to me about the situation with Alice, though they had a complicated story about why Marwell happened to be in town that was thoroughly unnecessary and utterly transparent. You would think that a man who taught psychology would be capable of coming up with something better—though come to think of it, the compounding of ludicrous fact upon impossible coincidence originated with Ethan, not with Marwell. At any rate, we three agreed that we were too much the old-fashioned fellows, stuck in our ways, rarely able to go along with the crowd politically or in any other way.

It is very difficult to write this. Marwell, it seems, is personally friendly with one of the more officious doctors at Alice's hospital. It *seems that not only has she been cursed with this breakdown, but that a physical problem has been discovered, as well. All of this inquiring was done behind my back and would quite annoy me except for Ethan's obvious devotion to me. It seems there may be surgery, which they expect to solve her medical problem. To get her in shape for this, they have recommended a series of two or three shocks to the system — Marwell says this is the accepted new treatment, painless, and quite effective. It seems they do not want to operate while she is in a depressed state. It appears there is uterine bleeding, and they feel they must act soon, so I am writing yet again to say that during the period when Alice is receiving the new anti-depression treatments, I will continue on at the Waldorf. It seems a difficult time to have the boys for a visit, but if you feel it is essential, I could certainly book a suite for you to stay in and would see you as much as business and hospital visits would allow.*

I gather that Alice has also been writing to you. I was under the impression she was too depressed — or perhaps I should say lethargic — to do so, but I am sure you are happy for her communications. I of course hope they reflect her progress and that they have not placed any undue burden on you. She has said very strange things to me, feeling a sort of generalized guilt and dread quite out of proportion to circumstance. I suppose she has expressed to you some of the same thoughts. At any rate, I thank you for your kindness, as apparently you have promptly replied to her letters, and that seems, according to Marwell's doctor friend, to have been much help.

I try to avoid a gloomy outlook, though some days it seems clear to me that slight errors on my part have resulted in rather extreme consequences. Though the boys prosper, and though you seem a pillar of strength, I must admit that my former conduct toward Alice has apparently been quite detrimental, declaring so firmly the way things should be, so I suppose I am hinting for your sympathy.

Here I find myself at the point in the letter when my thoughts usually turn to nature — in fact, the verdant world of the property in Maine, the roses, the lilacs. That beauty has certainly been no consolation to Alice, and now I wonder: though you move among it, is its loveliness important to you, or do you nurture the roses as you nurture the boys? What I mean is, when things are a mixture of duty and pleasure, how does one truly feel about one's actions?

Martine, without Alice at my side I do not know how I can return to Maine. It may be that we will have to be elsewhere, let the house go, the gardens. It is filled with memories that cannot be risen above, connected inextricably with the cruel blow of the baby's death. What is it like for you to be there? Do you feel as estranged as Alice does, as I now increasingly feel, and are you just soldiering it out? I will brace myself for your reply. Meanwhile, as always, my inadequate but deeply felt thanks.

With affection,

M.

11

CAFÉ LUXE, painted dark green inside, with exposed pipes painted black and tin ceilings painted pale pink, had been opened the summer before by a professor denied tenure. The waiters and waitresses—perhaps in mourning over the college's bad decision—dressed in black: shirts, pants, shoes. One of the waitresses even had black polish on her long fingernails. Sonja sometimes went to Café Luxe with clients, because they played classical music late in the afternoon. Marshall rarely went there, though, because there were too many students who might want to talk to him, but he felt the sudden need for a café au lait as he drove by, and a car was pulling out of a parking place right in front of the building. He parked and went in, waiting behind one other customer who was ordering something to take out. He flipped through an Italian fashion magazine, looking at all the models in black, who were only slightly skinnier and more abject looking than the waitresses picking up their orders. "Café au lait to go, please," he said, when the customer in front of him turned to leave.

"Hey, how's it going?" the blond man said.

The man looked familiar. Someone who worked in the library?

"Not ruining your café au lait with two-percent milk, I hope." The blond man smiled.

The cop. Worse than a student who wanted to talk, it was the cop. He stuck out his hand to shake hands with Marshall, calling over his shoulder, "Hey Sharon, float some cream on my friend's coffee. He just went off his diet."

Sharon looked skeptical. She turned a nozzle, and hot milk squirted noisily into a tin cup.

"You know, I'm not really a very curious fellow," the blond cop said. "I have to force myself to keep on my toes in the curiosity department. What I mean is, I lack certain instincts I ought to have, so sometimes I just zero in on details. To overcome my lack of natural curiosity, so to speak."

Marshall nodded. The cop seemed sincere. Slightly apologetic, almost.

"Wife doing okay?" the cop asked.

"Yeah," Marshall said. "Quite a shock. All of it."

"Caffeine to soothe the pain," the cop said.

"Absolutely," Marshall said.

"Great place here," the cop said. "Makes me happen to find myself in the neighborhood."

Marshall nodded.

"Orchids," the cop said, pointing to two orchids blooming on tall thin stems.

"Very nice," Marshall said.

"Wife likes orchids," the cop said.

"No," Marshall said. "Roses. She likes roses."

"Mine," the cop said. He tapped his wedding ring. "My wife," the cop said. "Brought her in here last weekend, she decided she wanted an orchid like that one. Owner sells them. Not inexpensive."

Marshall nodded.

"Sort of the giraffes of flowers," the cop said. "Does that sound like an accurate description, Professor?" He smiled at Marshall, who was pulling out his wallet to pay the waitress. He waited while Marshall pocketed his change, then walked ahead of him and held open the door. "I don't really care what anybody does with a lost hour or so," the cop said. "Just in case you were worrying."

Marshall's heart missed a beat. Was the inquisition about to start all over again?

The cop shrugged. "You don't look like you believe me," the cop said. "I want to tell you, though. I lose track of time myself. Half an hour, an hour—you're not looking at your watch, how do you know?"

A redhead in a black Toyota rolled down the window and said, "Come *on*."

"I take longer than she likes," the cop said. He stuck out his hand. "And so, farewell," he said. Instead of continuing toward the Toyota, though, he stood on the sidewalk grinning, watching Marshall all the way to his car.

Approaching his office, Marshall quickly registered that the door was open. Fear seized his stomach: more police awaiting him? He didn't trust that the door could be ajar without anyone's being inside, felt sure every space he inhabited was now going to be turned into a free-for-all, whether it was Cheryl Lanier's hallway, or his home, or his office, not believing the wedge of sunlight slanting across the corridor could wash through an empty room that contained no unpleasant surprises. That would be too much to ask: that he be allowed to walk into a sunlit room and sink down in his chair, with no further problems awaiting him. Or was it Cheryl Lanier—the initial messenger of the bad news that had started him on this exhausting routine he might never extricate himself from? Cheryl, of course. And the moment he saw her he would do what he should have done all along: draw back from the situation; apologize for some of his admittedly strange reactions; ask her—no: instruct her—to say nothing of his going to her apartment, to say nothing of the ride he'd given her to Dover, to please not keep him posted on Livan Baker's state of mind, because he did not want to be compromised, and he had had enough of Livan's and McCallum's, and even Cheryl's, largely self-inflicted problems. His house was a mess: furniture overturned, blood on the walls, specks of blood everywhere, so he had no idea how Tony Hembley could have reported the house was essentially fine. People were crawling all over it, measuring bloodstains; for God's sake, they'd sent the carpet-cleaning service away—his house was filled with unfriendly cops who stood staring at him like bulls staring at a matador, the blood-spattered walls having made them more frustrated and angrier, more reluctant to budge.

It was not Cheryl Lanier in his office, but Sophia Androcelli, sitting with her pleated skirt tucked between two large mounds of knees, reading from a spiral notebook. She registered no embarrassment at occupying his chair; she looked up as if she was slightly surprised and dismayed to see him—this girl who, he immediately understood, had come as Cheryl's messenger, just as Cheryl had once approached him as Livan Baker's. If she was slightly dismayed to see him, he was more dismayed to see her: if Cheryl had been there, he could have revealed how perturbed and imposed upon he felt and begun the process of his own salvation by laying down the new ground rules, but Sophia Androcelli's presence did him no good at all. That was why he simply looked at her, disappointed and vaguely bothered by her existence, saying nothing. For the first few seconds she met his eyes but said nothing, either. Then she ripped two pages out of a notebook and held them out to him, planting her Doc Martens on the floor astride the backpack as she rocked forward to look him directly in the eyes. Mickey Mouse stared up her pleated skirt from the red leather backpack dropped in front of his chair, and Marshall thought: *Yes, this has all been pretty Mickey Mouse.* Mickey Mouse except for McCallum's wife's version of let's-turn-Marshall-and-Sonja's-house into Frontierland.

"Just one thing before I go," she said, picking up one strap of the backpack with a sweep of her hand (the nerve! not even saying "Hello," let alone "Excuse me," as she rose from his chair!). "Cheryl thought I'd be a good person to talk to you and explain more than she explained in the note, but while I was waiting for you, I realized that even though you're a good lecturer and you've always been perfectly fine toward me, the bottom line is that I don't trust you. I think Cheryl made a big mistake getting involved with you, and personally, I'm glad it's over."

"You waited here to express your dislike of me and to hand me two pieces of paper?" he said.

"Buildings and grounds was waxing your floor; I said I had an appointment with you, you must be late. Somebody making minimum wage apparently didn't care to argue the point. At first I was going to sit at your desk and write you a note of my own, telling you what you'd done wrong, but before I'd even begun, it seemed like wasted effort. Because you condescend to people, you know? The look you get on your face when you start using 'Ms.' very histrionically. The 'Ms. Lanier, Ms. Androcelli' stuff, while at least the guys in the class you like get the respect of being addressed by just their last name. The minimalist approach to male bonding. The secret society wink."

"Sophia," he said. "In the past twenty-four hours I have noticed a remarkable lack of civility in my life. Perhaps you could enlighten me: You're saying you sense mockery on my part? Mockery, when I should take seriously, say, a teenage girl's accusations of sexual trauma that are quelled by the delivery of a Domino's pizza? Colleagues whom I should address seriously about matters of the human heart when they are so narcissistic that the simplest polite question from me results in a blow-by-blow account of their encounter with a bag lady near Boston Common, hoping to impress me with their deep sensitivity toward schizophrenics? Colleagues who have made the sort of marriages in which one member expresses herself by stalking her husband to my home and attempting to stab him to death because he is insensitive? 'My weariness amazes me,' to quote a prophet of my generation. My weariness fucking amazes me."

"Your weariness doesn't 'fucking amaze' you; it amazes you because you're fucked. Get it?"

"Sophia," he said, after catching his breath. "Look at it from my point of view. After too long a period of being involved in the problems of others, after a very traumatic event, I come into my office to find you having taken over my desk, after lying to the floor polisher about your right to be here—and let me point out that you are as guilty of stereotyping as you accuse me of being, if you assume that being paid minimum wage was necessarily the reason why the floor polisher did not throw you out—let me just say that it seems to me I should occupy less of everyone's attention, if everyone has the amount of equilibrium he or she claims."

"Cheryl was right," Sophia said. "You really are impossible."

"What does that mean? That I don't take shit?"

"Listen," she said, sinking back into his chair, pushing pleats between her legs, "you just don't get it. You don't get it that things have changed and now you're required to be a more genuine human being. For example: many people might look at what had been put in their hand before starting in with their own complaints. Even normal human curiosity might have set in with a lot of people. But all you want to do is banish me, like you've banished her."

This was the first time Sophia Androcelli seemed disturbed; he watched her bottom lip as if watching a once-tugged fishing line. But the fish went free, the lip relaxed into a ripple as her expression devolved from angry to blank. "Banished her" hung in the air, more perplexing to him the longer it hovered.

He sat in the chair beside his desk. He unfolded the pieces of paper and scanned what seemed to be a hastily scrawled note from Cheryl.

Marshall,

I'm writing this to explain, as best I can, some of my thoughts before I get the bus and get out of here. When Timothy came back from the library and found me gone, he hitched a ride to the house in Dover and we had a long talk that resulted in my realizing that I'd gotten very caught up in Livan's situation because it bore very strongly on my own life — things I was going to tell you that we never got around to talking about because everything got so hectic. You were the first person, male or female, I'd ever felt as mature as I know I am around, because in spite of the way you act sometimes, I could see that we were (forgive me) kindred spirits. I put up blockades too, and like me, I'm sure you have your reasons. It's not your fault that I also fell in love with you, but as Timothy says, I have to suspect that reaction, too. Let me tell you something you have to know. When Livan was telling me about what McC. did to her, it was pretty vague. I sort of told her how to embellish it, though what I thought I was doing was sharing some private things about my life with her, and then she picked them up and said them back to me as if they were hers. That thing with her godfather never happened, but it did happen to me, but not when I was very little, only five years ago, because my mother had me baptized and then later she insisted I have a godfather. I didn't want to leave without saying goodbye because next year I'm going to come back and I'd like us to be comfortable when we pass each other in the corridors. I understand that you didn't do anything to me and that you were just reaching out to me in the car, but it made me see that there was a subtext — that we weren't that far away from being Livan and McC. This is an apology as well as a confession, because if I hadn't told Livan about my experience with my godfather she probably would have chilled out eventually, but once I did tell her, and then she told it all back to me as if it was hers, it was like I'd really given it away and it was someone else's. I know that you're closer to McC. than you say, so I'm asking you to tell him about this because inadvertently I did cause McC. problems, and I'm very sorry for

*that and also sorry that you and I (I know this is going to sound
stupid, but I'm going to say it anyway) aren't the same age, that I
couldn't really be close to you. But we're close enough that I had to
write this note. Goodbye, and take care.*

Cheryl

He looked at the corner of the room, and out the window, familiar
with the sameness of what he looked out on, yet still hoping for something: a group of students passing, a car driving through campus,
Llewellyn's black dog in the snow. "So much depends upon a red
wheelbarrow" went through his mind—a line of poetry he had probably first read when he was Cheryl Lanier's age, the meaning of which
escaped him even as it stopped him dead. *So much depends upon
what?* he thought now. *What does it depend on? That people make
confessions and provide you with new understanding? Or that you
look high up into the corner of your office and see the dusty remains
of what must have been an inefficient spiderweb—that you take pride
in being more farsighted than your myopic middle-aged colleagues.*
So much depended on making eye contact with your fellow man, in
this case Sophia Androcelli, who clearly had read every word of
Cheryl's letter, who had become his accuser though her friend Cheryl
had not. How would she not be upset with him if she knew he'd
kissed her friend in a car? Jealousy, perhaps. High-mindedness. A
lack of sophistication about the way things were. All that was left to
him was to move his eyes to hers, to see if the situation was impossible, or if there might be a chance he could present his case.

"I'll tell you what she said when she gave me her notebook," Sophia said quietly. "She said, 'I wasn't totally honest. He deserves to
know the way things really are. He's got his problems, but he's basically a very kind person.' So I end up the messenger for her note,
delivered to a guy on the make who isn't worthy of her compassion.
Your weariness. Tell me about it," she said, picking up the backpack,
standing, and walking past him.

When she was gone, he looked back to the spider's web for any
missed signs of life, wrinkling Cheryl's missive the way he'd once
ruined schoolboy drawings he ran out of school with, taking them
proudly to Evie, the same way he'd pressed the life out of lecture
notes his thumb worried into blurred lines of type, practicing some

difficult new lecture by reciting it silently the night before he intended to give it, walking back and forth in his living room. His living room. His bedroom. The smeared blood in the hallways.

Okay: now it was known that Cheryl Lanier, for reasons of her own, had intentionally or unintentionally added her own unpleasant experiences to Livan's, thereby fuelling Livan's fury. Not the end of the world, but certainly worth factoring in. Though it was not pleasant to acknowledge that the world could be such a terrible place that well-intentioned Cheryl could at one point in her young life have been exploited by a man assumed to have her best interests at heart. What if he either rushed after Cheryl or paid a hospital visit to McCallum, to tell McCallum what Cheryl had told him—what if, instead of being made to feel guilty because he'd been compromised, he asserted his control over the situation by standing firm and insisting that enough was enough, that henceforth he was entitled to a private life, that he would not willingly accept other people's projections, that he had a right to his former life, that he was entitled to peaceful domestic tranquillity.

In that state of mind he shuffled some sheets of paper on his desk and looked at the telephone, dialled information, dialled McCallum's hospital, reached the switchboard, and was finally connected with patient information. In a pleasant, calm voice, the woman who answered the telephone told him that no information was available on the patient he was inquiring about. "That's NOS, sir. Although the patient is at the hospital, we are not provided with information, ourselves, about his condition." What kind of an answer was that? "It's marked NOS, sir; it's not on the screen, at someone's request. Perhaps the family. The doctor." He thanked her and hung up. Perplexed, he stared again at the spider's web without really focussing, brought his eyes back to the piece of paper. That long night of conflict seemed long ago. To remember it tired him physically, as if the episode existed concretely and he had brought it down on his shoulders like a boulder he should not have reached for. Should not, should not: Wasn't it the new accepted groupthink that people give up thinking in terms of what they should or shouldn't do and think, instead, originally? If so, what original thoughts might he have had? Perhaps a bit like thinking of a snappy rejoinder a day late, and yet he was tempted by his little challenge to himself. One answer might be that he could have turned his back on the situation. Or even that, setting out, he might have changed course, followed the car full of kittens being jostled about. He could have turned his life into an existential errand, an amusing bit for a farcical movie on the subject of middle-aged angst. Without his phone call, was there even a remote possibility McCallum would have ended up at his house? If McCallum had always considered him his friend, then just maybe. But couldn't he and Sonja have sent him on his way, wouldn't the drama have been diffused by sending him home after a brief conversation, and if he'd gone home, would his wife have become so enraged? Still, he did not feel personally guilty about what had happened to McCallum. At the very least McCallum probably knew the woman was violent, knew—or should have known—enough not to deride her over the telephone, reporting on her irrational actions to the first person who happened to call. How peculiar it was: that you could just edge over into someone's life, like a cat creeping through an open door, dashing in unseen, perhaps dashing out again, too, except that in place of the tinkling-bell collar of warning, McCallum had dangled words, and they had felt obliged to respond to them, to weigh them, and to consider them, instead of smacking their hands together and hurrying him out. McCallum had told a fascinating alternate account of what had happened between him and Livan Baker, and as he'd done it he'd been both in character and also enough out of character that the account had seemed convincing, much the way certain artists could pull things off, Marshall thought now—artists who'll tell you the quickest way to attain verisimilitude is to improvise, not to translate exactly. McCallum could have gone on stage with his Bag Lady monologue. Of course this was not to say that he hadn't told it the way it had happened, not to say the inherent awkwardness and the painful truths hadn't registered on him so that now he could show them to others, as easily as touching ink and holding up his hands to prove where he'd been. An image of a dirty-palmed McCallum came to mind— wishful thinking, or a true insight?—McCallum as the archetypal boy with his hand in the cookie jar, McCallum as the member of a species tagged to trace its eating habits, its migratory patterns. Well, for all that, a bird's wing could be tagged, some animal's ankle banded, and presumably by tracking it, you would have information—but McCallum had only tagged himself, and with no one to watch, or at least with no one but a bag lady and the clearly unbalanced Livan. So here it was: so-called real life, which he'd analyze totally differently than he would a text. He looked again at Cheryl's note and was surprised that he felt a little pang because not only the note, but also the slightly harried way it was written, let him know immediately that everything was heartfelt. The way her handwriting revealed that the writer was young—female handwriting, not male, though of course such things could only register privately; it would be anathema to reveal such politically incorrect assessments. If she was gone, so much the better. As he began the process of resuming his normal life, he could do without recriminations. He could also do without facing the guilt he felt—okay; he felt it—because, acting like a person younger than his years, he'd been too quickly taken in by overblown problems, found them perplexing and then compelling. He'd become a little tantalized by his increasing involvement, which he knew, deep down, had been tinged with another kind of curiosity—all right: sexual curiosity. And he'd known it before she wrote what she did about that moment in the car—that almost inconsequential moment that had registered on him as strongly as it had registered on her, the connection that defined a missed moment.

He folded the letter and put it in his pocket, because it wasn't something he would want to risk having fall into the wrong hands. The wrong hands: the police, whom law-abiding adults were supposed to respect; his wife, presumably his closest confidante. Maybe he would present the note later to McCallum, reveal his own vulnerability by letting McCallum see how he nearly got sucked in, empathize with McCallum a little. *Not on screen,* he thought, as he walked down the corridor. Technology was now supplying metaphors faster than poets ever had.

On the stairs, two girls he didn't know began whispering the second he'd passed them. It should have come as no surprise to him—though it did—that the local newspaper had a story about McCallum on the front page. He saw it in a vending machine at the entrance to the faculty parking lot, dropped in his quarter, and took the last copy from the box. He stared at the fuzzy picture of a younger, bearded McCallum. He read the report of what had "allegedly" happened in his own house. The adverb made his life seem absurdly like a TV police drama. On the jump page there was an equally fuzzy photograph of one of the angry-bull cops, standing in front of what he immediately recognized as his own couch, overturned. He, himself, he read, was "alleged" to have been out of the house at the time, as was his wife "alleged" to have been gone. He sat in the car with the overhead light switched on and read as much of the article as he could. It was a long article, and he found it terribly annoying, perhaps any assessment of this awful situation would be terribly annoying, but every fact seemed to miss the point, the story had no shape, the writer moved through official opinions and paraphrased or unattributed speculations ("Yes, she seemed strange, Mrs. McCallum") like an overwrought person navigating a minefield. Halfway through the piece, he read that his wife was a real estate agent, and that he was currently up for promotion (in fact, the promotion had been given him the previous spring). A neighbor was quoted as saying they were very quiet, pleasant people (he didn't recognize the name; neighbors on his street? did Sonja know them?), as if that were at all to the point. As if, had he and Sonja been big party givers, a madwoman crashing through their house might have been entirely comprehensible. He stopped reading when he got to the paragraph talking about "the early hours of dawn." He had not left the house until about nine-thirty, leaving behind a note for McCallum saying he would soon return, and driving to school to teach his morning class. A little drive before his life changed rather dramatically, it turned out. No good deed without punishment—as the uninspired reporter would have been happy to write, if she had been able to make contact with him. He could have given her clichés; she could have dully recorded them. The thing was, the situation really had to do with pent-up emotions, grievances, people's personal pain, their breaking points, and those who found themselves churned up in other people's storms, everybody suddenly as vulnerable as airborne particles, some chilly, uncontrollable wind propelling them. The real story was about storms that came without warning.

He had turned on the radio and was listening to the weather report. Colder that night, with warmer air moving in toward the end of the weekend. There was no mention of the snow that had begun to fall lightly. Then the weatherman segued into the sports announcer, and as he turned off the light and started the ignition he heard the crack of a baseball going off a bat. What would the sounds of McCallum's attempted murder have been, he wondered: the crash of the overturned sofa; the wife's hysteria; McCallum's attempt at reason, or just his fearful first scream, as she snuck up on him? The crowd—people at spring training in Florida—cheered wildly, and he scanned the radio for the classical music station, watching the green digital numbers roll until the preset channel came in and his thumb depressed the button, locking the station into place, the sound of a cello intensifying as if responding to his firm touch.

All his life, he had hated to visit people in the hospital. The antiseptic smell, the smell of boiled vegetables and recirculated air, made him gag. The rooms were at once empty and crowded, rooms impossible to personalize, made bleaker by flower arrangements and Mylar balloons blown about by the perpetual haze of hot air rising through metal radiator covers under windows that looked out over parking lots. He concentrated on the anonymity of the hospital, no doubt, because it pained him to concentrate on the patients. Easier to look at the floor than at the IV going into the arm; simpler to glance upward at the television than to make contact with a person's drug-fogged eyes. It was one of the reasons he hated to go with Sonja to visit Evie; the nursing home would inevitably remind him of a hospital. If all of this wasn't the life Sonja had imagined, it wasn't the life he'd imagined either, though he couldn't exactly remember having had a clear scenario, even at the beginning. They were compatible; they liked many of the same things, though they went about pursuing them differently: she liked to travel; he liked to read essays on travel; he loved talking about literature; she loved internalizing the books, keeping them as part of herself, those she really responded to—with the exception of what she always described, a bit hurtfully (though he knew she didn't mean to offend him), as her very "nonacademic" book discussion group. He once heard her describing herself as liking "major houses and music in a minor key," which did seem true of her: selling real estate had nothing to do with her admiration of certain rather grand architecture—grander, more unique houses than she usually ever had a chance to present to clients. Still, they were alike in that he tried to elucidate texts, and she tried to present possibilities—what might be called, and not in the pejorative, fictional possibilities about how people might inhabit certain houses so that the house, and the people, could assume more complex personalities.

He had come up with that late one night, not so long ago, rubbing her back, thinking out loud, trying to console her because business had been bad and she had been discouraged, claiming that she was interchangeable with some obnoxious salesman going door to door, no one wanting his wares.

At a red light, he realized the car that had been tailgating him was coasting around, saw that the woman inside was rolling down her window. He touched the button on the side of the door and his own window lowered so he could hear what the woman was saying to him. She was someone who worked at Benson, though he couldn't exactly place her. A tall man who was probably her husband was driving, and in the backseat was a row of grocery bags. "I'm so sorry it happened," the woman hollered, and he turned down the music, slightly surprised that now condolences were being shouted through snowy winds as he sat in traffic, nodding with a false smile, suggesting with an exaggerated shrug that soon this would all be over, what a mess but he understood that soon it would be over, perplexing and sad, but soon over. . . . Her husband was calling to him, too, but he could hear only a few words, among them the word "bitch," which caused the woman in the passenger's seat to turn away from Marshall and to begin lecturing the man. Then it came to him: she was President Llewellyn's secretary, Barbara. The President had been quoted about "the regrettable incident," that phrase Marshall remembered from the too-long newspaper article. It made him uncomfortable to be recognized inside his car, and when the light changed he accelerated too fast, which caused the car to veer off at an angle. Pulling out of the skid, he saw their faces bright under the streetlights, two faces staring over their shoulders, suddenly registering his nervousness, his awkwardness, if they had not before. What was it going to be like for McCallum when he got out of the hospital? Everyone would be watching, trying not to be obvious about it, while riveting their attention on him. Where was McCallum's son? Who had the boy if his wife was in custody and he was in the hospital? Though he quickly controlled his fear, at first it struck him with the force of an anxiety dream: like a person who found himself walking down the street without clothes, holding his breath and hoping he would not be found out, it seemed for a few horrible, irrational seconds that only he could know there was a son—everyone else must have forgotten and the boy would be somewhere, abandoned, frightened, starving, perhaps even dead. Surely that was impossible. Someone would have gotten him from school—a family member, a friend, the police. How ridiculous that he could be in a cold sweat, as though responsibility for the boy's existence rested with him. The boy would be (he went through the obvious possibilities again) with relatives, or with friends, with the parents of one of his friends, somewhere. Hadn't McCallum complained about his mother-in-law, whom he saw all too often? She must live nearby. The boy would be with his grandmother; McCallum's wife was in custody; McCallum was in the hospital. People were where they were supposed to be. It was all quite logical in its own terrible way. At the next light, though, he scanned the article for mention of the boy and found none before the light turned green. Why was that so upsetting, that his quick glance at the disorganized article gave him no information about the child, whom he was sure was with someone, not forgotten, like some waif in a sad fairy tale? Still, his heart went out to the boy, whose mother was suddenly gone, whose father had disappeared. Who knew what he had been told about what had happened. Children always thought they were responsible for what went wrong. What would McCallum's son, who must already intuit the difficulty he posed, think now that his parents had disappeared, what could he think but that whatever had happened to them was his fault? He had an image of the child, standing in the living room McCallum had recently described: the missing sofa; the ladder-back chairs; standing there quietly in the calm, stoically indifferent to what was occurring around him. It was an unshakable image, though Marshall tried to clear his head by rolling down the window. He tried to concentrate on the traffic instead of imagining— what a strong, strange image—the boy standing in an uncharacteristic way, like a paperdoll instead of like a real boy, arms at his side, paradoxically both peaceful and frightened, the fate of his parents unknown, his life changing because it was dependent on what did not exist anymore, or would not exist in the same way. Then another boy appeared, another paperdoll, and, fighting to overcome his sudden dizziness, Marshall coasted to a stop at the next intersection, steering with great concentration because an effort of will was necessary to bring the car to a stop. Like someone who was stoned, he was approximating the motions, concentrating excessively, imagining that

he had done a very good job in persuading . . . whom? The people in
the other cars? Beside him, in a red Subaru wagon, was a harried
young woman with a crying baby strapped into a car seat beside her.
Her hand went from the chest of the crying child to her hair; she was
looking at her hair in the rearview mirror, smoothing it, glancing
quickly at Marshall with embarrassment, because she had been
caught primping while her child wailed. Of course McCallum's son
would be fine. Eating dinner, perhaps. Taken care of by someone. At
the house of a friend. When the light changed, Marshall stole another
look at the woman; she was looking straight ahead, pretending not
to notice he still looked at her, and something about her forward gaze
shook him, took him back to the two paperdolls. As he drove off, he
watched brake lights tapped on, then off, ahead of him. He snapped
out of the reverie, and he realized what he had been seeing: it had
been himself, the smaller of the two paperdolls, and his brother, Gordon, in a room—not McCallum's room, but another room that he
now saw distinctly: a room with blue upholstered chairs, and on the
table a Bible, and on the floor a box of paperdolls. His mother, having
read the 121st Psalm, was explaining that she was going to die, looking not at them but straight ahead, out the window at the moon, and
then someone, or something frightening: his father, pacing, his head
obscuring the light from the moon. It was only his father. He and
Gordon sat inside, crushed by what they'd heard, while their father
moved outside, beginning the retreat he would make total once she
did die, once she was absent from the room, and the Bible had been
removed, never to appear again, as far as Marshall could remember.
My God: he was remembering the night—he must have been three or
four years old when his mother told them that they must be brave
and take care of each other, because she was going to disappear, and
he could remember clearly that he had tried to compress himself into
a smaller child, flatten himself into one of his paperdolls so he would
not be so noticeable, absent himself by making himself inconsequential: an unimportant person who would not be given such information. He could remember looking at Gordon, wanting Gordon to
deny what they had just heard, but Gordon had shrunk, too. The two
of them were very small and their mother much larger, almost a
ghost, she was telling them, standing there in the living room in her
long white flannel nightgown, at first looking toward the window and

then turned away from the window, and then away from them, where they had moved together as if magnetized. "Lift up your eyes," she had said—or was that the psalm? Was he remembering her reading the psalm, asking nothing of them, quoting the words "mine eyes" and saying nothing about what they were to do or where they were to look? What was it she expected them to do without her? What was she talking about?

Ahead of him, the parking lot attendant's lighted booth shocked him back to reality, though as he coasted to a stop the attendant waved him past, indicating that he should take a card from the automatic machine to activate the gate. He rolled down the window and punched the button and saw that it was 5:45 p.m., put the card on the dashboard, turned into the first empty space, and turned off the headlights and the ignition. He stared straight ahead, testing: he knew his image had been exact, though it tortured him that he could not conjure up more details, that he had only seen it as in a few moments of pulsing strobe light, first his father outside the window, then the flash illuminating the blue fabric of the chairs, shining in a nimbus around the two brothers huddled together, their mother in a nightgown he had just a few moments before seen distinctly and now could only remember as being long and white. Hadn't there been details? Endless details he was forgetting? "Lift up your eyes," he remembered her saying. He recalled the tone of her voice, the slightly skeptical way she said it, as if she, herself, was not sure this was the thing to ask for.

Ahead of him, through the snow-covered windshield, was the hospital, and as he got out of the car, locking it, grabbing his coat closed instead of taking time to button it, he reflected that because of the wind, no one would think that he was crying, but assume the wind had dashed tears from his eyes.

Martine, Most Dear,

I must hope your last letter was written in haste, and that you are not seriously suffering the distress you imply. I am certain — I say this most emphatically, and I do hope you will believe me in this if in nothing else — Martine, I am absolutely certain that there is no such thing as retribution sent by God Almighty, if God Almighty indeed exists, to rain down on the heads of those of us on earth who may have committed misdeeds. In our time, we have seen science come to the fore to increasingly provide answers to many mysteries, including the previously unknown medical causes of particular physical afflictions. Whether or not there is a just or an unjust god is a question men have been grappling with through the ages. I myself believe that it is a way to avoid personal responsibility, an obscuring of one's role in one's destiny . . . though I do not see this in any way as contradicting my position, which is to say that though painful things may be thrust upon us, in time science may reveal more cause and effect at work than we suspect. I am constantly upset by backsliding, such as the very unexpected stance taken by my brilliant acquaintance J. R. Oppenheimer, who has shown us the key to materializing one amazing creation but who has hesitated on alleged moral grounds about continuing to use his brilliant mind to provide others. I do not mean to compare you two, because I know you have exhibited great courage and will continue to do so, yet in your situation and in his I see some similarity. One must proceed by logic. It is our ally. I have been unfair in announcing my arrival so many times, but you must not feel that because you are alone there without Alice and me (you know she would prefer to be there; you know I prefer it) huge forces have conspired against you. Please think of each situation in its own context and do not do yourself the disservice of jumbling everything together so that one bit of bad luck and then another become a cumulus cloud hanging over your dear head. I am sure there are any number of explanations for why Alice's letters to you have suddenly ceased, by the way. I, too, have been carrying a *heavy burden, though I am certain that nothing that happens to you, or to me, or to Alice, has befallen us because it is justice dealt us by cosmic forces.*

Ever,
Your devoted M.

12

"WE'VE ONLY MET briefly," she said. "There's no reason you'd remember me."

The attractive young woman standing in front of him, clasping his hand, was Jenny Oughton, Sonja's busy friend he'd intended to meet with the day he found himself, in another hospital waiting room, holding Sonja's hand as they awaited word from Evie's doctor.

Jenny Oughton had called to him as he came off the elevator in something of a fog. He had been heading toward the nurses' station, as the woman at the patient information counter had told him to. Jenny had given him the shocking news that McCallum was back in surgery: internal bleeding—apparently a complication, and they suspected, also, a problem with his spleen. They might be removing McCallum's spleen. She had said all that without realizing that he didn't know who she was. "Oh, of course," he had said, but he was sure she saw through him. Then he wondered what she was doing there, this attractive woman with auburn hair and heavily outlined blue eyes, younger than he'd imagined, and nowhere near as cool as she'd been on the telephone. He found himself apologizing a second time: once, disingenuously, for not immediately recognizing her; again, for not keeping the five o'clock appointment he had set up with her days before. He suddenly remembered McCallum, late at night, in the living room, after he had thought of rescheduling the appointment he'd missed with Jenny Oughton—the moment when he had said to McCallum that they needed to go on the record with someone about Livan Baker's lies, McCallum looking at him, slightly bemused, saying, " 'The record'? What is 'the record'? Is it like 'the Force'?" Jesus: McCallum was back in surgery. Still, his eyes darted around the waiting room as if McCallum might suddenly appear, as if all this weren't really happening.

Jenny Oughton gestured to the sofa. He sat beside her in a chair. He realized Jenny Oughton was focusing on him and forced himself to assume a less alarmed expression. She seemed quite young to be a doctor, though increasingly everyone seemed younger: gas station attendants; airplane pilots. So: he had apparently met her once before, a face smiling as he came into the house after his night class, while Sonja's book discussion group was still meeting. "I know he's a very good friend of yours," she said now, her hand on his wrist. "I'm very sorry."

He had arrived at the point where he'd decided not to question this repeatedly. Also, although the assertion continued to perplex him, it didn't seem the time to disclaim any feelings for McCallum.

"But I assume since you're here, he must be your friend, too."

She smiled. "When I was still practicing, he was my client."

"Client?"

"In the old days 'patient' was the term, I believe."

There was something he could identify with; her sense of irony, though in her case she was obviously using it to put him at ease.

"Well, that's amazing, because when I suggested he and I"—he faltered—"I mentioned, or maybe I didn't mention, your name, and he agreed to consult with you, but he never said he knew you. I mean, that would have been bizarre. If we'd walked in and he'd been your former patient."

What did that quixotic smile mean? That he was somehow the odd man out in this situation, that there might be no end to the number of things she might fill him in on?

"You had been coming alone that day, I thought."

"I guess I had been coming alone," he said. "It seemed . . ." What had it seemed? What had that whole tedious episode with Livan Baker been about when obviously the real threat to McCallum had been his own crazy wife? "He didn't tell me he knew you," he said simply.

"Well," she said, just as simply, "if you didn't use my name, I suppose he didn't know it was me you'd be seeing."

"Yes, but I don't see why he didn't just call you about this problem to begin with."

"We terminated a couple of years ago. He was seeing one of the M.D.'s about the medication he was taking."

"Forgive me," he said, "but he didn't give me the impression he knew anyone at student health, except that he knew of someone who had apparently upset a student who had certain . . . who believed, rightly or wrongly, that McCallum had done certain things to her. I thought that student needed help, but the therapist had, well, the therapist had apparently not been the picture of compassion when . . ."

That smile again, but slighter. "I know the situation you're referring to," she said. "I'm aware of the determination regarding the therapeutic approach."

"Therapeutic approach?"

"Yes," Jenny Oughton said. "The student came for therapy."

"I know she came, went, for therapy, but are you aware that she was extremely upset following her first session and that she didn't return?"

"I did hear she didn't return. Yes," she said.

"Am I missing something here?"

"I don't think you're missing anything, per se." She looked at him, no smile. "I understand your confusion," she said. "I should add that I found myself with a conflict of interest when I was called in to consult. I no longer see clients privately, but I was called in as someone the therapist thought might offer some insight. I realized, then, that the client being discussed was describing a problem she felt had been caused by my former client. That might not have been definitive, in terms of my bowing out, except that more recently, Susan McCallum had been to see me. Susan McCallum was in treatment with someone else. Because of my going into research." The smile, again. "I'd appreciate your keeping confidential my mention of Susan McCallum as a client. The situation was naturally very puzzling to you, so I told you."

"Puzzling. Yes. Well. It was puzzling, yes," he echoed. He was deliberately stalling for time, yet he wasn't sure what might ideally happen: she might suddenly tell him everything about everyone, including, through her always infallible, omniscient view, what was true and what was a lie? Not a chance—and quite possibly, she didn't know. She might give him, at the very least, some clue as to why, by implication, the puzzle had been in large part resolved by what she'd said? Did she think he saw things more clearly after what she'd told him? Had McCallum, in effect, set him up, knowing full well that it was not in his best interests that Livan Baker's problem be analyzed at student health?

He watched as a heavy woman in a red coat walked down the hallway carrying a vase filled with red roses. He had begun to feel like someone pulled into an ongoing mystery, a passenger who'd happened to book a seat on the train the night an audience-participatory mystery was being staged. Or as if he were sitting in the front row, watching a bizarre comedy routine, and suddenly he had been pulled into the comic's routine—exactly what had happened to him years before, at a comedy club in Portsmouth, with a spotlight on his face as he tried to appear good-natured about the comic's insults. More bad-dream stuff: the anxiety dream of walking naked; the irrational conviction that he, alone, might be McCallum's child's savior; his obviously secondary position to Jenny Oughton and her world of what's-taken-for-granted/what's-helpful-to-know.

"What about this makes you feel genuinely helpless?" she said, her voice level, eyes filled with concern. My God—he must have spoken to her. She prompted: "The only person not part of the plot on the mystery train?"

"You know those games," he said lamely.

"Yes. You feel that involving you in this, McCallum has tried to take away your autonomy?"

"I feel awkward about getting a freebie," he said.

"Who's giving you the freebie?"

He said: "Did you mean to send a bill?"

"No, I didn't," she said. "I thought I was paraphrasing what you'd said, so I could be sure I understood. I wasn't entirely sure if you were speaking literally or metaphorically. I was trying to understand, not to offer an opinion."

"You know, this is going to sound really strange, but I just realized that something I do to keep my distance from people is just what you do when you mean to communicate," he said. "Conversationally, I mean. I often try to—it's not paraphrase, exactly, it's more a honed-down version of what the person has said. To see if the person still agrees with the statement in the simpler, or the starker, form."

This caused a frown. "Aren't those two rather different things?" she said. "I wouldn't think of simplicity and starkness as being the same."

"This is really a very strange conversation to be having in the waiting room of a hospital," he said.

"You don't want to address my observation." Her eyes sparkled. She meant it mischievously, a satire of the shrink playing shrink.

"You don't seriously want to keep this up," he said.

"You think I'm so different? You don't think it's possible I ever find myself in the middle of things without having anticipated everything?" She shrugged. "I have a problem managing my intensity sometimes," she said.

"What does that mean?"

"Do you want to know simply, or starkly?" she said.

He hesitated.

"I mean that we might have locked into a conversational mode that has more to do with personality—our specific personalities vis-à-vis one another, and my intensity, in particular—than with any externals. We might be speaking this way regardless of the situation, is what I'm suggesting."

"Do you think we would have talked this way if I'd kept our five o'clock appointment?"

"No," she said. "I'm on my second wind."

This made him laugh spontaneously, it was so little what he expected she'd answer. When he laughed, he was aware of the huge weight he had to lift off his chest to get more air into his lungs. That awareness took him back to the moment in the car when he had sat looking at the hospital; that had been the first moment he had registered the crushing weight, and suddenly he could remember how painful it had felt—his wondering how he would get out of the car and proceed, and the thought, as if perfectly logical, that he need not button the four buttons of his coat, but instead he could grab each side and close it over his front. All the better an image: the huddled man, braced against the wind, tears shaken from his eyes a response to the frigid wind, not tears of emotion.

This time, when he looked at her, he was convinced he had been speaking when he had not. He was convinced that he had let her in—ridiculous, but he meant it literally, not metaphorically—that she had been some airborne particle, and his coat had not been tightly held against him, so that she worked her way inside, the way mice find their way into walls in winter, the way cobwebs sometimes flutter onto your fingertips. He was thinking of her as a mouse? A cobweb? She was a real person, who must be contended with. Looking at him, as if they'd come full circle, with her eyes again narrowed so that he knew she saw him in sharp focus, and that she was waiting for something. He also knew what he wanted: he wanted her to be what she was not, a prophet, someone who could tell him, definitively, that McCallum would not die, the invincible authority figure he had always secretly questioned whether any therapist could be. Confronted with a smart, complex person, he had tried to make her a small, gray annoyance. Failing that, he had tried to see her as drooping tendrils of dust.

"Just between you and me. McCallum isn't going to die, is he?" he said.

"Whew," she said. "That's a slight departure from what we were talking about."

"You're a doctor," he said. "If they take out a spleen—they can remove a spleen without its being a big deal, right?"

"It isn't a good sign that when they've operated and things have stabilized, there's sudden internal bleeding."

"I wouldn't imagine," he said.

"I hope we find out he's all right soon," she said. She looked at her watch. "My son's picking me up in another five minutes."

"You have a son who drives?"

"Learner's permit. You can get them at sixteen. His father's giving him a lesson."

"They dropped you off?"

"I don't live with my husband. I took a bus, but my son and his father are going to pick me up and drop us at home."

"Ah," he said.

"He turned sixteen a week and a half ago, and already he's volunteering to pick me up because he knows he can hit his father up for the car, and his father will feel like he's doing a good deed to let him drive, then deposit us both safely at home."

"That's nice of him," he said.

"My husband and I divorced because he was an alcoholic, but for the last three years he has been sober, married to another woman who has given birth to two of their children, and he's very, very sorry and wants me back."

He stared at her. Such complexity, everywhere. For what seemed an eternity, he had been sitting in an orange plastic chair, talking to a pretty young woman who sat on the corner of a sofa covered in material that looked as if a cat-clawing contest had been held atop it. Some doctor, some nurse, must have brought the sofa from home— the sofa with the clawed arms, the nearly threadbare material, a bulge of foam rubber from the far cushion, one leg propped up—he now saw—with a cinder block, in place of a gold-tipped peg leg.

"That sounds peculiar?" she said.

"Not that so much—the sofa. You're sitting on a deteriorating sofa that looks like it's been used after hours for a cat fight."

"McCallum used to miss his own sofa," she said. "His son is hyperactive, and he jumped one too many times, and he wouldn't replace it. He put the old sofa with the broken frame by the curb for the garbage pickup, and then there were just the uncomfortable ladder-back chairs."

"It's a lot to have to deal with," he said. Which, to his mind, meant all of it: the hand you were dealt, fate, unpredictable meetings in anonymous buildings, even. The alcoholic who reformed too late. The sofa frame not built to withstand repeated impact.

He was so agitated that he did not expect the doctor to be walking toward them, up to the last second, when he looked up and understood that they, alone, were the focus of the man's attention. He asked if Jenny Oughton was McCallum's wife. Didn't he realize why McCallum was a patient? You always heard that doctors and nurses did nothing but gossip—could this doctor have no idea of the particular circumstances surrounding McCallum's admission? Or could he have thought McCallum's wife was out on bail, cooling her heels until her husband got out of surgery?

Jenny Oughton said she was not; she was a friend. Marshall said the same thing, because, again, it did not seem the right time to qualify anything.

The doctor told them the surgery had gone well. McCallum was in the recovery room, the internal bleeding stopped. He seemed to be searching their faces to see if he needed to elaborate. Then, in their muteness, he must have decided he could walk away. Marshall had risen, Jenny had not. Still, the doctor seemed more focussed on her, shaking Marshall's hand as he looked through him. *The guy's just tired,* Marshall thought. What havoc McCallum's wife had caused. What misery and pain.

"Well," Marshall sighed, sinking down onto the chair again as the doctor left. "Who would have thought we'd cross paths once when I walked in on a book discussion group, and the next time in the hospital? Did whatever you were discussing that night clarify anything about this?" He was mocking himself, repeating one of Gordon's annoying assumptions: that books did not pertain to real life.

"That was probably in October, wasn't it?" Jenny Oughton said. "As I recall, we were discussing *The Scarlet Letter.*"

He shook his head. Only fair that his inner-directed sarcasm had been mistaken for serious thought. This woman did not seem frivolous. She probably heard very few tossed-off comments during the course of any day.

"It was interesting that a lot of us who thought we remembered the book had forgotten the husband," she said. "We remembered her punishment by the community, but not by Chillingworth. It must have been wonderful to be able to give characters names like that. No writer could get away with that now."

She'd caught his interest. "What were you discussing about Chillingworth?" he said.

"That he returned to haunt her, and it turned out we'd all forgotten. I guess you grow up and you want to forget there can be real bogeymen. And the way Hawthorne presented him, he was so . . . well, chilling. Old and ugly. Absent. He'd wanted her youth and then deserted her, really. That's not terribly different from what Susan McCallum was protesting, I suppose. In the book, your sympathy is all for the one who's been abandoned: Hester Prynne. It's not as easy to see what the transgression was with McCallum, obviously. And he isn't old and ugly. He's actually quite attractive. But she thought he'd withdrawn, and then when he reacted the way he did about her pregnancy, I suppose Susan thought everything was going to be worse. I'm not sanctioning stabbing him. I'm just saying that when you don't see the thing that's stalking someone, often you forget to factor it in. But that thing can be as real as a person."

Was she talking personally? Not only about *The Scarlet Letter*, not only about the McCallums?

"Forgive me," she said, "I'm overstepping my bounds. This is conjecture. Not something I have any understanding of from both perspectives."

"But I thought he'd been your patient," Marshall said.

"He hadn't been there to talk about his home situation," Jenny Oughton said. "When something like this happens, you feel you've miscalculated, though. It does make you wonder whether you should let things evolve, let the client get around to what's really the problem, or be more directive. I've really said too much. It's not always easy to keep everything compartmentalized."

He liked her much better, suddenly, and was sorry she was getting up to leave. He helped her on with her coat, wrote a quick note to McCallum, which they both signed, saying they'd waited for him to get out of surgery (as if they'd known it was going to happen), that each would visit soon. They walked together to the nurses' station and asked the only nurse willing to make eye contact to give the note to McCallum when he returned.

In the elevator, the piped-in Muzak was playing a slowed-down version of "Age of Aquarius." Everyone looked straight ahead, lost in thought as the elevator stopped at almost every floor, slowly proceeding to ground level.

"You're sure your son is coming," he said.

"As sure as I can be of anything," she said. "It was nice to see you again."

He shook her hand. She had pulled on purple suede gloves with linings so thick he couldn't feel the hand inside. He felt slight frustration at not being able to register the handshake, at her retreat into the formality of her goodbye. Walking to the parking lot, he thought about partings: McCallum's odd two-fingered wave; Cheryl Lanier's attempt at a grown-up sign-off at the end of her letter ("Goodbye, and take care") that had seemed, instead of exhibiting maturity, to signal her youth with its slightly portentous formal good wishes. And his mother? How had she left the room that night so long ago? Certainly she hadn't waved, but how had she departed, since she couldn't have evaporated into air? One of the most upsetting things about having remembered that night was that the more he tried to remember, the more everything seemed to recede.

He put the key in the lock and opened the car door, slipped in quickly out of the cold, and pulled the door shut. Had something as automatic as that happened? Had she said what she meant to say and then said goodbye and left the room? He invented a hug, instead. That would make sense as what she had probably done. He invented her swooping toward him, hugging him as he sat in the chair, and then realized that yes, that was true. Probably true. Because the feeling that came back to him was his stiffness: she had put her arms around him, but he had not returned her hug. Of course: he had been punishing her for going away.

Martine, Chérie:

I am taken aback that you would think of taking the children to your parents' house in Canada for the remainder of the summer, though I can see that you would feel disheartened and would lack for companionship. I did not realize, either, that you had been the recipient of unwanted affections from my friend E.B. but feel sure that you can insist that he withdraw. Surely, this should not be a factor in your leaving what is, as much as it is Alice's and mine, your own home in order not to suffer unwanted advances. I can truly sympathize because for so long I have been a victim at the mercy of the doctors. If you have temporarily inherited a life you were not led to expect, so have I dangled like a puppet at the end of some doctor's string. Alice appears quite exhausted after her series of shocks, and not discernibly better, to me, though apparently she is now able to discuss with the doctors her fears about — well, we know this, both of us — about a continued life with me, and about her unjustly suffered guilt at the baby's death. Her melancholy had apparently silenced her for quite a while preceding the treatment, though now she seems more willing to communicate. I will get a firm commitment from the doctors about whether or not Alice will be able to travel to Maine in the foreseeable future, and will let you know at once. I know you would not want her to arrive to find the house empty of you, her close friend, and her two boys, as well. In my dreams I see vases of flowers, petals on the tabletops, and your exquisite fingers brushing them into your cupped hand. Yes, the summer grows long, and I must not delay longer. My apologies for leaving you without protection against . . . well: who would have thought he would harbor amorous intentions toward you? It comes as yet another of life's endless surprises. Say the word and I will see that this situation concludes immediately.

Across the miles,

M.

Dear, Dear Martine,

I have just this moment received your latest communication telling me that Amelia has volunteered to stay with the children while you visit your father after his tonsillectomy. I do realize that such surgery is very difficult when one is beyond childhood, and I am truly sorry for his discomfort. Naturally, if you feel you should be at his side, Amelia would be a most suitable person to watch over the children for a few days, which is what I imagine you are proposing. I must say that I am slightly vexed that she did not call me here at the Waldorf to say that all this might be going on, though I suppose that when one is long absent from one's routines, one's regular life, I mean, others tend to make plans of their own. I am sure I speak for Alice in saying that you must, absolutely, do what conscience dictates. I write only to say that I trust you have not abandoned hope entirely of our arrival. I cling to the thought of that moment as much as you must, Martine. I hope that you do not feel you have to escape the home in order to escape E.B. He has been a friend for so long that I hesitate to speak to him about this matter, unless you feel you cannot, or do not wish to, handle it. You seem quite clear that his affections are not reciprocated, and I cannot believe he would be insistent upon this. At any rate, I believe that even without Alice — there being only the slightest possibility she could travel for a weekend following her last treatment — I should like to come and check on things next weekend and see whether a discussion between the two of us might clarify some things. If you feel that you must go to your father before then, however, of course I would understand. Some say that visits are most appreciated when one has recovered a bit — but I leave that decision entirely in your hands. I will, of course, be happy to arrange a plane ticket.

Warmly,
M.

Dear Martine,

You must promise not to write me again in haste, as it causes me great pain. My opinion is still the same vis-à-vis punishment dealt from above. I simply do not believe this is true, and therefore the question of whether any penance can alleviate one's unhappiness becomes quite beside the point. Further, I feel that many different factors are responsible for Alice's collapse, including her early years, and her general approach to life, by which I mean the nervous disposition she was born with—not something thrust upon her. Science still knows so little about the causes of alcoholism, though some feel it may be a disease, the proclivity toward it passed on through the genes. At least, this has been the point of view currently considered most thought provoking by a group of doctors at Alice's hospital, I am informed. Please do not take on any burden greater than what you have already accepted. As to the other matter you mentioned, I am happy that you have felt free to share with me your innermost thoughts, but I hasten to add the obvious: that nightmares are not reflections of reality, but much changed versions of it (if versions is the correct word at all). What can you think it would do to me to hear that you hear the voice of a child crying repeatedly, that it startles you from sleep, that you check the boys' bedroom again and again? I understand you must have been quite depressed to say that you assumed even that cry would not register with me. This all registers with me, Martine, and every day I hope against hope that we can all regain a normal life. We cannot do anything for those who have died untimely deaths, except to give their memories the respect due them, seeing that scientific forces—call it even "fate," if you will—move, as "God" is said to do, in mysterious ways. But we must not see suffering as the product of some punitive agenda. You cannot think that I find it bearable that you suffer under such delusions.

Most fondly,
M.

Dearest Martine,

I write you instead of responding to Amelia, because I can only assume you are aware of her letter (which I enclose). I am happy she arranged for time off to go to Maine and be with you, though I am slightly taken aback that this happened just as I was considering arriving myself. I assume that now the two of you are together, you will not find my visit so necessary. I am pleased, also, that she can be there when you fly from Boston to visit your father. I do hope he is improving daily and send him my very sincere best wishes for a speedy recovery.

Can you imagine that from my perspective, Amelia's letter would appear quite intemperate? I understand, of course, women's sympathy for one another, but what value will her presence be if she encourages you in skepticism toward me and tells you your nightmares are quite logical? I am arguing only for the necessity of trying to triumph over circumstance. Of course I understand that I have made mistakes, and if you see clearly what I should do now to affect the outcome of situations that have arisen from those mistakes, I would welcome the information. I do not mean to be unkind, as I hope Amelia realizes I like her very much, and she has been quite kind to me in New York, but whatever you write me I would like to be an expression of your ideas rather than the result of conferring with anyone else. Speaking of which, I registered the information that the two of you had spoken to Dr. St. Vance. I think highly of his abilities, and if this mitigates your distress in any way, it was a good thing for Amelia to have encouraged you.

I am being as philosophical as possible about the good that may come of Amelia's knowledge concerning my intimate affairs. I assume that since she is so much a woman of intelligence and good taste that both you and Alice adore her, her discretion can be counted on.

With great affection,

M.

Dearest Martine,

I will be honest. I, too, have more than one scenario. There are, however, only two, and I keep returning to them — not in nightmares, as you do, or even in dreams, but during the course of a day, never deciding, always in a state of conflict. In the first, I walk away from everything. One cannot truly do this, but I imagine that in cowardice I could rationalize my behavior and avoid the pain of returning to the house, let those who cursed me for a coward curse me for a coward. I could join a business venture beginning in New York, arrange through lawyers, if need be, the care of the children, their schooling. I could send you a large check, which you might cash or not, however you decided, as a thank-you for all you have done. That would be irresponsible, at the very least. Entirely deplorable. But I know deep in my heart that I am capable of doing that. In the second scenario, I return not so much to the house and children as to you, feeling that there is still the possibility that after all the malingering, and in spite of my deficiency of character you would fold me in your arms. Though Alice might be lost to me — isn't she lost to us? — you would step forward as if out of the fog, and that fog would be the past, which would dissipate, wafting away as I stood with you in my arms. I feel that possibility within me.

You and Amelia have asked what I envision. One of the above.

M.

13

TONY HEMBLEY STOOD at the grave, beside the other mourners. She had asked him not to come, but when did Tony, headstrong Tony, listen to anyone, let alone a woman who had already been demonstrated to be unable to influence the way he thought about anything, herself included? What had he thought? That she'd be secretly glad to see him? Was he egotistical enough to suppose his presence might make it easier for her to endure the funeral, or just so guilty he had decided to intrude himself in a place where he had no business, perhaps even deceiving himself into thinking his presence revealed a man of good character, one who offered friendly support, who stood by in times of trouble.

Marshall was thinking: *This could quite possibly have been McCallum.*

She thought: *Not long ago, Evie was alive; not long ago, that man standing across the grave with his scarf flung to the side like a schoolgirl's ponytail and I were lovers.*

Sonja was surprised that the sausage nurse had come to the funeral. Dressed all in black, with a black wool scarf tied to hold her black hat on her head, the woman dabbed at her eyes as the priest spoke of Evie's many good qualities. A teenage girl stood next to her, equally fat, equally sad, a paisley scarf in shades of beige and brown draped over the shoulders of her long black coat. She stood close to her mother's side, staring straight ahead, shifting from one foot to the other, waiting for the funeral to end. Sonja had never seen the girl before she and her mother walked into the church, and she had never

seen the old man in the wheelchair—at the church, or elsewhere—
though she imagined it must have been the black man who had called
on his behalf to inquire where the burial would take place. Marshall
had taken the call; at first, he had been taken aback by the lengthy
explanation the caller gave about who he was himself: a caretaker; a
"student of life in our universe," he had apparently told Marshall.
Now, the black man held the handles of the wheelchair, his orange
leather gloves enormously puffy, as if two small life rafts had inflated
on his hands. The man was expressionless except when he bent forward to whisper to the old man, to quickly place one consoling hand
on the old man's shoulder, then withdraw to his official position. She
watched them out of the corner of her eye as the priest sprinkled holy
water on the grave.

As the true faith united her with the throng of the faithful on
earth, your mercy may unite her with the company of the choirs of
angels in heaven. . . .

"Who knows?" Marshall whispered, sensing her implied question
as she gazed—apparently, not as subtly as she thought—at the two
men. "Maybe Evie had a boyfriend."

"Very funny," Sonja said, with no trace of amusement. Across the
grave, Tony caught her eye and would have held it, except that she
looked away. Jenny Oughton stood several yards away from them,
alone, her violet coat (so that was why she had had such unusually
colored gloves at the hospital, Marshall was thinking) unbuttoned
and whipped by the now-steady wind, a large embroidered shoulder
bag hanging from her shoulder. She wore earrings that caught the sun
so that Marshall had difficulty keeping his eyes off Jenny Oughton.
It was as if she were signalling, flashing a message to him or, more
likely, to Sonja, who had earlier raced to embrace her, obviously
touched that her busy friend had found time to come, on this frigid
day, not only to the church, but also to Evie's burial.

The priest spoke, and many in the crowd blessed themselves. The
sausage woman elbowed her daughter, and her daughter repeated her
mother's motions, quickly, out of time with everyone else. Her scarf
fell to the ground, but when she bent to pick it up, her mother put
her hand on the girl's arm, and the girl straightened without having
touched it. The sausage woman's foot slid forward to pin it to the
ground, which caused the girl further dismay. Finally, in spite of her

mother's warning, she bent forward and snatched it up from under her foot. In the sudden, strong wind, the girl found that she was holding something that looked like an unwieldy towel swept up from a clothesline in a great wind, or a huge, flapping pennant. The priest saw it in his peripheral vision and missed a beat, then began again the drone of his prayer. If looks could kill, the girl's mother would have killed her, yet Sonja was relieved for the distraction, happy to have something to focus on so she wouldn't think of the sadness of the occasion, and of how bereft she was, and cry.

Take away out of their hearts the spirit of rebellion, and teach them to see your good and gracious purpose. . . .

It was a cold March day, the ground frozen, the trees leafless. Evie had gone into the hospital in winter and she had died in winter—Evie, who so loved flowers. Sonja regretted not taking her more bouquets. She regretted passing along one of the Godzillas Tony had given her, putting it on Evie's bedside table as if it had been her token of love to Evie, not a secondhand valentine from her lover.

She hadn't told Evie the history of the windup toy, but she had told her about Tony, confessed the way Evie confessed to the priest, though Evie had been Sonja's only priest, and she had spared Evie the details, spared herself the shame of making her story more specific. Just the outline: a man at work, a mistaken notion that she would go so far and then no further, followed by the mistaken impression that sleeping with Tony could remain a harmless game, having as much to do with being childishly silly, with letting go and having some fun, as with sex itself. Well: what had she really spared Evie, if she'd told her about their chasing each other through empty houses, playing hide-and-seek, going through the houses and closing the drapes or dropping the blinds as they discarded their clothes, the excitement building as the house grew darker, the potentially prying eyes of neighbors or passersby adding to the thrill? She had reassured Evie that it was something she'd done in the past—in the not-distant past, she hadn't told her. And the end of it? She'd made it sound as if their folly had finally impressed them with their silly, risky behavior; she'd implied that she had simply seen the light one day, regained her common sense, reminded herself that her marriage to Marshall meant something. It meant, at that moment, that he was standing at her side, head bowed in prayer. He hated funerals—didn't believe in them.

He was there because of Sonja, there because he was her husband, there because he loved Evie, however much he had been cowardly in avoiding her after her stroke.

What a disturbing winter it had been, with hardly anyone doing what was proper. The word came to Sonja's mind because Tony sometimes used it, as in "a proper tea." She had once found his Englishness charming and often amusing, his diction as arch as his behavior seemed uninhibited. *A proper fuck,* she had said to him once, turning down the bed in their motel room and smoothing the sheets, lighting a little devotional candle she'd bought while wandering through the drugstore in search of Evie's beloved Muguet des Bois dusting powder. Instead of wildly discarded clothes and a football tackle, she had wanted them to sit on opposite sides of the bed and undress, to make love with classical music playing on the radio and the candle glowing. To her horror, Marshall had come upon the candle in her purse several weeks before. She had left it unzipped and, passing by, he had sneezed, then sneezed again, then reached into her bag, which was on the kitchen chair, for a tissue, coming up with a handful of pens and credit card receipts and the candle, yet he'd acted as if scooping a candle out of her purse was entirely unexceptional. He'd stuffed it back along with everything else, without even commenting, dropping the little white candle back in the glass holder, extracting a tissue and sonorously blowing his nose. There it had been, the moment that could have changed everything, and he had simply blown his nose long and hard, his quizzical look a response only to her standing and staring at him, horrified.

Now the priest was standing next to Marshall, mentioning Evie by name: first name, middle name, maiden name, married name—all the endless, confusing identities of women born in Evie's generation—and then, his words obscured by a howl of wind, clasping Marshall's hand, the ceremony apparently finished, the Bible clasped in his gloved hand, the ungloved hand he had used to turn the pages extended to everyone who gathered around them. The priest offered further condolences as Marshall returned the priest's handshake. He thought how different this funeral had been from his father's, when he and Gordon had stood alone at the grave, listening to a soprano sing a song his father had loved, an a cappella version of Robert Frost's "The Road Not Taken." His father's lawyer had been the only other person present. The lawyer and the singer had come together, in a limousine. Where had the woman been found? She was short and not at all attractive—Gordon had joked that the lawyer had borrowed her from amateur night at some nightclub—wearing blue harlequin glasses and singing with a voice alternately glorious and shrill, her spike heels sinking in the grass during the laboriously prolonged song. It would have pleased Gordon, who loved ironies, to know that their father had mistaken a poem written to mock another poet for a deeply felt expression of conflict, but he hadn't told Gordon that. It had seemed too disrespectful of his father, who had been moved by something he hadn't known was ultimately a kind of joke. Evie would have been at the funeral except that she had the flu, and Sonja hadn't come because she had had a miscarriage the night before. Gordon had said with great relief that his wife was also ill. Marshall doubted it, though no doubt Gordon had also thought he'd been lying when he said Sonja was sick. Why had he hesitated to tell his brother the truth about Sonja's miscarriage?

A man and a woman about Sonja and Marshall's age, who had come late, reminded Sonja that they had often visited Evie when they went to the rest home to see the woman's mother. They were Catholics, Sonja had noticed during the funeral; they had genuflected, and now the woman greeted the priest by name as she reached out to clasp his hand.

Marshall excused himself and walked toward the old man, stopping to say hello and to hug Mrs. Azura, who had been Evie's neighbor in the townhouse she'd lived in before her stroke. Mrs. Azura was a kind woman who had brought jars of homemade soup to the nursing home, who had always insisted to Evie that she would eventually make a full recovery and return to her home, where they would be neighbors again. Mrs. Azura had been so emphatic with Evie in saying they would be living side by side again that Sonja had never been sure, until Mrs. Azura's house went on the market while she continued to speak to Evie as if her being away was only a temporary thing, that the woman knew better than what she was saying. Another woman from the townhouse complex was also at the funeral, but Sonja knew her hardly at all, and Mrs. Azura had to whisper her name to Sonja so she could greet her: Andrea FitzRoy, a divorced woman in her late fifties who had taught Evie how to do bargello.

She had strawlike dyed hair and clown circles of rosy color on her cheeks. As she offered her sympathy to Sonja, clasping her hand to communicate her sincerity, Marshall reappeared and said that the old man's attendant had explained that the old man had lost his voice to laryngitis. He had told Marshall that Evie had been a longtime friend he had known many years back, someplace in New England, the attendant thought. The old man's name was Ethan George Bedell, and he had been a college friend of Marshall's father. He had known Gordon and Marshall when they were little boys—too little to remember him, he was sure. Marshall did not remember, but he was surprised that Evie had kept contact with someone through the years who was such an old friend, but of whom she had never spoken. Mr. Bedell had asked the male nurse to bring several photographs to give to Marshall. He had brought them but left them in the glove compartment of the van, he'd told Marshall, not sure what would be the proper time to present them. As he delivered this information, he had obviously been torn between staying at the old man's side and immediately going to get the photographs. Marshall had, of course, asked them to join the others at their house for coffee. He reported this information to Sonja in bits and pieces, interrupting himself to thank people for coming, to make sure they understood the directions to the house. Listening, Sonja remembered the day not long ago when she had sat beside Tony in his car, imagining a fantasy garden, while he had questioned her about directions to the new motel. "Just follow me," the priest said to Mrs. Azura, who finally had to admit that she had no car, that she had taken a cab to get there. The priest insisted on giving her a ride, as Marshall gently scolded her for not calling them to arrange transportation to the funeral.

"He does not have good health," the man wheeling Mr. Bedell past them said. "He thanks you, but he is unable to continue on to your house." Standing behind the wheelchair, the man rolled his eyes upward. What was this? Dismay at not being able to stop for coffee, or a more general roll of the eyes about everything: old age, bad health, death?

"You and Evie were friends for many years," Sonja said a little louder, crouching to look into the old man's face. She nodded in agreement with herself, because the old man only stared. "I'm Marshall's wife. Evie's stepson's wife," Sonja said, gesturing toward Marshall.

"He does not hear well," the man behind the wheelchair said loud enough to startle Sonja. "He told me when he still had his voice that he knew all about you," the man said, in a more conversational tone of voice.

All about her. Wouldn't that have been distressing. Yet of course he did not; he had probably only heard some innocuous story from Evie. "You know about me from talking to Evie," Sonja said. It was half a statement of fact—of course that would be how he knew— and half an expression of her puzzlement: How was it she had never heard of Ethan Bedell? "You must have read about the funeral in the newspaper," she said.

At this, the old man vigorously shook his head no.

"He was contacted at his friend's request by a nurse at the rest home, I believe," the man said. He turned to Marshall. "Your step-mother, sir, was quite a favorite of the nurses. She did have a lovely way, and I offer my heartfelt sympathy."

Marshall nodded, only half following. He had begun speaking quietly to the priest, giving him detailed instructions about how to navigate a particular route. Then Mrs. FitzRoy spoke to the priest. She thanked him for his sensitivity and said she assumed he knew that the 121st Psalm was one of Evie's favorites, that she recited it so beautifully her friends often asked to hear it during their own times of trouble. Would it be at all fitting to recite that psalm at Marshall and Sonja's house, or was such a thing not done? The 121st Psalm came back to Marshall, fragmentized: *mine eyes; my help; neither slumber nor sleep.* He thought he knew the other words, the other verses, but at the moment it ran together as if it were something he had to race through to the end. Why had this suddenly set off such a strange reaction?

Because outside the hospital . . . when he went to see McCallum . . . Jesus Christ: How could he have forgotten? That night, just be-fore the snowstorm hit with real force, it had begun to come back to him, the memory of being a child, seated near his mother on a dark night, his father outside, his mother speaking earnestly to him and to Gordon, who had taken a paperdoll away from him. At first he had been quite angry at Gordon, but then, small as he was, he had understood that Gordon had his best interests at heart as he tried to make him pay attention. Gordon was also trying to placate their mother, whose eyes had moved more than once to the box of spilled paperdolls Marshall stared at with such fascination . . . the paperdolls on the floor, flat on the floor, dead, his mother had said the word "dead," she had spoken of herself as dead, as a paperdoll put in a box, they must not cry, they must listen . . . and outside had been the sound of his father crying, or perhaps talking; there had been that indistinguishable sound and also the cat scratch of branches scraping the windowpane. Like an actor rehearsing, she had walked back and forth in her white nightgown, reading, at once passionate and slightly perturbed, as if she could not quite get it right, starting over, trying for the right intonation, the only intonation acceptable to her ear, his mother telling them she was dying, reading the 121st Psalm. Yes . . . of course Evie would love the 121st Psalm, because what did she not love that his mother loved? Evie and his mother had often read the Bible to them at night—sometimes stories from the Bible in an illustrated children's book, but in time directly from the Bible. That night his mother had read the 121st Psalm, and Evie had stood in the doorway, visibly upset, not going toward either Gordon or Marshall to comfort them as she usually did, because they were crying too—first Gordon, then Marshall, imitating him, frightened at the way their mother appeared, astonished that he had had his paperdoll snatched away. From that night on, it would be what seemed an eternity until Evie comforted them again, and their mother . . . surely she could not instantly have disappeared, yet he couldn't remember what had come next, couldn't remember further interactions with her, or even how or when he had been put to bed that night.

It was not considered proper that young children be at funerals, so they had not gone to their mother's funeral. He could vaguely remember Evie crying when the day finally came, combing her hair and looking at herself in the tall hall mirror with the gilded putti trailing flowery sashes in each corner, crying as she yanked a comb through her hair, punishing her hair, it had seemed, Marshall's father ignoring her, ignoring his sons, who were taken care of that day, Evie had told him years later, by a neighbor woman who had always frightened them because of her long black hair. Both boys had been convinced they'd been left in the care of a witch.

After two years—a decent interval of time—their father had married Evie, providing a known quantity as a mother for his sons, having with her a much different marriage than he had had with his first wife. Not a business arrangement, exactly, but two people who seemed never to speak harshly, though neither did they seem to laugh—generic grown-ups, if such creatures could be said to exist. He had always been sure that his father thought he was doing the right thing, the logical thing, in marrying Evie and in trying to attain again a sense of stability for his sons, and therefore for himself. If they hadn't loved each other, though, that would have been a tragedy. If his mother, in her white nightgown, had become a ghost whose presence permeated the house. . . . Because it now seemed more than possible that this was the case, he tried to put such thoughts out of his mind. He could remember berry picking with his father and Evie the summer after his mother's death; taking turns climbing the ladder to string lights on the Christmas tree; hiking to a waterfall, laughing . . . she had laughed then . . . or had that been his own laughter, his and Gordon's, running ahead, Gordon sliding in the mud? Did he remember it, or had he only been told about it so many times it seemed real?

He was almost to the parking lot, lightly holding Sonja's elbow, talking—how, when he had been so lost in thought?—to Mrs. Azura, when he realized that Mr. Bedell and the male nurse were not coming to his house, the man had said not, so that he should follow them to the van and get the photographs.

The van was equipped to carry the wheelchair in the front, locked into place in the space where a passenger's seat would normally have been. He stood there as the man wheeled Mr. Bedell up the ramp, then rolled the chair into slats and locked the wheels. The man slid the door shut and came down the incline, turning to push a button at the side of the door to retract the ramp.

"He was too ill to come," the man said. "Cancer of the esophagus. We call it laryngitis."

"I'm so sorry," Marshall said. "It was very kind to come out to give me pictures when it was such an obvious effort."

"They're nothing," the man said quietly. "You hear about photographs being brought to a funeral, you assume it's a Perry Mason mystery and something's going to be cleared up. Mr. Bedell has me rerun those Perry Mason shows for him almost every night. Della Street always gets a smile from him, because he thinks she's a smart girl even though her role is to be confused and to ask questions. She's pretty, too. And the private investigator—did you know he was some famous gossip columnist's son? Paul Drake. Handsome man. I'm afraid your two pictures aren't much of anything, though: blurry pictures of a girl standing in a dress and sitting in a rocker. Don't get your hopes up."

"They're pictures of Evie?" Marshall said.

The man nodded. "He has another picture of her, or he says it's of her, that he didn't want to part with. I guess you and I both can play Perry Mason well enough to assume Mr. Bedell loved your stepmother. The love of one person for another, I mean: that much I can sense as a student of the universe. Wait here and I'll get them."

He went around to the far side of the van. Marshall looked over his shoulder and saw Sonja, talking to Tony Hembley. Poor Sonja: she'd loved Evie so, been so good to her, driving to see her all those times he hadn't gone along, bravely receiving the bad news so many days at the hospital. His heart warmed with love for his wife, his wife with her pretty windblown hair, standing and talking to her boss. Sonja made everyone comfortable. She had a way of getting on equal footing with people.

As the man had said, he could see at the first quick glance that the pictures were a letdown: a young woman, not recognizably Evie, standing and pinching out the sides of her skirt. "A Simplicity pattern definitely not simple" was written on the back of the photograph. In the second picture, the same young woman was sitting in a wicker rocker with an elaborately worked back in the shape of a heart, a baby on her lap who must have been either him or, because she looked so young, Gordon. "Martin," it said on the back of the photograph. Martin? He looked again, wondering whether the old man might not have been confused. It could have been anyone—it didn't seem to be Evie, but perhaps if her hair had been very different . . . He slipped them back in the envelope and thanked the man, calling up also to thank Mr. Bedell, his voice, he was afraid, loud but insincere.

"He does not hear well, even when you shout," the man said. "He communicates with me in writing, and I write back. He asked me to give you the two pictures of your stepmother some time back, but I neglected to get in touch the way I should have. He showed them to her in the nursing home, and when he saw that she didn't want them, he told me to look you up. Then I'm afraid the better part of a year passed, and then one day the nurse phoned."

"Evie knew this was her?" Marshall said.

"Oh yes. Picture number one, she described every step of making that particular party dress. Picture number two was upsetting, though, so that's when I took them back and changed the subject." The man looked up at Mr. Bedell in the van. "I guess we'd all better count on changing so much we'll be the only ones to recognize ourselves when we're old. I don't know about you, but I might cut some movie star pictures out of magazines, flash Denzel Washington and tell people down the line that was me."

"You assume he was in love with Evie," Marshall said.

The man shrugged. "Different times," he said. "Maybe the old gentleman admired her." He shook Marshall's hand. "He's got drawers full of things," he said. "Maybe he'll find some better pictures. If others pertain to you or your family, I'll send them along. You know, eventually," the man said.

Mr. Bedell, in profile, sat staring straight ahead while they talked. Marshall thanked the man and wished him a safe trip. He tucked the pictures in his inside pocket and started toward his car, where he could see that Sonja had already seated herself in the driver's seat.

"Wait one minute, okay?" he said to her.

She nodded and he quickly walked back to the grave, where the two men who had been waiting in the background had begun to shovel dirt onto the casket. Someone was collecting the folding chairs.

"Everything's okay?" he said to the man collecting chairs.

"Yes sir. My sympathies," the man said.

"How will you mark the grave?" Marshall said. "Until the tombstone is ready, I mean."

"Sir?"

"I mean—" What did he mean? "You'll . . . what, will there be some of those flowers on top? The tombstone isn't here yet."

"It will be delivered in a week," the man said. "I've personally spoken to the stonemason." He reached into his pocket and rifled through several pieces of paper. Marshall could tell that the man thought he was talking to a crazy person.

The man held out a typed-in form. Marshall read it with relief: the date ordered, the date delivery was to be made. As the man had said, it was to be delivered to the cemetery one week from today. She would only be anonymous for one week. He nodded as he looked at the form, and at the clearly printed letters in the rectangular space:

EVELINE MARTINE DÉLIA LOCKARD
APRIL 2, 1918
MARCH 22, 1994

14

———

MARSHALL LEFT HIS CAR in the faculty parking lot, nosed in toward a snowbank, blocking easy passage out for someone's dirty white Mustang convertible; only half the lot had been plowed, and there were too few parking places. It was the best he could do, and he wasn't about to walk half a mile from the shopping center. In front of the humanities building stood a snowman with a carrot nose, scarf, and top hat, and standing next to him a Botero-ish snow woman wearing a red gauze skirt and a sequinned vest unbuttoned not over snow breasts, but . . . upon closer inspection, he was seeing pumpkins embedded in her chest with pumpkin stem nipples protruding, painted red. She had no nose, but blue marble eyes: oversized marbles, sure to drop out the minute the temperature rose and the snow began to melt. The sight turned him momentarily sentimental: the many times he and his brother had fashioned snowmen, though they'd never been allowed to put clothes on them, they'd had to sculpt clothing or leave off the clothes entirely. As a child, Marshall had been fascinated by things that reproduced the human form: paperdolls; snowmen; dolls. His father, vexed, had finally snatched away his last doll when he was three or four—Gordon wasn't sure which, and Marshall certainly didn't remember its having happened. Snowmen and snow forts, streets closed off for sledding—on those rare days when the world seemed to have been turned over to children, he had felt exhilarated, empowered. Today, however, he'd felt only dismay at the struggle involved in driving poorly plowed roads, concerned and slightly irritated because Sonja had communicated her anxiety that something bad might happen to him. What did she want? For him not to show up at his job? Since Evie's funeral she had been withdrawn and out of sorts, alternately silent or filled with anxiety: the ceiling seemed to be bulging, it must be about to spring a leak (he squinted hard; the ceiling was smooth); a pane of glass was about to fall out of the bathroom window (nonsense: he'd used a bit of caulk and the slight rattling stopped). Sonja had said, after Evie died, that she intended to take a leave of absence from Hembley and Hembley and think about what else she might do, what might really be important, because she did not want to die feeling she had only marked time doing a job she'd fallen into and never rethought. What could he say? Of course Tony Hembley had also been quite upset by her decision, calling the house numerous times when she didn't return to work, though Marshall had heard her calmly announcing her decision to him more than once, and if Tony thought he could change Sonja's mind, he had another think coming. His own guess was that she would soon return to work, but he understood that she had been deeply upset by Evie's death, and because he felt guilty that he was not terribly upset (he'd known for so long it had been coming), he hardly felt he could criticize her. She had been so involved with everything, so unendingly loyal to the woman who had really been his responsibility. In a way, though, that pleased him: he liked to see a person act out of pure affection, rather than a sense of duty. In a way, he supposed it was Evie's payback for her kindness to him and to Gordon: two children she never expected would be left in her care, motherless, a huge responsibility befalling one so young. You would think that after marrying his father—the old days, the old-fashioned ways: making sure everything was done correctly—she might at least have started her own family. You would think she would have wanted her own child, though the way women talked now, it was almost an embarrassment to long for a biological child. He wondered if Sonja had ever talked about that with Evie, or about her own miscarriages, or whether such things remained private even between women. He supposed he wished Evie had had a child because that would have made it clearer that she wanted motherhood, instead of that she inherited it. As a young woman, she had left her own family in Canada to join their family: the idea was that she would teach Alice French, because Alice had such an interest in learning the language. No doubt, Evie had also wanted to have an adventure. But the language lessons never materialized, and gradually she was subsumed by responsibility for the children. She had become an au pair: an extra pair of hands. Some of his students had done that during their summer vacations—gone to places like Nantucket and the Vineyard to supervise children, going off to see their boyfriends on their days off. A pleasant enough way to get a free summer vacation, good training for the future. Then again, there were the recent cases of nannies who may have killed babies by burning down houses, or who had been caught abusing children when the parents secretly videotaped them, or those who had not been caught, but who were under suspicion because of bruises on a child's face, suspicious marks only in retrospect, bruises said to have been caused by falling on a toy, but who would believe that after the same child later died of a fractured skull? He and Gordon had been lucky to have Evie, and so had their father, and so, even, had their mother, who had died with the knowledge that her children would be well cared for.

Thinking about it now, that night when his mother had told them she was dying came into slightly clearer focus. By concentrating on what was happening outside—his father's pacing; the wildly blowing trees—even at that moment he had seen something important in his peripheral vision: Evie, coming quietly to the doorway, checking on them, disappearing, anxious to see how this traumatic event was registering on the boys, as well as seeing if there was anything she could do for their mother. However clear it was that she loved the two of them, it was even clearer that she loved their mother. It was a little strange—he thought that, now—that he and Gordon had not been prepared for the news in any way. Gordon said later that he knew their mother was ill, but surely he hadn't known she was terminally ill. Surely even Gordon must have been astonished, probably more than he, because he was older and could better comprehend what was being said. He could remember so clearly observing Gordon's expressions that night, trying to take his cues from his older brother. He was still reluctant to focus on his mother, and on her words, so that sometimes when that scene came back to him it could as well have been a scene that omitted her: just scattered paperdolls, his father moving outside the house, Evie appearing and disappearing. He and Gordon had had a magnetic disk and two small Scottie dogs, one white and one black; the top Scottie moved forward on the disk when the other dog was upside down underneath, drawing it along by magnetic force. Evie had seemed like the visible Scottie, probably the black one because his mother, in her nightgown, had been so white . . . yes; he had thought that back then. He actually remembered his half-formed, subliminal thoughts, not a feeling.

The building was overheated, with floor grates inside the vestibule that sent an eye-watering blast of hot air into his face as the doors swung closed behind him. Exiting the building at the same time he was entering was his student Dominic Ruiz, who came to a Wile-E-Coyote-at-edge-of-cliff stop to extend his hand and to say how sorry he was that Marshall's mother had died. Well, Evie might as well have been his mother, though he was surprised the department secretary had been so specific when she'd cancelled his class. "Everyone in my family is deceased *except* for my mother," Dominic said, as if this sad bit of information might offer Marshall some perverse consolation. Deceased, instead of dead. So: the family consisted only of Mrs. Ruiz and her not-very-bright son, Dominic. This nice young man who was gripping his hand sincerely. Dominic Ruiz had on leg warmers and cutoff jeans, his dirty knees visible in the space between striped wool and denim, a navy-blue parka zipped half-closed over a T-shirt revealing the soufflé of Bart Simpson's bright yellow hair. "Oh, man, I really feel for you," Dominic Ruiz said, straining to see past the teacher who was now his obstacle between hallway and door. "One thing I feel, at least you did the right thing to go to the funeral. I didn't go to my uncle's funeral and now I feel very bad about that. Oh, man, this stuff is difficult."

He nodded, clapped Dominic's shoulder, and moved away. *Kids and their ideas of profundities,* he thought, yet he knew that at Dominic's age he would have done no better. As Dominic ran out of the building a gust of wind swept through strong enough to cause a landslide of stacked newspapers in the corridor. He went to straighten the pile—if Dominic Ruiz could exhibit good manners, so could he. As he repositioned the papers he found himself looking at a photograph of Livan Baker. "D.E.A. Agent Arrested," read the headline. He stared from the photograph to the headline, then from the headline to the photograph. "Levann Baker," was written below it. So there it was: Livan Baker was a narc.

Instead of going into the department office, he went through the swinging doors, hoping no one else he'd be obliged to talk to would see him before he could get to his office and close the door and read this latest unfathomable piece of information. A stampede of six or seven students passed him, taking the stairs by twos and threes, screeching about a party they were on their way to, the girls in the lead, coats dragged, hats clasped in their hands, scarves trailing the ground. At what age did people start to actually wear their winter clothes? He looked down and saw a dropped glove, decided against giving chase to return it. The latest revelation about Livan Baker made him feel as if he'd taken a stomach blow; he also felt sure that he was going to feel even worse once he read the news story. He held the newspaper tightly rolled, feeling vaguely compromised by the presence of Livan Baker's story, though why should that be? He put the key in the lock and turned it, closed the door quickly behind him. He did not turn on the light. He went to his desk in the fading light, unbuttoned his jacket, and sank into the chair, smoothing the newspaper on the desk in front of him.

Livan Baker, twenty-five, of Chicago, Illinois, was an undercover narcotics agent. He read two descriptions of her: one by someone described as "a friend in the sophomore class," another from her landlord, who called her "irresponsible." The landlord commented that two other students shared Livan Baker's apartment, and that they paid their rent separately. Livan Baker's was either late or, more recently, never paid.

It could not be confirmed by official sources that Livan Baker was a narc. However, a Benson student, a former student from the University of Rochester, identified Livan Baker as the person who had been at the police station the day his best friend was booked for dealing dope. Someone described as "a source close to President Llewellyn" who would not speak for attribution was quoted as saying, "Well, what do you think? That there are people working undercover on campus Dr. Llewellyn doesn't know about?"

Caught driving on the wrong side of the road, DWI. Failed Breathalyzer. Search of car revealed cocaine in glove compartment, small quantity of marijuana in briefcase in trunk.

McCallum, you really pick 'em. That, or you have the worst luck imaginable.

Removed from jail by order of FBI. Paperwork about processing her release listed as "Confidential." Court date set. Nothing about him, nothing about McCallum, no mention of Cheryl Lanier or Timothy, the other roommate. No accusations of rape, no mention of anorexia, no quote from the bag lady at Boston Common. The car she had been driving was a white 1987 Cadillac Seville, registered in Chicago to LeRoi Franklin Brown, who could not be reached for comment. "Brown was her boyfriend," the same sophomore was quoted as saying. "It's hard to believe she was a narc, because, I mean, that's so straight, and you knew right away the two of them were wild."

Yes, the college president was quoted as saying; we have no choice but to accommodate the U.S. government if they suspect a drug problem on campus. It might be what he called "reasonable" to assume that from time to time there had been undercover work. "Of course they're undercover—what else would they be?" A statement on Livan Baker: "You should not necessarily assume that I, or anyone else, would necessarily know an agent's exact name." (As opposed to what? An inexact name?) Any denial, concerning Livan Baker? "No comment."

He read it again, and understood that Livan Baker, twenty-five, an undercover cop, had for whatever reason made the big mistake of calling attention to herself when she was drunk, had been caught by the local cops, found to have a stash of drugs, and then that she was sprung from jail by the FBI (nice of them; but what would *they* do?). This left unanswered many things, but what it did answer was any question anyone might have about her character. It would also either provide consolation to McCallum, showing him he'd been in over his head, or it would embarrass him because he had been such a fool, or it might even make him angry to think he'd been had in such a way. In any case, he felt sure that presenting McCallum with the paper would be better than taking him a bouquet of roses. What a terrific update McCallum was going to get, and how lucky he would feel that he hadn't been dragged in deeper. What if Livan Baker had been picked up with him, in Boston, what if she'd been busted in his presence? Either a very good actress or truly crazy. Older than she'd said, with a boyfriend who drove a Cadillac, probably had a fur coat back in Chicago, forget the bargain basement stuff. Just another out-of-control or deeply cynical person who'd tried to play both sides against the middle. A good enough actress that she'd sucked in quite a few people—more than necessary to validate her version of herself as tortured, pitiful. It was clear that Cheryl Lanier should see the article, also. It would wise her up, teach the lesson that everything shouldn't be taken at face value, show her that other people's suffering was sometimes less, rather than more, than it seemed to be.

He was angry at Cheryl Lanier. He was surprised at how angry he was. Angry because she was gullible, but then, he was angry at himself because he had been, too. Still, her leaving school had been an overreaction, and putting the blame on him, implying that he was in any way responsible, was . . . oh, maybe it had just been the panicked reaction of someone who could hardly be expected to see through impostors, who probably didn't have great experience in such complicated problems as Livan Baker had posed. She had flirted with him. Drinking his drink, talking the way she had. She had not been blameless and, hell, he hadn't done anything. One kiss in a car, one moment of letting his guard down, okay, one moment of letting her let her guard down. How amazing that she would drop out of school, go back to Virginia, go back to *what*? What could her parents think? He would pick up another paper on the way out of the building, send it to her . . . send it without comment, but with his return address, c/o the department, of course. This would be the perfect excuse to get in touch; he had not responded to her letter, because he didn't quite know how to respond to it. Thinking of Cheryl, he began to soften: whether or not Livan Baker had appropriated Cheryl Lanier's story of the rape for her own benefit, Cheryl had still suffered through that, and because she had finally had the courage to tell him about it, she deserved some response. What a difficult position: to have to write someone to console them about something words probably couldn't touch. She should talk to someone. . . . He realized he was thinking the way he had thought the night before the stabbing, urging McCallum to make sure that someone would be told what they knew. . . . Jenny Oughton. Jenny Oughton knew about Livan Baker, didn't know she was a narc abusing drugs herself . . . or wait a minute: Did she? Maybe Livan Baker had gone in there and told the truth, and all along, Jenny Oughton had known more than he, more than McCallum. The woman was hardly forthcoming. She had a way of looking at him that made him think she knew more about him than he knew about himself. Quite disconcerting. He hoped her much touted professionalism would keep her from speaking to anyone in the press. He hoped against hope that the whole ugly situation would eventually—no, quickly—just go away.

He saw that Sophia Androcelli had left several messages for him when he finally left the office and went to his mailbox in the department office. There was also a crayon drawing of a flower that looked vaguely like a flapping flag, and a lawn that looked like a deteriorating blue carpet. A Post-it note was attached: "My son and I are very sorry about your recent bereavement," it read. It was signed "Luftquist." He sorted through the pile of late papers, immediately discarded flyers advertising bargains on tire retreads. He assured the secretary that he and his wife were doing fine—a sad time, the death of a loved one, but . . . He thanked the secretary for her kind words. In the hallway, he opened a pink envelope that had no return address. On a pink sheet of paper was a poem, titled "I saw in the Obituaries."

> When others suffer grief
> It is so hard to say
> What we ourselves would likely do
> If pain spoiled our own day
>
> Conveniently we do assume
> That we would rise above
> From on high we'd take the long view
> And remember God is love
>
> But would we really do this
> Or would we weep and fret?
> We *think* we know what we'd do in
>   another person's shoes
> When we haven't occupied them yet
>
> It may be best to simply say
> Good times will come again
> Till then, dear Marshall Lockard,
> Accept the condolences of your friend
>   Mrs. Adam Barrows

Instead of heading off to see McCallum with the good news/bad news he went back to his office and, still stunned by the poem, unable to imagine any response to it, called Sophia. Facing whatever was in store for him would be good practice toward writing the letter to Cheryl.

Just when he was about to give up, the phone was answered. He asked for Sophia and was told to "hang on," loud music playing in the background.

"Finally," she said, when she heard who it was.

"I was at a funeral yesterday. I just got your messages."

"Yeah, well, I'll cut to the chase: a reporter from the newspaper is interested in talking to me about Livan Baker's involvement with your buddy McCallum."

"Sophia," he said, "McCallum isn't my buddy. We teach in the same department, but actually, I hardly know him. I'm pretty sick of all of this, and if McCallum's in trouble, I'm sorry, but McCallum's in trouble. I'm not McCallum." He waited for a response. There was only a slight sigh. "Why would they contact you?" he said.

"It's not exactly a secret that Cheryl's my best friend, you know. And Cheryl roomed with Livan. And Livan got busted, and Cheryl's gone. And I have another thing to tell you: I was in their apartment. Timothy and I were packing the things she didn't take to send to Virginia. Livan hadn't been there for days, but the night she got busted they got a search warrant, and Timothy and I found ourselves surrounded by cops."

"Well, I'm sorry you got involved. This has been a nightmare for all of us. I was on my way to see McCallum with the newspaper. I thought it would make him feel better to know who Livan Baker really was, but since the cops are no doubt going to be questioning him about her, I suppose he might have already heard it."

"I'll tell you what I called about," Sophia said.

He gave a nervous laugh. "I thought that's what I was hearing."

"No," she said, "what you don't know is that I took one of the notebooks—it was one she had rough drafts of her letter to you in— I took it to the apartment because she'd left it at my place, and I knew she'd want it back. It was there with everything else when the cops came in and it was like the movies; we had to raise our hands and be patted down, you know? We had to leave everything there when they threw us out and took over the apartment." She sighed. "It's not incriminating," Sophia said. "The drafts were just early versions of what you saw. I mean, she'd probably die if anyone but you knew about the letter, but what are the cops going to do? Read it on TV? Maybe they won't care about every single piece of paper in the place. They were looking for drugs, right? What would they care about her roommate's notebook?"

All he could think was that for the rest of his life he would be questioned by the police. Sonja would be sure to find out all the details about the whole messy situation. She might even wonder why he'd never written the girl, after she'd made such a painful confession to him. Sonja might wonder, in fact, how much of a secret life he had, since he hadn't mentioned anything before McCallum's visit about Cheryl Lanier, alluding only to the problems of her roommate, Livan Baker.

As if McCallum didn't have enough problems, now there was this.

As if Sonja weren't upset enough, with Evie just buried.

As if he'd get off the phone with Sophia Androcelli without one more zinger.

"There are two snowpeople outside your building," Sophia was saying, "both of which are incredibly offensive. One is stereotypically offensive and the other is sexually offensive. I've written an editorial for tomorrow's paper, but in the meantime I would appreciate your not disturbing them, so anyone who missed them can take a look once my piece appears. Just in case you were going to wring the pumpkin tits off on your way out, or decapitate them, or anything." She snorted. "Just a preemptive strike," she said. "If I were you, I think I might feel like demolishing something. Just don't go after my target."

God, they were all so self-absorbed: Cheryl; Livan; McCallum, Susan McCallum; Sophia. Whoever had built the two snowpeople was a jokester amid people who couldn't, or wouldn't, take a joke. Sonja, though, was not crazy, and he intended to give her the long version of everything once he got home. He would make her see that the students' problems had seemed too sad and bizarre—and, at the same time, inconsequential—to burden her with. Being sane, she would understand.

15

AFGHAN TUCKED AROUND her legs, Sonja listened as Marshall began at the beginning, giving her information she already had about Livan Baker, segueing into a discussion of Cheryl Lanier. She was his student, from a large family in Virginia: not brilliant, but dedicated; a person interested in learning. How he picked her up hitchhiking because she was young and poor and wet. How he'd taken her for coffee (*omit mention of food, Marshall*), how he'd been surprised when she confided in him (*will Sonja put two and two together, realize that the time he called, claiming to be with someone named Thomas, or Todd, or whatever name he came up with, it was actually Cheryl Lanier?*). He assumed Sonja's deepening frown was an expression of concern for the people involved.

Earlier that afternoon, Sonja had gone to the hospital to see McCallum, whose recovery was not progressing very well. First an infection had set back the course of physical therapy, then he'd become allergic to one of the medicines. He had fallen asleep after talking to her for just fifteen minutes, she said. It was as if McCallum, overnight, had become an old man. Her talking about McCallum, though, had seemed the perfect opportunity to fill her in on what she didn't know about his involvement (he thought, self-righteously: *I didn't sleep with her*) with the two girls (Sonja was his wife; he wasn't going to call two girls "women").

"Why are you telling me this?" she said.

"What?" he said.

"It's a pretty straightforward question. I'm not trying to trick you, Marshall."

"Who said I thought that? I'm just, I just . . . I'm not sure there's any reason to tell you these things now, it's just that I realized there were quite a few things you didn't know, and I wasn't intentionally keeping them from you. With all that's gone on, I guess I thought there was enough to deal with without including unnecessary asides."

"When did Cheryl Lanier stop being an 'unnecessary aside'?"

That gave him a moment's pause. He hadn't expected to have to go on the defensive (he hadn't slept with her; so what if he hadn't said anything about a hamburger and a beer, a Jack Daniel's—so what if those things had become "coffee"?).

"This other person . . . girl . . . a student of mine from the same poetry class Cheryl was in named Sophia Androcelli, very brash girl, can be quite bullish about announcing her opinions. . . . Sophia was in my office a while back, with a loose-leaf notebook of Cheryl's. She apparently had a crush on me. Cheryl, I mean. She wrote me a letter and actually, you'll be amused by this, said that while she was fond of me, or however she put it, I was too old for her. Anyway: an awful thing had happened to Cheryl. Really two awful things, pertaining to the same event. She said in the letter she'd been forced into sex with her godfather—this stuff is all so awful, it's what you hear about on daytime TV or read articles about when you're sitting in a waiting room, you really don't know what to say—and she told Livan about it, and the next thing she knew, Livan had appropriated the story. And she'd written the letter—well, she'd written it because she had a crush on me, I guess, but she'd also written to apologize because, inadvertently, she'd made the situation worse for McCallum, and like everybody else, she assumes McCallum's my great buddy and anything anybody might say to him, they might as well say to me. She wanted me to tell him about the rape, and about Livan Baker's parroting her story, so McCallum . . . I don't know; so McCallum would see how fucked-up Livan Baker was. As it turns out, it's quite an irony that his wife got furious at him about something besides Livan Baker. But anyway, Cheryl told me, and now I'm telling you."

"I don't quite get it," Sonja said.

"I know, it's so convoluted. It's just one kid who went through a traumatic event having the misfortune of rooming with a real loony, an undercover cop with a drug problem, for Christ's sake . . . and when she left school, she wrote her teacher a letter to explain. A confession, because she felt guilty, even though anything she'd done was unintentional."

"Her teacher?"

"Me," he said.

"Oh," she said. She was slouched in the chair McCallum had once sat in, little jumping embers sputtering in the fire, her feet, in the ballet flats, stretched out on the newspaper she'd read and then piled on the footstool. He could remember their former quiet nights of reading things aloud to one another from the newspaper, having leisurely dinners in which the only subjects of conversation weren't disturbing things, their planning vacations, talking about possible house sales before it became a buyer's market, relaxing. She tucked her hair behind her ears, which made him smile fondly at her. She looked rather like a schoolgirl herself, as she gazed up at him. Recently, she had been looking at him quite often—the night before, she had put down the book she was reading, propped up in bed, and simply stared. He had come out of the bathroom, mistakenly wearing her robe.

"Why did she leave school?" she said.

"I don't know. I think it had all been too much for her. Generally."

She shifted in the chair, glancing over her shoulder, probably considering whether to add wood to the fire. He hoped she wouldn't; the discussion had gone on long enough for one night.

"You know, McCallum feels the way I do right now," she said. "He says there's no way he can go back to teaching. He doesn't know what he wants to do. I suggested, sort of half seriously, that he think about selling real estate. It would give him plenty of time to read books, in this market. He was upset today because he still can't concentrate. It was worrying him that there was a pile of books on the night table and he couldn't remember which one he'd been reading. I think it's common after something like what he's gone through that the person forgets things and can't concentrate. I tried to tell him that."

"What about his son?"

"McCallum's mother-in-law doesn't want him to visit him in the hospital. Whether that's for her sake or the boy's sake, I don't know."

"How does McCallum feel about it?"

"Oh," she said, letting out a long sigh. "I don't know how McCallum feels. He's a pretty hard one to read. I'm glad he's your great buddy, not mine. I'd always wonder what he was really thinking."

He snorted a little laugh. It was cold in the room. He got up and pulled the screen away from the fireplace, lit a section of tightly rolled newspaper he took from a brass bucket, and laid the quickly burning paper on the last remaining orange-centered log, then placed two others on top. He replaced the screen, centering it on the tiles.

"Whereas, I usually think I know what my husband is thinking, although tonight I don't," Sonja said.

"What?" he said.

"You know. My husband. You. The same person as 'her teacher.' "

"What does that mean?" he said, dusting off his hands and sitting on the footstool, gently moving her feet aside to give himself a few extra inches. Her feet felt light, delicate. He was surprised at their weightlessness.

"Was that the whole story?" she said.

"What part do you think I'm holding back? My wild affair with Cheryl Lanier? My true sympathy for Livan Baker, probably only a product of her troubled times, not to blame for deceiving the enemy?"

"You're pairing the two because you want me to think it's ludicrous you'd have an affair with Cheryl Lanier. You're trying to put that on a par with feeling sorry for Livan Baker."

"Sonja, I never had anything to do with Cheryl Lanier," he said.

"Would it be the end of the world if you had?"

What a peculiar response. Was it a rhetorical question?

"Well, you tell me," he said.

"Not the end of the world," she said. She got up and poked a burning ember. "I have a certain interest in espousing that opinion." She leaned the poker against the firescreen and went back to the chair, raised her feet to the seat cushion, and brought them up beside her, tucking the afghan around herself. Evie had made the afghan for Sonja's birthday, in November, and Sonja loved it the way Linus loved his blanket.

"What do you mean?"

"For a while I was having an affair with Tony," she said.

As she spoke, he began to try to distract himself so he wouldn't hear what was coming; he wondered if the logs were catching fire, or whether he should have used more newspaper, or whether it might not have been a good idea to place the logs on one at a time; he tried blocking her words, though "Tony" slipped through, and also the word "affair." He felt a physical sensation, a scrambling in his throat. She had managed to astonish him.

"Off the subject, I suppose, but so did Evie. Did you know that? That she'd slept with your father when your mother was still alive? She said she looked at the Kinsey Report when it was first published—that sneaking a look at it in those days was the same as flipping through a porn magazine now—and wondered whether women had been honest, because so many more men than women claimed to have had affairs. She and your father began their affair before she left her parents' house in Canada, and it continued when she went to live at their house. Can you imagine Evie being so brazen? She said she'd never known how much her mother or father knew about any of it. That sometimes she thought they knew exactly what was going on. That they were looking the other way from the first and expected her to, as well. I guess I'm trying to divert your attention from what I just said. I mean this, for what it's worth: I never wanted to break up our marriage. I know I should have found a better way to tell you, but I hate him now, Marshall. I hate myself, too, but I could sort of, you know, move aside with my own self-loathing and let you take over. I'll understand if you hate me."

He looked at the floor and was surprised to see how bright the colors in the rug appeared in the firelight: the large, worn Oriental they had gotten years before, in Boston, that had once had to be folded over at one end because their room had been too small. It had been like a big, colorful wave, rolling over. That first apartment came back to him in startling detail: the drop-leaf table that now sat beside Sonja's chair, with the leaves down, formerly their kitchen table. The chrome chairs they'd found at curbside on Boylston Street with the red plastic seats were gone, but the ceramic planter, now containing a large fern, sat a few feet from the fireplace. The underside of the leaves glowed silver in the firelight, so that it seemed a magic plant, a plant you would read about in a fairy tale. Perhaps that was what McCallum needed in the hospital: not serious literature, but picture books—photography, or an illustrated book of fables. His thoughts hovered around McCallum, and he remembered with a shiver McCallum's blood on the walls. Was it possible, because of the colors within colors, that some blood might still be on the rug, indistinguishable in the complex geometric pattern? He was looking at the rug as if he held a great magnifying glass to his eye, yet the harder he stared, the more the details appeared fuzzily out of focus. He was quite certain that he should speak, say something immediately, yet it would of course be incredibly inappropriate to ask a question about the rug—an unanswerable question under any circumstances, how would Sonja know? Sonja. Her name made him realize her presence: she was slouched deep in the chair, biting her bottom lip, her hands tightly clasped on top of the tangled afghan. The fingers of her right hand, laced through the fingers of the left, nearly covered her wedding band. He looked at his own hand. He had never worn a wedding band. Did that mean anything, he wondered, though who should know the answer if not him? He looked again at the rug, thought the phrase: *Rug pulled out from under.* That was certainly what had happened to McCallum, and now it had just happened to him. Imagine McCallum's horror when he realized his own wife was intent upon killing him. Imagine the things wives could do, the power they had. Sonja had just changed everything. He smiled a halfhearted smile, certain that she was both friend and enemy, and also hoping she'd understand his thoughts had been drifting. He felt paralyzed by stupidity. What could he say?

"Did you think you were in love with Tony?" he said.

"No," she said. "It was a game. I realize that's terrible. I had started to think of myself as so, you know, programmatic."

"Programmatic?" he said, though he had silently resolved not to reveal the full extent of his stupidity by echoing her words. The words he had been most tempted to echo had been "Tony" and "over." He thought the name. It didn't have any good connotations. He remembered Tony had waited for them outside the police station, then had stood in the entranceway to the living room with him when the place was filled with police. But wait: What if they moved? What about leaving the rug behind? What if the two of them were cut free from the ordinariness of their lives—what if they *really* left the scene of the crime? Who knew how many times she had slept with Tony? Sane, stable Sonja. Sonja who had had an affair with her boss, whom she now hated, thank God, and it had happened because she'd felt programmatic.

"It's okay," he heard himself say.

Sonja's frown deepened. "It is?"

"I'm glad it's over. I'm glad—" What was he glad about? Nothing he could imagine. He finished the sentence: "I'm sorry you felt the way you did. I don't think this has been a very good year for either one of us."

"That's all you're going to say?"

"It does occur to me that it was rather odd you'd imply that I'd had an affair with Cheryl, while you didn't rush to volunteer you'd been fooling around yourself."

"I wasn't any more sure of the timing than you were. I almost blurted it out the morning after McCallum spent the night. That would have made for an interesting day, wouldn't it?"

"Do you think we could talk about this tomorrow?" he said. "I'm awfully confused. I didn't expect to hear what I just heard. If there were clues, I didn't pick up on them. I always thought he was an odd duck, so I guess on some level nothing he's done could really surprise me. Did you think you were in love with him?"

"You already asked me that. I didn't think that. We'd go into houses, houses that were for sale, empty houses, ugly houses, walking around with our checklist, I don't know. I mean, of course that was my job, but it began to seem like we were inspecting tombs, or something. Caves. Big houses with the pipes drained and no heat, and no signs of life. Or at least it wasn't recognizable life. They were like shells left behind when reptiles molted. It was the emptiness that started to get to me."

"Why did it end?" he said. He had gotten up. He'd walked halfway across the floor.

"It couldn't have gone on any longer," she said. An evasive answer, but he preferred to think that Sonja had simply come to her senses.

"Let's talk about it tomorrow," he said.

"Do we have to?" she said.

"Yes," he said. "Don't you think this is the sort of thing we might talk about for more than a few minutes?"

"He said you wouldn't care," Sonja said.

"Well, I do care, but I'm in a state of shock."

"It was stupid, wasn't it? I could have thrown all this away. You might have stormed out of the house for good. You seem to be going to bed."

"I am going to bed," he said.

"You would have cared if I'd thrown it all away, right?"

"Yes," he said. "But you're telling me that was never your intention."

"But if I had," she said.

"Sonja," he said, "I don't think it's fair that you're asking for reassurance from me after hitting me over the head. Do you know what I mean?"

No answer.

He said, over his shoulder, as he walked out of the room, "Come to bed. We can talk about this tomorrow."

When he left, she was a little in shock herself. Evie had advised her against saying anything. Evie's reason for urging her not to confide in Marshall had come as something of a surprise, but she hadn't been wrong. Evie had worried that Marshall wouldn't be sufficiently enraged or jealous; basically, Evie had thought that he would insult her by not caring enough, which meant that Evie thought essentially what Tony thought. "Unemotive," Evie had called him. Once out of childhood, it was the way he had always been. Evie accepted that—what did Evie not accept, once it was an established fact?—but also Marshall had been lucky. He had been raised by a woman who thought everyone made mistakes, and who included herself when she said that. How strange to think of Evie involved in physical passion—and with a person as cold as Marshall's father had apparently been. In the nursing home he had lived in before he died, she had found out that his nickname was the Emperor. A man given to haughtiness and self-righteous pronouncements . . . who could imagine being in his arms? Then again, who would look at Tony Hembley, who was short and nervous and not very good looking, and decide to slip off her pants under her dress, pull the dress over her head, stand there, having quickly unfastened her bra, so that when he turned around from peering in a refrigerator where something spoiled seemed to be moldering, permeating the room with a sudden, ghastly odor—who would think anyone would respond so impulsively to Tony Hembley? That look on his face. He had flirted with her, but the quick strip had been her idea. She had almost told Evie exactly what she'd done, but now she was glad she'd held some things back. Evie had died thinking that although it was inadvisable to tell Marshall about Tony, he could nevertheless be expected to forgive her if she did say something, and that was what he seemed to be doing. And Evie had been right, too, about his drawing inward. There had been no professions of love, no pleading that she stay.

She could hear him in the bedroom, opening a dresser drawer, and she could imagine the rest: his standing at the sink in his pajamas, brushing his teeth, a towel draped around his neck. The fire was still burning, but she didn't have Marshall's fear of going to bed before a fire had burned down. It was like being afraid of airplanes or enclosed places: if you weren't afraid, you weren't afraid. Still, she stood in front of the fire, which warmed her front as her back grew progressively colder. She picked up Evie's afghan and slung it over her shoulders Marshall style, looking through the flames to the andirons: two lions, paws raised, their blackened manes rivulets of ash.

As she expected, he was in the bathroom. The door was open, and he stood at the sink by the glow of the night-light, leaning forward, hands gripping the edge of the sink, the toothbrush replaced or not yet used. He heard her enter the bedroom but didn't turn toward her. Neither did he move away from the sink. He was thinking, again, about McCallum; how desolate he must have felt, with his life out of his control: the hyperactive son; the unwanted baby; a wife who loathed him—she must have loathed him to stab him. It was terribly sad. McCallum was terribly sad.

As she undressed, she looked quickly over her shoulder, twice, to see if he had moved, and the second time she looked he had and was standing with the towel pressed against his face.

"I don't blame you for hating me," she said, walking to the open door.

He shook his head no. That, or he was rubbing his face back and forth beneath the towel.

He was crying out of sympathy for McCallum. He finally felt a real connection between McCallum and himself.

The Flamboyant Tree

16

———

"'S WONNERFUL, 's mah-vel-lous, that you should care foooooor meeeeeee," McCallum sang.

McCallum was in charge of the tape selection. So far, they had been through both sides of Bobby Short, one side of Maria Muldaur, and ten or fifteen minutes of a Jean-Michel Jarre tape Marshall had ejected, because it was impossible to listen without speeding. They were on day two of their journey, instigated and largely bankrolled by McCallum, who sat in the passenger's seat padded with down-filled pillows: one behind him, one wedged between seat belt and door, another under his knees. In anticipation of their ultimate destination, McCallum was wearing black kneesocks, khaki Bermuda shorts, running shoes, a baseball cap he'd turned backward, and thermal underwear under a denim workshirt. "Wonnerful," McCallum sang, though that verse had ended several minutes before.

"You're grouchy because you're doing all the driving," McCallum said. "How is the doctor going to know I'm taking a turn at the wheel? You're also supposed to not cross the street on a red light. How much advice can anybody afford to pay attention to? Who's going to see me doing a little driving? It'll make me feel less like an invalid."

"I'd see you," Marshall said.

"Well, I wish you'd been my guardian angel when you-know-who was trying to kill me."

"I wish I had, too." He was thinking not only of the possibility of McCallum's having escaped physical harm, but how much better he would feel if his house had remained the pleasant, undisturbed environment it once had been. Sonja was there now, as he and McCallum drove south during Benson College's spring break. He had wanted her to come, and initially he had taken it as a bad sign that she hadn't wanted to. Though she'd assured him it was over, he'd begun to feel that her affair with Tony was the new subtext for everything—every new recipe she prepared, every silly, old romantic movie she wanted to watch on TV. If McCallum hadn't gotten so excited by the idea of getting some sun, he probably would not have left Sonja's side he was so worried she would pick up again with Tony. He felt ambivalent about seeing Gordon and Beth, and he was worried that McCallum might be—because suddenly this was getting to be the story of McCallum's life—an unwanted guest. None of which he had said to McCallum, because the last time Marshall had visited him in the hospital he had become as excited as a child at the prospect of getting out of town.

Already, he missed Sonja. He wanted to be angry at her, but he couldn't sustain his anger. She had at least acted on her desires—and, much to his relief, she had selected a slightly ludicrous lover. Still, how boring the house must seem, after her antics with Tony. She had considered going somewhere warm herself to "think things over," but then she had decided to stay where she was.

Between McCallum's ejecting one tape and plugging in another, the radio cut in with the theme from *Midnight Cowboy*, a movie that had greatly impressed Marshall when he'd first seen it. The song also immediately caught McCallum's attention, though it was frizzed with static, as well as fading in and out as if they were driving through a series of invisible tunnels. Marshall could have done without hearing it; the song conjured up the movie's ending—Ratso wearing his palm tree shirt, dead on the bus bound for Florida.

Florida was where the two of them were headed, after the stopover they would make first in the small town of Buena Vista, where McCallum, for reasons Marshall still could not comprehend, felt that he must, for once and for all, explain himself to Cheryl Lanier so that his soul might begin to heal along with his bodily wounds. McCallum had also tried to find out where Livan herself was, to no avail; if McCallum had been intent on contacting her, the best he could probably do would be to send a letter to Livan Baker, Planet Earth. To the extent he'd been involved with Cheryl himself, Marshall could hardly refuse to stop on their way to visit Gordon in the Keys. Though she hadn't responded to the note he sent her along with the clipping about Livan Baker—vanished, it seemed; or at least, in a follow-up article in the paper, the U.S. government claimed to be interested in finding out her whereabouts—Cheryl had phoned McCallum in response to whatever letter he'd sent her.

The tape deck swallowed the next tape McCallum pushed in: Eddie Fisher, singing "I'm Yours." It was quite possibly the worst song Marshall had ever heard. Eddie Fisher's soaring tenor was vehement; it would have paralyzed the intended recipient of his affections as certainly as Kryptonite would bring Superman to a screeching halt. He had read that during Eddie Fisher's brief marriage to Elizabeth Taylor, she had had him picked up from the piano bench aboard her yacht and thrown overboard. Marshall looked imploringly at McCallum, but his eyes were shut, his head dropped back on the headrest, a shit-eating grin on his tipped-up face. All he could hope was that it was a homemade tape and that next they might be treated to something less ridiculous. It turned out to be Kate Smith. Rolling along on the Beltway, as a pallid half-moon beamed through drifting clouds, surrounded by vanity license plates and cars that were either expensive and new or limping-along junkers, Marshall practiced patience by listening silently to McCallum's hit parade.

"I love it," McCallum said, keeping his eyes closed so that there was no indication he was talking to Marshall, rather than himself. "Here we are doing our update on the buddy film: would-be murder victim and concerned friend making a big circle around Slick Willy's Washington, on their way to making amends and soaking up some Florida sunshine. 'Greetings from sunny Florida,'" McCallum said. "Remember those postcards where you check one box in each category? 'I am: Fine; Sunburned; Fatter; Lonely; Horny.'"

"'Wish you were: Here with me; Farther away; Kissing me now; Back on Mars,'" Marshall said.

The events of the winter had been so extraordinary he might as well have been living on another planet, Marshall thought. He flipped down the visor to block the sun, a bright orange orb low in the sky, shining in his face. To keep pace with the traffic, he was going fifteen miles over the speed limit, checking signs for Route 29 South, not sure how soon the turn would come after taking the exit for Front Royal. McCallum, now apparently asleep, was sitting on the map, leaving only a small corner protruding. The man was a wonder: to be able to tune out Kate Smith's heartfelt, booming voice; to not even squint in the blaze of sunlight. Then again, considering what he'd been through, such things were probably rather delightful. The night before, McCallum had slept with one of the bedside lamps on, lowered to the floor so it wouldn't disturb Marshall. Wearing earphones, he had fallen asleep almost immediately, and in the barely darkened room, Marshall, unable to fall asleep quickly, had turned on his side and propped himself on one elbow to look at the odd spectacle that was McCallum: he slept wearing his socks and running shoes, though he'd stripped down to his Jockey shorts and thermal shirt before getting into bed. He could tell by the bright yellow butterfly on the cover of the cassette case on the floor that McCallum had fallen asleep listening to Brahms. Brahms's "Lullabye" seeping smoothly into his unconscious, where the listener also retained images of a knife rising and falling, the memory of sudden pain. McCallum had not so much been shifting in sleep as trying to avoid the knifepoint, Marshall decided. Looking at him sleeping so fitfully, he had remembered his own fatigue the night he returned home and saw him there, slouched in the chair like the comfortable old friend he was not, fingers raised in that odd, nonverbal greeting he'd watched McCallum poke into the air as they'd walked away from the motel registration desk the night before, or as he had signalled his appreciation to the convenience store clerk who'd come out and opened the newspaper vending machine after he'd inserted twenty-five cents and nothing happened. McCallum was following "Shoe," which he snorted over appreciatively, along with his daily horoscope (any publication's report equally credible). He'd had trouble following stories of any length; he still couldn't concentrate on a book, but his new strategy was to try to work up to serious reading by finishing newspaper articles. The *New York Times* had proved too much for him, so he'd backtracked to *USA Today*. He was also interested in the weather maps, happy that he'd persuaded Marshall to make the trip, glad to get out of the cold.

McCallum didn't wake up until Marshall had turned onto the Warrenton bypass. After Washington, the Volvos and BMWs had tapered off, and pickups began to speed alongside, with quite a few

Jeeps mixed in, and some old Fords and Chevys whose chassis almost dragged the road. The radio was mostly country, shot through with static. McCallum settled for "I Told You So," which he sang along with in a satirical Southern accent, not quite in sync with Randy Travis because he didn't know anything but the chorus. The dimming sun highlighted the grime on the windshield, but through the flecks of dead bugs and the haze of highway dust he could see the trees, redbuds budding and dogwoods almost in full flower. They reminded him of Evie, and her love of all flowers. Of Sonja, to whom he'd often given roses on Valentine's Day, though she always told him in advance of the day not to buy them because the prices were marked up. Had she secretly been flattered, or had she meant what she said? The past February, he hadn't been sure. He hadn't bought them, but he hadn't bought anything else either. Had he intuited something was wrong? Not wanted to appear a chump?

No. He hadn't had a clue.

So, what had Tony given her?

No doubt roses, which she kept on her desk at work.

It occurred to him that there was probably no middle ground: you either wanted to hear every painful detail, or you didn't want any specifics at all. He seemed incapable of selecting either attitude, though; even if he'd felt masochistic, Sonja's words had a way of jumbling in his head like Ping-Pong balls turned in a drum until, at unexpected intervals, the drum stopped and they bounced to stillness and he reached in and took one out, turned it over, and then dully repeated what was written there: *empty houses; programmatic; sorry.* There were quite a few *sorry* Ping-Pong balls. Smooth and cold, he could feel the shiny surfaces of the many *sorry*s. He had sat with her the night before he left, watching some TV show in which balls were churned in a transparent drum, had tried to focus his attention on the numbers the woman called out as she picked out ball after ball. The numbers corresponded to prizes: a cruise; a sheepskin coat. What Sonja had been saying corresponded to an indeterminate future, married people skeptical of one another. They never watched game shows, but that night they'd sat there riveted, neither of them really watching. During the show Gordon had called, wanting to double-check their "ETA." Though he'd already told Gordon Sonja wouldn't be coming, Gordon had either forgotten or else suspected something was wrong, though Marshall had decided that he would not tell Gordon about it. Gordon had a way of letting you know he didn't like to hear bad news. His usual response was to listen silently, then shrug and say something like "Life—can you beat it?" or "Hell—what can you do?" He knew Sonja thought Gordon was, as she'd once put it, "impossibly defended." In her opinion, Gordon was filled with a sense of futility about the smallest, as well as the largest, things, a man full of anger and resentment, a person imploding while speaking banalities. It was difficult to argue with her, but of course Gordon was his brother; he registered the contradictions in his eyes, interpreted the dismissive, rhetorical questions as answerable—it was only that he hesitated to cast a pall on Gordon's efforts to remain upbeat by getting serious. In a way, he respected the distance Gordon tried to keep between himself and problems. Sonja had told him, in bed the night before he left, that Evie had told her to leave her lover; Evie had advised her to say nothing to Marshall, to try, privately, to make herself happier in her marriage. At first, Sonja had been sure Evie had been speaking out of her own sense of guilt, from having slept with Marshall's father before she married him. But then, it turned out, Evie had worried that Marshall's reaction might insult her. "She says you've kept your reactions to yourself ever since childhood," Sonja had said to him. So there it was: Sonja had had an affair, and instead of his criticizing her, she—and Evie—had implicitly criticized *him*. Had Evie been right, though? An impossible question for him to answer: yes, she was right, because, as Sonja had seen from the expression on his face, which indicated he was about to cry, he was unable to handle it; no, she was wrong, because, as she could see from his ear-to-ear smile, he must be thrilled she confided in him, he obviously felt closer to her than ever, wished she had more of such interesting news.

"Fuck Tony," he said, pounding the heel of his hand into the steering wheel.

"Fuck what?" McCallum said, opening his eyes and shifting in the seat. "Oh," he said, answering his own question, "Tony the phony. Forget him. If she hadn't already forgotten him, you wouldn't have heard about it."

"You think so?" He could hear the tenuous acceptance of the idea in his voice. Not exactly Gordon, saying, "Life—can you beat it?"

but still, he was surprised to realize that he had sounded slightly hopeful.

"Absolutely," McCallum said.

"You're humoring me."

"It's what I believe. You've got to understand, I don't exactly idealize the union of marriage right now, with these sutures still dissolving and pinpricks of pain burning my gut like bees stinging me."

"How are you doing?" he asked McCallum—as if he hadn't just heard.

"Used to be a husband," McCallum said. "Used to like my color TV. Even had a pet. A turtle. Did I tell you some neighbor came in and found the turtle under the bed and donated His Highness to the third-grade class? Used to have *la vie normale*. Used to be a devoted daddy."

He waited for McCallum to continue talking about his son. He did not. He rose slightly, wincing in pain, then held the seat belt that crossed over his chest near his breastbone with his left hand as he sat upright, trying to ease some sudden pain, while looking through the windshield, taking in the budding trees, a tractor bumping along, plowing a field, the sinking sun. If it had been his right hand touching his upper chest on the left side, McCallum might have been pledging allegiance to those things. Pledging allegiance to daily life in Virginia, where the landscape, once they passed Warrenton, had begun to remind Marshall of New Hampshire. New Hampshire seemed far behind, farther than it was in actual miles, and he had to squint to bring back details of the roads he drove most days, narrowing his eyes to focus sharply on the remembered image of the ghostly dead elms crowding the road at the bend by Rimmer's Stream, to envision the swaying light blinking yellow at the crossroads. The season hadn't changed to almost-spring there; it was still winter, the light fading fast as evening came on, black ice a sheen that could surprise you on the roads.

To his right he saw a gun shop and shooting range that advertised discounts on fireworks. So many cars and trucks began to signal their turn into the parking lot that Marshall pulled into the left lane and slowed slightly to look, the way someone would decelerate to look at an accident: trucks were clustered in the lot, appearing as small as toys below the huge brown bear that loomed outside the store, its mouth opened in a red-tongued roar, its teeth the size of Roman candles. Beside the bear, he saw briefly as he glanced past McCallum, was a ride of some sort: a twirling disk with handles gripped by children, further dwarfed in the adult world by a thirty-foot bear. He thought again of McCallum's son—whether seeing children brought him to McCallum's mind, or whether, as it seemed, he'd written the boy off. Unless he asked, there would be no answer to that question, he could tell. He rolled up his window against the evening coolness, continued surveying the land. He thought that what he and Sonja might need was a change of scene, that they might explore the possibility of living elsewhere, someplace less harsh than New Hampshire, a place where spring came earlier. Though the problem didn't have to do with long winters, but with her infatuation with Tony. Which she said had ended.

"If you pass another one of those places, we should get some fireworks, set them off in a field. Celebrate my being alive," McCallum said.

"Do you think about your son?" he blurted out.

A moment's delay before McCallum spoke. "Probably as much as you think about your wife."

"I can't stop thinking about her. The situation, really. Not her in particular."

"Maybe that's the problem," McCallum said. "Maybe you've seen her as part of a situation, but you haven't seen her in her own right. Good armchair-shrink speculation, don't you think?"

"It might be true," Marshall said.

"Might be, but what do I know?" He looked at Marshall. "How come you used to get so mad when I said you were my friend, now all of a sudden it's just an accepted fact?"

"You persuaded me," Marshall said. "With your many virtues."

"Being?" McCallum said. "That the suggestion we hit the road came along at just the right time? Think things over yourself; see your brother; check out your sweetie."

"You've got to be kidding."

"You told me how guilty you feel about her dropping out of school. Come on—all I said was that you were sweet on her."

"Only in your mind."

"Not true, but I won't argue because backing down is another one of my many virtues."

"Your wife thought you were pretty domineering," Marshall said.

McCallum shrugged. "What's this?" he said. "You playing nyaa-nyaa-nyaa all of a sudden? For a while, she liked the way I was," he said. "Only thing I went too far with was keeping after her about getting the kid on some medicine, which she construed as my wanting to shoot tranquillizer darts in him like he was a charging rhino—and of course I hoped she'd abort the next one."

"I can't believe my bad timing, to call just when . . ."

"Bad timing, good timing, I don't know," McCallum said. "I sort of like the idea of her in jail. Excuse me: in the prison psychiatric ward."

"I still don't see how a person would do something like that as a response to another person's sarcasm."

"She didn't like criticism. All you can do with people like that is back off from them or keep your self-respect by saying whatever you want to say, whether you cross them or not."

"But you didn't suspect? Nothing made you suspect she might be violent?"

"What are you asking? Did I see her eating Twinkies?"

"What?"

"Twinkies. The Twinkies defense. Some lawyer went into court and—"

"Oh yeah," Marshall said.

Stores began to string together into larger rows to become shopping areas, the farmland disappearing, new roads poked into recently graded land. They were the warm-up act for the inevitable Wal-Mart that was sure to appear momentarily, the blunt-topped Taj Mahal rising out of the suburban blight, the long reflecting pool in front sensibly paved to provide convenient parking for thousands of cars. A palace that was not a monument to love, but to discounts. Sonja snuck off to Wal-Mart once or twice a year, he knew: not so much to save money as to take in the spectacle, bring back some souvenirs, though she stuffed the bags deep in the garbage so he wouldn't find them. All the problematic things we do that we don't care to discuss: where we shop; with whom we have an affair. Insult to injury: it had been Tony, an uninteresting control freak who could drop his pants and play tag with someone's wife, but heaven help the person who was improper enough to stay too long at his house, his precious, private house. He'd invited them, then flipped out. Sonja had told him about it: that childish proprietariness not acceptable to her . . . though hell: she hadn't objected to joining in to help enact his childish fantasies. And wait a minute: if everyone else was expected to be so proper, what about showing up at Evie's funeral, making Sonja uncomfortable, returning to the house, sipping coffee and making small talk, being nice to old ladies who would have fainted if they'd known what he spent his days doing with Sonja, suggesting all along he was Marshall's friend as much as hers. How long would it take for him to be in Sonja's presence and not think of Tony? When Tony picked out their house—he had, really, and Sonja had either loved it or pretended to love it—that early on, he now thought, Tony must have been conspiring to have an affair with Sonja.

Traffic was heavier, and he looked for an excuse to pull off the road. He turned into a gas station just as "Yellow Submarine" started to play on the radio, a song dedicated to Ms. Blair (much giggling, as the dj asked the caller to announce the dedication herself) from the M.F.A. students.

"Submarine surfaces, you get gunned down at the Dakota," McCallum said, loosening his seat belt and slowly, wincing, swinging one leg, then the other, onto the asphalt. He stood with more effort than Marshall expected, even given that people got stiff sitting for long periods in cars. Just when Marshall was about to help him, McCallum wavered to almost full height, leaning forward slightly, his hand on his side. He straightened his body as he walked toward the bathroom, suddenly swinging his arms and high-stepping as if he were doing a military drill, aware that Marshall was staring after him. A teenage boy in black leather, coming out of the bathroom, slowed down to take in the spectacle. McCallum marched on.

Paying for gas and a Diet Sprite, he saw McCallum exit the bathroom and walk to the car, neither marching nor walking normally, his legs rubbery. They were within sixty miles of Charlottesville, then it would be another seventy or so to Buena Vista. What was McCallum's scenario? Were they going to check into a motel and call Cheryl, get together with her that night? It seemed particularly pointless to be seeing Cheryl, who meant so little to him, when everything with Sonja was up in the air. He had not mentioned the planned stop in Buena Vista to Sonja.

"Want me to get you something to drink?" he called to McCallum as he approached the car.

"Yeah, thanks," McCallum said. "Ginger ale. Something to settle my stomach."

He turned, sipping from the can of Sprite. Though you could see nothing but shadowy shapes inside the store from outside, from inside the view out was clear. As he waited in line, he thought about using the pay phone he'd seen near the ice machine, calling Sonja and telling her he loved her, he knew everything was going to be all right. He wasn't sure everything was going to be all right, though, and the risk of having his voice ring hollow as he spoke made him decide against it. He paid with a dollar bill, got thirty cents change. Exiting, he looked through the glass and saw McCallum, head resting on his arm, which protruded from the open window, and was struck again by how strange it was to be travelling in this part of the country not with Sonja, but with McCallum. For a split second, he had wondered: *What is that man doing in my car?* What was he doing in the car himself? Had it been a good idea to leave, even though Sonja told him the trip would do him good, even though she'd insisted she wanted time alone? There wasn't even the slightest possibility she'd get back together with Tony, was there?

He handed McCallum the Schweppes, wiping his fingertips on his jeans before turning on the ignition.

"Hey, man, I can take a turn driving," McCallum said.

Marshall didn't answer him. He pulled around a Jeep, coasted to a stop, then accelerated to get onto the highway. This was fine, he'd decided: all of it fine except perhaps the Cheryl Lanier part. What few words of consolation he could redundantly offer her could be said quickly; he intended to claim fatigue, leave the two of them together, wherever they might be, and tell McCallum to call the motel so he could pick him up when they'd finished talking. It irritated him more the farther south they got: Why was McCallum so intent on being granted forgiveness by a girl who had never even been his student? How guilty could he feel when, along with many other students who for one reason or another couldn't hack it, she had decided to drop out of school for a while? McCallum hadn't made it impossible for her to continue. Neither had he; the silly flirtation, the imagined romantic connection, the overreaction to the situation, however unpleasant it had been for everyone involved, were all partly the result of Cheryl's own youthful inability to deal with problems. What was her motivation in agreeing to see them? Why had she responded to

McCallum's call, but not to his letter? It was going to be an effort to be kind, to pretend that how she was doing mattered.

A hawk flew over the highway, its large wings slanting a ragged shadow over the car. It took both of them so much by surprise, they ducked. McCallum snorted, an acknowledgment they'd been fooled, thinking a plane was about to crash into them—a snort to the Fates to indicate they knew that anything still might happen.

17

THE DECOR OF DOLLY'S was country eclectic: birds' nests hanging on fishline dropped from the rafters, taxidermy treasures (a deer head with tinsel dripping from its antlers; a fox striding forward on a shelf that also held a fishbowl with two goldfish too large for the small container); license plates hung next to chintz curtains. There was an old jukebox with a cardboard sign: OUT OF ORDER SINCE ELVIS DIED. At eight o'clock it was an hour until closing.

Marshall had ordered a bowl of beef stew and a side order of cornbread. McCallum ordered next: pork chops, mashed potatoes, and collard greens. When the waitress asked if he wanted gravy on the pork chops, McCallum said, "Absolutely."

"And on the potatoes?"

"You bet."

"What would you like to drink with that?" the waitress said.

"Iced tea. But don't forget a dollop of gravy on my collards."

"You serious on that?" she asked, tilting her head skeptically.

"I'm a man who loves his gravy," McCallum said.

"That so?" she asked Marshall, who was less than amused by McCallum's high spirits. McCallum had also bought a Texaco cap, which he wore with the brim pulled low, so the waitress trusted the look in Marshall's eyes more than McCallum's.

"I'm betting you don't want none of it in your tea, even if you do want everything on the plate to float."

"That's right," McCallum called after her. "Let me have the gravy on the side with my tea."

She turned, smiling as she hurried away.

"Lemon wedge can be right in it, but the gravy's got to be on the side," he said.

As he walked to the table, a spasm of pain had passed through McCallum, who'd reached out to steady himself on the coatrack. He'd washed down a pill the second the waitress brought the water. He kept them in his pants pocket. Marshall thought about it and decided that along with hating Band-Aids, men almost never carried medicine with them. When McCallum had emptied his pocket in the motel the night before, the pocket of treasures had contained the loose aspirin with codeine that Marshall was almost sure he was taking too often, a small compass, a wristwatch with half the band missing.

"What's left to say to Cheryl Lanier?" Marshall said—the second time that day he'd asked, though he'd tried to fight the urge and not keep after McCallum. It was irrational; McCallum had never come up with a satisfactory answer, and Marshall was sure he wouldn't. He thought, in the second after he spoke, that perhaps McCallum was still in some sort of shock; if he, himself, had been so physically wounded, maybe he'd have some unexplainable feelings too. "Never mind," he said instantly, though McCallum had not rushed to answer.

Music started playing, not from the broken jukebox but from a cassette player on top of an old sewing machine: Jerry Lee Lewis, doing "Great Balls of Fire." A man whose stomach had forced the waistband of his pants to his groin rose from a stool at the counter, held his hands above his head, and shimmied his hips, breaking into a wide grin as his friend walked back from the cassette player. He ducked when his friend lifted a hand to swat him, and their waitress, from behind the counter, pretended to be about to douse them with a pitcher of water. It was that way, with everybody at the back counter smiling and one taciturn family eating fried chicken at a table in the middle of the restaurant, when Cheryl Lanier leaned hard against the door and rushed into the restaurant. She was wearing the white ski parka. To Marshall's surprise, she was also wearing the scarf he'd given her the night he picked her up hitchhiking. It was coiled around her throat, one end dangling in front, the other tossed over her shoulder. She loosened the scarf as she approached their booth, looking more puzzled than pleased—though why should she be surprised to see them?

Because McCallum had lied; he'd never told her Marshall was going to be there. That was why. Marshall knew it instantly. And too late.

"Like nuns," McCallum said. "We travel in twos."

"Wrong sex," she said, after a long pause.

She took off the parka and hung it on the tall pole with coat hooks two booths away. On the other hooks hung the pink jacket of the little girl who was tapping a chicken wing on the edge of her plate and the parents' denim jackets, lined in black-and-white-checked wool. "How are you?" the man said to Cheryl.

She knew them. She knew the waitress, too, who raised a serving spoon in greeting from behind the counter. It was Cheryl who had suggested this restaurant.

"I'm fine. How are you?" Cheryl said, stopping at the table, her hand on top of the little girl's chair.

"We're about to sit here all night if she doesn't eat her chicken. She's had nothing but cornflakes for three days. Tell Cheryl Jean why you won't eat nothing but cornflakes," the man said.

The little girl squirmed in her seat. Marshall saw that her plate was almost untouched. The man's plate was empty, except for bones, and his wife had almost finished her dinner. She reached across to her daughter's plate and picked up a chicken breast, saying nothing to Cheryl in greeting, avoiding her husband's eyes, saying to no one in particular, "All she eats is cornflakes. You might as well get used to it."

"So how have things been back at the cloister?" Cheryl said, sliding in beside McCallum. As he slid sideways in the booth, he winced.

"Cheryl Jean, you tell Bobby to call me in the morning whether that part comes in or not," the man called.

Cheryl nodded. The waitress came to the table and put a cup of coffee down in front of Cheryl. "Eating, hon?" she said.

"No thanks," Cheryl said.

"You be in this Saturday?"

"One to nine," Cheryl said.

If the waitress had any interest in who anyone was, she wasn't letting on. Marshall had eaten only half his stew, but McCallum had finished. She cleared McCallum's plate, asking if he wanted "gravy coffee."

"One sugar cube, no milk, gravy on the side," he said, smiling.

"We charge extra for gravy with coffee," the waitress said. "Tell him," she said to Cheryl.

"So," Cheryl said. "What a surprise to get a call from you. I take it you're headed down to Florida too, Marshall? Doesn't sound bad."

"Spring vacation. Ten glorious days on the road leading to the southernmost point of the U.S. of A. Going to stand at land's end and have our pictures taken. Buy a coconut," McCallum said.

"I've never been that far," Cheryl said. "I went to Marathon to go fishing with one of my brothers a few years ago."

Though the waitress paid no attention, the man at the table never took his eyes off their booth.

"I wait tables here on weekends," Cheryl said. "During the week I've got a job in Lexington, working at a gift shop one of my cousins opened." She looked at Marshall. "I haven't thought about poetry in a while," she said.

Marshall shrugged. "I can't say I've thought about it lately myself. Cheryl—I thought McCallum told you I was going to be here."

"She's happy to see you. I knew she would be," McCallum said.

"I'm not exactly *happy* to see either of you. I hope you don't take that wrong."

"We don't understand why you left," McCallum said. "It doesn't seem right that because"—he lowered his voice to a near whisper—"because of what happened, you should be here, and Livan should have blown town, leaving whatever mess she left behind."

"You came to Buena Vista to sympathize with me," Cheryl said. It was the first time Marshall had heard the name of the town pronounced. It was "Buena" to rhyme with "tuna."

"We're stopping on our way to Key West," Marshall said.

"No, we came because we wanted to see you," McCallum said.

"Well, here I am," Cheryl said.

"Though I didn't know when I wrote I'd have the added benefit of meeting with your mother," McCallum said.

What was this? Marshall thought. Her mother was suspicious about why two college professors would stop to see her daughter who'd dropped out? It did sound strange. He could well imagine that Cheryl's mother would want to check them out.

"Why?" Cheryl said, ignoring the remark about her mother. "Why do you care how I'm doing?" It was loud enough that the man eating with his family heard the question. Marshall saw him kick his wife's leg under the table.

"I want to tell you the truth about the things Livan accused me of," McCallum said. "At the very least, you deserve to have an idea of what was true and what wasn't, and what was an exaggeration."

"Forgive me," Cheryl said, "but I've stopped thinking about the truth. She thinks what she thinks, and you say what you say. It's all over, as far as I'm concerned."

"Then what's this about, that you drop out of college—"

"You worried about falling enrollments or something?"

"Worried about you," McCallum said.

Cheryl sighed. She looked around the restaurant, taking it in as the odd place it was the same way they had when they'd first come in. Marshall could almost feel her sudden estrangement from the place. A woman came from the back and flipped the OPEN sign to CLOSED on the front door. She ruffled Cheryl's hair but didn't say anything. She looked through McCallum and Marshall as if they weren't there.

"Listen, this isn't about me. It isn't even about me," Cheryl said suddenly. "But since I've heard enough about you, and even from you, for a lifetime, let me tell you a couple of things myself. My mother has gray hair now, she had a baby last year, and she had to go half-time at the food plant. Daddy's doing long-distance hauling on runs between here and Michigan. He's got a girlfriend in Michigan my mother found out about, and she thinks it's just a matter of time until he'll find work out there and not come back. Since I've been home she's had two operations to tie off veins in her legs, but she's going back to work full-time next month. She needs the money. I've been taking the baby to my cousin's shop in Lexington, because the lady who was coming in while my mother worked ran away with the Amway salesman. It's not *The Bridges of Madison County* down here; everybody runs away all the time. It's nothing special."

"Makes it stranger you came back," McCallum said.

"McCallum," Marshall said, with exaggerated patience, "she wanted to help her mother out."

"Which I very much approve of—the idea of her getting some help—because the woman was once the love of my life. When I was sixteen years old. Seventeen. Not that much younger than you are now, Cheryl."

"I'm aware of that," Cheryl said.

"What?" Marshall said.

"Your mother tell you we almost got married?" McCallum said.

"She's got a picture of you two hidden in her dresser drawer. You probably know the one: the two of you in a canoe," Cheryl said, evading the question.

"She got a scholarship to a camp in Virginia. It was my last year there," McCallum said to Marshall. "I was a camp counsellor."

"She told me when I was in high school," Cheryl said. She looked at Marshall. "My mother and the guidance counsellor thought I should apply to Benson. That Professor McCallum here would be my ticket to getting financial aid."

"What in the hell!" Marshall said, shaking his head. What was he doing here, as if he had any part in this? He hardly knew McCallum, and had no desire to know about the intricacies of his life.

"I'm still ashamed," McCallum said to Cheryl. "I dumped your mother for no good reason and broke her heart. It's still painful to think about."

"Unbelievable," Marshall said. "Why couldn't you have given me a little background before we showed up here? What is this about that I'm constantly dragged into your life and your problems like my feelings don't matter? You think I love your revelations, or do you have trouble levelling with anybody?"

"Cowardice," McCallum said. "You continue to misunderstand me."

"We're both cowards," Cheryl said. "I didn't tell her you were coming."

"You didn't?" McCallum said. "You said you would."

"I changed my mind. I thought I'd leave it up to you—have you call her yourself if you were so sure it was the right thing." She looked at her untouched coffee as if she were considering something small and sad. "She has ten children, you know. She's at the free clinic with one of my brothers tonight, waiting to get his arm x-rayed. She's got enough troubles. I don't know how to say this except to say it: I don't know what happened in Boston, in spite of the fact that Livan turned out to be a real nut case. On the chance that you did that, though, I could hardly want you back in my mother's life. Your track record is that you proposed to her, asked her to wait for you, then took off with somebody else." She looked around the restaurant. The dancing man and his friend were sitting slumped forward with their arms around each other's shoulders. No sign of any waitresses, as they waited for everyone to clear out. "What do you think can happen?" Cheryl said. "You think you two are going to fall into each other's arms like all these years never happened? If she'd wanted to do that, why didn't she make an attempt to get in touch with you when she drove me to Benson?" She didn't wait for McCallum to answer. "I told her about Livan Baker—what she accused you of. She wanted to know why I'd felt under so much pressure; I told her exactly what I'd been through. Courtesy of her white knight." Cheryl shook her head. "She was so horrified. I guess—" She pushed the coffee aside. "She clearly didn't think you would have done such a thing," Cheryl said, in a very matter-of-fact tone. "You say you didn't. Let's say you didn't."

"Let's take her home and give her a bowl of cornflakes," the woman said to the man. "Tomorrow's a workday."

"Don't need to remind me of that," the man said.

"They're closing," Marshall said, stating the obvious, looking around at the too-bright, sparsely populated restaurant.

"I want to say one more thing," Cheryl said. "Two things, actually. Up until a few years ago she was still very pretty. Her hair's gray now. She hasn't lost the weight she gained with the last baby. She's had one medical problem after another since Sara was born. I don't want you to be unprepared. The other thing I want to say is something I've already told Marshall. If you don't talk to him about what's so meaningful in your life, maybe he doesn't keep you posted. It's not such a big thing, but I think you need to hear it. The things Livan said you did to her. Does he know where she got a lot of those things from?" Cheryl said.

"No," Marshall said.

"Does he know you kissed me that night in the car?"

McCallum smirked, raising an eyebrow in Marshall's direction.

"He didn't until now," Marshall said.

"Well, the thing is, I'm pretty sure my mother had a lover. Either that or she and this man had a crush on each other. My mother got religion a while back, and she had me baptized. She would have baptized the older ones, but two brothers are gone and the other one put his foot down, and Daddy backed them up. I wrote Marshall that this boyfriend, or whatever he was—he was somebody she'd met at church. She got all excited about the idea that he become my godfather. When I was going to look at colleges, he drove me to a couple of places not too far away—we'd go there and come back the same day. I didn't like him. On one of the rides, before we got there, he said he felt sick; he pulled off the highway and said he needed to take a walk. I went with him. He raped me in the woods."

"They don't talk to you in school about being a vegetarian, do they?" the man at the table said to his daughter.

The answer was inaudible. The two men from the counter picked up their jackets and started out, slapping each other on the shoulder, trading insults about how ugly the other one was. One waved to the man at the table, the other picked up a free real estate guide from a stack inside the door. "Put that back, you ain't buying nothing," the man at the table hollered. "You expect some tree to have got chopped so you can wipe the ice off your window?" Behind them, the waitress sponged the counter.

"The reason I'm telling you is because considering that man, and considering my father, it makes me think she doesn't have great taste in men. I'm not saying you're that man. Livan apparently thought you were, or decided to make you into him. But she didn't even know him, and I did. He was singing in the choir the next Sunday, and afterwards when we were filing out, he looked right at me when she stopped to talk to him, swung one of my little brothers up on his shoulders and looked at me like nothing had happened. A whole year went by before he tried it again. That time I told him I'd tell my brother in the marines, and my brother would kill him. He would have, too. He was betting on me being too ashamed to tell anybody, but when he found out I would, that was the end of it. I'm over it now. He comes in here and I let somebody else wait on his table. I mention all this because I still have that brother in the marines, and if you do anything that upsets her, you're going to wish you'd died when your wife meant you to."

"Think about it," McCallum said. "She's still got my picture, she's having a rough time—how could I come all the way here and not call her? What's that look for? She got in touch with me when she needed a favor, didn't she?"

"You know, Marshall," Cheryl said, touching her scarf, "it would be bizarre if I hadn't stopped kissing you. If I'd gone to bed with you"—she looked at Marshall, whose attention had been drifting, but whose eyes immediately shot open—"and then, after that, if my mother got together with your best friend. Everybody willing to fuck everybody else. It could have been the way it probably was for you guys in the sixties."

"It was such an awful night," Marshall said. "It was one quick kiss. You only imagine we might have slept together."

"Describe it to your wife," she said. "See if she'd draw the same conclusion."

"Temper, temper," McCallum said.

"It really is unbelievable that you'd think about coming back into her life," Cheryl said to McCallum. "She's married. She has—" she faltered. "She has a life, and everything about it is difficult enough without you."

"Think about it: you want to maintain the status quo. You're also pretending I have power I don't have. Do you really think that against her inclinations I could take her away?"

"You'd have to take her away, because you could never hack it in Buena Vista," Cheryl spat out, gesturing around her as if the restaurant represented the entire town. Which it might, Marshall thought. He closed his eyes and tried to imagine his house in New Hampshire. Instead, what came back to him was the green bedspread in the motel room, the bed sagging under him like a badly inflated float.

"Cheryl," McCallum teased. "Have I made you feel insecure? Are you afraid you won't be my Dulcinea?"

They'd snapped at each other so fast Marshall hadn't been able to interject a word; he hadn't been able to object to McCallum's pushing this frightened girl too hard—couldn't he see this was her notion of protecting her mother? All she must feel she had at this moment was her mother, her life with her mother—the same person who had compromised her without realizing it.

"Cheryl," Marshall said, "I'm going to do my best to see we leave without any call being made to your mother. I want you to know I agree with you."

"Can you imagine it?" Cheryl burst out. "Don Quixote and Sancho Panza at Dolly's restaurant in Buena Vista, Virginia? I mean, poverty like this would bring down even Don Quixote. How would anybody"—she looked at McCallum—"*nobody*," she said, "could believe in resuming a great romance in Buena Vista. I'm here while she recovers from her leg surgery, and that's the end. In another few months, I am out of here."

It was the first time Marshall had the sinking feeling that she was trapped.

McCallum paid the bill, smoothing wadded-up bills on the tabletop. "You might both dislike me right now, but at least it should prove to you that I can be transparent," he said, putting a saltshaker on top of the money. "See? Willing to let my friends know my failures, see my flaws. Willing to admit my shortcomings, to try to make amends."

"I don't see it that way," Cheryl said. "I don't believe what you say. You're a barnacle. You attach yourself. You stick on, like a parasite. That's what's most important to you."

"I had no idea in hell about any of this," Marshall said to Cheryl.

"You seem not to have an idea in hell about a lot of things," she said.

"You're mad at him. Don't be mad at me," he said.

But her comment had been on target: he had no idea what Sonja was doing tonight; he'd never had a clear idea about what to do in the face of Livan Baker's problems. He remembered the night he'd talked to McCallum about their talking to someone in an official position, when McCallum had derided the entire concept, saying, "What is 'the record'? Is it like 'the Force'?" All his life, he'd stayed the younger brother, looking to someone else for cues. Two days into the trip, he didn't know whether he'd done the correct thing in leaving New Hampshire, or if Gordon was really looking forward to seeing him. There seemed every chance Gordon had called the other night half hoping Marshall's plans had fallen through. He was also unsure whether, the more he knew him, McCallum receded farther or began to seem more comprehensible.

"I want things to turn out well for all of us," McCallum said, pushing open the restaurant door. Over his shoulder, Marshall saw that the family still sat around the table, the man stubbornly remaining until he was asked to leave, the little girl powerless, the mother fatigued, resigned. My God, Marshall thought: Were those people so different from their own trio? McCallum bullish; Cheryl trying to resist intimidation; himself, sitting silently for most of the time they were there at the table, under the weight of a situation—a constantly unfolding situation—that seemed never to stretch to full length, so it could be examined and understood.

The cold air might as well have literally smacked them, the impact was so powerful. It took Marshall's breath away. In the parking lot was an old pickup, a Toyota, and a black Ford station wagon. A sheet of newspaper blew across the lot, followed by a can of Coke that rolled from underneath the pickup. Back in the restaurant, one light was turned off, then another.

"If you didn't know me, if you didn't know anything about me," McCallum said, "would it bother you as much that she had a place in her heart for me, and that I still cared for her?"

"You don't care for her," Cheryl said, hunched in the wind. "This isn't some cosmic coincidence either. Your marriage is over and you're doing what's expedient. You were driving through on your way to Florida anyway." She gestured toward Marshall. "Wasn't that what you pointed out earlier?" she said.

"Don't confuse me with him. Please," Marshall said.

"I don't," Cheryl said, arms crossed over her chest. "I remember you, too."

That night, as McCallum slept curled against the pillow he clung to like a life raft pushed against his stomach to ride out another stormy night, the flashlight from the road emergency kit sending an oblong beam along the dirty gray shag carpeting because there was no bed-side lamp, Marshall played back in his mind the night he'd left his house intending to go to Livan Baker's rescue. Had he really been going to the apartment because of her, or because of Cheryl? Cheryl more than Livan, to tell the truth. In the moment, though, that trip had seemed to be about something else; it had been convenient not to think it through. Now he thought Sonja might have been with Tony. Was that why she wasn't home, though it was late? Was that why she'd said, "Happens" with such resignation, sitting tiredly on the bed, still in her clothes, after McCallum's long night of revelations?

"Happens." Well, that was indisputable. Things happened, situations materialized and transmuted, changed of their own accord, it seemed, as if they were not within people's control. Maybe, he thought sleepily, everybody in the face of life's power, its tragedy and its absurdity, its changeability, became the little brother, looking to someone else for explanations, confirmation, guidance. That would be one of the reasons people procreated: so they'd have someone impressionable to tell their stories to, someone who would believe them, at least for a long time, an audience to whom they could recite their stories instead of introspecting. All those little dramas, made huge because they were personal: How Dad Met Mom; Your First Brilliant Statement; Why Our Family Has Special Reason to Fear Thunderstorms; Gentlemen Open Doors for Ladies. Family myths, passed on from generation to generation, along with a tendency toward tooth decay, or genes determining baldness.

He could remember distinctly lying in bed, a twin bed far more comfortable than the bed he was lying in now, taxing Gordon's patience by wanting everything the adults had said that day verified or refuted by the one person he trusted absolutely. What a reluctant interpreter Gordon had been: caught in the middle, Marshall now understood, having to decide whether it was better that Marshall believed what they said, because that would make things easier on everyone, or whether he should respect his little brother's intelligence and give him more information, allowing him to see through the adults' rhetoric, their shaky scenarios passed off as absolutes, their parents no more convinced what direction to take than their mapless children. For years, Gordon had pointed out the fallacies in their parents' logic, kept from sleep by the necessity of setting Marshall straight: the parents needed to believe in Santa Claus, so it was best to pretend; their father had sent them from the table not because they'd had inappropriate fits of giggling, but because he wanted time alone with his wife. In retrospect, he had been a burden—more than he'd suspected, thinking over their nighttime debriefings this many years later. He could remember Gordon saying, *She's really dying,* and *He doesn't think you're a sissy for playing with paperdolls, he wants someone to blame for her getting sick, because he can't blame her and he can't blame himself. You just happened to have your stupid paperdolls out.* He could also remember climbing into Gordon's

bed, when no amount of reasoning would work to make him feel
better, and Gordon's deep sighs, as if Marshall's presence were a boulder rolled onto his tiny island of mattress to displace him, though
another part of him knew that Gordon was flattered to have him
there. *Yes, she's sick; she's dying,* he remembered Gordon saying,
whispering it with real urgency, *but there's something else,* he had
said. *I can't figure it out, but there's something I don't know.*

It was Marshall's last conscious thought, sliding lower in the bed,
fastidiously turning back the green bedspread he automatically assumed was soiled, settling himself in the bed's deep crease as well as
he could, the hum of a headache boring into him. The idea of being
on his way to see Gordon was at once comforting and discomforting;
he had asked so much of Gordon—probably too much. And then
when they became adults they had drifted apart. He had drifted away
from the person who had been his life raft, yet he had the idea now
that he needed, at least temporarily, to return; that even if McCallum
hadn't seized on the idea of a trip, he would have made the trip alone.
It was a time in his life when Gordon shouldn't have any power over
him; everyone knew that at some point the complexity, the sheer ac-
cumulation of experiences, evened out age differences between
people. He supposed it was not so much his insights that he wanted as
his guaranteed sympathy: his burdensome friend; his disenfranchised
wife. Though he wasn't talkative on the phone, face-to-face he would
become again the Gordon Marshall had always known, the brother
he could still turn to.

He looked across the room, as he had when he was a child, though
instead of seeing the reassuring sight of his brother asleep—the explanations all registered, Gordon leading the way even into sleep—he
saw the lumpish mass of McCallum.

18

MARSHALL— the note from McCallum began. *I wouldn't do this if I thought I'd really be leaving you stranded, but I'm afraid I've been getting you down. I do have to see Janet Lanier, but am not going to end her marriage (I guess that's been done already) or force myself on her sexually, and if I do, I won't tie her up (joke). Got up a little after five, found diner across the highway just opening. Looked at my horoscope. Scorpio must "trust those from the past to provide knowledge about your present." I don't suppose I have to justify this to you, but it's pretty hard to see myself as Prince Charming— Cheryl's wrong about my power—but what I'm hoping for from Janet is some acknowledgment I'm not a monster, either. I got some money out of the cash machine (behind 7-Eleven, if you're interested; it's one of those new ones. Screen says* HELLO, MR. MCCALLUM *when you slide in card) that I'm going to press on her. Not my cock, my money. As if I could get it up feeling this bad. One more addendum, slightly embarrassing: the same way you were telling me you still look up to your older brother, I look up to you. I know there are problems in your marriage right now, but I also know they're going to blow over. Hey—at least you didn't marry Susan. If she loved the kid as much as she said, she wouldn't have gone after me, landing herself in jail, leaving him stranded. Can still hear the old lady's gasp when I called her from the hospital and told her what her daughter had done.*

Marshall turned to the other side. He looked at McCallum's little arrow, surprised that McCallum might think he wouldn't have the

sense to turn the bag over. On the flip side, McCallum's writing became smaller, sloppier.

*About Boston: felt guilty cheating on Susan, though as you might
suppose, our sex life wasn't great. That trip wasn't the first time Livan
and I had sex. Afterwards, I had a nightmare in which Susan's greatest fear (along with doing anything positive to help the kid, that is)
materialized. I was Prince Charming, or at least somebody richer
than I am, and Susan was a bag lady, which is always what she feared
she'd end up. She wanted me to join the Masons, so she'd have a
decent old age home to go to if I died. Not in the dream, in real life.
We had fights because I wouldn't join the Masons. A guy who writes
in "Gore Vidal" on every Presidential election ballot, a hippie who
spent his college years in SDS, and she wanted me to join the Masons.
In the dream, I was kissing Livan, walking pretty much where we
actually walked, area around Boston Common, and the b. lady
threatened us with a gun. I talked the b. lady into dropping it. Then
I kissed her, and suddenly it was Susan standing there. I grabbed her
hands. Then she was handcuffed by the police for causing a public
disturbance. Livan woke me up because I was grabbing her wrist.
Bits and pieces of what Livan later accused me of are true, but they
weren't done to her the way she said, they were things I'd described
to her from nightmares.*

*You've been more of a friend to me than anybody since I lost
Livan. No kidding: I once thought that despite her age, despite the
fact she was a girl, she was my best friend. Trust you know me well
enough to know that I know what I'm doing. This afternoon will get
ticket back north from Roanoke, try to pick up pieces. I appreciate
everything you've done.*

*What do you sign a note written on two sides of a takeout bag?
Best Wishes? Best wishes, Happy New Year next year, Hang loose,
God bless. — McCallum*

It was an incredible document. The obvious thing to do would be
call the Laniers' house. McCallum would be glad to hear from him,
reassured to know Marshall worried about him after receiving the
note; he'd also no doubt want him to go there and sit around the
kitchen table, listen along with him to the woman's story, or even—
God forbid—he'd want him to listen to more of his own. He sat in
the car, where he'd been sitting since he looked through the window

and saw the note on the driver's seat. The first thing he noticed was that without a passenger the car was quiet and seemed infinitely spacious. He tossed the bag in the backseat, rubbed his hands over his face. McCallum had mentioned Roanoke. Where was Roanoke, and how had McCallum known there was an airport there?

He went back into the dingy motel room. A maid's cart sat on the blacktop outside, and a fat black maid was cleaning in the room next door. He wanted to be gone from the room as much as the maid wanted him gone. He decided to forget about shaving and tossed the few things he'd brought in with him into his duffel bag. As he picked up his shaver, he saw that one of McCallum's dirty shirts hung on the back of the bathroom door, and when he saw it a feeling went through him almost as if he'd seen the ghost of McCallum. It wasn't a pleasant feeling. Neither was he proud of himself for leaving the shirt hanging there until he felt ashamed—of course he would have to turn around and get the shirt. He zipped the duffel bag and picked up the shirt, exiting the room just as the maid came to the open door. He said good-morning to her; she returned his greeting. He tossed the duffel bag on the backseat—no more McCallum, who'd stretched out there for naps periodically—and got halfway to the office, on foot, before he realized McCallum had taken his denim shirt. It had been in a plastic bag on the floor of the backseat, a last-minute grab on his way out of the house in New Hampshire, Sonja thoughtfully having decided to go to the cleaner's the day before he left. His next-to-favorite blue shirt, and McCallum had just helped himself.

Behind the desk was a thin woman with a missing front tooth. She stood behind dish gardens and potted plants that had a lavender Gro-Lite aimed at them from a bulb clipped near the top of a coatrack. He saw that a philodendron had been trained to grow coiled around a toilet plunger, which had been painted white. At the top, with nowhere else to climb, the plant looped down and was headed for a pink ceramic elephant with a begonia planted in its back. Small pots of African violets were dotted amid the larger plants, rounds of cotton underneath the bottom leaves, padding the rims. Stuck in some of the pots were drink swizzle sticks topped with pink plastic mermaids, or bright green sailboats.

"Your brother paid the bill," the woman said.

Was it the woman's supposition they were brothers, or had McCallum told her that? If he had, he'd probably guessed there was a good chance the woman would repeat the information.

"Just need the key. I already given him the receipt," she said.

"My brother," Marshall said. "Was he able to find out from you where the nearest airport was?"

"Would have been, but didn't ask," the woman said. He saw that there was also a tooth missing on the bottom.

"Okay," he said. "Thanks."

"Thank you," the woman said.

He went back to the car and drove to the diner across from the motel. Climbing the steps, he saw at the top a plaster rabbit and three small plaster bunnies clustered around an empty terra-cotta planter into which someone had thrown a beer can and a used rubber. Inside, on a metal stand, the local paper was piled up, with a canister attached to the side of the rack marked 25 CENT HONNOR SYSTEM. A child's doll lay on the bottom shelf, its blue dress folded under its head. He passed through the fog of cigar smoke rising into the air from the man paying his bill at the register and walked to the back counter. A short man in a denim jumpsuit was crumbling saltines into a bowl of tomato soup. Two seats away, a woman looked straight ahead and puffed a cigarette, a full cup of coffee in front of her.

"I'd like one of those bran muffins," he said to the waitress, pointing into a hazy plastic container on the counter, "and a coffee to go. Light."

"Tuesday," the woman said. "Second muffin, Danish, or cream horn half price. Only one cream horn left."

"Oh," he said. "Then I guess I'll have a Danish too."

"Apple raisin strawberry."

"Apple, please."

She poured coffee, put the top on the container. With plastic tongs, she lifted an apple Danish from a tray, centered it delicately on a precut piece of foil she pulled from a box, and wrapped it. Then she opened the container that held the bran muffin, lifted it with the tongs, and dropped it, unwrapped, into a white bag. She carefully placed the pastry in the bag, closed the top, and handed him the coffee separately. "Cream's at the register," she said.

"I think my brother came in earlier," he said. "Walked a little funny? Nice looking, about my height. I wondered how he was feeling this morning."

"Feeling like he meant to leave town!" the waitress said. "I gave him our biggest takeout bag to write on, and I thought: I never seen a man write for so long about how to get to the airport. Either that is the most forgetful man in the world, or I gave such detailed directions I scared him to death."

"Let me have a beef barley soup and more of these crackers," the short man down the counter said.

"Let me once in my life live someplace where people eat breakfast at breakfast and lunch at lunch and dinner at dinner," the woman two seats away said to the waitress.

"I heard that at Donald Trump's Atlantic City casino, if you're winning big you can call for poached eggs on toast at two in the morning and have them carried right up to you on a silver platter as long as you don't push back your chair and walk away with your winnings," the waitress said.

"You thinking about rejoining the fire department?" the woman said. It was the first indication she knew the man.

"Might," he said.

"Silly snit, if you ask me. This isn't a community where one person taking exception to another person can ruin things to the point where we don't have enough firemen."

"Beef barley," the waitress said, lifting the pan off the burner and pouring it into a bowl. She put the bowl on a plate and carried it to him, doing a deep knee bend to pick up one package of crackers on the way.

"I order more crackers, tell me no," the man said.

"That's what I like," the waitress said. "A man who tells me what to tell him. You want to put the words right in my mouth, Randall?"

"'Oh, Randall, you look so handsome today,'" Randall said in falsetto.

The woman on the stool laughed.

"Hear me repeating them?" the waitress said. "Then everybody'd really have something to laugh about, because Betty would have finally lost her mind."

Marshall smiled, taking the bag and coffee container to the cash register.

"What do you think it is about banana nut?" the woman said, peering into the bag, then punching cash register keys. A dollar and fifty-one cents came up, and the woman automatically reached into a dish for a penny as she gave Marshall two quarters. He pocketed them, thanking her, then took two small, wet half-and-half containers from an ice bucket. "Used to be everybody preferred banana nut."

In the car, he broke off a piece of muffin and ate it while looking at the map. He wasn't sure that he shouldn't call McCallum and wish him well, just for the sake of closure. There was a phone booth in the gas station, beyond the diner, but someone was inside. Marshall moved his finger along Route 84 toward this day's destination: somewhere in South Carolina. It couldn't start to get warm fast enough. Just walking from the diner to the car, his feet felt frozen. He scuffed them back and forth on the floor, trying to warm them a little with the friction. He turned on the radio and searched for a station, stopped when he heard music he thought was Beethoven. The person was still in the phone booth. He took another bite of muffin, dropped the remaining lump in the bag. He peeled back a little rectangle of plastic from the top of the coffee container and sucked up mostly air, deliberately, testing to see how hot the coffee was. Hot enough to make him shiver, because his body was so cold. No McCallum up front, so he could leave the map unfolded on the seat. On the floor, he saw one of McCallum's pens. Thinking about that, and about the shirt, he had the sudden image of a snowman that had melted and could be conjured up only by the carrot on the ground, the black coal eyes. That brought to mind the snowman and snow woman on campus he had seen when he went back after Evie's funeral. He thought briefly about the snow woman's breasts with their spoutlike nipples, then remembered Sophia Androcelli's irate letter to the newspaper, preceded by her equally irate comment to him that he shouldn't dismantle the snowpeople when he went outside. The person was off the phone, so he started his ignition and drove onto the road, then immediately turned off, coasting to a stop in front of the phone booth. When he got there, he was sure he didn't want to call McCallum. Instead, suddenly and surprisingly on the verge of tears, he dialled his own number, to talk to Sonja. His hand was shaking. An automated voice asked him to reenter his card number. Then the call went through, and he heard the familiar double ring of his home phone, over and over, ringing in the empty house. She wasn't there. It seemed more than possible she wouldn't be, but it made him suspicious that she might be with Tony. It seemed completely far-fetched she would be buying groceries. Ludicrous to assume she would have returned to the dry cleaner's so quickly. Then, taking a deep breath, he hung up and began rationalizing another way. What if he had reached her? What was there to tell her? More about McCallum's odd behavior; chitchat in a diner. He drove away, but was only on the road a few minutes when he decided he'd made the wrong decision; it was the sound of her voice he needed to hear, not Beethoven, not his own roiling thoughts, the silent conversations he'd begun having with himself. He dialled the area code, but couldn't remember the number of Hembley and Hembley. The thought of Tony made his fingers tingle, so he took another deep breath and reminded himself that except for calling, he wouldn't need to have anything to do with Tony ever again. Even Sonja was fed up with Tony. Hadn't she said that? Forcing calmness into his voice, he reached New Hampshire information and asked for the number, tracing the numbers on the dusty metal shelf under the phone. His fingers were so sweaty, the numbers were perfectly legible. He called the number, hoping Tony wouldn't answer the phone. Gwen, the other agent who worked there, answered, but he didn't want to talk to her either; he disguised his voice, finding it very little trouble to sound tremulous and slightly high-pitched. And she was there. Sonja had gone back to work. Sonja was there!

"I'm so glad I got you," he said. "I miss you. I'm standing beside the highway sweating, and it's not that hot here. I'm—"

"I know you hate it when I do this, but I've really got to put you on hold," she said.

Her voice sounded official. She did not sound delighted to hear from him. Probably Tony was standing right in front of her. Probably she and Tony were having a discussion. Even Gwen might be in on it.

"Hi," she said. "Sorry."

"You're sorry? I'm sorry. I don't know how things went so out of focus"—he saw the white line painted up the center of the highway running along, as if it were a conveyor belt—"I'm here without you. This doesn't make any sense."

"I thought you had to see your brother, and McCallum had to have a vacation," she said.

"You're furious at me," he said. "Why? Why are you?"

"I'm not," she said. "I thought a trip would do you good."

"Why?" he said.

"Have you called to start a fight about a trip you told me you wanted to take?"

"Is he standing right there?" he said.

"'He' Tony? No, he's not in the office. He does own the place, though."

"I don't care what he fucking owns, he doesn't own you."

"I realize that," she said.

"You just don't realize that I love you," he said. "And maybe you shouldn't. Maybe I've really blown it. McCallum—McCallum went off to apologize to some woman he knew from years ago when they were kids in summer camp. After all this time, he needed to apologize to her. I understand that. It's not easy, sometimes. Too much time passes. You don't know what to say. I don't exactly know what to say now."

"Write me a love poem," she said. Her voice softened slightly.

"I'll build you that tree house and climb up into it with you and read it to you there. How's that?"

"It's funny you teach poetry and you never write poems," she said. "Do you write them and keep them hidden from me?"

"No," he said. He shuddered as he remembered the grotesquely inept poem written by Mrs. Adam Barrows. "What are you doing?" he said quickly.

"Sitting here, waiting for an electrician to stop by and explain something to me about an exploding stove," she said.

"You could fly to Key West," he said. "Meet me."

"Maybe we should take another vacation. Another time." A pause. "McCallum is setting right some wrong? New lease on life and all that?"

"He jumped ship. He's flying back."

"And you wouldn't be calling just to get me to pinch-hit for McCallum, would you?"

"I love you. Don't you know that I love you?"

"Yes," she said quietly.

He looked again at the highway. The line was no longer moving, but cars were. The sun had begun to shine on his back. He turned away from it, facing into the phone booth. "The reason I called was to say I loved you. I'm afraid you're going to leave. Have you been thinking about leaving?"

"I've given some thought to a brief vacation in Santa Fe, floating over the desert and eating blue corn tortillas."

"That would be great," he said. It sounded terrible. Far away, and pointless.

"I think I'm going with Jenny. Maybe after you write me your poem, you and I can go to, oh, Niagara Falls."

"Anywhere," he said.

"Okay," she said.

"I love you. Can you say you love me even if you're at work?"

"I love you," she said.

"You'd say it if Tony was there, right?"

"I'm not in love with Tony," she said.

"Does Gwen know about this? Did everybody besides me know?"

"You mean, did I confide in McCallum that night we had our little chat?"

"You did?"

"In fact, I didn't. Listen: here's the electrician. Once this stove situation gets fixed, everything's going to be fine. We'll be fine. Write the poem. Buy the lumber."

"Niagara Falls. Hell, I really will take you, if you want to go."

"I was kidding," she said.

"But not about the other?" he said.

"No," she said, lowering her voice. "I do love you. You're always so distracted. I mean, you didn't even pay attention to Evie. I don't know if it was your class you were thinking about, or—"

"Don't say any more," he said. "This isn't sounding as good as when you just said, 'I love you.'"

She laughed. "You do make me laugh," she said.

"I didn't do well enough by Evie. I haven't done well enough with you."

"We'll talk about it when you get back," she said.

"I will," he said. "I'll get back."

He looked around him, smacking his lips dryly to send her a small kiss as he hung up, his hand still shaking as he replaced the phone in its cradle.

It would be good to get to Gordon and Beth's. That would be his own version of McCallum's sitting by the hearth, nestled in a chair, himself the center of attention, a drink on the table, forget the coffee and tea, a drink. It would be interesting to start from the beginning, with two people who knew nothing about the situation except its outcome—its ostensible outcome, since who knew what McCallum would do, and who knew what would happen to Susan, when and if she was released from the prison psychiatric ward to stand trial?—to discuss how McCallum had for reasons of his own decided he was entitled to be a part of Marshall's life, which was in counterpoint to Marshall's having decided he would distance himself from Gordon. Absenting yourself was a decision made by default, wasn't it? What had happened that he and Gordon had for years kept a distance from one another? Wives? Geography? Their jobs? All those things, though Sonja had encouraged him to see more of his brother (more time for Tony?), and he'd always had the same amount of vacation time he had now, he could have gotten on a plane. It was too far to drive. He'd just driven because McCallum had stars in his eyes about being out on the road, though now he saw that McCallum had an ulterior motive. That left the category "jobs." Okay: his had allowed him to turn inward, to spend his time passively, reading and thinking. Things that had once seemed a great luxury had become habit. Following the complexities of books had ultimately made him naïve about what was happening around him: everyone's complicated lives; their difficult-to-articulate desires. Perhaps, having no ability to compete with his brother, he'd taken the opposite path, learned vocabulary while Gordon was learning skills, surrounded himself with other thoughtful people, while Gordon had concluded the optimal life was about more action and less thought.

He was worried that he'd dropped out of Gordon's life too long, that it was going to be difficult to reconnect. There was every possibility Gordon thought that too; that Gordon was signalling he'd left not only Marshall, but the whole family behind when he didn't come to Evie's funeral. Gordon had said that exact day was when a Japanese businessman would be meeting with him to discuss buying the dive shop. But who knew? And what should his brother have done? Put everything on hold, since no doctor would say whether she was getting better or worse? Truth was, Gordon had never been as attached to Evie as Marshall. He had liked her, but not loved her. As a child, Marshall had thought that admirable: that Gordon was still loyal in his thoughts to their mother, while Evie's kindness eroded more and more of their mother's memory. It had been easier, probably, for Evie to embrace the younger child—physically embrace him—because Gordon was standoffish; Gordon saw his mother's death as a way to increase his independence, because the adults were so preoccupied. And Gordon didn't want his father to have any excuse to think him the sissy he thought his younger son. They had both known that was the way he had thought of Marshall. His father had asked Gordon to repair things, while he'd asked Marshall to help Evie wash dishes. It was to Gordon's credit that he deemphasized his own achievements, that he had so convincingly made their father seem silly in his reactions toward Marshall. Well, Marshall thought, what if the payoff for having been such a good person was that one day Mr. Watanabe from Tokyo, Japan, made Gordon a rich man. What if Mr. Watanabe was an original thinker—no taking over Hollywood, no buyouts of companies in Silicon Valley: acquiring a diving-supply and boat-chartering business in Key West, Florida, the end of the line, Cuba floating ninety miles away, across all the gleaming water filled with million-dollar fish that were loaded onto airplanes still flopping, flown to Japan to be filigreed into sashimi. According to Sonja, who had talked to Beth, Mr. Watanabe's other businesses included a drugstore chain in Kansas, and a meatpacking factory in Omaha. That sounded so dreary that the guy was probably looking for a business that would provide a little excitement.

The music had gotten lugubrious, so he pushed the "seek" button, thinking wryly, *Yes indeed; yes indeed—that's what I'm out here on the road doing, all right*. It was the McCallum mentality, communicable, like a cold. He pushed his thumb against the tiny button above which a green light quivered, locking in Bette Midler singing "Skylark." Another song that should make him watch his foot on the accelerator. A cop car sat in a gulley where the road sloped, but he'd seen it in time. He looked at his watch, saw that it wasn't time yet for lunch, and reached into the bag and broke off another piece of muffin. The muffin disintegrated, which made him think again of McCallum, who, the night before, reaching for Marshall's leftover cornbread, had found himself holding bright yellow crumbs.

The prospect of days without McCallum, the idea of sun, palm trees, ocean breezes, lifted his spirits. He flipped down the visor as the car moved in line with the sun.

19

IN CHARLESTON, South Carolina, he decided to call it a day. For the past three or four hours driving rain had pelted the car, the jagged patches of light between clouds narrowing until early darkness erased what Sonja would have called "the fill-in parts of the puzzle"—the maddening, uniformly toned blue pieces of the one puzzle they owned, which depicted a small, colorful desert below an enormous, even-blue sky. The puzzle had been a gift from Gordon and Beth several Christmases before. Usually they sent a carton of grapefruit and oranges, but that year they had sent the desert, the orderly little desert with its one prairie dog peeking from its hole and its red-flowered cactus blooming. More than he wanted to, he had thought for much of the ride about McCallum, imagining scenarios in which Cheryl's mother raced into McCallum's arms, or, alternatively, the woman's husband taking exception to his presence, going after him the way McCallum's wife had. He thought that maybe he had gotten addicted to McCallum's life the way other people got addicted to soap operas, though instead of being allowed to tune in to watch, he had been given constant synopses of what had happened, as if McCallum were reading from outdated issues of *TV Guide*. It was nothing he and Sonja would have watched on TV, he was sure of that. The jigsaw puzzle had been such a novelty, and they'd been snowed in just after getting it. But other people's despair and ongoing confusion? It didn't seem titillating, didn't figure in their lives.

He stopped outside a small building with a canopy above the entranceway, using McCallum's shirt to cover his head as he made a mad dash for the front door.

Inside, a man in a three-piece suit was talking to a young woman behind the counter. The counter was flanked by potted palms aglow with tiny coral lights. A woman in a long black raincoat stood peering out the window. It was as different from the motel in Buena Vista as anyone could imagine, which meant that it was exactly where he wanted to stay. When he heard a room was available he didn't ask the price. He said, "Good," and waited while the man went behind the counter and got a registration form and put Xs in the two places where Marshall was to sign. The man wore a silver signet ring on his third finger and, on the other wrist, a Rolex. He feigned interest in the young woman's paperwork as Marshall filled out the form. "We have complimentary continental breakfast in the lobby or in your room between the hours of seven and nine," the man said. "There is a hot tub in the courtyard I don't think you'll be using tonight, and there should be a duvet in your armoire, which also contains the television. I'll be happy to provide you with a list of complimentary movies you might view on the VCR. Alicia will show you to your room." He placed an index card of movie titles on the registration desk. "I believe there should be a duplicate list in your room, but you might want to glance at this now so you could take one with you."

He selected *Betrayal,* which he'd never heard of, because it starred Jeremy Irons and Ben Kingsley.

"May I help with any luggage?" Alicia said.

"No, no," he said. "I've got a duffel bag in the car I can bring in. I can take the key and find the room myself."

"I'll be happy to accompany you. House rules," Alicia said.

"We don't want anything not up to standard when you enter the room," the man said.

"Of course," Marshall said. "I'm parked right outside. I'll get my bag."

"You're checking in after turndown, so let me give you a Godiva mint also," the man said.

"Thank you," Marshall said. He felt as if he were doing a kind of charade: a reenactment of Halloween, from an old-fashioned gentleman's perspective. There he had been, knocking at the door, and here were these civilized people, offering him mints and movies.

"Please place this inside your windshield in order to avoid parking penalties," the man said, handing him a laminated card with the hotel's name on it.

"Certainly," Marshall said. "Thank you."

He turned and went outside, reluctantly. It was raining harder, and McCallum's already damp shirt was almost no protection. He quickly got the bag and locked the car, slightly embarrassed to be reentering the lobby looking like a drowned person.

"There will be chamber music tomorrow at twelve-fifteen," the man said. "Checkout time is one p.m., which we would be happy to extend."

Marshall felt the foil-wrapped mint in his pocket, jiggled it like a good-luck charm. *Maybe I could live here the rest of my life,* Marshall thought. To the man he said, "I'll have a better idea in the morning."

"Please," Alicia said, holding out her hand for his bag. She wore a thick silver cuff bracelet between two narrower gold bracelets. Though he was reluctant to hand a woman his bag, he extended his arm.

"Sir," the man said, "it would be possible to have your shirt laundered and returned by checkout time."

He looked at McCallum's shirt, feeling as if he'd carried in a grease rag. "No, no," he said. "Thank you very much."

"Please follow me," Alicia said, opening a side door. The building, two tiered, stretched behind them. Just outside the overhang, two redwood tubs held palm trees with something flowering at their bases. Pansies? Purple pansies in April? The elevator was about twenty feet away; the doors opened immediately when Alicia hit the "up" button. They rode in silence to the second floor. When the doors opened, she said, "Please turn left," then came up beside him and overtook him just outside room 44. Before the key turned in the door, he felt sure that room 44 would be as close to heaven as he could imagine. He saw it in advance, felt the carpeting beneath his feet, almost drank in the pale light from the table lamp Alicia switched on. It sat on a lacquered chest just inside the door. As she switched on two more lights, he looked at the cherry armoire, saw the large bed with its enormous bedposts and scalloped back. On a brass tray were a digital clock, a flashlight, a thick black pen, and the request form for the morning's breakfast. He reminded himself that he was not an unsophisticated person: he had stayed in other good hotels, seen these things before. But tonight it was as if velvet were replacing sandpaper. He realized the extent of his exhaustion. It was the strain of being with McCallum, not only the days of driving, and in that large bed he could lie spread-eagled, dreaming it all away. Maybe he really would stay for the chamber music. Maybe he would extend his stay, recuperate, use this extremely nice place as the springboard for re-entering the world.

"Thank you," Alicia said, as he slipped his billfold from his back pocket and tipped her.

She left, telling him to call the desk if they could provide anything further. She had already lifted the duvet from the armoire and placed it at the bottom of the bed. As she closed the door, he poked it with the heel of his hand, watched the down cover sink and slowly rise. McCallum's shirt was draped over an arm of the chair. His bag sat on a luggage rack. Over the bed, flanked by sconces, was a framed Audubon print of a flamingo. For the first time, he felt he had truly left New Hampshire behind. Something indescribable about the room, which was at once comforting and impersonal, relaxed him. He decided to take a hot shower and stretch out on the bed, to decide then whether it seemed the right moment to call Sonja, or whether he felt more inclined to watch *Betrayal*. He ate the mint, rolling the foil between thumb and finger, dropping the little ball into the trash basket in the marble bathroom. On a tray he saw cotton swabs, small bottles of lotion and shampoo, a Bic shaver, a small sewing kit, a shoeshine cloth. Above those things, in the long rectangular mirror, he saw his face: haggard; showing the signs of the skipped morning shave; a small red pimple or bug bite on his temple; his sideburns, now almost completely white. It had been a while since he'd scruti-nized himself in a mirror. He'd developed a way of more or less look-ing through mirrors, so he didn't consciously register what he was seeing. Who would love a person who looked so ordinary? he won-dered, smoothing his rain-matted hair. Not that Tony Hembley was any movie star. Not that he looked this bad every day. *Not as though you have to keep looking if you've seen enough,* he told himself.

A thick white terrycloth robe hung from a hanger suspended from a hook on the back of the bathroom door. He removed the robe and draped it over the top of the shower door, spent a few seconds figur-ing out how the faucet worked while admiring the heaviness of the brass. The bath mat was rolled and placed in a deep, chrome-plated basket attached to the tile at the back wall of the shower, along with a back scrubber enclosed in plastic. Standing under the strong force of the shower, he unwrapped the soap, tossing the wrapper sideways, over his head. The soap smelled of roses and cloves, he decided after some thought; it smelled like something that might be ingested. Tempted to put the tip of his tongue to the heavy oval bar, he touched it instead with the tip of his nose, then smeared it over his cheeks and forehead before placing it in the soap dish and spreading the soap with his hands. If he had brought the razor into the shower he could have shaved, though he was glad he'd left it on the counter because he was enjoying the sybaritic shower. He washed his hair with the soap—something Sonja deeply disapproved of, saying it made his hair look like it had been struck by lightning—then massaged each shoulder as he dialled the showerhead clockwise, increasing the force of the water. What if he looked for another job? What if he went into business with Gordon, assuming Gordon wasn't retired himself? What if he and Sonja had an adventure? What if this time they bought a more expensive house, one with a marble bathroom, the floor matte-black tile, a brass hook on the back of the door strong enough to haul Moby Dick out of the water? What if he got out of the shower transformed, combed his hair straight back in the fashionable European style, put on fresh clothes and went down to the lobby and charmed Alicia, lured her back to the room to spread herself on the bed beneath the impossibly long, swooped neck of the pink flamingo. Maybe instead of being an artistic exaggeration, the flamingo's neck had grown like Pinocchio's nose, responding to all the lies told beneath it, all the breathless *I love you*s. *Cynical, cynical,* he thought. *McCallumesque.*

He stepped carefully from the shower, turning off the water after he got out. He reached for a towel, ran it over himself lightly before pulling on the robe and tying the sash. With a serious expression he faced the mirror again, considered shaving lightly while his skin was still wet, decided to grow a beard. He opened one of the small bottles and squeezed, discharging a tiny slug of bright yellow lotion into the palm of his hand, swiping it over his cheeks and down his neck. It felt strange, as if it were about to sting, though it did not. He massaged it in with awkward delicacy, went to his duffel bag, and rummaged for his comb, taking it into the bathroom and combing his hair back, stepping back from the mirror to look at himself a second time.

He turned up the robe's thick collar, then became suddenly self-conscious, as if this middle-aged man might presume to be Humphrey Bogart in his trench coat. Instead of telling Ingrid Bergman she should leave him, though, he would be urging Sonja to stay. He thought: *We'll always have New Hampshire.*

Sitting in one of the two overstuffed, flame-stitched armchairs, he tucked the robe between his legs and flipped through a magazine that described tourist highlights of South Carolina. He looked at a close-up of a peach, flipped to another page that showed a close-up of a wrinkled black hand holding a puff of cotton. On another page, Marla Maples, Donald Trump, and Marla Maples's mother stood in a line, Marla smiling, Donald either trying to look enigmatic or else dragged down by the weight of his extra-long tie, Marla's mother in profile, no doubt telling the photographer to hurry up before Donald jumped out of the frame. Another page gave recipes for étouffée.

He stretched out on the bed and looked at the ceiling. White, un-marred, a round, unilluminated lightbulb hanging from the center of the ceiling fan. He thought again of *Casablanca.* A couple, arguing, walked down the corridor past his room, their Southern drawls miti-gating the seriousness of what they were saying. He seemed to be objecting to her only liking expensive restaurants; she seemed to be objecting to his objecting. They were thin shadows cast ceilingward, the white enamel fan paddles briefly beheading them.

Dorothy Burwell, he thought. She had been the first girl he had ever argued with. She had said she'd go to a school music concert with him, and then she'd cancelled. Evie had gone with him instead, and there Dorothy Burwell had been, on stage with the sopranos, dressed in a pink dress with pinker flowers, right up there on stage as part of the performance she'd said she'd attend with him. He had said afterward, driving home with Evie, "How could it ever have been possible that she'd be my date when she was part of the choir?" and Evie had tried to make light of it, saying that probably Dorothy had wanted to be with him so she'd practiced a bit of self-deception, pre-tending until the last minute that it was a real possibility. It hadn't seemed very likely to him at the time, but now he thought perhaps Evie had been right. He had not had any experience with conflicted people at that point, or run into many people who responded to things in terms of the way they wanted them to be instead of the way they were. Though there was still the chance Dorothy Burwell had said yes because she didn't know how to say no. Dorothy had spent the first ten years of her life in Savannah, Georgia; she had a Southern accent some of the other kids made fun of, but he had loved it, the way she'd drawn out words as if sentences were a taffy pull.

He looked in the phone book, but Savannah wasn't listed. He rolled over, picked up the phone and called Savannah information. Dorothy's mother had left Dorothy's father when she moved north, but he remembered how proud Dorothy had been of her father and how much she'd missed him. Her father had run the Ford dealership there. Maybe he still did, if he hadn't retired. Or the Ford dealership would be closed; he would think better of calling Dorothy the next morning; the idea could be dispensed with in one quick call. Information gave him the number, the recorded voice telling him to "Please hold for your num-burrr." He wrote it on the pad by the phone, then looked at the phone, wondering if he really wanted to do this. He dialled. He reached a recording, giving the hours when the shop was open. When the beep came to leave a message, he said, "Mr. Burwell, this is a friend of Dorothy's from high school. I remembered that you ran the—"

"Hello?" a man's voice said.

He hadn't expected that. "Hello," he said. "I'm trying to reach Mr. Burwell."

"Speaking," the voice said.

"Hello, sir," he said, becoming again an adolescent. "We've never met, but I went to high school with your daughter Dorothy—"

"Graduated with honors. Very proud of her. Seems like yesterday," the man said.

"Yes," Marshall said. "I was wondering if you knew how I might get in touch with her. To discuss old times," he added lamely.

"Got a few dollars, I hope."

"I beg your pardon?"

"You'll have to call Frankfurt, Germany. She's married to a German fellow and has two German children, one sixteen years old this month, the other one adopted. Just born."

"Oh, I see," he said.

"About the way I look at it. What can you say? She fell in love with a German at the University of Santa Barbara."

"Oh," Marshall said.

"She'd love to hear from you," the man said. "I don't have the number at the shop. I'll give you my home phone number and you can call me. I'll be bowling until ten p.m."

"Thank you," Marshall said. He would never call the man. He would hang up and forget all about it.

"Speaks perfect German," the man said. "Talk fast. Don't let them hang up on you."

"No, sir," Marshall said.

"Here's my number," the man said.

Marshall wrote it down and drew cross-hatches beneath the number.

"Reminds me of the time I looked up an old army buddy. Took about twenty phone calls and when I got him, you know what he said? He said, 'I thought you'd call.' Thirty years later, that was his reaction."

"Did you get together?" Marshall said.

"Meant to, but didn't."

"Uh-huh," Marshall said.

"Not impossible. Don't have but one toe in the grave so far, and I'm not wiggling that one, as they say."

"I'll call you later," Marshall said. "Thank you."

"No problem," the man said. He hung up.

Marshall replaced the phone and rolled over on his back. It had only been a strategy not to call Sonja, he decided. He had no real feeling for Dorothy Burwell. He had not felt disappointment when he heard she was married; he had felt relieved she was out of the country.

He got up and opened the armoire, studied the VCR, opened the box, and slid in *Betrayal*.

By the time it was over, he had decided he could not possibly speak to Sonja. The movie was gripping, a love story that went backward in time, Ben Kingsley the mischievous but calculating husband, wiser than he seemed, revelling in the pain he inflicted. Jeremy Irons was Ben Kingsley's friend as well as his wife's lover, outdone in his game of pretense by Kingsley, the master gamesman. A spectacular scene in a restaurant in which Kingsley, coming apart in Irons's company, speaks about another issue, his voice careening out of control like a runaway car. Marshall was transfixed, admiring such acting talent, in awe of Pinter's script, but also personally rebuked. The woman had fallen in love with Jeremy Irons, at least. But what would he prefer—that his wife have an affair with someone interesting and handsome: Jeremy Irons? Still, it was annoying and slightly puzzling that she had selected Tony Hembley. Even Sonja felt dismissive of him now. She really did; he had seen it in her eyes. He was grateful that she had had the affair with someone who wasn't a personal friend of his. Though, to be honest, he had no personal friends. He thought about McCallum writing on the white bag that Livan Baker had been his friend. He doubted it, though maybe McCallum had felt that, in which case McCallum must have been willing to settle for very little. Even he did not say Livan Baker had depths that were not apparent.

He stood on the bed and pulled the fan's chain, which set it gently spinning. More people passed by, murmuring. He got up and closed the shutters, went back to the bed and thought again of Alicia, not really desiring her, but desiring to desire her. Sort of like Eliot's "distracted from distraction by distraction." What he really desired was something to eat. He closed his eyes, imagining himself dressing, walking out the door, asking at the desk for a recommendation of a good restaurant. He awoke an hour later, the ceiling fan stirring warm air that came through the ceiling vent, the duvet he must have pulled over himself unconsciously shed, the thermostat apparently set for heat without his knowledge. The previous occupant, or Alicia's idea of the perfect temperature?

He decided to forget about dinner, because the rain was still pounding. The problem was, he would probably never fall asleep again, and all he had in the room was the guide to South Carolina. He got up, turned off both the fan and the heat, pulled the duvet back up on the bed, rechecked the drawer in the bedside table: the magazine and the Bible. He picked up the Bible, read randomly for a minute, then found the 121st Psalm and read it. It was inseparable from the context in which he'd heard it years ago, his mother quietly reading, the long time he and Gordon had sat in the room, and then the rainfall that had finally driven their father in from his pacing, Evie holding out a closed umbrella to him, he now remembered—Evie's assumption he would be going back out into the rain, his mother's struggle to take the umbrella away from him, though that wasn't it, she had been trying to take away the bottle in the deep pocket of his coat, saying to him that he was more like her than he admitted, he accusing her of being drunk, Gordon's sliding closer as if the two of them might meld to intensify their strength for the battle that was about to break out. He and Gordon as still as stones, Evie snatching the bottle away from their father, opening it, and pouring the contents out, the stench of alcohol as strong as the smell of vomit as it slushed into the sink. So many things passed from hand to hand, as if a mad version of hot potato were being played; the umbrella first in their mother's hands, then grabbed by Evie; their father reaching for it and stumbling over the table; more paperdolls and coloring books spilled; the ripping off of the paperdolls' arms, and their mother staring, suddenly still and staring, saying, "Is that what you'd really like to do? Don't you think you've done enough to destroy us all already?" He had destroyed them, their mother had said, and Evie had tried to quiet her. The umbrella had flown open, and then their father was gone, the wind blowing in the front door as Gordon sat with his leg pressed against Marshall's. Marshall had stopped watching. In the darkness he heard the rain, heard their father cursing, and then the sound of his car, motor racing, then tires skidding on wet pavement, followed by Evie's deep sigh that seemed to have absorbed much of the outside wind, her exhaled breath a barely registering whistle as she collapsed on the sofa and turned to them, looking through them instead of meeting their eyes, saying to their mother, who had rushed to the window to watch the car disappear, "My God, they're terrified." He remembered their mother turning toward them then, coming back toward the center of the room but then stopping to carefully pick up the paperdolls and put them back in the box, the mother and father, son and daughter, dog and cat paperdolls she had helped him carefully cut from the pages, tucking the torn pieces in the side pocket of her white nightgown, leaving to Evie the job of comforting them and getting them to bed. The umbrella lay on the carpet, and Evie had muttered something about how absurd it had been to care if he got wet, why should either of them care that he had rushed off in a senseless fit of anger, what did it matter if a person got wet? In bed, they had heard their mother quietly crying, Evie whispering, their mother's crying abating. Gordon had whispered, "I don't think they want him to come back," and Marshall had nodded silently in the dark, thinking: if someone had to go, best that he was the one. He had been sure he would never see his father again. His presence would be extraneous to their family, like the little girl paperdoll, the dog and cat paperdolls. "He was drunk," Gordon had whispered. "Maybe she was, too," Gordon had said. "I'm not sure she's going to die." But that turned out to be wishful thinking. Like a shred of paper disappearing into a pocket, she had died the following year.

All his life, Marshall had connected rain with death.

20

—————

JANET LANIER'S VOICE, when she answered the phone, was weary. "Jack McCallum's friend. My daughter's teacher. Right," she said. In the background, children's voices shouted responses to something on TV. "Do you have children yourself?"

"No," he said.

"I don't suppose you need to be a parent to be a teacher," she said. "Teaching at Benson College—is that like teaching children or teaching adults? I understand you do have a wife," she added. When she slurred the word "understand," what he understood was that Janet Lanier was drinking. Then he heard her sip from her glass. One of her children raising his voice to her, or to someone else. A door banging. "Jack isn't here," she said. "As to how you can get in touch with him, I'd say to call Lexington information and ask for Lenore Brighton's number on Pine Street. That will get you my cousin. I don't think they'd have a phone. Maybe you can persuade Lenore to go across the street and knock on the door."

"I'm sorry?"

"You don't know?" Genuine surprise was mixed with her weariness.

"He left the motel before I woke up. He left a note saying he was going to your house to talk to you."

"Ah," she said. On the TV, someone got off a round of gunfire. Then: "So he did."

He listened to the confusion of her house, as if, by focussing, he could sort through that and determine whether she might have said what he thought she'd said. He could almost see it: the children, excited, taking the opportunity of Mom's being on the phone to act up, quarrel, change channels, slam doors.

"I would never have recognized him," she said. "Handsome Jack McCallum. Now he's underfed and has such a haunted look. I think he's haunted himself, if you know what I mean." She put her hand over the phone, spoke inaudibly to whoever was speaking to her. "His injuries are quite serious, though I could have done without seeing the gash in his side." She cleared her throat. "Would you like to come over?" she said. "Might as well talk about this face-to-face."

He looked at the highway. Across the street was a discount boot store. A large pink neon boot repeatedly kicked a falling star. Next to that was a liquor store with an unlit neon sign of a huge martini glass tipped almost on its side. At the base of the sign was a tangle of pink and orange bougainvillea. "I'm in Islamorada," he said.

"Then I guess you wouldn't like to come over," she said. "I don't find that many people do come over, including my husband."

Marshall decided to ignore that remark. It was as if flames leaped from it. "He said he'd known you years ago at camp," Marshall said hollowly.

She laughed. A small dry laugh, or a cough—he couldn't be sure.

Why was it, he wondered, that involving himself in any aspect of McCallum's life always made him perplexed and vulnerable? "Perplexed" was too mild a word. He was so shocked by McCallum, so often, that now he was trying to quell his reactions by downplaying what his emotions really were. Yet again, McCallum had omitted significant information. He and Cheryl were together, in Lexington, Virginia. This was what Cheryl's mother had just said, surely it was what she had just said. He looked at the ground, at the asphalt strewn with dropped blossoms and crushed cigarettes. Across the highway, the star descended toward the boot's pointed toe. He was standing at a phone outside a seafood restaurant in Islamorada.

"I won't keep you," he said. "If you see him, tell him I called to see how he was doing," he added lamely.

"Did you think I might be having them to Sunday dinner?"

"Excuse me?"

"Jack and Cheryl. Did you think I might roast a chicken and have them for Sunday dinner?" She covered the receiver again, but this time her words were audible: everyone in the room was going to go straight to bed if there was any more fighting over Nintendo. He imagined her there, stuck in the chaos of her life, a woman who had just gotten the information that her ex-boyfriend from about thirty years ago was now her daughter's lover. "Hang on. I have to switch to the extension," she said.

As he waited, he thought of hanging up. He was embarrassed that he was both too shocked and too curious to do it. What a story he would have to tell Sonja when he next spoke to her. He could imagine no way to tell her this on the phone.

"Hang it up, Richard," Janet Lanier hollered.

The phone was hung up. When she spoke to him, the absence of background noise was stunning, almost surreal, like trees becoming still in the wake of a storm.

"I assumed you knew. Cheryl said you knew she'd been raped—how would she not have told you about her great savior Jack? Did you know Cheryl had been raped?"

"She told me," he said.

"By one of the nicest people, I thought, I'd ever known. I have to believe her. I wish she'd said something at the time. But now I find that I was the last to know." She cleared her throat. "Of course, I have to believe her," she said again.

It was incredibly perplexing. So Cheryl had known McCallum all along? Known him when Livan Baker made her accusation? Known that he had come to be with her the night she came into Dolly's restaurant, and that was why she was so troubled when she discovered both that Marshall was present and also that he meant to contact her mother? McCallum had instigated this trip knowing he'd jump ship in Virginia. Why hadn't he just flown there? Why had it been necessary to involve him, to mislead him by saying the rendezvous with Cheryl was for his sake, too?

"You knew that he arranged financial aid for Cheryl, didn't you?" Janet Lanier said. "All those years we kept in touch, and he was so helpful. So 'supportive,' I believe the current term is. He sent me so many letters years ago. Do you know, I began to fantasize we'd get together when he finished college. We'd get married, we'd have nice lust instead of backseat lust. All these years later, suddenly there's Jack, standing in my kitchen. The two of them, come to set me straight about what I didn't know. And the worst thing is, I forgive her. She's foolish, but I'm stupid. Do you know what I thought as they stood there, my Cheryl so brazen, trying to change the conversation by blaming me for having her baptized and naming her a godfather, as if those things were the same as arranging to have her raped? I thought: He'll stop at nothing. A boy from summer camp, who once taught me to swim. He used to stand out there in the water, hollering instructions, blowing his whistle, and then before we got out of the water he'd always do the same thing: the dead man's float. He could hold his breath so long, we'd all race for him in a panic. I can still see him in the pond, not moving a muscle. Then he comes to Buena Vista and takes my daughter's hand, claiming to be in love with her. Whatever she thinks she's doing, I know he's still doing the dead man's float. What does he think he's going to do to support her? He'll have to take her back to New Hampshire. Is that what's going to happen? Is she going to live with him down the street from you?"

"I don't live anywhere near him," he said. He was grateful that there was finally something he could say.

"A thought like this doesn't even cross your mind. It reminds me that most murder victims know their murderer. Or is that an old wives' tale? I think they know them, that they're lovers or aunts or uncles or whatever they are. The same way so many people get broken bones from accidents right in their own house. People walk fine when they're outside, then they slip in the tub. Have you heard this, or am I imagining it?"

He said, "I have heard that." He wanted to get off the phone. He had called someone who was drunk, whose life was a mess, who had been deceived all her life and then slapped in the face.

"And to think: I used to write her letters asking if she had dates. I thought she might be at dances, or going to parties and building snowmen—the pictures I'd seen in the Benson College catalog. Are you sure you don't want to come by so we can cry on each other's shoulders? You don't exactly seem to be holding up your end of the conversation."

"I'm eleven hundred miles away," he said.

"You are? Where are you?"

"Islamorada," he told her again. He wouldn't blame her for not believing him; it sounded like an invented name for an invented place.

Islamorada. How about Uranus? Just some strange point on the planet where he was standing in a parking lot, talking on the phone. Why? Why had he not learned that McCallum and everything associated with McCallum did nothing but cause him pain. He was a compulsive liar. Dangerous, probably. Set on a trajectory he sucked people into, tossing them aside at his convenience. He felt humiliated for both of them—for himself, and for Janet Lanier. To know McCallum was to be humiliated by your own vulnerabilities.

In the parking lot, a windblown couple got out of an old Oldsmobile convertible, the woman taking off her visor and running her fingers through her hair, the man in a tank top and white Bermuda shorts bending forward and backward to stretch himself. Though the lot was mostly empty, it held quite an assortment of cars: a blue Miata with New Mexico plates that read GOERNER; a Jeep; Toyotas; BMWs. There were window boxes filled with bright pink flowers and drips of dark green ivy. Over one of the window boxes a monarch butterfly hovered. Two monarch butterflies. He thought of a photograph he had once seen of Vladimir Nabokov running with his butterfly net. He thought of *Lolita*. What a second-rate Lolita Cheryl Lanier had been—not particularly pretty, but most of all, distinct from Lolita in that she had not been genuinely needy; she was just another person who wanted things.

"Do you believe me when I tell you I didn't have the slightest idea that McCallum and your daughter—"

"That makes two of us," she said. "I'm glad to know it doesn't have something to do with my lack of sophistication."

"Sophistication," he said. "I don't think it's a lack of sophistication. It's just not possible to keep up with him."

"You get thrown off by people who go to great lengths to explain themselves," she said. "What I mean is, you take what they say to be explanations. I kept his letters explaining himself from the end of that summer until about 1975. I got rid of most of them when we moved. While I was packing boxes I reread them, and you know what? I was a grown woman by then, and I didn't believe any longer I'd been the great love of his life, but I believed he still missed me. That I was special."

"I'm sorry," Marshall said. It sounded lame, inconclusive. It was probably the last time he would speak to Janet Lanier.

The man in white Bermudas came out carrying a bag of takeout food. The woman in the visor held his hand. *An ordinary couple,* he thought. Then he immediately wondered if there was such a thing as an ordinary couple.

"Your husband," he said to Janet Lanier. "Is it true he's got a girlfriend in Michigan?"

"True," she said.

Why had he asked? He stared after the couple, the woman giving a little skip as she leaned into him and appeared to be saying something joking. He could not remember the last time he and Sonja had seemed close—close and casual about the closeness. They had let too many things from outside influence their moods: the routine of their jobs; Evie's illness. Then he had an image of Cheryl Lanier, appearing like an apparition in the snowstorm, his pulling over to give her a ride, the moment when he involved himself in something from which he felt he was still trying to retreat.

"Why do you ask?" she said.

"Because I can't believe anything either of them has ever told me. I wondered—generally, I sort of wondered whether you're going to be all right," he said.

Were those awkward words really the ones that came out of his mouth: "generally, I sort of wondered"?

"Yes," she said. "I'll be fine."

"I'm sorry I'm so far from Buena Vista," he said. "Right now, I think I'm probably the only person who could understand exactly what you're saying, and you're the only person who could understand—"

"That'll change," she said, a little abruptly. "Your wife will be very sympathetic about the hoops you've had to jump through."

"We've had some trouble lately," he said. "But you're right, of course. She won't believe the continuation of this story. Which I don't think we've probably heard the end of, have we?"

"No. I can't imagine we have."

"Your husband," he said. "You aren't worried about being physically harmed, are you?"

"What would make you ask that?"

"Well, clearly not intuition," he said. "I don't seem to have any of that."

"Men don't have it the way women do," she said. "That's true. But don't blame yourself for not understanding Jack. Jack has to have an audience. He always did. He always finds it, too. Even if it takes doing the dead man's float."

"You were kids," he said.

He and Janet Lanier had so clearly been an audience for McCallum's madness. But he had been the audience for other things, too: if he stood behind a lectern and lectured on literature, he was still only speaking publicly about works for which he had been a passive, willing audience. As a child, he had followed instead of leading. It was always someone else—his mother, that night in the living room; Sonja, in a discussion he thought had been only that, an exchange of ideas, dropping the bomb about Tony; all the way back to Gordon, who had explained things, like Sherlock Holmes to the young Dr. Watson. He would have believed anything his older brother said. It was as if things were not real until Gordon discussed them. He could remember, with slight humiliation now, asking Gordon whether it was true it was going to rain the next day.

He said goodbye to Janet Lanier, vaguely aware that she had not answered his earlier question, but taking her evasion as a dismissal of his concerns. Cheryl had seemed so protective of her mother, but in thinking it over, maybe what she said, even about her mother's physical appearance, had been untrue. Maybe she knew her mother was still pretty, but she wanted to pretend otherwise because she feared McCallum's affections might waver. Maybe her hair was attractively gray, but Cheryl had needed to emphasize her mother's age, as opposed to her own youthfulness. She was a seductive girl. He remembered sitting with her in the restaurant, her drinking his drink while he was on the phone. There he had been, telling a white lie to Sonja about whom he was with, while she had probably spent the day fucking Tony Hembley.

Everywhere he looked, there were couples in the restaurant. Couples in booths, everyone with someone else, only a few tables filled with people clustered together who seemed to be friends: the odd man out, the unaccompanied woman. The customers seemed happy, smiling, and tan, vacationers taking time out, intent on having a good time.

The waitress handed him the menu and a list of specials. He ordered a scotch and water, changed it to a gin and tonic before the waitress walked away. It seemed more tropical. He was somewhere called Islamorada. Out the window he saw the window boxes, the pink pansies, the monarchs, he saw now, plastic butterflies on springs, bobbing in the breeze.

21

DRIVING INTO KEY WEST he passed what seemed like endless shopping malls, filled with building-supply stores, open-air nurseries, discount liquor stores, stores selling aloe products. In spite of the state of the economy, the building boom was still on in Key West. Its advantage to Gordon was that it had allowed him to move off a distant key onto Key West itself, which Beth had been lobbying for since she'd married Gordon on a sailboat at sunset five years before.

The previous night, after talking to Janet Lanier, Marshall had called from the seafood restaurant. Beth had answered the phone after so many rings he'd been about to give up. A party roared in the background: the Byrds, he had decided, as the music overwhelmed Beth's voice. The best he could make out was that Gordon and some friends had gone on a late-night sail. She urged him to come immediately, while there was still seafood pizza. He heard people yelling, splashing in the pool. "What will you give me. . . ." he heard. It was the Byrds.

He told a white lie. Told her he'd run out of steam, was stopping to spend the night at a motel he'd just checked into; he'd be in Key West before noon the next day. It sounded as if a tractor had toppled into the pool. "Oh God!" Beth said, the rest of her sentence drowned out by women shrieking and music overlaying the Byrds—live music, he guessed. He wondered who the neighbors were.

Gordon's first wife, Caroline, had left him after five years, taking their daughter with her, moving to Mexico. Gordon had heard, from Caroline's cousin Rawlins, who passed through Key West and went into the shop Gordon worked in, that Caroline had remarried another American while she was in medical school in Mexico, and that they'd gone to Rome to join a group of American and French doctors. When Caroline left the United States, Gordon decided to, as he put it, "cut my losses" and not have further contact with Caroline or with Julia. Caroline had been bitterly opposed to his having a relationship with his daughter. She had done everything she could to thwart him, but leaving the country had finally been successful.

Gordon's second wife stayed married to him for about two years. She had a teenage son when they married, but the boy was in military school and visited infrequently, usually for a week or so during summer vacation. They'd lived in Fort Lauderdale then, and Gordon had been a late-night weekend disc jockey for the local radio station, as well as assistant manager of the bar Lissa worked in. Sonja had asked Lissa, when she married Gordon, what the boy's interests were. She wanted to send him birthday presents. She was very thoughtful about that sort of thing. The answer, as best Marshall remembered, had been pornographic magazines and fencing, which had pretty much stymied Sonja in her pursuit of appropriate gifts. That marriage had also ended badly, with Lissa getting a quickie divorce and marrying a much older man. About that time, Gordon had started to work for the dive shop he'd stayed at until he started living with Beth. Then he'd gone into partnership with another person, borrowing money from Evie, which had slightly shocked Sonja, along with five thousand dollars from Marshall and Sonja after a desperate late-night phone call, which he'd paid back after a year, with interest. Sonja had returned the interest part of the check, and Gordon—whether he'd been sincere or meant to be funny—had sent a "thank-you" gift of a pitcher shaped like a parrot, a set of glass swizzle sticks topped with pineapples, cherries, and bananas, and a box of instant margarita mix. As far as Marshall knew, Gordon had lived alone in between Lissa and Beth. He'd married Lissa in a large wedding in her hometown of Memphis, wearing a rented tuxedo to accompany his bride, in an ornate white bridal dress she'd told Sonja her mother had kept on a dress form in her sewing room from the day Lissa turned sixteen. For her first marriage, Lissa had eloped, but her mother had never gotten rid of the dress. Once a week—this was true years after the second marriage and was probably still the routine—Lissa's mother set her hairdryer on "cool" and blew air on the dress to remove any dust. The curtains were kept pulled in the room so the dress wouldn't yellow. Sonja had related this to him with amazement, late one night in bed. He and Sonja and Evie had gone to the wedding, flying out of Boston and staying at the Peabody Hotel, which was famous for having a flock of ducks that got off the elevator and marched into the lobby to swim in the fountain twice a day. The day before the wedding, Sonja and Evie had gone to Graceland and bought plastic place mats depicting Elvis in his various jumpsuits, smiling. He could remember the place mats propped up on the window ledge, Sonja shaking her head at them as she sprawled on the big bed: all those views of dead Elvis in his sparkle suits.

He had only met Beth twice: soon after her wedding, and a year later, when she flew to New Hampshire with Gordon to attend Evie's birthday party. She was now in her early forties, a short, slim woman with streaked blond hair and inch-long red fingernails who seemed to him a mixture of simultaneous shyness and extroversion. She had blushed and mumbled when anything resembling a personal question was asked of her, but she'd also brought a big suitcase filled with Mary Kay cosmetics, which she sold, and had insisted the women who had come for coffee and birthday cake stand under falling mists of various fragrances to see which most suited them. Evie's birthday present had been a bottle of perfumed lotion and a small pink kit containing blush, eyeshadow, and lipstick. Evie wore no makeup. She gave it to Sonja after Beth left.

He passed the dive shop on Route 1 where Gordon used to work, recognizing it from the time he'd been in Key West years before, with Sonja. The dive shop was his landmark; Marshall set his odometer and began to look for the other markers Gordon had given him. In five minutes, he'd pulled onto Simonton and found the house: a white frame house with a new roof and rotten boards and broken shutters piled in the front lawn next to a banyan tree whose trunk took up half the front yard. Two long, splintered window boxes sat at curbside, along with a recycling container loaded with beer cans and upside-down liquor bottles. One window box was empty, an end broken off. The other held one yellowish hemp plant. The brackets were on the back, rust bleeding through white paint. One high-heeled shoe lay on its side in a puddle. The front door was ajar. A rooster, bobbing out from behind water-soaked cardboard boxes thrown under a dead palm, crowed piercingly as Marshall approached the gate, surprising him so he jumped back, grabbed the sunglasses he'd just removed so hard he feared he'd broken the arm. He hadn't. He blew on his glasses, cleaned them on his shirttail. Back on his nose, they were only slightly less smeared.

People on mopeds sped by. A truck carrying lumber, with a white handkerchief dangling from an end of a board, crept along behind the mopeds. Behind that came an elderly man pedalling a bicycle. He wore blowsy swim trunks, a white Isadora Duncan scarf dangling down his bare chest, and green clogs. A small brown dog hung its head out of the bike basket fastened to the front; behind him, he pulled a slightly larger dog in a basket on wheels. That dog also wore a scarf. A bandanna. What difference did it make? He moved backward to lean against the hood of his car and look at the house. A new window had just been set in beside the front door; plywood covered a hole to the left of the door. A wicker chair and a chair with several broken brown and beige plastic straps sat on the front porch, where a work table was also set up. A palm grew out of a plastic garbage can, pushed up against the plywood window. Above the door was a curved window of etched cranberry glass. From inside, music that sounded like the vocal equivalent of a whirling dervish floated out, though it was nowhere near as loud as the music from the night before. The neighbors, he saw, were a small bodega and, on the other side, a boarded-up house with a rotting boat in the front yard. Several cats watched him from the bow of the boat. A hula hoop was draped over one arm of a lamppost twined with faded red tinsel. A stocky man wearing a leather cap, leather jeans, and leather vest walked by, his chains jingling. Marshall looked back at the house. Three roosters followed their mother out Beth and Gordon's gate, heading for the next yard. This was the neighborhood Beth preferred to the cluster of contemporary houses on the channel on Duck Key? The singer's voice soared, repeating the same phrase over and over as he went up the walkway, trying to avoid tripping on scattered bricks and heaved-up cement. The first step was two thicknesses of board; the other steps were cinder block.

"Oh, great!" Beth yelled, as he rang the doorbell and "The Star-Spangled Banner" played. "Great, great, great," she yelled, rushing to greet him.

As he remembered, she was short and thin, but her hair was now very pale blond, streaked with pink. She was wearing enormous gold earrings and a silver choker. She had on a tightly knotted white halter top that revealed half her rib cage, and striped sultan pants. Her toenails were painted bright pink. She leaped into his arms.

"Don't say you didn't get a warm welcome," she said. The earrings swayed, making a cacophonous noise inside his head.

"Well, I appreciate it," he said, returning her hug with slightly less strength.

"What is this, are you having some crisis like Gordon says? He's gone to get briquettes to cook your dinner. You missed the clam pizza with white sauce last night. Best you'll ever eat, brought all the way from Miami. Come in. I'm a little wired because I just got out of my step class. Come in, Gordon would hate me for holding you in the doorway."

His first thought was that it was good Sonja wasn't with him. His second thought was that he was surprised—inside, the house was in very good shape. He followed her through a long pine-panelled hallway with a central ceiling fan. He glanced into several small rooms on the right side of the hallway as he walked past. In the first, where the door was propped open with an iron Scottie dog, he saw a dressing table and mirror on a white shag carpet and several white folding chairs. That was the Mary Kay room, he thought. Next was a dark room with the door almost closed. After that, the bathroom, the track lights glowing, steam on the mirror, a pleasant, fresh, wet smell. The largest area of the house was the main room, a room about twenty by thirty, at the end of which were sliding screen doors, through which he could see a raised hot tub and black iron benches with flowered cushions. She pushed open the screen and motioned for him to follow. In several large terra-cotta pots on wheeled platforms, variously colored bougainvillea bloomed. A seven-foot-high wall surrounded the back deck, hung at intervals with mirrors, in ornate picture frames, that needed to be resilvered. Several orchids hung in pots suspended from a tree limb that stretched from the bodega's backyard to overhang the deck. Standing beside him, she smiled brightly as he looked around. Beside the steps leading up to the hot tub he saw the mate to the high heel in the puddle outside the house. An aluminum garbage can held discarded liquor bottles and beer cans. On the redwood table, a pitcher held birds-of-paradise.

"It's beautiful," he said. "A real surprise."

"We're going to eat out here tonight," she said, ducking back into the house and turning down the volume of the boom box that sat on the kitchen counter. "He wants it so picture perfect, he even keeps the grill behind that fence, there." She pointed to a bamboo screen.

"This is amazing," he said. "How long did it take you to do this?"

"Helped along by my winning at blackjack," she said. "No kidding. They might get me later, but that time I had the sense to take the money and run."

"Well," he said. "It's really wonderful. You'd never think this was back here."

"He wants to keep the front looking like shit so people won't break in. I've got to get you to persuade him that stuff has got to go. There was a bathtub there until the day before yesterday. If people are going to break in, they break in. You can't spend your life trying to protect yourself." A little lizard darted from the hot tub to the bamboo screen and disappeared. Above them, the sky was a cloudless, deep blue. "I don't see any point in fighting obstacles," she said. "The climate here is perfect, as far as I'm concerned. And in the summer you just go from air-conditioning to air-conditioning. The bedroom's air-conditioned," she said. "So are we going to convert you to Key West? If everything goes right, your brother could be retired and a rich man and you could sit around on the back deck with him, shoot the breeze. I'm going to get you a drink. What kind of drink would you like?"

He began to think the parrot pitcher hadn't been a joke.

"Corona," she said, before he could answer. She walked to the long narrow kitchen bordering the living room. The floor was tiled a deep green-blue; a counter divided the kitchen from the rest of the room. A big ceiling fan stirred the air.

"Are you upset about Evie's death?" she said, coming toward him, holding two opened beers. "Is that a subject I should avoid?" she said, before he had time to answer.

"No, not at all," he said. "I mean, it isn't a subject you should avoid. We both—I'm glad we found a nursing home that seemed like a good place. Sonja visited her often. I'm afraid I didn't go as often as I should have."

"I'm always making mistakes in what I'm not supposed to say,"

Beth said. "Remember when I gave her a makeup kit? I knew when she wasn't wearing makeup on her birthday, when we first walked in, that I'd made a mistake." She relinquished one of the beer bottles to him. "I hope she used the lotion," she said.

"I don't really know if she used it," he said.

"I like you," Beth said. "That's a good answer." She fingered the silver choker. "She was very kind to remember me," she said. "Is this something that has a history in the family? I asked Gordon, but according to him, he doesn't remember anything."

"The necklace?" he said, following her back outside.

She nodded.

"You mean it's Evie's?"

"Yes," she said, a little put out. "You don't remember it either?"

"I'm not the right person to ask. I don't notice things like jewelry, usually."

"Well, that makes two of you. You and your brother."

She sat on the black iron bench. He sat in a chair. In the distance, he heard a dog yapping. A plane passing overhead.

"When did Evie give you the necklace?" he said.

She fingered it. "When she died. There was a nurse friend of hers who packaged some things from her room and sent them to us. I hope I haven't said something I shouldn't have said. This nurse said she was supposed to pass on things to both you and Gordon. She said Evie reminded her all the time, and they had a joke: the nurse would pretend to scold her, saying, 'Is that the only thing you keep forgetting? You mean that's the one and only thing you're senile about?' She'd promised her a hundred times she'd do it, she said." She sipped her beer. "She seemed quite nice on the phone," she said.

"Yes. I know who you mean. She was very nice. She did bring us things, come to think of it, on the day of the funeral."

"I feel bad we didn't come to Evie's funeral," Beth said.

He shrugged. "To come all that way for someone you didn't really know," he said.

"I know, but I was surprised Gordon didn't go. He went and sat on the floor of the ocean. That's what he spent the day doing."

"Well," he said, "that would have been a long way to come just for the funeral."

"He doesn't like to face some things," she said.

"No, I suppose none of us do," he said.

"But he just doesn't do it. I had a lump in my breast biopsied last year. Everything was fine, but the day he was supposed to go to the doctor's office—we weren't even going to hear right then, it was just a biopsy—he had somebody call from work to say he'd gotten tied up. He didn't even call me himself!"

"That's unfortunate," Marshall said.

"It is unfortunate. He has more capabilities than he calls on."

Marshall nodded. He would just as soon not hear these things about Gordon.

"Maybe a lot was expected of him when he was young," Beth said. "It was that way with my older brother. I have an older brother, too. He works for a conservation group in Africa. He'd do anything for an animal, but he doesn't even send my mother a birthday card. Sometimes a postcard, but there's never much information on it. She was going to visit him once, and he told her there were too many diseases, not to come."

"He was probably telling her for her own sake," Marshall said.

"Men stick together, they really do." She sighed. "I don't even believe that you believe that."

"I don't," Marshall said.

"I like you," she said again. She looked around. "I was thinking about getting a few ficus, or something like that. Do you think there's enough greenery, or would more look nice?"

"It looks perfect to me, but I'm not very good at envisioning things when they aren't in place."

"Hmm," she said. "Gordon's very good at that, usually. You know what he does? He gets a piece of paper and he draws polka dots on it. He says doing that allows him to envision what things will look like before he breaks his back moving everything."

He nodded.

"Did he tell you about the letters?"

"Letters?" He had been thinking about ficus trees. Were ficus the ones with small, wrinkly leaves? The ones they sold sometimes in the supermarket in New Hampshire?

"He didn't tell you," she said, matter-of-factly. "I don't suppose I thought he really had." She slid forward, placing her feet together, the beer bottle half-empty. "Don't tell him I told you," she said.

"What about letters?" he said.

"The nurse. That woman, who was so nice. She called to say they'd be coming. I really shouldn't tell you this, because you almost got the letters. Evie was going to give them to Sonja and you until just before she died. She changed her mind, the nurse said, and wanted them to be sent to me and Gordon. I hardly knew her, so she was sending them to Gordon, not to me."

He frowned.

"Don't tell him," she said again.

"Okay," he said.

"Well, she called to say how sorry she was, but to say she'd heard from the nurses at the hospital that she didn't die a painful death, and all of that. Gordon told her we'd see her at the funeral. I was going to go. If he went, I was going to go with him. Anyway, the nurse was calling to say she was sending the things by Federal Express, because she didn't feel right about putting jewelry in the mail and just mailing it. I told Gordon he should send some money to reimburse her, that that was probably what she was hinting about. Well, she did send it. This necklace was in its original box, from a jewelry store in Boston. I kept the box, because it's beautiful too. I started to read the letters, but I didn't understand anything in them. Sort of business letters, about somebody's delayed arrival. They were boring, to tell you the truth. I put them aside and thought maybe I'd look at them again some other time, and then Gordon got home from work and started reading them. They were in three packages, tied with ribbon. He read about half of one pack and then he said, 'You know, the truth of the matter is, I don't much like surprises.' He doesn't, either. He likes to know in advance what I'm getting him for his birthday. He told me right out, when I hardly knew him, that if I ever gave him a surprise party, he'd never speak to me again. I wish you'd gotten the letters, because then I could find out if that stuff meant anything. I saw them and they didn't look like love letters. I think he was just teasing. But he didn't like having them, so do you know what he did? He took them with him when he made a night dive. He and his buddy went out together, and when he went down he tucked the whole pile of them under a rock on the bottom of the ocean. Littering the Atlantic! At first I thought he was kidding me, but then it turns out to be true. He took a bunch of her old letters and drowned them."

"Jesus," Marshall said. He remembered, now, the box the nurse had brought with her to the house the day of the funeral. With the exception of the necklace, Evie had given Sonja the entire contents of her jewel box. His father's pocket watch had been in there. Sonja had given that to him. It seemed almost obscene that Tony Hembley had looked at it admiringly—that he had stood in the living room, joining the little cluster of Sonja and Marshall and the nurse, and peered into the pink satin jewel box and looked appreciatively at the watch Sonja drew out, his father's octagonal watch dangling from its platinum watch fob. The nurse had done just what Evie had asked. Her timing might have been better, but he supposed that if someone other than Tony had gazed in, he wouldn't feel so cantankerous. It was hardly a private matter, really: a box filled with an old lady's brooches and rings, bracelets and necklaces, costume jewelry with only a few precious stones dropped in among the tangle, Sonja had told him later. It wasn't as if the Hope diamond were hiding in there.

"I think maybe it made him sentimental," Beth said. "Letters from so long ago."

A bird began to shriek, its piercing cries making Beth spring up, grabbing the top of the fence and hissing at a cat that had begun to prowl the bird's cage in the neighbors' yard. "They hooked up some electronic thing that was supposed to keep that cat ten feet from the birdcage," Beth said. "It works all day until late afternoon, and then I just don't know. The cat's right in there like there was nothing set up at all." Next came a recorded voice, as he watched her, white-knuckled, clinging to the fence. "You have entered a secured area," the voice said. "Oh, fuck you," Beth said to the recording. "If I didn't grab the fence and hiss, that three-hundred-dollar bird would be dead, and that would be a very happy alley cat."

"Where are the people?" he said.

"Oh, they don't ever do anything about their hair-trigger alarm. They're probably inside smoking dope."

"Really?" he said.

"Oh, I don't know. The owners keep going back and forth between here and Boca Raton, and they've got some Rastas staying in there who don't care about anything but dope and sunshine. Why they'd leave the bird that way, I don't know. The guy really likes the bird. He's out there every evening he's home, trying to get it to say things."

"What does it say?" Marshall said.

"It says 'Margaritaville' and 'tropical breeze' and things like that. Now it says 'good weed.' His girlfriend's the one who rented to the Rastas. Now he's gonna be furious at her."

"Hey, beauty!" the bird hollered. "Hellooooooooo."

"I save your life every day. Can you say, 'Save my life?'" Beth hollered.

Silence from the bird.

"I do," she said.

Marshall sloshed the last inch of beer around in the bottle. He could see living this way: blue skies; warm winters; flowers.

"Hey, Marsh!" Gordon hollered, appearing at the end of the long hallway. He was backlit, just a shape, his features indistinguishable as Marshall went toward him. Gordon embraced him one-armed; the other held a bag of charcoal and a string bag dangling from his thumb, filled with things from the store.

"Hey, I hope the party didn't keep you away last night. You didn't check into a motel just because those idiots hadn't cleared out, did you?"

"No, no," Marshall said. Gordon smelled of alcohol. Beth stood smiling at him, having picked up both empty beer bottles.

"Corona, babe?" she said.

"Yeah, sweetie. Thanks," he said. He put his arm around Marshall's shoulder. "Very good to see you here, man," he said. This time he sounded more enthusiastic. "Hey, quite the transformation, don't you think?" he said.

"He never saw it before," Beth said.

"Oh, right. Right. We were out on Duck Key when you and Sonja came down a few years back. Right," Gordon said. "Well, nothing would do for Beth but to be a townie, hey, hon?"

"I didn't want to live my life driving in from Duck Key," she said.

"She doesn't appreciate the fact I have to work for a living," Gordon said. "She wants us to live like it's our twilight years right now, today. Maybe I can hunch myself over and limp over there near the kitchen and get me a beer for my twilight years. Toast them the way we bring New Year's in."

"People retire in the United States before they're old," Beth said. "What's so wrong with having money and deciding how you want to spend your days? Some of us, rich or not, prefer to spend them kicking along parallel to the ocean floor. I guess I understand that by now."

"Don't give me that shit. You see me plenty. Plenty more than you want to sometimes. He'd shown up last night, I could get more of a report on what a party girl you are than you might provide me with yourself."

"I have never flirted with a human being since the day we tied the knot," Beth said. She had opened three beers and put the bottles on the kitchen counter. She opened a jar of peanuts.

"Vacuum-packed," Gordon said, taking the jar from her. "Close as she gets to a vacuum." Gordon laughed.

"This place is fantastic," Marshall said.

"You got yourself a new house, didn't you?" Gordon said.

"No. We've been in the same place since we moved to New Hampshire."

"Is that right? I thought you'd gotten yourself another place."

"No," Marshall said.

"I guess you'd know," Gordon said.

"Honey, did you get any food?" she said, unloading the string bag.

"All the way down," he said.

She pulled out a package wrapped in white wax paper. "Oh, snapper," she said. "Good. Do you like snapper, Marshall?"

"Very much," he said.

"You look just great. Come on outside and we'll drink these beers," Gordon said. "Outside, by Mount Vesuvius."

"He calls the hot tub Mount Vesuvius," Beth said, rolling her eyes. She pushed two of the beer bottles toward them. Gordon, like Beth, was thin—thinner than Marshall had last seen him, and slightly wobbly on his feet. His hair was combed strangely, a crooked part dumping long bangs over half his face. His nose was red: drink, or sunburn? His brother was in constant motion: wiping his hands on each side of his jeans, passing the bottle of Corona from one hand to the other as he dried his hands; tucking the long flap of hair behind his ears, freeing it; scratching his chest, adjusting his shirt.

"She tell you how she got that hot tub?" Gordon said.

"He loves this story," Beth said.

"She had it delivered; never mentioned the first thing about it,"

Gordon said. "Her girlfriend came down with meningitis. What happens but Beth starts waitressing for her. Don't outguess me here: she does *not* make the money in tips. She makes the money—this is gonna kill you—a guy comes into the Hyatt, sitting at the bar, he's got a cold. Miss Health-Conscious gives the guy her jar of vitamin C out of her bag, tells him when he gets back to his room to take the vitamins, then put a hot washcloth on top of his head, and sit in a chair for ten minutes, thinking positive thoughts about the disappearance of the cold. You know what happens? This'll make you laugh, but the first time Beth tells you this, I swear by it: it works. She presses the vitamin C on him—"

"One thousand milligrams a pop," Beth said. "You have to have a high concentration to make it work."

"Yeah, babe, but you say that's also not good for your kidneys," Gordon said, pushing the screen door farther back, walking out on the deck. Marshall followed.

"Here's what happened," Gordon said. "She goes into work the next day and the guy has left an envelope for her, doesn't even know her name, just writes on the outside it's for the blond-haired waitress with the flower earrings who was on the previous night at ten p.m. The bartender takes it, writes 'Beth' on it. She gets there and opens it: four thousand dollars—a buck for every milligram of vitamin C. The guy thinks he's found a miracle worker, someone who's got the cure for the common cold. Says so, in his note. It used to be hung on the refrigerator with one of those refrigerator magnets: a pink cow holding a nice, handwritten note that accompanied four thousand dollars cash. You know what Beth did? Went to Tropical Tubs right after her shift ended, picked out what she wanted looking through the gate, next morning in she walks with her money, and here it is."

Beth shrugged. "It works more times than not," she said.

"Hey, listen," Gordon said, turning his attention to Marshall as if he'd just walked through the door. "How the hell are you? How've you been?"

"How have I been?" Marshall echoed. "This has been a very confusing year. I haven't been all that well."

"You haven't?" Gordon said. Marshall could hear the trepidation in his voice. He drained his beer, his eyes darting to a lizard heading for one of the bougainvillea pots.

"I'm fine," Marshall said halfheartedly. "I had a friend along on part of the ride. He was having health problems."

"He try the Corona cure?" Beth said.

"No," Marshall said. "As far as I know, he didn't try that."

"Hey, babe, how far ahead should I light those coals?" Gordon said.

"Better dump them in the barbecue first," she said.

"Notice that I married a wise ass?" Gordon said. "I love her, though. Babe, tell him how we got the ceiling fans in the house."

"No," she said. "It'll sound like bragging."

Gordon shrugged. The bird shrieked again.

"Get away, you fucking asshole!" Beth yelled at the cat, racing toward the fence. She bypassed the beer bottles, stepped over Gordon's discarded T-shirt, Marshall's kicked-off shoes. "And stay away!" she hollered.

"Pretty boy!" the bird shrieked. "Pretty boy. Pretty boy."

"Oh, my long-suffering ass you're pretty," Gordon said, picking up his empty bottle and throwing it into the yard.

"Gordon!" Beth said.

"Yeah?" he said.

"What do you think you're doing?"

"Is it my fault if our friends the Rastafarians have a problem with picking up after themselves when they've been drinking beer?"

"Don't do that again," she said.

"Pretty boy, pretty boy," Gordon said, puffing out his chest. He smiled at Beth. "How is it you think that bird lives through every night? You're not awake all night long to protect it, unless that book you were reading on astral projection finally took."

"All I know is I've stopped that cat from getting it approximately one million times."

"She sends protective thoughts to it during the night," Gordon said.

"I say a prayer for it. That's all I do," she said, handing Marshall a dish filled with nuts. The dish was in the shape of a flamingo's head, nuts filling the shallow pocket of its beak. A bright blue eye stared up at Marshall as he reached for the dish. Gordon's fingers dipped in. Some of the nuts scattered to the deck; others made it into his mouth.

"Here comes the part where he objects that I'm mystical, as he calls it," Beth said. "I meditate before dinner. Watch him make fun of me once I turn my back."

A new tape was clicked into the boom box: the sounds of the sea, Marshall guessed. The sea, with chimes intermittently ringing. Marshall watched her disappear into the house, heard a door close behind her.

"She meditates in the Mary Kay room," Gordon said. "You know what I tell her? That she's in there meditating for money."

"Pretty necklace she got from Evie," Marshall said.

"Say what?"

"Her necklace," Marshall said. "She said it was Evie's."

"That what she was wearing?" Gordon said. "Yes, very nice of Evie."

Marshall waited, hoping he'd say something else. Finally, Gordon said, "Hey. How about some colder-than-cold beers? Friend of mine is tending bar tonight down at the Green Parrot. What do you say I light these coals and we duck out while she's meditating?"

"Sure," Marshall said.

"That all right with you?"

"Sure," Marshall said again. He was slightly drunk and didn't intend to drink more once he got to the bar, but he decided he'd go along for the ride.

"Hey, I can tell you all about the buyout," Gordon said. "I got my hopes up."

"This might really happen, huh?"

"Might happen. Yeah, might happen. If so, I'm going to think something from living with Beth rubbed off. She's got the most amazing good luck of anybody I ever met, let alone a pretty woman. Women don't have much luck at all, in my personal experience. Listen to them long enough, you'll think no one woman ever had a moment's luck, ever."

"Yeah," Marshall said. As he spoke, he wondered exactly what he was agreeing with.

"Okay, we're out of here," Gordon said. As he passed the boom box, he turned up the volume slightly. "I know just how she likes it," he said. "Music, at least. The rest, you go figure."

This seemed not to require a reply.

"You mind hanging on to the back of a motorcycle?" Gordon

said. "It's not mine, it's borrowed. I'm giving it back to the bartender. We can walk back."

"How far is this place?"

"Across town, but town's about as wide as the *Queen Mary* sideways. You know about the fish that saw the shadow of the *Queen Mary*'s bottom, right?"

Searching for his keys in a fishbowl of change on the floor near the front door, Gordon forgot to expect a reply. *If that's the Queen Mary's bottom, then God save the King,* Marshall thought. If someone had asked him for the punchline of the joke—that joke, or any joke—he wouldn't have thought of it. Amazing, the irrelevant things stored away that could be tapped into, spontaneously.

The motorcycle was a big black Harley. When Gordon turned the key in the ignition, it sounded like something large exploding; then the engine settled into a burbling, growling monotony. Instead of a helmet, Gordon pulled on a baseball cap that had been stretched over the fake leopard-skin seat. Marshall jumped on and the motorcycle took off at a forty-five-degree angle, Gordon hollering something into the wind he didn't understand. "When I lean, don't lean with me," Gordon said a second time. "Sit back there like you're Queen Elizabeth on the throne. Sure ain't gonna be Prince Charlie, all the trouble he's gotten himself into. Whoo-ee!"

Gordon zigzagged between two cars, turned right on a red light after a second's hesitation. "This is Truman," Gordon shouted. It was the same road Marshall had taken into town, but he was experiencing it differently now. He decided to let out a big breath and trust Gordon's driving skills.

"You see that *Saturday Night Live* skit about Prince Charles wanting to be his lover's Tampax?" Gordon shouted. Every third word was lost in the wind. Gordon seemed to realize this. "Prince Charles. Camilla Parker-Bowles: Tampax!" he shouted. "*Saturday Night Live.*"

"I did, actually," Marshall said. He was slightly surprised that his brother remembered Prince Charles's lover's name. He hadn't remembered that himself, though he did know what he was talking about: the woman gets a gift from the Prince and it turns out to be a Tampax with Charles's head talking at the tip. Maybe everything and everybody was just fucking crazy. Maybe riding on a motorcycle with Gordon made as much sense as anything else. Wasn't that exactly what the recondite McCallum would do, hooting with pleasure? Sonja, herself—apparently she liked a wilder time than she let on.

The motorcycle veered right onto Whitehead, steeply banked as it cornered, a few blacks on bicycles looking up as the two men roared past on the big black Harley, one clinging to the other's shirt as if it provided a secure grip, the driver hunched over, barrelling forward in yellow aviator glasses and a backward Mets cap, shirt billowing. He slowed for a red light, then coasted through, accelerating when he passed the intersection. "Oo-ee!" Gordon hollered. "Hate to return this baby."

The Green Parrot was on a corner several blocks up: a big bar with open shutters and a deeply overhanging roof, specks of light inside from pinball machines and the lights dangling over pool tables. The wall art, Marshall saw as he climbed off and walked limp-legged into the bar, consisted of hand-painted beer bottles and framed pictures of parrots. The rectangular bar took up almost the entire room and was worked by one bartender, who did things faster than the eye could register them. "Hey, man," he called, in greeting to Gordon. "You got my machine fixed, I see." He raced to their end of the bar, setting down two open bottles of Rolling Rock and pouring two shots of vodka that slowly settled after he left like water calming in the wake of a boat. Gordon nodded, tossing down the vodka. Marshall did the same, tears springing to his eyes.

"So you tell me, man," Gordon said. "Have we got the right life down here, or do we not?"

"Seems great," Marshall said.

"Beth upsets herself about the place, though. Says the reef is a cesspool. Everglades almost gone. Hell, she won't go into the Audubon House because it turns out he killed birds. She's got quite a rant against Audubon. But luck? Does that woman have luck? She got four ceiling fans off the back of a truck in trade for her spare tire. No fuckin' way you can figure out what that's about, right? Guy driving a Ford pickup is getting gas the same time Beth is, tells her he'll give her four ceiling fans in exchange for her spare. She didn't even question him, man. She is some cool customer. You know her philosophy? It's better not to ask. Which is a hard philosophy to argue with. Jackson!" he hollered to the bartender.

Jackson raced to their end of the bar. "I had a customer you missed by ten, fifteen minutes. He was going to Paris to jam with Jim Morrison. Hope he likes playing music leaning up against tombstones—that's what I didn't tell him."

"He doesn't contradict a lot of ideas," Gordon said to Marshall.

"Heard that, Gordo," Jackson said, opening a cluster of beer bottles and racing with them in two different directions.

"He hears real good. But he doesn't hear. You know?" Gordon said.

Jackson raced back. "What about the machine, man?" he said, pouring two more shots.

"It was nothing. Got it fixed in half an hour. My guy admitted it couldn't count as repayment for his debt. Have it break down a couple more times, he might be even with me."

"Gordon built this guy a brick courtyard," Jackson said.

Marshall nodded appreciatively.

"Hey, this is my brother," Gordon said.

"No shit. He's your brother? Where you here from, bro?"

"New Hampshire," Marshall said. The words stuck in his throat.

"Isn't that where Jean Louise went the time she ran away?" Gordon said.

"Nah. Seattle."

"She get that tattoo lasered off okay?"

"Nah, now she's decided she likes it."

"We going diving or what?" Gordon said.

"My ear's still no good," Jackson said. He pivoted to take a drink order, dunking glasses in soapy water, then clear water, putting them upside down on a towel to drain, reaching for drier glasses to squirt drink mix into, while scooping in ice cubes left-handed. "Gin tonic, vodka tonic, liiiiime for everyone," Jackson said, opening two bottles of beer, grabbing them by their necks, palming slices of lime onto the rims, setting all four drinks in front of two people standing and two sitting.

"Is Beth going to mind if we're not there when she's through meditating?" Marshall said.

"Beth? No way. Beth'll start 'em all over again, let the burned-out coals be dust to dust. She knows I'll be home eventually."

"So you really like it here?" Marshall said. "You think you'd retire here even if you sold the business?"

"Oh, I don't know," Gordon said. "Is that gonna happen? Am I gonna sell that man the business? Hank's not even sure he wants to be bought out. I expect if he saw it in writing, he'd change his tune. But retire here? I don't know. I've heard Maui is pretty nice. For all that, I've heard Costa Rica can be beautiful."

"Really?" Marshall said. "You'd think about those places?"

"Yeah, why not?" Gordon drummed his thumb on the counter-top.

"Guy down there's a friend of the boss," Jackson said, picking up their empty shot glasses, indicating with a roll of his eyes he couldn't refill them again.

"His wife is gonna leave him," Gordon said as they left. "Came to the wife or the motorcycle, I think I know which he'd miss most, though."

"His wife, who went to Seattle?"

"That was the girlfriend," Gordon said. "She got a viper tattooed on her butt. So I hear, anyway." Gordon coughed a long, dry cough. His face was red, and there was a scar above his left eyebrow, pink and puckered. Off the motorcycle, Gordon looked suddenly smaller. He had gotten quite thin. Marshall felt protective; he was glad Beth would be feeding Gordon dinner.

"You remember that night Mom told us she was dying?" Marshall said.

"Shit, man, I knew you were going to mention that. Sitting in the bar, it came to me that that is exactly what you were going to ask about. I've gotten psychic since I've been with Beth." He kicked a stone, stepping far to the left to do it. "What about it?" he said.

"Did you know that was what she was going to talk about that night? It just occurred to me that you might have known what was coming."

"Well, Evie had told me she was sick, but it was the first time I'd gotten it from the horse's mouth." Gordon turned slightly to look at two girls passing by, both in short shorts and tropical shirts tied at the waist. "Jail bait," he said. As they got to the corner of a more crowded street, Gordon said, "This is Duval. The main drag. We take you sightseeing when you were here before?"

"Yeah," Marshall said. "We ate on Duval one night. At an out-door place."

"Claire," Gordon said. "Closed. Became something else."

"Good jukebox," Marshall said. He looked at Gordon. "How did you do that to your eye?" Marshall said.

"Hit the fucking reef," Gordon said. "She's putting vitamin E on it. Healing it pretty damn fast." Gordon pointed to something ahead of them. "This street we're walking up. Faustos is on it. I'm always trying to get her to go out on the highway to shop, but now she's a townie, she feels she's got to be loyal to local establishments. Watch: she'll say whatever vegetable she's cooked came from Faustos."

"I swear I won't keep talking about this, but lately I've been thinking about that night, and some things are very distinct, but other things are blurry."

Gordon looked at him with mild interest. Not because of the night, Marshall guessed, but because he was so intent on discussing it.

"Our father—he was outside? In a storm?"

"Overcome with grief," Gordon said. "Didn't you ever see *Wuthering Heights* on the tube? One of those old movies like *Rebecca* or whatever, trees blowing, clouds streaming over the moon. Cliffs. Stuff like that. The big house lit by lightning."

"What was going on?" Marshall said.

"You think I know?" Gordon said. "He didn't want her to tell us. He thought we shouldn't have to hear it, or something. She had cancer. People didn't use the word in those days. Look, she was crazier instead of better after what they did to her in the hospital. My opinion is that he'd rather she'd faded away, but she decided to pull out all the stops. Those two were going to have their show, and so they did. She'd started drinking again, you know. She did not stop drinking the day she got home from the hospital. Quite the opposite."

"What do you think was wrong?" Marshall said.

"Oh, Marshall, forgive me, but why would you look for some one thing to be wrong? The two of them could blink in unison, and suddenly they were actors in a soap opera, and to tell you the truth, I think they got off on it. They understood each other. They got off on the pain. Forget the fact that real things might happen to other people that might be painful; all they could think about was themselves. There was a summer night on the back porch that I remember. . . ."

"You understood so much more than I ever did," Marshall said. "Just those few extra years you had on me—they gave you a perspective I never could have had."

"Don't kid yourself," Gordon said. "I might have been around to observe some unfortunate stuff. I might have known some things they would just as soon I didn't know anything about. But don't assume that gave me any advantage. Whatever I saw, whatever I knew, the only way to keep the peace was to shut up about it. So what good did it do that I had their number? They closed down, and I was expected to do the same."

"Because the marriage was bad, you mean?"

"Because the marriage was bad," Gordon echoed. "Yeah. That's a good way to put it. When I think about them, that certainly comes to mind: that their marriage was bad."

"But what are you remembering?" Marshall said. "You saw them fighting, but you weren't supposed to let on? They were fighting on the back porch?"

Gordon looked at Marshall. "What do you want, Marsh? You want me to fill in details? Tell you about every tragedy, major or minor? Look: he married somebody who was nothing like him, didn't he? Not that Evie was much more like him, but he wasn't afraid of her. All I remember about that particular night when he went out into the storm was that Evie thought she was having a heart attack and Mom was drunk, going into one of her religious fits, and the two of us were sitting there as their captive audience. I mean, give me a fucking break. You were so scared I thought *you* were gonna have the fucking heart attack. That place was a fucking zoo sometimes."

"Do you think he married Evie so we'd have a mother?" Marshall said.

"I think that sounded as good as anything else he could come up with. Do I think that? No, not really. I never knew him to do anything except for himself. I think he was boffing her long before Mom died. I mean, think about it. All that running around at night. It used to wake you up. You were the lightest sleeper in the world. You'd wake up and get afraid and wake me up. I still never sleep through a night, man. Beth was feeding me pills with a name I can't pronounce—Tryp-something—that worked pretty well, and then they got yanked off the market. I'm not complaining, I'm just telling you: I do not sleep through a fucking night, no matter how tired I am." Gordon looked at Marshall. "So now you know everything I know."

Marshall was walking fast to keep up with him. Past Faustos,

Gordon had turned right, onto Simonton. The conch train passed by, filled with tourists. Alongside it, a one-armed boy on Rollerblades kept pace. They caught up with him at the next red light, wheeling in backward circles.

"Do you wish you knew more?" Marshall said.

"More?" Gordon said. "Do I wish I knew more? No, I don't wish I knew more."

"Don't think it would help you sleep?" Marshall said.

"Maybe it would. Never thought about it."

"But you don't wish—"

"There was more to know. I realize that," Gordon said. "You know what I think? If I knew *that* stuff, there'd still be more to know. I talk to Beth more than I've ever talked to every other woman combined, and you know what? I will never know it all. I'll know what she says that day. I'm not saying she's a liar, or that she doesn't want to talk to me. She'll talk till she's blue in the face most of the time. But every time she surprises me, I realize that I am simply never, ever going to have enough information to predict what she'll do. Here in the Conch Republic, there's a tradition I've come to depend on. Stand down at Mallory Square, or anywhere the tourists are, and when the sun sinks below the horizon line, everybody claps. I take it as a sign that people like a grand finale, but when they've had one, they've had one. Something like the sun gradually sinking is very distinct. You figure things out about people when they rush off or you see them stick around to see the sky get more colorful, because that's what happens. The colors deepen. It gets orange and bright blue and battleship gray. It gets real pink, and sometimes the pink's shot through with lavender. A pink and purple sky. If you applauded all the while that spread out above you, you'd never get to drink your drink."

A cat tried to rub against Gordon's leg. He raised a foot in its direction, and it darted away.

"Fuck, man, you just got here, and look what I did. We missed sunset," Gordon said, pushing open the front gate. "Can't have you missing dinner, too. Hey, babe! How are those coals coming?" Gordon hollered.

They had burned to ash, they saw, but Beth, still meditating, had not restarted the fire.

22

HE SAT IN A canvas butterfly chair behind the dive shop, waiting for Gordon to get off the phone. The phone was a cordless, and Gordon kept wandering in and out of the store, so there wasn't any way to tell from his end of the conversation whether Gordon was pleased or displeased by what Mr. Watanabe was saying. Marshall picked up Gordon's sunglasses from the seat of another butterfly chair, put them on, and looked at the water, and the boats docked nearby, through the yellow lenses. The dive shop was closed for the day while Gordon's partner, Hank, took inventory. Altiss, the Trinidadian roofer, was installing a skylight in the loft above the store. Mr. Watanabe had called from Fort Lauderdale and would not be coming to have dinner with Gordon that night—that much Marshall had understood.

"This is the good life," Altiss said to Marshall, climbing down to get a cold drink from his Styrofoam cooler that sat near the cluster of butterfly chairs. "I recommend to you the profession of roofing. Very good money, and not as dirty as plumbing. I go once a month to Orlando to Walt Disney World, where there is always work to do on the roofs in the Magic Kingdom." Altiss wore khaki shorts, a red T-shirt, and a many-pocketed vest. He also wore argyle socks and purple basketball sneakers. He grabbed his boom box and took it with him when he climbed the ladder to the roof.

Four days spent driving to Key West; three in Key West, four days until he would be home again in New Hampshire. Today, day three, when he had just begun to unwind, was his last day in what was alternatively referred to as Paradise or the Conch Republic. There had been a sunset sail planned with Mr. Watanabe, but when that plan fell through Gordon had rented the boat to a Texan and his girlfriend. Though the store was officially shut, Gordon hadn't been able to resist answering the door when the man knocked, grinning from ear to ear and holding up his wallet, pointing his thumb in the direction of the boats moored off the dock. His wife or girlfriend had flirted with Gordon as Gordon pointed out the reef on the navigational map. "Check his bank balance before you turn your attentions, sugar," the man had said, cupping his hand over her ass. It was all good-natured: the flirting was as obvious as her sparkling gold jewelry. The woman had been surprised when she couldn't draw Marshall in. He had never liked being the object of someone's flirtation. It usually had an edge he distrusted. He remembered Cheryl Lanier, drinking his Jack Daniel's as he talked to Sonja on the telephone. If it was McCallum she'd been interested in, why had she bothered to flirt with him? Maybe he had been a backup flirtation. Or a flirtation within a flirtation, like a play within a play. A sailboat with PUCK written in fancy calligraphy had caught his eye, making him think of *A Midsummer Night's Dream.* As he watched the boats bob, he realized he'd been wrong: it was a too fancily drawn *L,* not a *P.* What did that mean, he wondered—that the person who owned the boat had good luck, or that the person hoped to invoke it?

"He's going to buy this place. I really think he is," Gordon said, sprawling in the chair beside Marshall. "Apparently his secretary wants him to buy a Thai restaurant in Fort Lauderdale instead, but I said to him, 'Why would you listen to your secretary?' He's Americanized enough to be pussy whipped. Thinks her opinions are as interesting as her snatch."

"What's the first thing you're going to buy when you get rich?" Marshall asked.

"Ticket to Hawaii," Gordon said.

"Two tickets, I presume."

"You hinting?" Gordon smiled.

"No, not for myself. For Beth," Marshall said.

"You think I got it right this time?" Gordon said. "I don't know. I sure am fond of her, but I don't know if she's the lady I want to spend the rest of my life with."

"You're kidding," Marshall said.

"I'm serious."

"Does she know it?"

Gordon shrugged. "She likes more action than she gets with me. I'm fourteen years older than Beth, you know. I shouldn't be so cocksure she'll always be around, even if I want her to be."

"I thought you two were really in love," Marshall said.

"Who's really in love past the age of twenty? You and Sonja really in love?"

"We haven't had a very good year," Marshall said.

"I haven't noticed you burning up the phone lines," Gordon said.

"I've spoken to her," Marshall said. "I called her before I got here."

"Yeah? What did she say? Missing her hub and sorry she wasn't in the Florida sunshine? Sonja doesn't like me," Gordon said. "She thinks I'm a lowlife."

"She does not," Marshall said.

Gordon lowered the yellow aviator glasses dangling from a red cord around his neck, raising one eyebrow. "I hereby indicate skepticism about what you just said," Gordon said. "I also ask you to look at me impartially. I am a lowlife. I drink too much, I take a shower once a week, maybe twice, I skip out on work whenever I can, sit around topless bars out on the highway, and if I sell this damn business I'm out of here. I'm going to be draping orchids around my neck and dunking my butt in picturesque swimming holes below cascading waterfalls, attended by dark-haired Hawaiian beauties who live to give head. It's the American Dream, bro: going to the westernmost point in America. Fuck this southernmost point in the United States bullshit. I want what's across the water, and I am *not* talking Fidel Castro."

Marshall did look at him impartially. He saw Gordon, drunker than he'd realized, so that now he understood Gordon had been drinking as he'd talked to Mr. Watanabe. The years of sunlight and drinking had permanently reddened his brother's face. He was losing his hair, and he'd aged—it seemed as if he'd aged ten years in the time since Marshall had last seen him. When Beth first met Gordon, Gordon had probably looked worse than Marshall realized. Yet he did not think he was the only impartial observer who would understand that Gordon was acting a part. He was playing a role, using language that did not come naturally, but doing a credible imitation of a lowlife, all right. He had the right clothes, the macho bravado, the beer bottle prop, even the right wife. Beneath the facade, Marshall saw the watchfulness, the steadiness, of his older brother. It was interesting that as they became adults, both of them had chosen a slightly mocking attitude: Marshall mocked himself, he supposed, in the way he addressed his young students by putting their names in implied quotes, communicating that they all—himself included—had become marginal people, attempting to better understand the human condition through the careful reading of literature, which for all intents and purposes was no longer a currency in which the real world traded. "The real world," of course, was also something deserving of mockery: the masses—idiotic tourists who could not understand what they were looking at, let alone what it signified, as they regarded the big fish at the end of *The Old Man and the Sea*. Literature was the study of Them by Us. It was undertaken by people smart enough to make a microscope of the page—or, more fashionably, to assert that things could shake out any number of ways because the page was a kaleidoscope. That was what they were taught by McCallum. He, too, tried to instill a sense of self-doubt in his students, though his approach wasn't as fashionable as McCallum's. It was his strategy to point out to them that they were America's elite, to stress that the future was in their hands. The students smart enough to understand his tone would get the real message almost immediately—that he actually meant to instill doubt about one's importance by pretending to insist on the supremacy of the self. So amusing, to send them out of the classroom having proved to them they were the elite, while having twisted that term into a dirty word; graduate, and they become the entirely dismissable elite—those who have seen the world in its variety and its complexity, but once their little group disperses, no one in that now opened-up, fascinating, complex world would care any longer what questions they raised, what conclusions they reached. The world would continue to operate in terms of dirty politics, opposing religions, wars, insider trading, freakish accidents, and the sale of lottery tickets. His benediction to them, last class: Goodbye, and good luck. Watch out for Answered Prayers. And if you must pray, don't eat lunch with the next Truman Capote.

Well, all right: interesting that once Gordon was seen clearly, he could see himself more clearly, also. Two mocking people: he used a vehicle, language, to mock; his brother lived his life by invoking a stereotype he knew was absurd. Gordon had done Marshall one better; he had lived his entire life in apologetic quotes to call attention to the absurdity of his position. This much was entirely clear. The only problem was that he couldn't announce this revelation to Gordon, because Gordon had invested everything in keeping people at a distance through the pretense of being crude.

Their father had excelled at keeping others at arm's length, also, but his method had been to intimidate by imperiousness, while Gordon had decided to be a beer-swigging good ole boy. Their parents—their father, their mother, Evie—would not recognize Gordon now. It was only an act, though, meant to be repellent. Underneath, Gordon was still observant and insightful. He looked at his brother and thought about what Gordon had said the first night he arrived in Key West. It was true: their father had married someone not at all like him. Though Evie had not been much like him either, the friction between them had still never been as obvious as the contention between his father and mother. If his father had put his hopes in either of them, it had been Gordon, but he sensed his mother cared more what became of him. Or should he see it differently now? Was it just a case of a mother's favoring her baby? That had been what his father said to his mother, that night. He had heard them arguing—had run upstairs because they were arguing. He had been in the kitchen with Gordon, and then he had pushed his chair back from the table and run upstairs—how embarrassing, to remember his endless cowardice—and Evie had risen to leave as well, only to be called back into the kitchen by their father. It became a three-way argument, Evie calling his father a bully, his father complaining about their mother's love for him, Marshall—all her love reserved for the person he humiliatingly called "the baby." All she cared about was the baby, he remembered his father saying. She was obsessed with the baby, ruining their lives with her preoccupation with the baby—though it was an unfair criticism; she had not been as focussed on him as his father insisted. It might have been true that Evie fussed over him slightly more, but his father had not been objecting to that—it was quite specifically his mother's attentions toward Marshall "the baby" that had infuriated their father that night.

A plane coming toward the airport descended quickly, motors roaring, and Marshall looked at it, there below the clouds. What a sky, blue with white clouds, the ideal sky, the sort of sky that was supposed to make people feel life was miraculous. Instead, the vastness of the mesmerically blue sky made him think that his birth had been an accident. Of course it had been: the perfect son already existed, and his mother's attentions toward him—her attentions toward Marshall-the-Baby—clearly incensed his father. There was every probability his father had not wanted a second child; especially not one who was emotional, cowardly, his nose always in a book, welded to his brother's side—not even clinging to their father, but dependent on Gordon, which must have offended their father. He had blocked out that night for so long for the obvious reason that he found it all so painful—his role in disturbing the family, his being the center of attention even when he absented himself, the thorn in his father's side. That was why their father had insisted on talking about his wife's having favorites when she was terminally ill—that was why he insisted on telling her her deficiencies as she was preparing to tell her sons she was going to die.

"Gordon," Marshall said, "do you think he loved her?"

"The Texan?" Gordon said.

He looked at his brother. Gordon had pulled the brim of his cap low over his eyes and was resting, one knee crossed over another, hands clasped on his stomach. Amazing but not surprising: Gordon's thoughts really did not return to their parents—to that time or that place. Certainly not to that night.

"Yeah, the Texan," Marshall said, for the hell of it.

"Mm," Gordon said. "He probably loves her. Yeah."

"Do you think our father loved our mother?"

He could hear the slight annoyance, mixed with resignation, as Gordon sighed, "No. I doubt it."

"Evie?" Marshall said.

"What's this? Cupid's love survey?"

"What do you think?" Marshall persisted.

"What does it matter?"

"I'm curious."

"I realize that. How about going into the store and getting us a couple of beers? I want to take a ten-minute catnap, then maybe we can wander over to Mallory Dock, give you the required touristic experience of watching the performers and the tourists strutting their stuff as the sun goes down. Beth's selling air plants for a friend who's out of town. You know what? I think Beth is a good person. I'm fond of her. I admire her. But I don't think I love her, if I ever did."

"You've read all those things," Marshall said. "About your early life and how you form relationships later on, I mean."

"I form relationships to get laid and to have one woman who doesn't hate me, who isn't after me night and day to marry her because I already have," Gordon said. "How's that for the confessional mode?"

"I'm not saying that anything that happened to us makes us unique," Marshall said.

"I fucking think you *are* unique," Gordon said. "How about two Coronas?"

Marshall got up, limping slightly on the first few steps because his left leg had gone dead sitting in the chair. Gordon probably did have the right approach to life: stretch out beneath the sky, don't cause yourself any unnecessary problems in Paradise, have a cold beer and a brief nap. He and Hank nodded silently as Marshall passed him, heading into the office to get beers out of the refrigerator. He stepped carefully through the clutter, looking briefly at a calendar that had not yet been changed from January. A bare-chested woman holding a pink heart-shaped lollipop between her enormous breasts smiled down at him from the wall to the left of the refrigerator. On a bulletin board to the other side hung a photograph of Mr. Watanabe, Gordon, Hank, and six women in sparkling evening gowns with plunging necklines. They were in a nightclub somewhere, clustered around a small round table. Mr. Watanabe's eyes, on closer inspection, looked like pinwheels. Gordon's eyes . . . it frightened him to look at Gordon's eyes. With a hand curled halfway around one of the blond women's jewel-studded breasts, the other arm dangled at his side as if it were a useless appendage. Looking at the arm, you would be certain the limb had no feeling—that you were looking at a handicapped person's flaccidly dangling arm. The more he looked, the more he realized Gordon was just very drunk; he seemed to be propped up in the chair, more like a mannequin than a real person, except that his eyes told you he was human. They weren't just empty, they were dead. They were eyes that had died.

He shuddered as he pulled open the refrigerator door. A blast of cold air hit him, causing him to double up as he reached quickly in, taking two beers from several dozen bottles crowded onto the top shelf. He shut the door quickly and looked around for an opener. He saw one on the wall, under the calendar, and opened both bottles, letting the bottle caps fall to the floor amid ant traps, crumpled paper, and many other bottle caps. He carried them out, looking down so as not to meet Hank's eyes again. It was as if he'd seen something shameful in the room, or as if he'd partaken in something shameful— a thought he didn't want to come any closer to articulating.

A breeze had blown up outside, disturbing the surface of the water. From the roof, the sound of a staple gun punctured the silence. Gordon reached up for the beer without changing his position in the chair, and Marshall's heart missed a beat, he was so delighted to see Gordon's right arm move. *My God,* he thought: *I must have convinced myself something was really wrong with Gordon's arm.* He stood there as if he'd awakened from a bad dream, grateful to be back in the world, silently embarrassed he'd been elsewhere. He handed down the beer, fascinated at Gordon's hand as it gripped the long neck of the Corona. Elbow bent, he moved his hand to his mouth and swigged from the bottle. It was ordinary—the most quintessentially ordinary thing Marshall could imagine—but the motion seemed beautiful, inherently fascinating, and beyond that a relief. It was a huge relief. Gordon was not the Gordon of the photograph; that had been a sudden flash that produced a deceptive photograph.

The rooftop reggae devolved eerily into Jim Morrison, singing "Wishful Sinful." For a minute, amid hammering, he listened. A stronger station had overtaken Bob Marley. It was Morrison in the lead, Marley second, darting in for a fuzzy word, a sung phrase, Altiss loudly rooting for Marley until a Skil saw overwhelmed both words and music. When it resumed, Marley had triumphed, though Marshall's thoughts were no longer on the music. Hearing Jim Morrison had reminded him of Gordon's friend the bartender. He was replaying going into the Green Parrot, watching the ambidextrous bartender perform, frantically keeping up with drink orders while washing glasses and holding simultaneous conversations. It seemed that in Key West everyone was either completely wired or very laid back. How amusing, then, that high-energy Gordon was pretending to sleepwalk, turning over the possibility of leaving his wife, travelling in his mind to places like Hawaii while he sat sprawled in a butterfly chair near the water's edge, picking under a fingernail with one of the toothpicks he always carried in his shirt pocket. *What a shirt*, Marshall thought, appreciating the bizarre colors—a shirt that reminded him of a tequila sunrise, pinks settling into orange, a watery concoction of electric color that blurred more the harder you tried to focus.

"Man, with my eyes closed, I can tell you're lost in thought," Gordon said. He hunched his shoulders and sat up, raising the yellow aviator glasses, rubbing his arm over his eyes, pushing the glasses back on the bridge of his nose with two fingers. "You understand I don't have any special knowledge about what never got said when we were kids, right? But you want my opinion anyway. Okay: my opinion is that if he ever loved our mother, he stopped loving her pretty fast. He felt bad when he knew she was going to die, but that's something else. And Evie—as I've said, looking back, I think Evie was always his squeeze on the side. Guy needed to get laid, is my guess. Our mother seemed like a ghost long before she got sick and died. I don't remember her in any season but winter. That Bible she carried around. Always so unhappy. I know what he felt like: if something doesn't work out, next time you go to the opposite extreme." Gordon rolled his head to the side, looked up at Marshall, standing with his back to the water, holding a bottle of beer from which he had not yet sipped. "Are all these questions because your marriage to Sonja is breaking up? I mean this quite sincerely: I've been through this stuff before. At the moment it seems like the end of the world, but it won't be. Whatever happens, I don't think you're going to get any answers about the present by raking through the past. By thinking about the previous woman, yes—but you've only been married one time."

"I don't care about what I'm doing for a living. I don't—with the exception of a madman who's no longer my friend, I don't have any friends except you. Sonja and I had a bad year, but I should have seen it was going badly. I should have cared, and I didn't. I'm shutting down."

Gordon shook his head. "You make it sound like you're a dangerous nuclear reactor, man. Who do you know who loves what he does, loves his wife, loves every fucking thing in the world? Things will work out. You've got to think forward, not back."

Marshall nodded.

"I should also mention that you find yourself in a slightly strange place, bro. Boats bobbing out there on the water, people on their rented pink motor scooters. It seems easy. People talk like it's easy. There's flowers and sunshine. It's like an illustration in a fucking children's book. The Conch Republic's not necessarily the best place to find yourself when you're undergoing self-doubt. You pick up that conch shell and hold it to your ear, you know what you hear? A roar. A hollow roar. If you're already down, you'll take it as the absolute truth."

At Mallory Dock, the air was suffused with the odor of meat and onions frying on a grill, the roar of fruit and juice liquefying in a blender, the triple blast of a cruise ship calling for the last passengers so it could sail away before dark. Smaller boats crisscrossed the water, sailboats and motorboats, people clustered on deck as the boats blew back and forth, turning to keep the sun in sight, bands playing at the open-air bars on shore, recorded music or an amplified guitar drifting off the water toward land, people drinking swampy margaritas and cheap wine included in the price of the sail that would give them instant headaches. Near where they stood, a bagpipe player puffed his cheeks and began to finger his next song, drowning out the Bob Dylan imitation undertaken beside him by a barefooted man who stopped singing every half minute to berate people in the crowd for walking on the cord that attached his guitar to the amplifier. People grabbed each other's hands, snaking through the dense crowd, yelling over their shoulders for others to follow, evading jugglers, backing off to provide a small circle of space to a man who raised a shopping cart containing four bowling balls, with a bicycle tied to the cart, from his shoulders to his forehead, then moved it from his forehead to his mouth, taking small, bent-kneed steps while finally tipping it enough to balance the entire shopping cart by its handle on his teeth. Children were lifted to parents' shoulders, teenagers tumbled against each other's bodies, using shoulders and legs as springboards, their T-shirts rolled to reveal tattoos of the setting sun inked into their biceps, along with skulls and crossbones, Merlins with crystal balls, long-haired, big-breasted women galloping on unicorns. Dirty, shoeless men with caved-in chests stood squinting in the background, looking for abandoned hot dogs or half-full cans of Pepsi left on the ground. Dogs nosed through the crowd while others of their kind performed: a white dog in a bandanna who jumped over three Vietnamese pigs in graduated sizes, their tails braided, who in turn jumped over the expressionless dog, landing in a perfect line, one-two-three; a cat in red booties who jumped, at the crack of a whip, through a flaming hoop. He thought, suddenly, of Janet Lanier, telling him, "Your wife will be very sympathetic about the hoops you've had to jump through."

As the sun inched down in its descent below the horizon line, music reached a fever pitch, soprano sax scuttling the bagpipes as stoned teenagers released Mylar balloons to drift over the Gulf and mingle with swooping seagulls and flapping sails. Piercing whistles and applause continued for a full half minute after the disappearance of the last sliver of orange sun, caps thrown up and clambered after as they landed in the infinitesimal spaces between bodies, or perched rakishly on other people's heads. One man danced in place, shaking his tambourine, as the pigs once again flew forward to make their perfect nose-to-tail line. Quite possibly, this would be the most ludicrous place on earth to come if you were hoping for an epiphany. Though it made Marshall uncomfortable to think in those terms, he *was* looking for something, and furthermore, Gordon realized that he was. It was not an accident that Gordon had suggested this gaudy party at land's end. If Mr. Watanabe had come, the plan had been to sail past Mallory Dock as the sun was setting, to be out there with the other boats, looking toward shore through binoculars, but when Watanabe cancelled, Gordon had still been intent upon showing his brother a sight he couldn't miss.

He and Gordon had parked several blocks away, walked down Duval Street, then fought their way through the crowd streaming onto the dock, heading toward the table where Beth was selling her friend's air plants. Marshall recognized her from behind, the tie-dyed tank dress she had put on that morning with its interlocking cobwebs of maroon and deep purple suddenly sedate in comparison with the extravaganza in the sky. Beth was barefoot, a gold clip in her hair, still damp from a shower. The air plants grew out of conch shells, to which her friend had glued button eyes and red felt lips: the green-gray plants looked like odd, miniature toupees. Playing grab-ass with her, Gordon had caused her to lose one sale, so she tried to send them off to watch the performers, telling Marshall to be sure to see the cat who jumped through a burning hoop. "Just like Morris the cat," she said. "It was saved from a shelter."

He trailed after Gordon, trying to stay calm. Moving deeper into the crowd, he had begun to feel claustrophobic. Faces began to take on a sameness: a fixedness of gaze; sweaty skin; people snaking forward without looking at one another. He was suddenly reminded of the travelling carnivals they'd been taken to as boys, the ones they begged to be able to attend, where they'd watched Punch-and-Judy shows and been given rides on straw-hatted donkeys. This spectacle was as unrelated to those summertime travelling road shows as crawling was to space travel. As he walked, passing dusty traveller's palms and thorny sprays of bougainvillea growing weedlike in narrow patches of dirt near the buildings, he saw the brightening sky, lavender streaks dissipating like smoke, dark gray clouds like so many submarines rising to the surface. From where he stood he could not see the water at all, but the sky seemed a kind of sea, the clouds devolving into sea creature shapes, tentacles spiralling out and then retracting, nets of white flung toward the sinking sun.

Below a tree Beth had told him the second day he was there was named a flamboyant tree, a drunk lay on his side, a broken pint bottle still clasped in his hand, blood speckling the ground where he had cut himself as he passed out. Marshall took a deep breath, needing air to avert a swarming dizziness. The place had sent him into a near panic. He was looking for reference points, landmarks, familiar things that would provide a buoy on which he could affix his attention. In another flamboyant tree he saw two balloons. In a store window, a gargoyle draped with shiny necklaces. Trash in the gutter. People still rushing toward the dock grabbed for flyers flicked in their direction—flyers advertising discount videos, massages, two-for-one drinks, trips to the same reef Beth had told him the first day he arrived was all but dead. His life had been sharply proscribed, he realized, and he was the one who had done it; he had been the one who'd chosen to circle on the slow donkey, going round and round but going nowhere, and then what had happened but someone had galloped into his life on a high-spirited horse, and he had found himself on the road, a most unwitting and highly unlikely Sancho Panza. Okay: Cheryl had been right about that—following after . . . what? Whatever unarticulated quest McCallum had decided must be enacted.

Suddenly, a man, in a parody of an effete conductor, raised his hand and poked a burning stick of incense toward his nose, which he tried to ward off. Still, the musky smell seemed to clash unpleasantly with the sunset, the near-fetid smell making him squint at the sky's harsh brilliance. Behind them, people continued to crowd toward Mallory Dock: excited tourists; indifferent day-trippers who'd been told this was the place to go; the homeless, who might as well drift in that direction as another. The dock was by now punctuated with fire: jugglers tossing torches, animal trainers raising burning hoops, people holding sparklers that fizzed with silver fire, the cacophonous music as loud as sirens in the night. Whistles and shrieks continued, along with balloons released to float upward and intermingle with the coming stars, until that time when they would inevitably explode or deflate, to become a deadly food for fish. If McCallum had made it this far, Marshall thought, he would have loved this lurid spectacle. With an increasing feeling of claustrophobia and an adrenaline rush that made his heartbeat echo in his ears, the noise of the after-sunset revellers became white noise, just as—in a place that seemed across the universe—drifted snow disguised the landscape of New Hampshire in his absence. He thought of New Hampshire. The snowy woods. The icy hoarfrost on his own front lawn. Every man's house his castle. New Hampshire, blanketed in white. Returning, he would have to drive carefully. Gingerly, back to the gingerbread house, real icicles its white frosting.

Cocoanut Grove

WE MIGHT HAVE BEEN there that night, the night of the great fire that burned the Cocoanut Grove, except that Miles received a business call at the Ritz, and when Miles received a business call, you could always gauge its importance by whether or not he untied his shoes. That night, not two minutes into the call, he stepped right out of them: soft black leather lace-up evening shoes he'd had mailed to him from Lobb's in England, just before the war broke out. He always ordered shoes in duplicate, so although he couldn't get the shoes any-more, he still had a brand-new pair he'd never taken from the box that he'd just taken out of the suitcase a few minutes before. Lobb's shoes: how he loved them. He wanted to look dashing at his friend's wedding. It was winter, 1942. Holy Cross had just beat Boston in college football, and he was in a very bad mood before he answered the phone, because he'd made a rather large bet that Boston would win. At first he thought the phone call was from his friend, wanting to collect. Then he realized it was something that would take a while and he waved me away, as if he were dispersing cigarette smoke—as he so often did when he took a business call. I think he was convinced women could die of boredom. I think he thought his standing there, holding the phone, was as dangerous to a woman's well-being as her being on a battlefield. It was not that usual that a lady visiting Boston would be sitting alone in the lobby of the Ritz, but I wasn't silly about things like that. I knew I'd be perfectly safe, and who cared if an eyebrow or two was raised? I had on a peach silk dress and nylon stockings and a pair of black high heels he'd bought me. It was a coincidence that I wore the same size, exactly, that she wore. It's very hard to find a AA shoe these days, but then it was a common size. Women's feet were narrower. So I had on shoes not terribly dissimilar from shoes she'd picked out for herself, though mine had higher heels. My hair was auburn, and I knew the peach silk set off the highlights in my hair. I was so excited to be going to the Cocoanut Grove. You'd think the party was for me—though many years would elapse between that night and the night of my marriage. I was never sure I'd be married at all, to tell the truth, and it certainly never would have crossed my mind I'd be married to Miles. I thought about our relationship the way he had presented it to my parents long past the time I should have; I realized I wasn't there in Maine to help take care of Gordon and to teach Alice French. She had no interest at all in learning French, and I felt so silly, bringing it up, as if it were my own obsession. "*Bonjour,* Alice!" I would say, and she would sigh, or tell me, "*Bonjour, chérie. Ça suffit,*" which was her little joke about not intending to converse in any language but English. But in spite of the way things were, I kept thinking about the way my parents had been told things would be, and I tried to pretend that was the reality. They would have been stunned, of course, if they'd ever known my real position in the house. And certainly they would have been shocked to think that from the winter of 1937 until 1941, when his courtship resulted in my pregnancy, and I finally realized I would have to go with him, to do whatever he said . . . they would have been stunned to know I'd been courted by letter and in person by Miles, for years. That I'd gone to a hotel with Miles would have been inconceivable. I was no different than a whore in that hotel room, though nobody but the two of us knew that. She knew it too, of course, but she didn't know at that very moment where we were, didn't care to know, is what I think now, because she liked me. After all, if it hadn't been me, he would have had some other indiscretion. She had no idea she might have lost both of us in the horrendous fire that was to kill 492 people that night. A busboy stood on a stool and lit a match to replace a lightbulb. The headlines the next day blamed the busboy, but really: he was working in unsafe circumstances; he'd made a simple mistake and suddenly one of the artificial palm trees caught fire, went up like a torch. There were luxurious silk draperies that caught fire, and before anyone could react, the entire nightclub was aflame. When it was over, the firemen would find the partygoers, Miles's good friends, the bride and the groom, dead inside. Some people said they were lying six deep, scattered like garbage dumped from a trash can, piled one on top of the other so the firemen found it all but impossible to enter the nightclub through the revolving doors. The bar was downstairs, the restaurant and dance floor up above. There was no sprinkler system, there were no marked fire exits. It became an inferno, the palm trees burned, the drapes sizzled into sheets of flame, the tables went up as if they'd been doused with gasoline, they burned so fast, everything contributing to the explosive heat that was to kill more than half the people who had gone there with so many pleasant expectations. If not for that call, we might have been among them. Maybe we would have been among the lucky—the ones who crawled out a bathroom window, or who found some other way out. But we never went to the Cocoanut Grove. I sat in the lobby for a while, then returned to the room. Ten or fifteen minutes into his call, he wasn't happy to see me, but what could he do? I was slightly relieved, after all. People at the party knew his wife. However he introduced me, they would suspect. Deceptions of that sort just did not bother him; he only felt obliged to say something perfunctory—not necessarily to state the truth. He was so charming; you could see it in people's eyes that they didn't believe him, but neither did they contradict him. "If they say nothing to my face, they'll surely say nothing to yours," he said, and that was one of the truest things he ever said. I only saw it in their eyes, or in their exaggerated politeness. Alice was another matter—as well she might have been. Imagine any married woman finding out her husband had a twenty-three-year-old lover—being presented with this person as a fait accompli, and then being told later the same day that the twenty-three-year-old girl, the daughter of her husband's Canadian friends, who'd come to help them set up a summerhouse on the coast of Maine, was pregnant. I wasn't sitting in any lobby in a silk dress with my hands folded neatly in my lap during those two encounters with Alice several hours apart, you can well believe that. She threw a glass of orange juice in my face and stomped her foot on the empty glass, cutting her hand as she picked up a big shard to throw at him, screaming words I never heard her use again. I was terrified. Simply terrified. She was only three years older than I was, but she was so sophisticated. She had been so nice to me when my parents and I had first joined them in New York. She'd brushed my hair for me in the ladies' room, told me she'd heard I was very skillful on skis. That was in 1936, in the Plaza Hotel. It was snowing outside, just as it had been when I left Montreal by train with my family. Miles and my father were business acquaintances. It never so much as crossed my mind that he had his eye on me. It never crossed my mind any more than it did Alice's. The only love talked about that day was the love of the Duke of Windsor for Wallace Simpson, the divorcée he could not marry and still ascend to the throne. George V had died, and his son was supposed to be the next King of England, but he had already fallen in love with Wallis Warfield Simpson. Some said he wasn't fit to be King, and that it was all for the best, but there was much concern between Miles and my father about what would happen to the English economy if Edward VIII abdicated. My mother thought it was all wonderfully romantic. I don't remember that Alice had much to say—only that England was so far away, a truly foreign country. It was a place her husband brought her sweaters from. Sweaters and tea, fine English teas that were not imported in those days. This was December of 1936. Early December. In February Miles came to Montreal, and he and my father took me to an elegant French restaurant, where I sat quietly at the table as they discussed business. Until the last minute, my mother had also been expected to come, but suddenly she was taken with a chill. I made her hot tea with lemon and took it to her in bed, but she said she felt cold all over—that there was no way she could attend the dinner. I must go in her place, she said. And she let me wear her beautiful lace dress, the tawny-colored dress I'd always admired, but which she'd said made me look too mature. Surely she couldn't have known what was going on—though why do I think that? She might have known. She might not have thought it would have such disastrous consequences. A flirtation, a little titillation—what was that? Indiscreet, on the part of a married man, but hardly calamitous. In truth, she did whatever my father told her to do.

That night in the restaurant Miles was very solicitous of me. He wanted me to take him skiing the next day, before he left Montreal. My father had an appointment he could not break, though he left the table twice to telephone, hoping things could be rearranged so he could come along. Did he really want to come along? I'm not saying he could see the future, only that he deferred to Miles, respected him greatly and quite simply deferred to him, as so many people did. He might have guessed that Miles would prefer to be on the ski slopes with me, alone. There is no reason to imagine that my father, in the restaurant bathroom, smoking a cigar, pacing back and forth to allow time to elapse, only pretended he was trying to rearrange the next day's business. Yet I do have that feeling. It's because he told me when I was a little girl that he did that, sometimes: had the men's room attendant light a good cigar for him, so he could have a few puffs and allow whatever was happening at the table to reach a certain crucial point before he returned. Then, later, he'd go back to the men's room and have the attendant relight the cigar, so he could have a few last puffs. Miles, himself, did not smoke cigars, but he did enjoy brandy. He and my father ordered two brandies before the night ended. My mother would have hated being there. The brandy was always her cue to leave the table, and she hated to be sent away just when things were getting interesting, she said. Yet my father did not give me a cue that I should leave, so I sat there, not quite understanding what they were saying about Haile Selassie, I think it was. A name almost forgotten now. "It is us today," I remember my father intoning, shaking his head and raising his brandy snifter in a toast. I sat there in my mother's dress with its dropped waist that no one could see once I was sitting down, but I knew it was lovely, with a drooping bow at my left hip, and I felt so grown-up. *She would be proud of me,* I thought. I had graciously and immediately agreed to take Miles skiing *le jour prochain.* I had not been asked to leave the table when the conversation turned serious. Neither my father nor Miles felt sympathy toward Haile Selassie, as I recall. Noses buried in their brandy snifters, they snorted instead of inhaling. "You understand that the man is asking the age-old question, 'Am I my brother's keeper?'" my father said to me. I had not been fidgeting. I had been trying to follow what they said, though they spoke so elliptically, or at other times so softly, that it would have been difficult, even if I had known the exact subject being discussed. I had assured my father I understood entirely. What I must have looked like, sitting there in my grown-up dress, speaking so seriously. The next day, on the ski slopes, Miles asked me: "Don't you smile?" A strange question, I came to think when I knew him a bit better, because he so rarely smiled himself. At any rate, he was not

smiling when he took the call in the hotel room that evening when he
stepped out of his shoes, loosened his bow tie. When he stood there,
saving his life, saving mine, though he had no idea that was what he
was doing. I felt bad enough about being there, about going to Boston
behind Alice's back, on the day she had gone to Rhode Island to visit
her friend Amelia. I mean, there I was in my peach silk, and she had
a slight cold, herself, and of course she also had Gordon and baby
Martin. Still, there the two of us were, sitting peacefully in the Ritz
sipping champagne, to say nothing of the fact we were about to go
to a lavish wedding reception with oysters Rockefeller and other wonderful food and enjoy a night of dancing. We were all preoccupied
with the war, tired out by the children, exhausted, frustrated and exhausted, yet she'd dressed Gordon in a new outfit and put the baby
in the stroller and insisted upon setting off by train to visit Amelia
at her parents' house in Rhode Island, refusing to listen to Miles's
suggestion that she wait until the weekend, when he could take us all
by car. She could have been in Rhode Island when she got the news—
if such news had been forthcoming. It wasn't, though. We did not
burn in the fire. Having missed too much of the festivities, we made
love in the big bed inside our room at the Ritz—only the second time
since I'd given birth to Martin—and it was not until much later that
we heard the news, shouted by someone in the hotel corridor, that a
terrible fire was raging. This came to mind because tonight a folksinger—a long-haired folksinger, a perfectly nice young man with
long hair and daydreams in his eyes—came to the nursing home and
entertained us after dinner by playing the guitar and singing. He sang
songs by James Taylor and by Carole King. I recognized most of
them. One of the women, feeling mischievous, asked for "Hot Time
in the Old Town Tonight." He had a nice way about him, and he
tried to play it, but none of the old fogeys, myself among them, could
remember the name of the woman who'd put a lantern in her shed. So
it was: "Old Mrs. Something put a lantern in her shed / Cow kicked it
over, and this is what she said / 'There'll be a hot time in the old town
tonight.'" The man's voice announcing the fire at the Cocoanut Grove
seems like yesterday. It was almost unprecedented to hear anyone
speak above a whisper in 1942 in a hotel corridor.

In 1936 I was such a naïve girl. What I knew about sex was that
when a man and woman married, the woman must listen earnestly

when the man explained something important to her. That was what my mother had told me; that one day I would be told "something important." Though I menstruated, I did not connect that with sex. How it ever came clear to me, I don't exactly recall. Because when I was pregnant with Martin, the doctor, unsolicited, volunteered that after giving birth to a baby, my cramping would end. "Cramping?" I asked him. "Yes," he said. "You don't have menstrual cramps?" I was shocked to hear him say the word aloud. He was quite affable—a friend of Miles's who had attended medical school at Yale during the same years Miles was there. I think he talked so much because he was trying to be friendly, though actually he was quite uncomfortable: his friend's mistress—well, I'd never known the word had that other meaning, until it became obvious by the context in which Alice used the word that awful day we sat in the living room of the house in Maine and he told her everything, that I was someone's *mistress*. Whatever name she gave me, I was terrified. I was certain I was going to be sent back to Montreal, and as much as I feared my parents' disappointment—they thought the United States was another world, a superior country, and I would have been ashamed to have failed there, to have failed at making Alice like me, in spite of everything I'd done setting up the house, in spite of the bulbs planted, the dinners cooked—if you can believe such a thing, there was actually a time when I thought that it was fine to sleep with a woman's husband because he requested it. I assumed that was my responsibility toward being part of the family. There were secrets my mother had kept from my father: money put away in food jars; the scrawny cat she some-times set a saucer of milk out for, at the same time he was trying to run it off. In my innocence, I simply thought that sex was a secret Miles and I were keeping from Alice, like a saucer of milk placed under the bushes. It seems difficult to believe, but you have to take it on faith I didn't know any different. I believed in Santa Claus as a real man who came from the North Pole until some girls set me straight when I was eleven years old. I thought fairy tales were inter-changeable with stories in the newspaper long past the time when everyone else understood they were just made-up stories. Though I did not like sex, and I certainly did not want to be pregnant, espe-cially because I had been horrified to have to spread my legs in a doctor's office and feel his hand inside me—although I considered it a personal failure that had caused misery to everyone and would no doubt cause further misery once my parents found out, I nevertheless did like Alice, so when she raged at me, my heart was broken. If she had not spoken to Amelia and gone through a sea change, I would have died of a broken heart. This many years later, I can only wonder what Amelia must have said to her that caused such a change. Suddenly Alice accepted everything, taking both my hands in hers and apologizing to me, though I don't remember her apologizing to him. While Martin was just a tiny fetus inside me, it had been decided that the child I carried would be their child. No one would know any different. We would go abroad, and I would give birth there. That plan did not materialize, of course: the war continued, and everything changed. We ended up hiding from people, beginning in my fourth month, in the house in Maine. Miles's friend from Yale arranged for a doctor to watch my pregnancy, and to send a young colleague of his to be present, along with the local doctor, at the birth. It was decided that nothing would be said to my parents. I was so grateful for that, it was the biggest relief of all. When I wrote them or spoke to them, the baby was the one thing I never mentioned. In all the world, the only people who knew—except for Gordon, who was too young to understand—were Amelia, the doctors, and Miles's friend Ethan Bedell, who came unannounced and opened the front door without knocking and walked in on us, when I was hugely pregnant. It is so easy to forget that people have their personal preoccupations. When they encounter the unexpected realities of others' lives, their preoccupations nevertheless continue just as strongly. He was there, if you can believe it, because he feared for the health of the painter Grant Wood; though he did not fear for Wood's mortality, he feared Miles would fail to acquire important paintings before Grant Wood's death. "You didn't listen to me about *The Black Flag*," I remember him saying. "You must absolutely listen to me now." Alice always maintained that Ethan Bedell was the only man she'd ever heard of who went to fortune-tellers. A fortune-teller had predicted the untimely death of someone very talented, known to Ethan only through his work, not personally, and Ethan had jumped to the conclusion the man was talking about the death of Grant Wood, whose painting *Death on Ridge Road* he interpreted as a curious departure, a harrowing vision of the painter's own death. After registering his initial shock in how he found us, he recovered himself quickly, then launched into a heartfelt description of the paintings of Grant Wood, pulling one photograph after another from his briefcase, seizing Miles's hand as if he could, in the moment, press him into buying whatever paintings were available. Alice and I had to leave the room, we were so overwhelmed by Ethan's fervor. "God—that awful picture of the farmer standing by the ugly woman and the pitchfork!" she had squealed, as we went upstairs.

Martin was born on December 8, 1941—the day after Pearl Harbor. That was when the Americans acknowledged there was a war; everyone in Montreal knew that in 1939, of course. On Christmas Day, Hong Kong was taken by the Japanese. The radio and the fire crackled constantly, and we waited, day after day, for information. I think we all forgot ourselves, forgot our individual lives had real meaning. Strange, the names you remember. Like a song that was being sung by everyone, Miles and the people he talked to on the phone seemed to be in constant contact with a Harvard chemist named Louis Fieser. For a while, it seemed the miraculous substance he was developing in his laboratory would be the solution to the war, and Miles and Ethan Bedell were convinced Fieser should have investors behind him, private investors, as well as the ear of the press, rather than working alone and trusting that the U.S. Army would deal correctly with his product. There were numerous calls every day, instigated by Ethan and by friends of Fieser, who for some reason would not communicate directly with Miles or with Ethan Bedell.

When the baby was born, he was the most wonderful distraction for everyone. Even Gordon loved him from the first. Alice and I would pass him back and forth, taking turns walking with him, rocking him. I felt only a momentary pang of regret when the birth announcements went out saying that Alice and Miles were the parents. I thought we would all be together, always, and that the baby had been born into the most wonderful family imaginable. Instead of seeming an enormous burden, he had suddenly become a great gift. Gifts arrived every day: booties; buntings; toys; a copy of the song "There Will Never Be Another You," from Ethan Bedell, who had been sent the lyrics by his good friend Mack Gordon. It later played in the film *Iceland,* and everyone started humming it. It became a classic. I remember sitting with Alice, one of us taking care of the baby, the other reading aloud from *Liberty* magazine, that song playing in our heads even when we weren't hearing it. Though we never saw *Iceland,* we did see, and love, *The Palm Beach Story,* with Claudette Colbert and Rudy Vallee. Such sweet melodies, such pleasant movies going on while the world was at war. It was like receiving a beautiful infant into our arms and finding that some little thing, still so unformed, yet so wonderful and fascinating, could change all the adults' personalities. We were all at our best. I would have gone on that way forever. I was so perplexed when Miles declared his love for me, when he suggested we "undo the wrong." He would have left his marriage, risked social opprobrium, for nothing more than exchanging one wife for another, and nightly sex with me. I thought he was mad, and by then I had the courage to tell him so. Things were fine the way they were. I had no intention of causing any more unhappiness to the woman who had been consistently kind to me, except for a brief moment of shock when she lost sight of the fact that all of us were a unit, saw what her husband and I had done—naturally enough—as betrayal. So there was a time when she had great equilibrium; if she lost it later, that is another matter. Everyone changes through time. When it was most important to have it, she had great equilibrium.

I think he had some mistaken notion of punishing me for not doing what he wanted. The closer she and I became, the more he tried to drive a wedge between us. He gave us a book called *Generation of Vipers,* which caused a scandal in its time—a book about "Momism" ruining male children! We couldn't take such a thing seriously. He doted on Gordon and never wanted Martin out of his sight, yet the book said that siblings were essential because *women* would dote unhealthily on infants!

The next child, Marshall, was her child with him: a beautiful boy born in 1944. This time she showed off her pregnancy, friends gave her showers, and only toward the end did she wonder aloud whether she should have allowed Miles to persuade her that three children were not too many. In a magazine I flipped through today in the activity room, I read about a woman who was already a grandmother giving birth to her daughter and son-in-law's child after having been inseminated with the embryo, begun in a test tube. I mentioned the article when Sonja was visiting, and she said: "Don't worry. We won't ask that of you." Such a sense of humor. She also seems to have come to terms with her inability to have children. "You're not supposed to say such things, but I think I'm happy to be spared the pain," she said. I almost agreed with her, automatically, but then I remembered that I *had* had a child, that it would not be respectful to his memory to state otherwise. Bad enough not to have set the record straight after so many years, but why say I knew just what she meant, why compound the lie? In her eyes, I am another version of her: a childless woman. Whereas, I had a child in 1941, and he died in 1943, walking toward us on the porch in Maine, having gotten out of bed because the noise of the Fourth of July fireworks had frightened him, the fireworks in the distance, lighting up the sky. At first we thought he had tripped. He was walking toward us in the dim light of the porch, carrying a toy he'd brought from bed, and then he went down, with our arms outstretched and Gordon calling his name, he went down, struck by a cerebral aneurysm, a weakness in the brain that might well have been present at birth. From the time he recovered from colic as an infant, he had never been sick, and there he lay, with all of us so stunned that little Gordon was the first to actually reach him. I fell apart, seizing Gordon, in my panic, as if he'd done something wrong, refusing to acknowledge my child lay on the floor. Apparently, after riding with him in the ambulance to the hospital—I am told Alice jumped in with me, and wouldn't budge—apparently, after insisting to the doctor that what had happened was because of something I had done, while Alice insisted otherwise, I blacked out, and when I came to, I said nothing for two days. Before I did speak I apparently hiccupped nonstop, while the doctors discussed further sedation and Alice begged them not to do it. The next thing I knew, I was out of the hospital, in their bedroom. For some reason, they had put me in their room, as if I were a frightened child who could be soothed by being taken into the adults' bed, and when I awoke I had the terrifying, confused sense that a war had begun; that the house had been hit by a bomb, which would account for the darkness, for the sheets tangled on the floor, the discarded clothes, and for Alice's body, dead in the chair. She was asleep. Not a sound in the house, and not a sound I could bring forth. I kept working backward, fixating on the war, trying to remember when the war had begun. *December 1941,* a voice said inside my head. Then I skipped ahead to the porch, to the fireworks, the bright explosions in the sky. I saw Martin walking toward us in slow motion, not a gun in his hand, but a toy tiger, the tiger on the ground, Martin dead—actually dead—beside it.

We lived, all of us, in a trance. I would look down and expect to see him, take a nap in the rocking chair and awaken to feel a pressure on my thighs as if a small child had just sat there, and got up to go elsewhere. Certain colors reminded me of toys he had loved; the color yellow saddened me because he had slept in yellow pajamas. I became convinced Martin's death was punishment for our sins. They tried to reason with me. If it would make me feel better to declare that the child had been his and mine, Alice said, she would understand completely. It was making her miserable, the way people rushed first to comfort her before turning to Miles or to me—she, who was least important. Miles became angry, telling her to stop dwelling on what he called "biology." Did he not want the secret told, or did he—quite probably, he did—think that the child's parentage was hardly an important issue, we had all loved him so much? It did not seem that any of us would ever be happy again. We could not even sit on the back porch. We turned inward, became cross with one another, went to bed ourselves as soon as Gordon was tucked in. And do you know what saved us? I thought of it when Sonja visited, bringing little presents with her. We were saved, looking back, by butter. In his blundering but insistent way, Ethan Bedell arrived at the house with a bottle of French cognac, which, when uncorked, smelled to Alice and to me like nausea itself, and with a large crock of butter. Bread and butter had become such a delicious treat, because we almost always used our red stamps for meat. But there was Ethan, with a large quantity of butter and the promise of an almost endless supply. Eating our buttered bread, we began to cheer up. That tells you how desperate we were.

Marshall was born in 1944. Alice said to me—prefacing it by saying that although she was about to overstep her bounds, she still had to tell me what she was thinking—that she hoped it was not lost on me, the fact that quite soon after Gordon's birth, Miles had gotten me pregnant with Martin, and now, so soon after Martin's death, she had given birth to Marshall. Next he would want me to have another child, and then he would turn to her again. It was the beginning of her becoming unbalanced. I remember also, that she read, that summer, a book by Wilkie Collins called *The Woman In White,* and that she imagined that her finding it on a bookshelf was no coincidence, and she became profoundly depressed at the actions of the dastardly Sir Percival Glyde. Miles gave away the book, and also *The Moonstone,*

by the same author. He even got rid of books by Charles Dickens—
as if that would protect us from any further misery! I think he did
not get her help as soon as he might have because she had also had
mood swings after the birth of Gordon—that, and naturally he did
not want to think about the serious implications of her behavior. I
can remember him telling me, quite sincerely, it seemed, that paranoia
was in the air, and he later reminded me that he had seen this trend
long before others did. When later the nation got caught up in the
Communist scare, he saw Nixon's persecution of Hiss for what it was,
deplored the irrational witch-hunt, became angry at a zoologist he
had known years before for publishing a book called *Our Plundered
Planet,* about the alleged dangers of DDT. He thought there was
much unfounded paranoia in America, the paranoia of certain fame
seekers who knew how to capture the media's attention, so that their
mass paranoia had seeped into sane minds, polluting them.

Actually, he was the one who never recovered. She and I adapted,
had our highs and lows, but he became entrenched in his ideas.
Americans became worse than fools for believing stories about micro-
film hidden in pumpkins—why, next they would believe that the stork
would be scared off from delivering babies by people prowling
through pumpkin patches. In 1941, when I first went to Maine, he
was already raving about Thomas Hart Benton's having said he hated
museums, which Miles saw as a subversive plot to keep people away
from culture. He later became furious at the appearance of Abstract
Expressionism, saying that now *there* was a Communist plot, if
people had to have their Communist plots: Pollock was only a madman, according to him; his so-called action painting a farce he meant
to put over on credulous critics, while pandering to the lowest common denominator of Americans' credibility by dripping paint on
enormous canvasses and claiming that what Miles called "skunk
sprayings" were works of art, important personal statements controlled by unconscious forces.

For a while, though, things went along. Marshall was born, and
he was a joy to us. Things went along until Alice became too incapacitated to really function, and then he did what men think to do: he
took her on a trip to New York, and when he sensed that hadn't done
the trick, he hedged his bets by contacting the doctor she and I had
seen, briefly, after Martin's death, yet he also kept her in New York,

far enough away that the doctor could not do her any good, which to him meant any harm, and where I also could not exert any influence. I could shame her into stopping drinking, and he knew it. But he enjoyed it himself. Didn't want to be told it was harmful. He thought he could re-create the past simply by cutting her off from the present, but she was too smart for that. Still, she must have felt very vulnerable, very uncertain about her own capabilities, if she let him convince her for so long that she should be apart from her children. It wasn't until she was actually hospitalized that any of my letters to her got through. She wrote back and said she'd heard nothing while they lived for that long time in the hotel. Who would prosper, when they were upset, by living out of a suitcase, being dragged to business dinners, kept away from their children and from everything that provided them with stability? It was wartime. The entire nation was upset to begin with. He had always been so overbearing, but through time he also became smooth. As he aged, people began to think him a charming, if slightly out-of-touch, gentleman of the old school, which of course implied he was an upstanding fellow. It was no different from the way he had first appeared to me, clasping my hand meaningfully and then kissing me discreetly on the cheek, so as not to frighten me. He seduced me sexually, and he proceeded to seduce anyone else he wanted, in any area in which he wanted to seduce them, whether it be for business or for pleasure. Amelia, for example, was a gratuitous seduction. Did he think I'd be flattered he wanted me so much more? Did he think he'd take her to bed and buy her silence? Amelia and I sat together in Dr. St. Vance's office, during that long time he kept himself and Alice exiled from Maine, and I heard what she had to say. I had guessed there was something between them, just as Alice intuited he still slept with me from time to time, of course. What he hadn't counted on was how much Alice meant to him. How much his own wife meant. Because when she faltered, when Amelia couldn't reason with her, when my obvious devotion couldn't quell her anxiety, he started to realize he had quite a problem on his hands, and that it was a problem none of us would be likely to want to help with: his further subjugation of his wife. She was the one he was reluctant to let go of: not his little children; not his secret affairs on the side. That she had become capable of doing the things he did almost killed him. A woman, having an affair! Drinking! For a long time, he refused to see it. I think he thought that if he could make their world anonymous enough, she would change her behavior, cling to him. So he set up housekeeping in the Waldorf Hotel, exiled both of them from their familiar world that he realized, too late, had caused her such pain, and tried to pretend a different context would allow them to begin a different life. I think he wanted us to vanish: for the boys to disappear; for me to return to Montreal. I did go there, briefly, though I understood he did not really approve of my leaving. My father had had surgery, and my mother seemed disproportionately upset. How strange that the sight of me was not so much soothing in its own right, but that he was reassured I was prospering. That was what he saw, in spite of the fact that my hair had grown long and straggly, I had lost weight, I was at wit's end, really. Yet when my father looked at me he saw only the prosperous child he had sent to New England. He wanted to see the pictures of the children I carried in my wallet. He showed me their Christmas card, as if Miles's signature, alone, ensured that all was well. My mother would hardly meet my eyes: she offered me her prettiest dresses, in spite of my description of rural Maine; when I hinted that Miles and Alice had been gone much too long, she equivocated, suggesting that she and I could not understand the complexities of business. I stayed three days. I felt too guilty about leaving Amelia, who knew nothing about children, alone to care for Gordon and Marshall. I think I also feared she might stay. Her staying would validate the desperate circumstances, I felt. On the plane, I actually thought about accepting Ethan Bedell's proposal of marriage—not because of any feelings toward him, but because . . . God—there was a time when I cared deeply what people thought. I had internalized my guilt so much that I wanted no one to have anything objective to latch onto with which to criticize any of us: Wouldn't they be astonished by two women raising children, as opposed to a woman and a man? Now I read about lesbian communities, festivals celebrating modern-day witches, single parents, businesses owned exclusively by women. Then, I would have felt like Hester Prynne. I would have felt entirely conspicuous, and certain that people's eyes would have followed me wherever I went. Curious, when I think back on it: that I would have gone to a party at the Cocoanut Grove, where everyone would have known I was not merely an au pair, yet nothing would have convinced me I could live alone, or with the help of another woman, in raising Miles and Alice's children. The simple difference, in my mind, was that if Miles was there at my side, whatever he said would get us through, but anything I did alone, or with Amelia, would be a transparent masquerade that would inevitably disgrace me.

"Mail call!" Patty the nurse always says, when she pokes her head in the door and has a catalog for me, or a postcard from Sonja of some pretty scene she knows I'll enjoy seeing. Or in the days when Ethan was still able to write. I said to her that it was as if one snowflake made her herald a snowstorm! I shouldn't have, because she, herself, seems cheered when she has mail to deliver. So different from years ago, when I didn't know what to hope for: more lies, about Alice's progress, letters announcing his or their imminent arrival, or an empty mailbox, no boot tracks leading to it, no false promises inside, flap closed, like a trap empty of animals. They can be quite beautiful, if you come upon them in the snow: a trap transformed into some harmless igloo, pleasantly insulated by whiteness. You forget what it might contain—what terrible pain. What bad luck. The other day a young woman, a new person, a social worker, came to see what she could do to "facilitate my adjustment," as she put it. Is one supposed to adjust to loneliness, to old age? I found the question quite stupefying. Well: if it had been years ago, she could have helped by being Amelia, and she could have stood her ground, and stayed in spite of my protests; if the social worker had been Ethan she might have construed my puzzled silence as wavering—a sign she might insinuate herself with me. If she had been Madame Sosos, a woman who was as oddly charismatic as she was lunatic, she might have flattered me and then played poker for my soul with the doctors. I think about that, sometimes. Ethan not knowing what to do, sending his fortune-teller into Alice's hospital with instructions to look at her palm and predict a long and happy life. She must have been so happy to see any outsider that she wanted to believe what she heard: a full recovery; good health; a quick return to her loved ones. Apparently, the doctor in charge was willing to buy Ethan's lie that Alice had consulted Madame Sosos for years. Alice was responding so poorly, and indeed she did manage to cheer her: she knew her devoted husband's name; where she lived; where she'd grown up. Madame Sosos's mistake was to name only two children, Gordon and Marshall, which devastated Alice because then she was certain that Martin did not even live in the spirit world. Before leaving, Madame Sosos was lured into a game of poker by some of the doctors—who could imagine how or why?—and won every game she played. They never let her in again. The second time she went there she had a special message from Martin, but she couldn't get into the hospital. Miles had made an enormous fuss. The doctors who'd been beaten at poker pronounced her a charlatan. Alice would never have heard from her again if Madame Sosos hadn't been clever enough to have flowers delivered, with the gift card saying she'd been contacted by Martin, who was fine, and who sent invisible kisses on each pink petal of the roses. She said she touched them to her lips—not so crazy she believed it true, but liking the idea of holding soft, fragrant rose petals to her lips. After her shock treatments her lips were always parched. Long after she got out of the hospital, she kept jars of Vaseline around the house which she'd dip into to moisten her lips. All day, we would sip tea.

That was what we were doing, sitting and sipping tea, Marshall with his paperdolls, Gordon with his book of fairy tales, with the stories printed on the left side of the book and the right-hand page to draw on. He would draw pictures that were improvisations on what he'd read, drawing mountains when there were no mountains in the story, or drawing the world underwater, though he didn't even have a snorkel mask. To my knowledge there were no such things for children in those days. He would read the fairy tales and leave the pages empty most of the time, but sometimes, to amuse his brother, he'd demonstrate his skill with drawing, and then we'd see some of the fairy-tale figures in imaginary landscapes, along with a fox, say, that simply hadn't appeared in the story, or an enormous tarpon he'd decided to put on land, underneath the castle under which Rapunzel had let down her hair. He was always adding to the fairy tales, not just illustrating what he'd read, and Alice and I would be so fascinated: What was that crow, sitting on the bonnet of the wolf in "Little Red Riding Hood," or the snake peeking out of the shoe in "Cinderella"? They were very original drawings, quite well done, but Miles didn't like them; he always wanted Gordon to stick to the facts, and he took it personally, as if all those stories he'd read aloud so many times had been misunderstood by his son, or as if the boy must have been bored, if he felt the need to add to what was there. This reaction, if you can imagine, from the same person who so admired Magritte. Fine if a train was rushing out of a fireplace, or if an apple floated in front of a man's face, but let his son draw a bird sitting on a wolf's bonnet and he was absolutely at a loss to understand what such a thing could mean. I think it's possible he saw Alice as unbalanced, and he greatly feared it might also be true of his children. At any rate, that day in the kitchen, where he'd come to sit with us as she was knitting and I was making a list of things we needed to buy to make raisin pudding, he saw the book open on the table and he picked it up and started flipping through, asking us questions about what Gordon had intended, as if we had any idea. Alice said that perhaps Gordon actually *was* illustrating the characters he read about, but they were in a different form; she thought it possible that he might be including creatures that existed in their reincarnated forms. Alice had come to believe in reincarnation. If only she could have lived to hear authorities on dying: Elisabeth Kübler-Ross, for example. Well: Miles didn't want to hear about religion, so he certainly didn't put any stock in reincarnation. She was needling him by mentioning it. He'd come into the kitchen and we both could tell the call he'd just hung up from had upset him—business was his deity—and poor thing, she had nothing but vague reports from the doctors, she was no fool, she knew the news was bad, knew more than I did, certainly, because I never believed she was so terribly ill, I thought it was just taking time for her to mend, and what use was he, coming into the kitchen, where we sat peacefully, suddenly starting an argument about his son's very nice illustrations in a book? Now I think I should not have been so unrealistic as to believe that any surgery simply cured the problem, but he was so insistent that this was so: he claimed to be stating the doctors' certainty, too. She had been through so much—who could believe there was anything worse in store for her? We were having tea when he pulled up a chair, sat backward in it—which was always a sign he was going to start in on some serious topic—and he said to her, "Tell me that you do not have delusions of an afterlife." Imagine: she was terminally ill, and he was intent upon disabusing her of the notion there would be an afterlife. I wonder what would have happened if the whole subject could have been turned aside. If we hadn't taken everything he said so seriously. Sonja tells me the expression "Get a life" is popular now. I wonder: what if one of us had had the nerve to tell him to get a life, if we'd gone on with what we were doing. But she was having none of it that night. She looked so frail in her white nightgown. So haggard. And yet, she had already forgiven so much. She said: "I won't come back as a person, Miles. I'll come back as an animal." She fingered Gordon's drawing of the fox. "You can marry Evie," she said, "and I can be your cat. Or your dog. I could be a bird, in a birdcage you could put over there, in the corner. It could be like the secrets we keep now, but then everyone would be thinking how sad that I'm dead, not just sorry you had such a crazy wife. Wouldn't that be fun, with only you two knowing the cat was really me? I could bring a dead mouse to your doorstep. Or come back as a dog that's rolled in carrion. I could enact what you really think of me. If I come back as a bird, be sure he clips my wings, Evie. Have it be the same way it's been in this life." We were astonished, of course. I understood, though I'm sure he did not, that she was imitating the manner of Madame Sosos. Ethan had insisted I meet her and I'd agreed, intending to put my foot down if she was too obviously crazy and would be sure to upset Alice. He'd driven to Maine with Madame Sosos. The boys were out of the house, which I thought was better. I expected someone in a turban, with a crystal ball. Instead, she had on the prettiest sterling-silver earrings from Georg Jensen. I'd seen them in a magazine, and I recognized them immediately. She had on those earrings, and a little rouge and lipstick, and all she wanted to talk about was how far away Maine was from New York. The car trip had really tired her, and of course she must have been slightly hostile: she was going to see Alice, at the hospital in Connecticut, so why did she first have to see the woman who took care of Alice's children? We had tea together, while Ethan very kindly fixed a shelf that had fallen in the basement. She'd examined the palm of my hand, lit incense, and found meaning revealed in the rising twines of smoke. There Alice sat, some time later, doing a perfect imitation of the dreamy voice of Madame Sosos, whom Ethan had sent to see her, after all, not Miles, though I don't blame her for being angry she was condescended to. I think I let out a little laugh—a sound, anyway— but Miles was too astonished to react for quite a while, so we were both shocked when he swept his hand across the tabletop, knocking everything to the floor, our tea, the saltcellar, the book, the ashtray. It made me sure, in that moment, I didn't want to ever be married to anyone. I was thinking that I was so glad I wasn't married, I was so glad I was not a person who might say such things, or another person who might react as he just had. I'd witnessed too many such scenes between married people. That was what I thought, sitting there with the smell of ashes in my nose, my ankles wet from toppled teacups. It had started to rain. Gordon stood in the kitchen doorway, having rushed from the living room to see what had happened. He looked confused, then stricken. The book was upside down in a puddle. He rushed to pick it up, but Miles got there first, opened the book, and shook it at Gordon, demanding that Gordon explain the made-up animals. Gordon was speechless. Miles was not a violent man. Even Miles recovered himself the instant he saw the expression on his son's face. Miles blotted the book with his sweater. Apologized for his outburst. Held out the book to Gordon with one hand and held out the other hand hoping Gordon would put his hand in his, forgive him. But nothing was explicit, and Gordon simply turned and walked out of the room. Marshall had run upstairs. Gordon was very protective of his brother, and he was probably setting out to talk to Marshall, but Alice got up and called him, asked him to come back. She went up and got Marshall. He was too heavy for her to carry, but she did anyway. I put my hand on Gordon's shoulder and guided him into the living room, hating Miles. Hating him, but at the same time sorry that Gordon had not taken his hand. I knew what that emptiness felt like: it was as if emptiness had weight, and texture. There had been so many times I'd looked down, thinking I felt Martin's little hand in mine again, only to see nothing. The air. Yet my fingers tingled. My palm was warm. It was as if he'd clasped my hand and vaporized, leaving his bodily warmth. Of course, I never, ever, would have mentioned this to either of them. Her most recent hospitalization had been a terrible time for everyone. We were not up to such a scene as had just exploded. He had tears in his eyes. Things from the tabletop were strewn everywhere. Miles bowed his head and said he was going out. Out in the rain? It was a storm: thunder; lightning. I wanted to take his hand myself, not so much for his sake, but out of sympathy for all of us. Instead, I got the umbrella from the stand and handed it to him, and that was what he used to sweep away everything else in his path on his way to the door, pushing Marshall's paperdolls off the table, breaking a vase, scattering paper. It was the baby she thought of constantly, he said. She lived in the past, cared only for the baby, who was she kidding by talking about the future, when she was fixated on the past?

When he left, she became quite composed. Quite calm, with Marshall in her arms, his chin on her shoulder, his legs dangling. She read to them from the Bible, told them she was going to die, walking back and forth in her nightgown. I thought it was a private moment between them, that I shouldn't be there, but as I backed away I saw the look in Gordon's eyes and lingered. I blotted the book dry. Because he'd used crayons, the drawings themselves were not ruined—except that later, the pages puckered. Not that he ever looked at the book again. Or that she ever read aloud from the Bible again. Though I looked at the 121st Psalm the other day, when Father Molloy brought me a Bible as a gift, and I could hear her saying the words, hear her voice as if she stood in the room. What would she make of such a room as mine? She, who had lived in such spacious houses. Lately an old movie has come to mind when I think about houses. *Holiday Inn,* with Bing Crosby and Fred Astaire, with all those wonderful songs by Irving Berlin. It was a movie about two friends who turned their home into a roadhouse, so they could perform for visitors every year. Fred Astaire did his Fourth of July number accompanied by torpedoes and firecrackers. I was told they had to call in technicians to build an organ that would set the firecrackers off electrically, so the organist could play the explosions at exactly the right moments, and the fireworks would be coordinated with Fred Astaire's feet. If I think of the Fourth of July, I like to remember that movie, not what once really happened on the Fourth of July.

My favorite nurse always gets involved in whatever old movie I'm watching on the VCR. Never to have seen *Casablanca*! Nineteen forty-two was such a vivid year, in part because that was when we first saw that unforgettable movie. The young are made weary by being told they're young; it's as rude, I suppose, as pointing out to someone old that they're old. It seems so many young people are cursed now with weighing too much. Patty is a pretty girl, but she's always worried about her weight—as well she should be. Sonja has stayed the same pretty, slender girl she's always been. It wouldn't have been insecurity about her looks that led her into an affair, I hope. I hope both boys were raised to give a lady a compliment when she deserves one. Who knows what Marshall really sees? Marshall is such a solitary person; it makes him self-absorbed. And Gordon is unobservable, like life on a star. There it is, shining, but you don't know the first thing about what goes on there. Frustrating, not to be able to find out how time will change them. Yet beyond a certain point, I think the world changes so much that no one can predict. An old person's intuition doesn't operate as it once did, because the rules change, familiar faces disappear, the things you came to count on to provide a context aren't there anymore—not even the music. No one ever hums "Moonlight Becomes You," and it was one of the greatest songs of 1942. Even before that, Frank Sinatra singing "This Love of Mine," the year Martin was born. That was also when we first heard "Blues in the Night" and Duke Ellington's "Take the 'A' Train." Of course, there was also Ethan's favorite: "There Will Never Be Another You."

It's difficult to imagine that Gordon or Marshall have particular songs that evoke romantic feelings. Sonja loves classical music; Beth tells me she likes "New Age." I thought to leave Miles's letters to one of the boys—Marshall, I thought, at first, because he is a college professor, words are his love, his business, but hesitated because he already thinks too much about everything. Neither of them would know that landscape. That haunting music. The resonance of the world in which we lived. Giving the letters to either one of them would be like giving them a silent film, based in a foreign land. Which made me think that Sonja should have them. Yet she is dismayed, now, at how men act. They would only reinforce her skepticism. So: Gordon. Better to give them to Gordon, along with something pretty for his wife, and hope that the person who so patiently explained things in his youth—who explained to his brother, at the same moment he was improvising stories himself—would discover things in them worthy of his attention. Gordon has spent his life on the run. He might be interested to know that there was a period of his father's life when he, too, kept himself apart from everyone. When he wished to reinvent his life.

I've been wondering, lately, what it might have been like if I'd never left Montreal. That first day we spent together alone, when I was still a teenager: Miles jumped off the lift and spread his arms, stood at the top of the mountain and whispered *Paradis,* then drew his arms in tightly as if to embrace the air. If I had drifted away like hot breath hitting cold then. Or skied down the slope, away. What if I had never started with him, let alone been won back through the years by fragments of romantic melodies. Or by an avalanche of letters to which I added a P.S. that was not there: that he loved me. If I had not responded, on the ski slope, or later, sealing my fate as easily as I licked an envelope, I could have had a different life. I could have been the white space between words.

THE BURNING HOUSE

In *The Burning House,* Ann Beattie surveys the lives of young men and women who are ruefully discovering the truths of growing up in an age that promises eternal youth.

Fiction/0-679-76500-X

LOVE ALWAYS

A satiric work about the nature of love "among the semi-beautiful people of late-twentieth-century media-fringe America" (*Chicago Sun-Times*), focusing on the lives of Lucy Spenser, a latter-day Miss Lonely Hearts, and her fourteen-year-old niece, Nicole, a child actress packed off from Hollywood to Vermont for the summer.

Fiction/0-394-74418-7

PICTURING WILL

Picturing Will unravels the complexities of a postmodern family. There's Will, an inquisitive five-year-old; Jody, his photographer mother; Mel, Jody's perfect lover; and Wayne, the father who left Will without warning. Beattie explores how these lives intersect, attract, and repel one another with moments of heartbreaking directness.

Fiction/0-679-73194-6

WHAT WAS MINE

These shimmering and emotionally complex stories combine painterly detail with an uncanny feel for the submerged rhythms of the heart.

Fiction/0-679-73903-3

Available at your local bookstore, or call toll-free to order:
1-800-793-2665 (credit cards only).